About the Author

Morris West was born in Melbourne, Australia, in 1916, the oldest of six children. After completing secondary studies in Melbourne, he joined the Order of Christian Brothers, took his vows and spent eight years as a teaching monk. In 1941, just before he was due to take his final vows, he left the Order. He joined the army and during this period he wrote his first book, MONEY IN MY POCKET, under a pseudonym. After jobs as a publicist and as a radio producer he began writing novels again, but his first real success was CHILDREN OF THE SUN, a non-fiction account of a Naples orphanage which became his first bestseller. Other famous books include THE SHOES OF THE FISHERMAN, THE DEVIL'S ADVOCATE, and most recently, THE CLOWNS OF GOD and THE WORLD IS MADE OF GLASS. After many years in Britain and Europe, he has now returned to live in his native Australia, where he has been appointed Chairman of the Council of the National Library of Australia.

Cassidy

Morris West

CORONET BOOKS
Hodder and Stoughton

First published in Great Britain
in 1987 by Hodder and
Stoughton Limited

Coronet Edition 1988

British Library C.I.P.

West, Morris
Cassidy.
I. Title
823[F]   PR9619.3.W4
ISBN 0-340-41141-4

Printed and bound in Great Britain
for Hodder and Stoughton
Paperbacks, a division of Hodder
and Stoughton Ltd., Mill Road,
Dunton Green, Sevenoaks, Kent
TN13 2YA. (Editorial Office: 47
Bedford Square, London WC1B
3DP) by Richard Clay Ltd.,
Bungay, Suffolk. Photoset by
Rowland Phototypesetting, Bury
St Edmunds, Suffolk.

For
our grandchildren
Jonathan, Gemma and Nicola
a parable of the follies of their elders

Author's Note

This is a work of fiction, a fable and not a history. The characters are figments of the author's imagination. Those who seek to distinguish real persons under the masks of the fictional characters will find themselves astray.

M.L.W.

He hated a fool, and he hated a rogue, and he hated a Whig. He was a very good hater.

(Samuel Johnson on the Earl of Bathurst)

1

Charles Parnell Cassidy – God rest his soul! – was the perfect specimen of an Irish politician. They're a migratory tribe, so you find them everywhere: Boston, New York, Chile, Vatican City, Liverpool, Peru and Sydney, Australia. They're hardy, longevitous, resistant to infection by disease or new ideas, little modified by regional influences.

The accent drifts a bit, maybe. The dialect adapts itself to the local patois: but that's a chameleon's trick: protective colouring, no more. The rest of it, the sinuous mind, the easy passion, the leery eye, the ready smile, the fine, swaggering, billycock-and-shillelagh walk, the flexible moralities, the bel canto oratory, the black bilious angers, these never change.

Charles Parnell Cassidy could have been anything, from horse-coper to Cardinal – except that he was too bright for the one and not celibate enough for the other. He wanted two things: money and power. First he became a lawyer: taxation and corporation law, what else? Then he made money. How could he fail, with the parcel of brewery shares his old man left him, and his own connections in commerce? After that it was politics – Labor politics of course. Make the loot among the privileged and then get the proletariat to protect it!

He rose like a rocket: one term on the back bench, one in Opposition. Then, with an election looming up, Caucus made him leader of the Parliamentary Party in the State of New South Wales which, as the whole world knows, was founded as a dumping ground for British felons and

11

dispossessed Irish. With golden oratory and charisma poured out like balm in Gilead – not to mention a lot of leg-work and a lot of money spread around the depressed areas of the electorate – Cassidy led Labor to a landslide victory and a ten-year term of office.

It sounds like magic; but it wasn't. He was a natural. The game was in his genes. He was bred under the same blanket as the Kennedys and Fitzgeralds of Boston, the Moynihans of New York, the Duhigs and the Codys in the Church and the Reagan who used to act in California.

The great Brian Boru sired them all, in the old, far time which is still 'now' for the Irish. Cassidy knew them all too, had dined at their tables, corresponded with them – or their womenfolk! – learned how their precinct machines were run and how they paid their scores and exercised their patronage. Then he came back to Sydney and worked up what he had learned into a revised version of the Gospel according to Cassidy:

'Document everything. If you can't write it – don't do it. Let some other mother's son carry the honey-bucket.

'Collect all debts in kind or in tax havens. Cash in the local bank is too easy to trace.

'Never get mad, get even! Remember Shakespeare: a man can smile and smile and still be the son-of-a-bitch he wants to be!

'Never bet on cards or horses. The electors love a sporting man; they're suspicious of a gambler.

'If you need more sex than you're getting at home, stay away from the whores and find a discreet mistress. The public love a little romance; but they don't want their elected representatives turning up on pornographic postcards.

'Nominate your own Police Commissioner; but let another Minister appoint him and run him. That way you're always the clean-skin and you've still got the police in your pocket.

'Make sure you've got a good Party man in every migrant

group. You'll never forgive yourself if the Croats or the Turks cost you a swinging seat.

'Get some bright women on the front benches. Let them field the curly ones, like abortion and battered wives . . . A man always sounds like an idiot when he's talking about a woman's right to her own body.

'Never debate political theory. That's an exercise in futility.

'Stay clear of professional economists. They can lose you an election and still have tenure at their universities.

'The law is the ultimate instrument of power. So long as you're the lawmaker, you're the man who wields it.'

With a gospel like that, and the gall to practise it, there was no reason why Charles Parnell Cassidy couldn't have led the country. The Party tried hard to get him into the Federal bull-ring; but his ambitions stopped at the State borders.

'This is my bailiwick,' he would say in that soft, blarney-ing brogue. 'I know how it runs and how to run it. Why should I want to blow myself up like a great horned toad in the capital? That's a short-term lease at best – and the tenant always ends under the executioner's axe. Here' – an eloquent shrug and smile of deprecation – 'here I'll know when it's time to quit, and I'll not wait to be pushed.'

The locals cheered him for it, of course. Round the parish pump, the simpler you are, the more they love you – and Cassidy was as simple as a biblical serpent. Of course he didn't want to quit, for a long time yet; he was coining millions.

I had no idea then – though I have now, by God! – of the size of the empire he was building, through interlocking enterprises inside and outside the country. But during his lifetime the image remained unsullied. He was rich when he was elected. He was entitled to a natural increase of his substance. He wasn't venal; he wasn't gaudy. His private charities were generous. He drank little, looked fit, was always coherent. He kept the traffic running, the hospitals open, the streets as safe as they could be in a violent age. The electors felt they were getting their money's worth.

Of his home-life little was known. While Parliament was in session he lived in a harbourside apartment, cared for by a husband and wife. His hostess at official functions was a young back-bencher whom he was grooming for a junior Ministry. Mrs. Cassidy was said to be a semi-invalid, living in seclusion on their country property. There was one daughter, Patricia, married long since and residing abroad. Clearly the poor fellow had a lonely life but he was respected as a man who carried his cross bravely. The press had given up their routine attempts to ferret out a scandal.

It was all beautifully tidy and stable. Even I, who had stolen his daughter and given sanctuary to his wife when she left him, had to offer a reluctant salute. Once, in a fury, I had called him 'bog-Irish on the make, trying to buy lace curtains'. Well, he'd made it now. The bogs were generations behind. The lace curtains were long past, too. Charles Parnell Cassidy was the lawmaker, the Lord High Panjandrum, and his writ ran further than I could then imagine.

We went a long way back, Cassidy and I. He gave me my first job after I graduated. In those days he was senior partner of Cassidy, Carmody, Desmond and Gorman. I devilled for him, on the affairs of the Archdiocese of Sydney and the big Catholic Assurance groups. When he saw that I was interested in his daughter he warned me off the course. I was too old for her, he told me, too poor in money and prospects – and, besides, he didn't like fortune-hunters who expected to marry money instead of working for it.

He could have been testing or teasing, or both; but I've got some Irish in me too and I don't like people treading on the tails of my coat. I told him what he could do with his money and walked out.

A week later I had a job in the legal department of a

merchant bank with connections in Switzerland, Paris and London.

Pat and I married soon after, in a civil ceremony, because we couldn't risk the local clergy forewarning Cassidy or calling the banns from the pulpit. Her mother was in the plot, but when we called to tell Cassidy the news and invite him to a reconciliation dinner, he told us he'd see us both in hell before he'd break bread or drink wine with us. If children were born they'd be bastards in the eyes of Mother Church and he'd want no part of them anyway.

It was as rough and dirty as only the Irish can make a family squabble. It got dirtier still when Clare Cassidy left him two years later and came to join Pat and me and the children in Paris, where I was working for Lazard Frères.

Cassidy, she told us, was a man driven by demons. His case-load at the office had doubled. He was out four nights a week, dining with union leaders or lobbying Party pundits or arguing in committee over strategies and speeches for his campaign. He was playing hard, too, golfing on Wednesdays, racing with the Squadron on Saturdays, hosting or guesting at Sunday barbecues, always with a gaggle of pretty women in attendance.

When Clare protested his philandering, he accused her and us of conspiring to unman him, blacken his name, tear his career to tatters. When we sent him photographs of the grandchildren – a pigeon pair, both beautiful – he handed them to Clare with a shrug and told her, 'Poor little bastards! I feel sorry for them!'

That was the straw that collapsed the fragile structure of their marriage. Clare Cassidy packed her bags and left. She briefed a roughneck lawyer who convinced Cassidy that if he wanted a fight, he would get it; but if he wanted a separation without scandal and a divorce on demand, the price would be steep, but fair. Cassidy was too bright to push his luck. He was being offered the best of both worlds: a marriage of convenience that kept him clean with the Catholics, a bachelor life-style, a reasonable bill of costs and no one to hold him to account for his later profits. He signed the agreement and trotted on down the triumphal way.

Only Pat refused to be thrust out of her father's life. Every Christmas she sent him a letter with a sheaf of photographs of the children. Every year the letter was returned unopened. She was hurt, but she took it calmly enough. Duty was done. She was holding the door open. It was up to her father to walk through it.

I believed he never would. He had turned hating into a fine art. For my own part I'd ceased to care. The children were teenagers now. They had three grandparents in working order. One black Irish curmudgeon wouldn't hurt them too much. We were living in London at that time. I had moved up in the banking hierarchy, with half a dozen well-paid directorships, good friends in the best houses and a crack at the market for the soundest floats.

Then, one bleak Tuesday in February, a note was delivered to me by special messenger. There was no address, no superscription, no 'Kind Sir, kiss-my-foot' – nothing but Cassidy's emphatic script.

I'm supposed to be in New York. I'm here in London. Except for the last rites and the last gasp, I'm a dead man. I'd like to tell my girl I'm sorry and kiss my grandchildren before I go. I'd like to shake your hand, too. If you're willing, pick me up at the Jesuit church in Mount Street at 5.30 this afternoon. I'll be sitting in the last pew – like the taxgatherer in the Gospel. If you're not there by six, I'll leave and I won't blame you. Cassidy.

I don't think I ever hated him so much as I did at that moment. Even if he were dying – and I wouldn't believe that until I saw the undertakers! – he had no right to sneak back into our lives like some errant schoolboy. Something more was called for: a letter to Pat, flowers, a phone call – some kind of prelude, for Christ's sake! And what about Clare? Was she to be included in the reconciliation? She was in Paris until Monday. I saw no reason to expose her to needless hurt.

I telephoned Pat, read her the note and asked her what she wanted to do about it. She thought, as I did, that 'the last gasp and the last rites' were at least half rhetoric. For the rest, between laughter and tears, she told me: '. . . He never steps out of character, does he? Of course I'm glad he's come round at last; but I'd still like to spit in his eye for all the good years he spoiled . . . The children don't get out of school until the weekend, so you and I will have the worst of it over . . . I'll serve a roast of beef for dinner. He'll like that. And do you have any Glenfiddich in the liquor cupboard? It's the only Scotch he'll drink . . . Mother? We don't have to worry about her yet. I had a card from her today. She met an elderly American art scholar at Giverney. She likes him very much and she's going down to Arles with him . . .'

Great! Mother had her scholar. The kids wouldn't be home. We'd have the old monster all to ourselves. If I thought it would help – but I knew it wouldn't – I'd pickle him in Glenfiddich and donate him to the Museum of Natural History: *elephantus hibernicus malitiosus*, a real rogue elephant from Ireland.

. . . Which shows you the tricks that memory and an angry imagination can play. When I saw him in the church, huddled in a heavy greatcoat, I was surprised how small he was. When I touched his shoulder I could feel the bones under the thick tweed. The face he turned to me was yellow and emaciated, the eyes sunk back in the skull. But he could still raise the old mocking Cassidy grin.

'Surprised, sonny boy?'

I was shocked to the marrow. My voice sounded unnaturally loud in the empty church.

'Charles! What the hell's happened to you?'

He gestured towards the sanctuary and the altar.

17

'One of the Almighty's little jokes. I've just been talking to Him about it; but it's cold comfort He's offering. Help me up, will you? These pews are damned hard, and there's small cover left on my backside.'

There was a briefcase on the pew beside him. As I helped him to rise he pushed it towards me. It was quite heavy. I wondered how far he had carried it.

He leaned on my arm as we walked out of the church and I had to ease him into the car like an invalid. He was shivering, so I switched on the engine and waited while the inside of the vehicle warmed up. I needed to talk to him before we got home. There was protocol we had to agree before I let him into our house. The words sounded stiff and graceless, but they were the best I could muster.

'You're welcome. I'm glad for Pat's sake that you've come. We're alone in the house just now. The children are at school until Friday, Clare's in France. So we'll have time to talk things out and get to know each other again. But there's a warning, Charles. Don't play games – with any of us. I won't stand for it.'

'Games?' He gave a small, barking laugh, with no humour in it at all. 'Games, is it? I'm under sentence of death, sonny boy. Can't you read it in my face.'

'Living or dying, Charles, the warning holds. You've caused enough hurt. So mind your manners in my house – and don't call me sonny boy ever again! My name's Martin; Martin Gregory, in case you've forgotten. Pat and our children are Gregorys too.'

'Well, now . . .' The words came out in a long exhalation. 'I can't quarrel with the proposition – and I'm too tired to fight with you. Do you want to shake hands on it?'

His skin felt cold and clammy. I had the feeling that the bones were fragile and would snap if I pressed too hard. I asked him: 'What's the sickness, Charles?'

'Secondary hepatic carcinoma. The primaries are in my gut somewhere. Nothing anyone can do. I'll stay mobile as long as I can, then I'll go into a hospice. The arrangements are all made.'

'How long have you known?'

'Three weeks. My doctor in Sydney did the first scans. There was little doubt what I had. I swore him to secrecy, flew to New York and went into Sloan-Kettering for more tests. Once the diagnosis was confirmed I sent word back to Cabinet that I was taking a month's holiday in the Caribbean. Instead I came here.'

'So, nobody knows you're ill or where you are.'

'Not yet. Parliament's in recess. It's mid-summer in Australia; my Deputy Premier's holding the fort. So nobody's missing me too much. Which is just as well, because as soon as I break the news all hell's going to break loose. The heavies will be out gunning for me. With any luck, I'll be dead before they find me.'

'What in God's name is that supposed to mean?'

'Just what it says; but I'll explain it better with a couple of drinks under my belt. Can we go now?'

'In a moment. Where are you staying in London?'

'With an old and dear friend, a lady of title in Belgravia. She's got a good doctor close handy and he's promised to rush me off to St. Marks at the first signs of dissolution. Now will you get me out of this bloody weather? . . . I hope you've got a decent whiskey in the house. Some of the stuff they're peddling now is like turpentine!'

'Are you sure you're allowed to drink?'

'I'm allowed to do any damn thing I choose. I'm going to be a long time dead!'

As we crawled home to Richmond through the peak-hour traffic, I told him: 'Pat's going to be very upset.'

Cassidy shrugged wearily.

'There's no way to break it gently. One look at me and she'll read it all.'

'Why didn't you get in touch before? Why did you wait so long?'

He was after me instantly; snap-snap like an old turtle.

'Because I didn't need you then. I need you now.'

'Your manners haven't improved, Charles. I hope you've got a gentler answer for Pat.'

'It isn't Pat I'm talking to; it's you, Martin. You were the stone in my shoe always: too bright by half, and righteous as bloody Cromwell. The only way I could get to my daughter, my grandchildren – even my own wife! – was through you. I gagged on that. I still do.'

'You're past me now, Charles. Soon you'll be face to face with your daughter. Be gentle with her.'

'I've got a whole stable full of speech-writers,' said Charles Parnell Cassidy irritably. 'I need a new one like a pain in the arse!'

As it turned out, very few words were needed or said. When Cassidy walked in, Pat's face crumpled into a mask of grief and she clung to him, sobbing helplessly. Cassidy held her against his shrunken body and crooned over her. 'There, child, there! It's all for the best. You'll see. It's all for the best.'

I didn't see it that way at all. I've always thought that piece, about everything being for the best in the best of all possible worlds, was opium for idiots. But this moment belonged to Pat and not to me; so I took myself off to the study, poured myself a large drink and waited for father and daughter to join me.

Cassidy was up to something, though I was damned if I could see what it was. I didn't believe one word of his blarney about kiss and make up before he passed on to bargain with his maker. He wasn't made like that. If he couldn't cheat the headsman, he'd have a damned good crack at cheating the devil – and I was the patsy he'd picked to help him.

Churlish and obsessive as it sounds, I knew the old monster too well. Give him half an opening and he'd have his thumbs on your windpipe – and you'd be dead before he was.

He came to the study alone, lugging the heavy briefcase,

which he pushed under the desk with his foot. As I poured his drink he told me: 'Pat's putting on a new face. She'll call us when dinner's ready . . . She tells me you're a good husband and you make her happy. My thanks for that.'

'We make each other happy.'

'Good. I'm leaving the bulk of my estate to her and the children.'

'What about Clare?'

'She's a beneficiary under a trust. The provisions are quite generous. I've named you as executor of the will. I hope you'll accept the job.'

'If you want. of course.'

'Thanks.'

'Now I'd like you to do a favour for Pat and me.'

'And what might that be?'

'Call Clare. She's still your wife. She has a right to know what's happened – what's going to happen to you.'

'I don't know.' He shrugged wearily. 'We dispensed with each other a long time ago. Anything more is just courtesy.'

'You owe her that, surely.'

He was instantly hostile.

'After I'm dead you dispose of my affairs! Until then, I tally my own accounts, thank you!'

'I'm reminding you of a debt, Cassidy!'

For a moment I thought he would attack again; but, to my surprise, he grinned and raised his glass in an ironic toast.

'To all the bloody righteous! Christ! You're a stiff-necked son-of-a-bitch, Martin. You won't give an inch, even to a dying man!'

'With your record, do you blame me?'

He laughed and I laughed too. Then he was off on another tack.

'Tell me, Martin, do you have a strongroom at your place of business?'

'We do indeed, the latest and the best. Why?'

'I want you to deposit my briefcase there first thing in

21

the morning. The combination is set at the day, month and year of Pat's birth. You open it only after my death.'

'Any special instructions about the contents?'

'The instructions are inside in a sealed envelope, with my will. Everything else is on microfiche, classified and cross-indexed, with access codes to the original documents. You'll find everything very clear. I've always been a methodical fellow, as you know.'

'I'm sorry I didn't get to know you better. I mean that.'

He shrugged and shook his head.

'Don't apologise! It was I who wasted the years, not you.'

'Is there any reason why you can't spend the rest of your time with us?'

'Yes, there is. Her name's Marian. She's a great lady. We're comfortable together and I don't want to hurt her feelings. Which reminds me . . . I don't want the scandal of dying in her bed, or being carted away in an ambulance from her apartment. So far as the press is concerned, I want it reported that I've passed away peacefully in the bosom of my family. It's not too much to ask, is it? A small white lie or two for the sake of posterity?'

Then I saw his ploy – or thought I did – and it set me laughing until the tears rolled down my face. Cassidy was only mildly amused.

'What's so funny? Everyone rewrites history. Why shouldn't my part of it have a happy ending? . . . Besides, you ought to be thinking of Pat and the kids. They'll be the ones hurt by a scandal. I'll be dead and past caring.'

He'd made his point. I told him I'd do my best to give him a pious send-off. I don't know why I used the word: but Cassidy was pleased by the flavour of it.

'Pious! That's good . . . "*iustus piusque*". It fits, don't you think? Charles Parnell Cassidy, just and dutiful even to the end. You might find a Latinist good enough to build it into my epitaph . . . oh, that's another thing! I've got a

State funeral coming to me. I don't intend to miss it. I've left orders to embalm me and fly me back so I can enjoy the spectacle of all my enemies crowding around the graveside to make sure I'm buried . . .' He held out his glass. 'Anyway, no more of death tonight. Pour me another drink, a large one, if you please, and I'll tell you the marvellous tale of the three girls in Piccadilly . . .'

By the time Pat came to call us to dinner, I was beginning to warm to him as I had in the days when I devilled for him in Sydney. Call him all the names in the book, the man still had style. He was suffering. He was humiliated by his infirmities. He was dissolving every day towards extinction. Yet he could still manage that louche, loping strut of the Celtic playboy.

His daughter had style too. I knew her as I knew my own pulsebeat. She was bleeding for Cassidy, crying for the years he had stolen from her, but she still chatted happily and chuckled at his jokes and was instant with small solicitudes. I have to admit that he was tender with her too. The old rasping wit was tempered to an elegiac humour. If he didn't exactly beat his breast with a stone, he did have the grace to say *mea culpa* for the failure of his own marriage and the mischief he had tried to do to ours.

I couldn't love him but I wanted to trust him. I wanted to pay him filial respect and smooth out the last rough days for him, but I dared not do it. Every instinct told me I had to be wary of him until the stake was driven through his heart and the flowers were growing on his grave. The best I could manage was a show of cordiality so that Pat's dinner party would not be spoiled.

We had finished dessert and Pat was in the kitchen making coffee when the key word I had heard and lost popped back into my head.

'The heavies . . . You said the heavies would be gunning for you, Charles. What did you mean?'

'Oh, that!' Immediately he was back in the greasepaint,

the old ham playing to his gullible public. 'A trade-word, nothing more! You know the way a Labor Caucus works. If you don't toe the line they wheel in the heavies to twist your arm and stamp on your toes and call in your IOUs and remind you of the nights you spent in Minnie Murphy's whorehouse. I knew how to deal with them; so they didn't worry me too much.'

'But they're worrying you now.'

'The hell they are!' His indignation had a fine terminal flourish. 'What can they do? Dig up my coffin and scatter the bones?'

'I don't know. I'm asking you.'

'They can do nothing. It's just that I'm tired of arguments and deals and whiskey oratory and the smell of cheap cigars at midnight. If Caucus knew the state I'm in they'd have a deputation in London within 48 hours to talk succession and ask for my private papers. I don't want that. I can't cope with it . . . Do you have a respectable port in the house?'

I knew I'd get nothing more out of him. That Irish two-step is a foolproof act. They teach it in seminaries to candidates for the priesthood and there's an intensive course for bishops and Ministers of the Crown. Cassidy had passed it *summa cum laude*.

I offered him the decanter of port but he asked me to pour for him. When he raised the glass I saw that his hand was trembling and that there was a dew of perspiration on his forehead and his upper lip. Clearly he was in distress. I suggested he lie down and let me call a doctor. No! He would finish his port. Then I could drive him to Belgravia. And he didn't want Pat to come with us. He hated fare-wells. Amen, so be it!

To tell the truth, I was glad Pat wouldn't have to cope with him, and I wouldn't have to argue myself through my quite paranoid dislike and distrust of the man. I would deliver him back to his Lady Marian, then come home and make love to my wife. Which was another thing I didn't like to dwell on: my dislike of Cassidy made me lust the more after the woman I had taken away from him.

We drove the first part of the way in silence. Cassidy was getting worse. He lay back in the seat, eyes closed, sucking in air to oxygenate his thickened lungs and steady his heart beat. Between gasps he managed to tell me that he was lapsing into cardiac arrhythmia and that I should notify his doctor and then drive him straight to hospital. He fished in his pocket and brought out a card with his physician's emergency number on it.

I pulled into a small garden square with a telephone booth on the corner and called the doctor. He told me he would meet us at St. Mark's. As I went back to the car I saw Cassidy take a capsule from a small enamelled comfit box. He palmed the capsule into his mouth, shoved the comfit box back in his fob pocket, then lay back, panting for air. I pulled away from the kerb and drove as fast as I dared towards St. Mark's Hospital, whose grim, Victorian buildings belie the mercy that is dispensed there to cancer sufferers.

Just past Harley Street, a motorcycle patrolman pulled me over to the kerb. He told me I was twenty miles an hour over the speed limit. I told him why. He took one look at my passenger and then rode in front of me all the way to St. Mark's. By the time we got there, Charles Parnell Cassidy was dead.

2

Cassidy's doctor, an urbane grey-haired fellow in his middle fifties, gave me a brief greeting, asked me to wait and then went into conference with the house physician. Half an hour later he came back and asked me to join him for coffee in the staff room. He offered his sympathies – and a summation as bland as butter.

'. . . These sudden collapses are quite common with terminal patients. Quite frankly, I'm surprised the man stayed on his feet so long. He was riddled with secondaries. There was minimal hepatic and renal function. I'd say it was a happy release . . . There are no problems about the death certificate. I've seen all his X-rays and the reports from Sloan-Kettering. I've been treating him long enough to issue the document without qualms. You can pick it up on your way out, and sign for his personal effects at the same time . . . He told me you were his executor. I presume you'll inform his government and make arrangements for the obsequies . . . I understand you've never met Marian . . . I'll break the news to her. She's prepared, of course, but she'll need someone to hold her hand. She and Cassidy were close – very close . . . Well, if there's nothing else, Mr. Gregory, I'll be running along. My card, in case there are any queries, though there shouldn't be. My respects and sympathies to your wife. Try to explain to her that it was a happy release. Cassidy was spared a lot of pain . . . Goodnight.'

'Goodnight, doctor.'

And goodnight to you, Charles Parnell Cassidy, cold and pallid on your mortuary slab . . . Now I'm the guardian of what they used to call your relicts: your wife, your daughter, the grandchildren you never acknowledged, whatever secrets are locked in that briefcase you kicked under my desk . . .

It was one-thirty in the morning when I got home. I had hardly set foot inside the door when Pat challenged me.

'He's dead, isn't he? He was dying when he left the house. I wanted to be with him but he wouldn't have me!'

I reached out to take her in my arms but she pushed me away.

26

'Don't touch me! Not yet . . . Please, Martin!'

I was stunned. In all the years of our marriage neither of us had ever rejected a caress from the other. Then a small cold finger of fear began probing round my heartstrings. It was as if Cassidy's implacable spirit had taken up lodging in his daughter's body and was challenging me from her tearless eyes and her tight, pale lips. This time, however, I was in no position to fight. I suggested gently that we could both use a drink.

She poured a stiff whiskey for me and a glass of mineral water for herself. We made no toast and the liquor burned my gullet as it went down. Then Pat made an apology so formal and detached that it hurt more than the rebuff.

'I don't mean to hurt you, Martin. Truly I don't. I love you, but that's beside the point . . . Here and now you threaten me . . .'

'You don't believe that!'

'It's true. Tonight at dinner you were trying so hard to be civilised and compassionate, but you were just as unforgiving as my father was. I felt as if I were watching two stallions battling to the death.'

'And that's why you can't bear me to touch you? – You blame me for your father's death?'

'No, it's something else.' She went on reasoning it out in a flat, bleak monotone. 'I feel like an object shunted eternally between the two of you. I can't stand it any more.'

'Sweetheart, please! This isn't you. It's a woman in shock. Two hours ago your father was alive. Now he's dead. He died beside me in the car – and there was nothing I could do about it except drive faster . . . Now I've got to go through the motions of telling his colleagues. That helps me; but you must let me help you. Don't lock yourself away. You need . . .'

'I don't need anything – except my own space.'

'You have it . . . you've always had it.'

'I know.' It sounded off-hand and dismissive. 'I'm

27

worried about Mother. She mustn't read this in a newspaper.'

'I'll call our Embassy in Paris first thing in the morning.
They'll get the French police to trace her . . . Now why
don't you go to bed. I'll come and tuck you in and give
you a knockout pill.'

'Don't worry. You have enough to keep you busy . . .
Just don't hate me too much.'

I held out my hand to draw her into a goodnight kiss.
She touched my palm lightly with her fingertips and left
me. I made no move to stay her. I was glad to be alone,
to brace myself against the new presence which had taken
up its abode in my house.

I closed myself in my study and made a telephone call
to Sydney, Australia. Cassidy's natural heir, the Deputy
Premier, was at lunch. His secretary was unwilling to
disturb him. A few blunt words convinced her that she
should. I was patched through to the Cabinet dining-room.
The Deputy Premier choked over the news.

'Dead! I don't believe it! Christ, this is a hell of a thing!
It couldn't have come at a worse time. We're in recess.
Some of my Ministers are abroad. The others are on
vacation. We've got two criminal trials of public officials
coming up in March. Why in God's name didn't Cassidy
let us know he was ill! . . . Anyway, that's our problem.
We'll handle it. I'll call our Agent-General in London and
have him take care of the protocol – Palace, Parliament,
the Commonwealth Office, the press – and of course the
transport of the body back to Australia. If there's anything
he can do for Mrs. Cassidy or your family, don't hesitate to
call on him. By the way, did Cassidy leave any Government
papers with you – official correspondence, documents, that
sort of thing?'

My answer was truthful if incomplete.

'I'm the executor of the will; but I haven't even seen
that document yet. It'll be a few days before I can determine how and where his records are kept. Then there'll

be the normal probate searches. If I come across any Government material I'll let you know – unless, of course, there's anything special that you need traced immediately.'

'Would you know where to find such material, Mr. Gregory?'

'For God's sake! My time is two in the morning. Cassidy died only three hours ago. My wife's in shock. I'm out on my feet. A document search is the last thing on my mind!'

'Forgive me, Mr. Gregory.' The Deputy Premier was suddenly bland. 'I'm in shock, too, and I'm being quite unreasonable. Obviously, my people and I will need to talk with you again; so perhaps you'd be good enough to give me the telephone numbers of your home and your office.'

I gave them to him. He thanked me hurriedly and hung up. I picked up Cassidy's briefcase, laid it on the desk, and set the combination at the day, the month and the year of Pat's birthday. I was just about to snap open the lock when a new thought struck me.

Cassidy had been a high man. He had driven hard bargains in his private and his public life. All sorts of people therefore would have an interest in his papers and in me as their legal custodian. Those who felt threatened might well threaten me – or my family. Those who sought power or profit might well see me as the keeper of the magic talisman.

And then, before I had scanned a single line, I saw the real nature of the joke Cassidy had played on me. Whatever messes he had left behind I was legally bound to clean up. Whatever scores he had left unpaid I would have to settle. Whatever secrets he had, I must guard under the cloak of legal privilege. The friends he had would look to me for protection. Sooner or later his enemies would come knocking on my door.

For one brief moment of madness I saw him, perched like a leprechaun on the lid of the briefcase, mocking me with another verse from the Gospel according to Cassidy.

'Virtue brings its own rewards: starvation rations and the backside out of your breeches . . . Now lift up the lid, sonny boy, and take a look at Charlie Cassidy's candy store!'

So I did just that. I opened the briefcase to find it filled with cassettes of microfiches, numbered in sequence and labelled with a list of contents. Laid on top of the cassettes was a heavy manila envelope containing Cassidy's will and three trust deeds, each with its own schedules and annexures. There was also a handwritten note addressed to me.

. . . As to the will, even you, Martin the Righteous, must agree it's a tidy and generous document. The usual bequests to servants and old retainers, then four million in diversified assets to my daughter and her offspring. No problems for my executor either. The schedules of assets are updated to December 31 last year. The title deeds and script are lodged with the bank at head office. There's money for taxes and other current liabilities and no taint or stain on a single dollar bill.

Then you come to the trusts, which require no work from you, merely an acquaintance with the documents. There's the Clare Cassidy Foundation which, during her lifetime, takes care of my wife in the manner to which I have accustomed her and devolves after her death to the benefit of the City Mission. The Gallery Endowment comprises my own art collection – not a bad one either, for a country boy who saw his first picture on top of a chocolate box – and a handsome annuity for future acquisitions. I'm no Paul Getty, but they won't be cursing me in the streets either, especially when they see the size of the gift to the Children's Foundation Fund for the care and education of the handicapped.

It all adds up to a round ten million, which is just about what my adoring public will expect and approve by way of posthumous benefaction. The trick is to be rich enough so they know you've made good – but not filthy rich, so it sticks in their gullet. And if you think I'm taking a lot of care of my reputation from the wrong side of the grave, you're right! Who the hell wants to be immortal in infamy?

But given that infamy is always predicated of politicians, I decided long ago to come to terms with ill-repute and, wherever possible, turn it into profit. So I started the little collection which you now have under your hands. It looks like a ragbag of letters, documents, diary entries, accounts, *obiter dicta*, snippets from telephone taps. In fact, it's a highly systematised summary of the life, times and unofficial diversions of Charles Parnell Cassidy. But before you delve into it, let me give you fair warning. All of it is dangerous, some of it lethal, material. So I'm offering you three choices.

First, you can get rid of the stuff, at a nice profit. You deliver it in care of Nordfinanz Bank, Zurich, for consignment to one Mr. Marius Melville. You will hear no more of it, and the bank will credit you immediately with five million US dollars, which is the price I agreed wth Mr. Melville if I should ever decide to sell.

There's only one problem with that arrangement. It puts an awful lot of power in Melville's hands and, with me gone, he wouldn't hesitate to use it. If ever you meet him, show respect. He merits it. And never forget that while he keeps iron faith with his friends, he's as ruthless as Caligula to his enemies.

The second option is to deliver all the material to the Attorney-General of the State of New South Wales. He won't pay you for it. He won't even like you once he sees what's in it! He'll hand the whole collection to his senior staff for what he'll call 'verification and assessment'. Which is another way of saying he'll be very happy if they can make it go away. Then, after great gurglings and rumblings and leaks to the press and calls for yet another Royal Commission, it will do just that.

Material will be abstracted, key documents will be lost until the whole potent pattern is destroyed. You, of course, won't have to worry. You'll be Martin the Righteous, sleeping the sleep of the just, with the receipt for a failed reformation tucked under your pillow.

Your final option is to examine the material yourself and make your own decision as to its use or its destruction. You'll be the potent one then – if you want to be. You'll be the rich one – if that's what you want. You'll also be the target for anyone who fears what I know about him – and that's a long list with a lot of big names on it.

Interesting situation, isn't it? I'm sorry I won't be here to know your decision. But maybe the Almighty will grant me one backward look before he boots me down to the Fifth Circle of Hell. Why the Fifth? I'll give you Dante's answer:

'*Lo buon maestro disse: Figlio or vedi
L'anime di color che vinse l'ira . . .*'
That's me and that's thee, sonny boy:
'The souls of those overcome by rage.'

You never knew and it's taken me fifteen years to tell you, that you were the son I always wanted and never had. Like every father with his first-born, I wanted to mould you to my own image, or at least to the undefaced image of myself. But you rebelled. You wanted to be your own man at any cost – and the costs came high for all of us. When first we quarrelled I thought you would break yourself on me. Then we would all kiss and make up and be happy in mutual malice, the way the Irish like to be, wherever they live.

Instead, I broke myself on you. I lost my daughter. I lost my wife. I lost all joy in my grandchildren. I came to hate the man I wanted to love as a son. The only satisfaction I had was that I'd left a drop of poison in your cup too. Stupid, isn't it – but that's the way the human animal is made. Comes a time, as we both know, when things have gone too far to mend, when love dries up and the heart hardens in rejection. That's why I've cut you out of my will and made you a backhanded gift of the worst side of myself.

That's another reason why I'm resolved not to linger through the last bad days. Marian's doctor friend believes in tidy and painless exits. He's given me a pill so that I can terminate myself before the going gets too rough and he'll sign the death certificate without a blush.

What more is there to tell? The rest is cliché.

Moriturus te salutat . . .

Charles

Suddenly I was choking with anger at the bitter, fruitless folly of it all. I marched upstairs with the letter in my fist, thrust it at Pat, who was lying sleepless on the pillows staring at the ceiling.

'Read it!' I told her harshly. 'Read it and tell me which of the stallions won the fight.'

Then I left her and went back to my study. I poured myself half a tumbler of whiskey, gagged on the first mouthful and hurried to the bathroom to heave my heart out.

When I came back, sweating and nauseous, Pat was waiting. She stretched out her hands to me and I grasped them gratefully. She said: 'I'm going to ask a big thing of you, Martin. I want you to say a prayer with me for the resting of his soul.'

I never felt less like praying. She knew it, but she talked on quietly.

'He used to quote an old proverb. He said it was Gaelic. "A wolf must die in his own skin." Well, he's done just that. I wish I could cry for him. I can't. But I owe him at least a prayer. You see, he wanted to be forgiven, but he was too proud to ask. That's why he took the death-pill. He wouldn't burden us with a care he felt he didn't deserve.

Can you believe that? Will you try to believe it, for both our sakes?'

'I want to: but what about this – this collection he's left that can make me rich, powerful and dead? It sounds like the apples of Sodom that turn to dust in your mouth.'

'I think it's something else, a service he needs done. I don't believe a life like his can be wrapped up in a will and three trust deeds. There must be other debts to pay, obligations of one kind or another. He couldn't ask you straight out, so, in his letter, he tried to goad you into helping him.'

'Maybe we should say two prayers – one for him and one that he's not playing another dirty trick on us.'

She rummaged in a drawer of the bedside table and brought out an old Roman Missal which she had used as a girl. We recited a Pater and an Ave and the De Profundis. Then we went to bed and made a strange fugitive loving that ended in our own little death and we slept afterwards separate and cold as marble effigies on a cathedral tomb.

I woke in the small hours, out of a comic nightmare in which Leprechaun Cassidy, with his fists full of dollars, danced on our marble slab to the tune of the Rakes of Mallow.

3

Three days later, I left London on Qantas Flight QF2, bound for Bahrain, Singapore and Sydney. Charles Parnell Cassidy flew with me, his embalmed body sealed in a stainless-steel box and coffined in a mahogany casket with silver-gilt ornaments, his secret history locked in the brief-case under my seat.

My travelling companion was not much livelier: a good-looking girl in a grey jumpsuit and big owl-glasses who, the moment after take-off, downed a couple of pills, wrapped herself in a blanket and went to sleep. I regretted her absence. I like company when I am travelling. I like women's company at any time. Tonight, of all nights, I should have been glad of some diversion from the black imps dancing a jig through my brain-box.

I was damnably depressed and more afraid than I wanted to admit. I didn't like the sound of Cassidy's heavies. Australia has a long history of rough-neck politics and Sydney has bred more than its share of professional frighteners. If they intervened they would begin with an offer to trade. If I refused the rough stuff would begin – and I would want my family as far away from the action as possible.

We had agreed, therefore – though not without some sharp argument – that I should be the one to take Cassidy home to Australia and bury him. I was kin enough to discharge all the public pieties: attend the Requiem Mass and the State funeral, toss the first sod into the grave, shake the hands of the distinguished mourners. For the rest, common prudence dictated that Pat and Clare and the children should stay far removed from publicity and gossip.

Already the Australian editorials were saying that Cassidy had picked a good time to die. The air was rank with scandal: drugs, violence in gangland, corruption of the police, of the judiciary, of Parliament itself. Cassidy, dead, was beyond attainder. The Opposition could not impugn his reputation without damaging its own. The Government could dump all its messes on his grave and walk away with clean hands and virtuous smiles – unless, of course, one Martin Gregory got a sudden attack of conscience and decided to go public with Cassidy's private files.

I had been a servant of the law all my life. I believed I had been a good servant. Cassidy himself had trained me. So, when he handed me the record of his works and days, he knew that he was giving me a hairshirt that would scratch and chafe until I stripped it off. As I tossed uneasily through the small hours of the morning, I half expected him to pop his head through the floor like Jack-in-the-box and thumb his nose at me.

This was the paradox of the man. Time was when he had loved the law. He understood its ancient principles. He cherished its refinements. No shoddy drafting for him, no chancy interpretation, no slipshod research. 'If you want to gamble,' he would say, 'go to the dog-track and use your own money, not the client's. You are dealing with sacred things here, matters of trust, matters of decision that will bind future generations. And get it into your thick skulls: we make our money out of the mistakes of other attorneys.'

It was high-minded, heady stuff and we juniors loved him for it, even while we hated his rasping tongue. But somewhere along the way he had turned traitor. He had sold out. I had to know why and to whom, before I could make any decision about the documents he had entrusted to me. I had to find out the true identity of Marius Melville who would pay me five million dollars, cash on the barrel-head, for the same documents. The alliteration made the name sound maddeningly familiar, but I could find no real man to hang it on. Drifting between sleep and waking, I played association games, matching the sounds to the pulsing rhythm of the jets . . . Marius, Mario, Marionette, Melville, Melitta . . .

A steward nudged me awake and whispered: 'Sorry, sir; but you're talking in your sleep – rather loudly, I'm afraid. It's disturbing the other passengers.'

I mumbled an apology. He gave me a wide, toothy grin and faded into the blackness like the Cheshire cat. I lay there, feeling confused and foolish, wondering whether I could make it to the toilet without falling over my own feet and disturbing the passengers again.

The girl beside me stirred under her blanket, tilted her seat upright and switched on the reading light. She turned to me and murmured, 'I'm sorry he woke you. Your pillow-talk was just getting interesting.'

'That could get me into a lot of trouble.'

'I know. I once lost a very adequate boyfriend that way.'

Her eyes were innocent behind the big owl spectacles, but I knew – or thought I knew – a baited hook from a leaf in the water. So I chuckled dutifully and asked if she were going through to Sydney. She told me, yes. I decided that if I were going to be picked up I might as well freshen myself before the rush to the lavatories started. Stubble and a stale mouth are unavoidable in marriage. They do not conduce to agreeable intercourse on a crowded aircraft.

As I shaved and brushed my teeth, and dabbed lotion on my jowls, I remembered another pearl of wisdom from the lips of the great Cassidy: 'It's the exiles who own the earth, sonny boy, because they're tough enough to walk without shoes and eat stale crusts, and mate in strange beds with women they can't even pass the time of day with . . . Walk any road on the planet and you'll find a Greek or a Celt or a Jew or a Chinese making money out of the locals. Look up in any sky and you'll see the wild geese flying across the moon . . .'

And that was another thing to note about Charlie Cassidy: he was committed, body, soul and breeches, to local politics, which is a game as bloody as cock-fighting. Yet, in a fashion rare among his ilk, he had managed to remain an international. He was a polyglot, too, with a passable fluency in Italian, French, Greek, German, Mandarin and Dutch. The languages were his passport into the migrant groups who now made solid voting blocs in every State of the Australian Continent. They were also the key that would open the doors to the underworld – to the Sicilian mafiosi and the Chinese triads who ran the girl traffic and the drug networks and battled for control of the gambling territories with the back-alley boys from Balmain.

But, give the devil his due, there was a lot more to Cassidy than political calculation. Under all the fustian, there was an old-style Celtic scholar, greedy for knowledge, a Renaissance man, too, tempted always outward to the Spice Islands and far Cathay . . . At which point I stopped in my tracks. Why should I write a eulogy for Cassidy? He had cheated the hangman, but he had left my neck in the noose, and his daughter and his grandchildren in jeopardy.

By the time I had finished my toilet the stewards were serving breakfast. My Lady Owl-Eyes was sitting up and taking hearty nourishment. She looked like a new woman. Her hair was brushed, there was colour in her cheeks. She smiled readily. Clearly, she was one of those precious creatures who know how to be agreeable at breakfast. We introduced ourselves formally.

'Martin Gregory.'

'Laura Larsen.'

I told her I was a lawyer – which closed out further questions. The usual response is 'How interesting'. The wittiest I've heard is 'Scored any good briefs lately?' which isn't exactly a laugh-line.

Laura Larsen was an easier subject. She was eager to tell me she was in the hotel business. She had worked for CIGA in Italy, for Forte in London and Paris. Now she was on her way to Sydney as sales manager for the Melmar Marquis, a new harbourside hotel in the five-star category. She presented me with a business card which carried a coronet over a double M monogram and the legend 'Melmar Hotels, a legend in luxury'.

Miss Larsen embellished the legend so skilfully that I thought she would have every room sold out in a week. Inside five minutes she was urging me to change my hotel and book in at the Melmar Marquis – with an introductory discount of course!

It was a good-humoured pitch and I was happy to go along with it. At five in the morning vitality is low and self-esteem even lower. Ever since Cassidy's death there had been a curious constraint in my relations with Pat. I began to imagine her in the role of silent accuser. I was the man who had invaded her primal family and ruptured it beyond repair. Mine was the hand that had held her back from the last journey with her father. True or false, it made a sadness between us, a small, veiled anger that neither of us dared to admit.

So, a mile-high first-class flirtation with an attractive woman was an agreeable diversion. Besides, why not be cosseted at discount rates in a new, luxury hotel?

I was just about to accept the offer when a warning bell sounded inside my skull. This was all too pat. I wasn't just being picked up. I was being set up, fitted out, for an old-fashioned badger game. We hadn't yet hit Bahrain. If we played it by the book, we'd be friends of the heart by Singapore and bedfellows the moment we unpacked in the Melmar Marquis in Sydney.

Once again, there was Charlie Cassidy chirping at me out of the past:

'. . . oldest trick in the book, sonny boy, and it still works. It's the easiest way to suborn a witness, frighten a judge, buy a Cabinet vote . . . A man is never so vulnerable as when he's caught bare-assed in bed by hostile witnesses – never so damn ridiculous either! . . .'

I tried to tell myself that I was getting paranoid about the whole thing. The girl was just a happy extrovert peddling hotel space. I was your normal male traveller with the mid-life blues, ready to talk to anyone who would give him good morning . . . Like hell! I was Martin Gregory, with a briefcase full of secrets at his feet and a whole pack of powerful people itching to get their hands on it. What more natural move than to plant a minder on me – and if she could do night duty as well, so much the better.

To my Lady Owl-Eyes I told half a lie and half a truth. I would love to lodge at her hotel, but I was on Government business and I had to defer to the arrangements of my hosts. However, I'd be delighted to visit and see the wonders she was selling. That led to some amiable talk which lasted until we slid down through the desert dawn to the flat sea and the sterile shoreline of Bahrain.

At six in the morning the transit lounge offers no attractions and precious few amenities. The toilets are precarious and the coffee shop a silent menace. There is a motley mob of passengers: Koreans, British, Japanese, Pakistanis, Palestinians and Australians. The dusty stalls display Arab newspapers, dolls stuffed with God-knows-what, fake pottery and hideous brassware. Five minutes is more than enough to complete the circuit; then you are stuck in the place for the best part of an hour. So, the safer option is to stay on board, let the cleaners sweep under your feet, and relax until take-off.

I was doing just that, and making desultory talk with Laura Larsen when a member of Qantas' ground-staff hurried me into the terminal to take a telephone call from Zurich. The line was surprisingly clear. The voice of the caller was a warm, soothing baritone with only a hint of European formality in the phrases and intonations. But when he spoke it was as if a cold hand had closed around my heart.

'Martin Gregory?'

There was no honorific, no preamble. I tried to keep the tremor out of my voice.

'Yes. Who is calling please?'

'Marius Melville.'

I said nothing. Cassidy's warning had been clear. 'Show respect . . .' Besides, I needed a second or two of silence to compose myself. The voice prompted me.

'I think you are familiar with the name.'

'Familiar? Not at all. I have seen only a brief mention of it in the papers of a gentleman recently deceased. There may be others, but as yet I have done no more than glance at the documents.'

'How long will it take you to study them?'

'God knows! All I've read so far is the will, three trust deeds and an index. I would say it'll be a week after the funeral before I can even make an informed guess.'

'But then you will be in touch with me?'

'If that is what the documents dictate, most certainly. An executor is bound . . .'

'I know what an executor does, Mr. Gregory.' The reproof was tempered by a compliment. 'I admire your professional discretion. Charles Cassidy was an old and cherished friend. We had many common interests. I know you will respect his wishes in my regard.'

'It is my duty to do so, Mr. Melville. Where may I reach you?'

'In care of Nordfinanz Bank, Zurich. But I shall communicate with you very soon. Meantime,' the rich voice was full of concern, 'please be most careful. You are in great danger.'

'From whom?'

'You carry bad news, Mr. Gregory.'

'I'm not yet aware of that.'

'You will become so. Then beware, lest they try, as they did in the old days, to kill the bearer of ill tidings.'

'Who are *they*?'

'Cassidy's documents will tell you . . . One more word, Mr. Gregory.'

'Yes?'

'Don't worry about your wife and family. They are under my protection. No harm will come to them. As for yourself, I urge you to trust Miss Larsen. She is a clever and courageous young woman . . .'

Suddenly I was boiling with anger at the cold presumption of the man. But Cassidy, dead, still counselled me:

'He keeps iron faith with his friends . . .' So, instead of shouting at him, I thanked him.

'I appreciate your concern for the family of an old friend. However, I do have to say –'

He wasn't about to listen. He had already broken the connection. The receiver was whining in my ear.

When I tried to reboard the aircraft, a surly policeman ordered me to wait and embark with the rest of the passengers. I wandered around disconsolately, staring at strands of cultured pearls, Japanese watches, worry beads and glass charms against the evil eye. Then I sat down next to a migrant worker who stank like a desert goat. I felt, as I had never felt in my life before, diminished to dwarf-size. I felt that I, too, must be stinking of fear, a cowering victim of powers too large to define or control.

When finally I was permitted to reboard, Laura Larsen greeted me, with a smile of blandest innocence.

'So, you've spoken to Mr. Melville.'

'Yes!' I was in no mood for small-talk.

'That makes our relationship easier.'

'Do we have one?'

'Oh yes. I have to keep an eye on you, make sure you're not bothered while you're in Sydney, put you in touch with Mr. Melville when you're ready to talk to him.'

'And suppose I tell you and Mr. Melville to mind your own bloody business!'

'You are our business, Mr. Gregory.'

'So all this talk about your big hotel job is so much eyewash!'

'On the contrary: Mr. Melville owns the whole Melmar chain – fifty hotels worldwide. That's how it gets it name – Melville, Marius, Melmar, just like that. We offer our guests the best security service in the world: bodyguards, electronic surveillance, protection against bugging and theft of commercial secrets. That service will be at your disposal.'

'But I don't want it.'

'You need it . . . Please don't be angry. You're only making things more difficult for yourself, and for me.'

If I hadn't laughed I might have shouted my anger around the cabin.

'Miss Larsen, understand this. I don't give a damn about you or Marius Melville. I didn't ask for your protection. I don't want you or your employer dabbling in my life . . . Let's have that clear and we can both enjoy the rest of the trip. Well?'

Before she had time to answer the steward was beside us, offering cool drinks. He was followed by a girl with iced towels. Then they were rehearsing us again in the exits-oxygen-life-jackets-and-rubber-boat routine, after which a disembodied voice from the flight deck recited our route to Singapore. By then Laura Larsen was a very calm, very soft spoken lady. She laid a cool palm on my wrist and told me: 'I want you to listen carefully, Mr. Gregory. Don't say anything until I've finished . . . I've worked nearly ten years for Marius Melville. He's a very formidable man. I knew Charlie Cassidy too. I travelled with him more than once, as Mr. Melville's representative. I liked him – most of the time. But that's not important. The fact is that he and Mr. Melville did a lot of deals together, all over the world. You're settling Cassidy's estate, therefore you have to be a focus of interest for Marius Melville. You've got him in your life whether you want him or not. Because you've got him, you've got me – and a lot of other people you don't know, and some you wouldn't want to know. So why not recognise that first of all? Then we can talk openly.'

'No secrets?'

'Of course there are secrets. You should be damned glad there are.'

One of the arts of the law is to drop an argument that is leading you down a blind alley. I managed to be polite about it.

'You've made your point. Here's mine: I'm handling the

estate of a public man, who was also my father-in-law.
There are legal rules about that. I can't bend them for you,
Marius Melville or the Queen of Merrie England!'

She gave a small, rueful chuckle.

'My God, you're like Charlie Cassidy. I've seen him at
meetings in Nassau and Hong Kong, when the air was so
electric you almost expected lightning and a thunder-clap.
The next instant he'd have them laughing their heads off
at some silly joke – and he never surrendered a position
either. Mr. Melville used to say, "Cassidy's a genius. When
he comes to a deal discussion his pockets are stuffed with
give-away points. He gets people squabbling over them
like monkeys over a bag of peanuts. At the end that's all
they've got – peanuts, while Charlie walks away with the
gold, the girl and ten per cent of the futures. It's not that
he's greedy. He knows what he's worth and he sticks out
for it." Mr. Melville is so different, you wouldn't think
they'd get on at all. But they were close friends. Mr.
Melville was very distressed by his death.'

'Do you mind if I ask a personal question?'

'Go ahead.'

'Are you scared of Marius Melville?'

'Why do you ask that?'

'You call Cassidy by his first name, but you always speak
formally of Melville.'

'He's a formal man. He doesn't invite intimacy.'

'He sounds like a cold fish.'

'Oh, no. He's like a dormant volcano with all the fires
hidden inside.'

'So I repeat the question: are you scared of him?'

'Not scared. Respectful.'

'Obviously he respects you, too.'

'I'm good at what I do.' She said it with a shrug,
then hesitated a moment before uttering an oddly
plaintive afterthought. 'Please, you're not going to mess
things up, are you? You're not going to be tricky and
devious?'

'I have no reason to be. I'm a simple soul, who likes to be friendly and hates to be pushed.'

'Good!' It sounded like a long sigh of relief. 'Now I can enjoy my lunch and the movie!'

And there we dropped the whole discussion. Through lunch we exchanged one-line banalities. I dozed through the film. We slept in separate silences from Singapore to sunrise over the Australian desert. On the final descent, with the red-tiled rooftops of Sydney spread beneath us, we said our farewells. I was sorry to see her go – and almost fool enough to say so; but my Lady Owl-Eyes had the last word.

'When we meet again I hope we can both be more relaxed. As soon as you're ready to confer with Mr. Melville, let me know. If you're in trouble, call and invite me to dinner at Mario's. That's the codeword – "dinner at Mario's". If we get it, we hit the red button and call out the riot squad . . .'

4

Charles Parnell Cassidy's welcome to his homeland was brief, bleak and ironic.

While we passengers sat in the aircraft, waiting to be sprayed with insecticide, Cassidy's mortal relics were lifted out of the hold, shoved into a black, windowless panel-van and driven swiftly to an undertaker's mortuary. Thence they would be delivered, early on the morning of the funeral, to St. Mary's Cathedral. The protocol officer who met me explained the curtness of the proceedings.

'It's a business day. The police don't want crowds at the

airport and along the traffic routes to the city during the morning rush. The Premier – he was sworn in yesterday – felt we shouldn't take the edge off the State funeral . . . He was sure you'd understand. He'd like you to dine with him tonight at Parliament House. Seven-thirty for eight. The Attorney-General will be there too. His name's Loomis. A limousine will pick you up at seven-twenty at your hotel. We've booked you in at the Town House. I've checked the suite. It's very pleasant . . . The funeral's tomorrow. The ceremonies begin at ten in the morning with a Requiem Mass in the Cathedral . . . Here's a schedule of the ceremonies and a list of dignitaries . . . If there's anything else you need . . .'

After a twenty-four-hour flight, gravel-eyed and reeking of fatigue, all I needed was a shave, a hot tub and a sleep. However, the sleep would have to be deferred. I had to rid myself as quickly as possible of Cassidy's briefcase. So, as soon as I had bathed and changed, I took a taxi into the city and presented myself at the offices of the Banque de Paris, our principal correspondent in Australia.

The Director, Paul Henri Langlois, was an old friend. We drank coffee and exchanged reminiscences. He provided me with a large safe-deposit box, an office, access to his microfiche scanner and the services of a multi-lingual secretary. Then, drunk with fatigue, I went back to the hotel, put a block on the telephone until five in the evening and tumbled into bed.

At five-thirty there was a knock on my door and a boy from the porter's desk presented me with a sealed envelope which, he told me, had just been delivered by courier. The envelope contained a message handwritten on notepaper from the Melmar Marquis.

Dear Martin G. – Hope you're comfortable. You were wise to lodge your papers with a foreign bank. Enjoy your dinner tonight. Watch your step with Loomis. He's a Cassidy man and will be very anxious to know where the bodies are buried. Mr. Melville has telexed his best wishes. Mine come with this note. Call me when you feel like it.

Best – Laura L.

Taken at face value, it was a very sinister missive. It told me I was under close surveillance, that my future movements were being plotted, that a senior minister – one with great legal powers – was potentially hostile. Read from the underside, it became a token of concern, an earnest of friendship. I have to be honest: that was how I wanted to understand it. Twelve thousand miles from wife and children, a stranger in my own homeland, a bearer of bad tidings to people I had never met, I wanted to be comforted and diverted, even if the diversion were a trap and the comfort a treachery.

The need was so strong that I sat down at the desk and wrote a lighthearted note of acknowledgment to Laura Larsen. Then my lawyer's caution prevailed. I tore the note into shreds and tossed it into the waste basket. Anger with myself made me clear-headed. I remembered the old lessons of the jungle patrol: the thickets were ambushed; there were snipers in the trees; the pistes were tiger-trapped; the clearings were mined; one incautious step and you were a dead man. Suddenly I was stifled by the onset of that most primitive terror, the panic of a lone traveller, lost in an alien landscape.

My early service with Cassidy, my later experience in the money markets of the world, had taught me hard lessons about the root systems of power, how deep they drive into the earth, how far and how tortuously they spread across frontiers, through blood lines and caste lines, and past the most ironclad defences of treaties and ordinances. 'A bear coughs at the North Pole –' so ran the ancient proverb – 'and a man dies in Peking.' A boardroom decision in Detroit could wreck a South American economy. A rumour floated in Delhi could kill a man in Delaware. I had once known a Lebanese banker, custodian of tribal millions, sent bankrupt by an oil man in Texas to pay off a grudge over a woman.

Another lesson I had learned: no one is invulnerable – no nun in her cell, no tyrant surrounded by his legions, no stylite on his pillar in the middle of the desert. The nun can be seduced from her loneliness, the tyrant can be cut down by his bodyguard. The stylite can be toppled by an earthquake or a clown with a crowbar.

But what of myself, Martin Gregory? By what stratagem, by whom plotted, could I be most quickly undone? A woman might coax me into folly. She could not easily blackmail me. A man could threaten me through my family. I had more fear of that than of violence against my own person. But the traitor inside? That besetting fault which could tumble me head over heels into disaster – what was it?

I had to know, because my life might depend on the knowing. I was like the captain of the watch in some old fortress town, making the rounds of the battlements, prodding the dozing guards, alert for those too wakeful for trust, too drunk for caution, wondering at the end whether he himself might be, witting or unwitting, the man who sold the gates.

So, for my own safety, I was forced to admit it. I had been ambitious always. I needed to be top man on my mountain, were it low or high. Charlie Cassidy was willing to make me his heir, but he wanted me humbled and needy and complaisant before he made the endowment. That price was too high for me; I would not pay it. But I was not then tall enough, strong enough, rich enough to face him down. I could not walk into the Cardinal's parlour and thump the table as Charlie did and make deals for votes and patronage and land grants in undeveloped areas. I could not – not yet anyway – stroll around the old harbourside tenements and pass the time of day and end up buying pints for the constituents in the corner pub . . .

But fight I could and fight I did, a quiet assassin, sleek and silent and oiled in every limb, so that no one could hold me. I took Charlie's daughter, whom I loved but he loved too. I sheltered his wife in her exile. I put a price on their heads and on the heads of his grandchildren . . . and the price was this: 'Now you bow to me, Charles Cassidy. Now you plead, presenting your petition on bended knee.'

God knows it wasn't declared so boldly as that – but it was true nonetheless. I had to win, if not by force, then by stealth and cunning and the secret calculations of the gambler. What else was my present career but a daily battle to outsmart the currency dealers in Hong Kong, guess the equity market in New York, pick up the slack between Sydney and Tokyo, balance out with commissions on insurance funds, and still be sitting on top of the heap at close of business on Friday?

The only place where I didn't want to win was in my own home, with Pat and the children, with Clare Cassidy the matriarch, widow of my dead enemy. There, however, the irony caught up with me. A family in exile, they demanded a leader. Colonists from a new world, they needed a bulwark against the strangeness and hostility of the old. I provided it. I was proud that I could. It made me an honourable man who paid his debts and cherished his loved ones. They cherished me too, open and warm in their affection.

But sometimes I chafed under the burden. I wanted to toss it off and ease my cramped muscles. I craved the luxury of irresponsibility – as I was craving it now, alone in Sydney town, with a political dinner looming up, and a funeral that would be splashed across the front pages of the press, and a very tangled estate to settle, and the glint of a sword-blade hanging over my head.

It was a depressing thought, dangerous to entertain too long. I shoved it to the back of my mind. I shaved and dressed with extra care, then took myself off to dine with the Premier and his Attorney-General.

The Premier was the new breed, tailored to specifications by a big advertising agency and a very skilled public relations outfit. He was young, still on the right side of forty. He was lean, flat-bellied, tanned, bright of eye, with a ready smile and a firm handshake, every young matron's dream of the man of confidence. He 'talked pretty', as Cassidy used to say, but he had a ready command of vernacular vulgarity which would go down well with the crowd. I called him 'Mr. Premier', which he liked. He called me Martin, which I loathed.

Loomis, the Attorney-General, was another animal altogether, pudgy, crumpled, slow of speech, shrewd of eye, with a handshake that felt like limp whitefish, and a furtive smile that twitched at the corners of his mouth and then lost itself in the furrows of his jowls. Cassidy had appointed him, so he had to know the law and the thousand and one ways to use it as an instrument of power. He called me Mr. Gregory but invited me to call him Rafe. The Premier offered me a drink, which he himself poured with a generous hand. Then, more brusquely than I had expected, he came to the point.

'We've got big problems, Martin.'

'What sort of problems?'

'A man dies.' It was the Attorney-General who answered. 'He can't sue for libel any more. We've been told the press are only waiting until Cassidy's buried, then they're going to plaster his personal and political history all over the front pages.'

'And you're scared of that?'

'Personally, no.' The Premier sounded unsure.

'Politically, yes.' The Attorney-General was emphatic. 'Charlie Cassidy had a very simple philosophy. If you're in the business of government, you live with what you've got – hookers and junkies and hit-men and honest Jack and Jill Citizen all included. You want a tourist trade, you take the call girls and the pimps with it. You want a gambling industry and the taxes it brings in, you get standover men on the same bill as the bookies. Charlie never flinched from that. He didn't do a bad job of keeping the peace – and he made the villains pay through the nose for their privileges.'

'But,' said the Premier, 'these last few years, things have been getting out of hand.'

'What sort of things, Mr. Premier?'

'Drugs,' said the Attorney-General. 'And all the shit that goes with them.'

'Forgive my mentioning it, but you're the man who administers the law. What's holding you back?'

'Dirty linen,' said the Premier.

'Cartloads of it,' said the Attorney-General.

'And we're wondering what you've got or may get to add to the pile.' The Premier was in command now. 'You're family. You're the executor. All Cassidy's papers have to come into your hands – if they haven't done so already.'

'And we want to make sure we see them and the press doesn't.'

'Let me be quite clear with you, gentlemen.' I tried hard to be polite. 'My family and I were estranged from Charles Cassidy for years. He came to me *in extremis* and told me he had named me executor of his estate. The only documents I've read so far are the will and three trust deeds, which are, on the face of it, simple and quite innocuous documents. So, until I begin my searches as executor, I have no idea what I'll discover. But, everything that does come into my hands is privileged until I am subpoenaed to display it in court. With the best will in the world, I don't see that I can help you very much.'

'Don't be too sure about the privilege,' Loomis' smile came and went swiftly. 'If you were concealing documents relevant to criminal matters, I could argue a good case against you for misprision of a felony . . .'

'Not a felony committed by a dead man!'

'But one compounded by the living, yes!'

51

'Only if you could prove I had incriminating documents, recognised their import and knowingly withheld them. Don't play games with me, please Mr. Loomis . . . I'm jetlagged and running out of jokes.'

'Sorry!' He apologised instantly. 'I've had a bitch of a day, too. Couldn't even take a piss without tripping over TV cables or microphone leads. Perhaps I can help you by expediting probate procedures. A word from the Minister, that sort of thing.'

'For that I'd be grateful. I don't want to hang around here too long. I'd like to get home to my wife and family.'

'Let me know as soon as you've filed. Who will be acting for you in Sydney?'

'The old firm: Cassidy, Carmody, Desmond & Gorman.'

'I wouldn't touch them with a barge-pole,' said the Attorney-General.

'I wouldn't either,' said the Premier.

'Why not?' I was all innocence.

'Because,' said Loomis unhappily, 'Carmody's damned near senile, Desmond's representing two of our choicest villains and Micky Gorman is counsel on retainer for our most colourful press baron. They're not the safest repository for your material.'

'Why not Standish and Waring?' It was the Premier's suggestion. 'They're more your style.'

'I have no choice, I'm afraid. They acted for Cassidy. All the documents are deposited with them.'

'Let's eat,' said Loomis. 'I missed lunch today.'

It was clear that they were both under stress and that we were still a long way from the core of the discussion. As we settled ourselves at table the Premier said, 'I know it's early days, but can you guess at what Cassidy's estate may be worth?'

'It's better than a guess and it will soon be public knowledge anyway. There's a bequest to his daughter and our children. There's a trust fund for his wife which devolves to the City Mission, a donation of his art collection to the

State gallery and separate provision for the Children's Medical Foundation. All in all, it's about ten million.'

'Handsome!' said the Premier drily. 'Very handsome.'

'But wearable.' Loomis was obviously relieved. 'He was elected rich. He died rich. The City Mission and the Children's Medical Foundation are worthy causes. And the art collection is very valuable. On the score of benefactions, I'd say Charlie goes out smelling of roses.' He turned to me again. 'Are you sure there are no contentious bequests – to mistresses, kids born on the wrong side of the blanket, that sort of thing?'

'None.'

'I wonder what he did with the rest of it.'

'The schedules of assets are up to date as at last December. The documents show no other funds.'

'Loomis is guessing.' The Premier sounded irritable.

'The hell I'm guessing! It stands to reason –'

'You're tired, Rafe!' There was real anger in the Premier's voice. 'You're making reckless talk. Nothing stands to reason unless it can be proven in court.'

I decided it was time to play the peacemaker. I gave them a shrug and an amiable grin.

'You both knew Cassidy better than I. He's been out of my life and my wife's for many years now. But wasn't that his style, to make mysteries, create illusions like a magician at a children's party?'

For the first time, Loomis laughed and the tension relaxed.

'You're right, of course. That was Charlie to a T.'

'So what are you really concerned about? It will save us all a lot of time if you can be open with me.'

'Save it for the coffee.' The Premier gave a furtive glance at the waiters hovering in the background. 'This place leaks information like a sieve. If I had my way I'd staff it with mute slaves!'

'Don't let the press get hold of that quote,' murmured Loomis gloomily. 'They'll never let you forget it.'

Over the coffee cups they came to the point. They had the grace to be embarrassed; but, true-blue politicians, they were dedicated to the principle of survival at any cost. The Premier laid down the first premises.

'Loomis and I – in fact, all the new Cabinet – are Cassidy men. He was a great leader. He had the gall of a con-man and the guts of a street fighter. He gave you a clear brief and, provided you stuck to it, he'd protect you right down the line. However, if you started writing your own variations, or quizzing Charlie about whys and wherefores, you'd suddenly find yourself in the middle of an empty paddock with the press baying after you like blood-hounds . . . It was dictatorship, of course, but benevolent dictatorship – most of the time!'

'But now the dictator's dead,' said Loomis, 'and we're accountable to the Party and the electorate. The only way we can survive is to let Cassidy take the rap for what were, after all, his own policies! How do you feel about that?'

'I'm wondering why the ground doesn't open up and swallow you!'

'It still may.' The Premier shrugged ruefully.

'But I still don't understand what you want from me.'

'I'll spell it for you,' said Loomis curtly. 'I want access to all Cassidy's papers – right down to his laundry lists. I want to take possession – and I'll give you a legal receipt! – of everything that could possibly interest us. Hand it over without argument, and you'll get probate for the will in double quick time. Stall me, and you'll still be screaming for your wife's inheritance ten years from now. Clear?'

'Very clear, Mr. Loomis.'

'Well, what do you say?'

'Thank you for the dinner and some instructive talk. I'll see you both at the funeral.'

I pushed back my chair and stood up. The Premier tugged at my coat-tails.

'Please, Martin! Please sit down!' He snapped at Loomis

savagely. 'For Christ's sake, man! What are you playing at?'

Loomis shrugged and gave that flabby half-smile.

'Just tactics. Forensic fun. You understand that, don't you, Mr. Gregory? We have to know what kind of witness we have.'

'Tactics be damned! Threats and menaces, more like. You have one minute to withdraw the threat and come clean. What am I supposed to have that scares you?'

There was a long, hostile silence until the Premier prompted Loomis.

'Apologise! Tell him! We didn't come here for a dog-fight.'

'I withdraw the threat,' said Loomis reluctantly. 'I'll guarantee a speedy handling of your probate application. For the rest, here's our problem. Cassidy carried the keys to this State. In a sense, he had the keys to the whole nation – because we've got the biggest port and the busiest international airport. He ran everything, legal and illegal. He dispensed the favours and collected the payoffs from drugs, gambling, prostitution, land deals, patronage, Government contracts. We were happy to let him do it, because – give the bastard his due – he kept the peace and was an honest paymaster. Everyone got what was promised, payment or punishment. The monies were dispensed by safe routes and there was always some good advice as to where to put them beyond the reach of the tax man. Cassidy had a lot of the legal profession in his pocket, too; lawyers who could lay out your loose change and get you twenty per cent return . . . The problem is that only Cassidy knew how the whole system worked. We all knew there were overseas connections. There had to be, because hot money was exported and cool money came back. But the nature of the network and the identity of the people concerned . . . only Cassidy knew those things.'

'And you want to know whether the knowledge died with him.'

'Or whether he passed it on to you,' said Loomis. 'And if he did, can we make a deal for it.'

'So you can start reforming the system, rooting out corruption in high places, that sort of thing.'

'Precisely,' said the Premier. The word came out on a long exhalation of relief. Loomis gave me an ironic salute and a backhanded compliment.

'You're a good man, Charlie Brown! Cassidy, wherever he is, must be proud of you. So, to put the question simply: How much do you know and how much does it cost?'

'It costs nothing – because at this moment, I know nothing.'

'But the probate searches might – just might – turn up something.'

'In which case, I'll take appropriate action.'

'Which is to bring the material to me.' Loomis was wasting no time on politeness.

'That's one option. There may be others.'

'You're playing games!'

'No. I'm simply reserving my position. Do you blame me? Not half an hour ago you told me that Cassidy ran everything in this State – legal and illegal – and that you, his Cabinet colleagues, were happy to let him do it. What does that make you? What does it make me if I commit evidence into your custody?'

'A prudent servant of the court,' said the Premier calmly.

My private opinion was that it would make me the village idiot; but we had traded enough insults and it was time to call off the argument. I made a pretence of reflecting for a moment, then I told Loomis: 'You seem to have forgotten one fact. I've been out of Australia for more than a decade. I've lost all interest in local politics. I wouldn't know a criminal from a Cabinet minister. So if you want information from Cassidy's files, the least you can do is supply me with a reference list of items and subjects. Without that I'm in the dark.'

'I could appoint a man to work with you.'

'No way! No how!'

Loomis and the Premier looked at each other. The Premier nodded. Loomis gave a grudging assent.

'For the first time this evening, you've begun to make sense. I'll hand you a check list after the funeral.'

'Thank you for your co-operation, Martin,' said the Premier blandly.

'Thank you for a pleasant dinner, Mr. Premier.'

'You're just like Cassidy,' said Loomis. 'You stall all night, then hand out a few scraps and expect us to call you Lady Bountiful . . . I hope the bloody funeral is rained out tomorrow.'

As it happened, the last rites of Charles Parnell Cassidy made a first-class production. The Governor-General was there, taking precedence over the State Governor as representative of the Crown. The Prime Minister was there, playing second fiddle to the Premier. There were union men and diplomats and sporting eminences and clergy and press, Cassidy's old partners and the staff from his office and his household. A contingent of mounted police acted as an honour guard, because the States of Australia have no armed forces except their police and their criminals.

There were a few of those in the crowd, too – but only the successful ones whose names were always mentioned in Royal Commissions, but never seemed to show up on a police charge sheet. There was a whole omelette of immigrant tribal groups – Lebanese, Italians, Greeks, Turks, Chinese, Viets, Celts, Anglo-Saxons, Dutch, Serbs and Spaniards – all acknowledging their debt to Charlie Cassidy and showing their voting strength to his successors.

The Requiem Mass was said in Latin – 'a tribute,' said the Cardinal, 'to Charles Parnell Cassidy, a fine Latinist.' Then he launched into a eulogy so stuffed with platitudes that Cassidy must have been writhing in his coffin. He talked of 'distinguished public service and charities dispensed in secret . . . a Christian life maintained amidst all the temptations of a political career . . . a colourful

personality in whom resided a spirit of extraordinary sim-
plicity.' He talked of 'those quiet dinners at which Charles
Cassidy opened himself to me and told me of his hopes
and fears and his ambitions for this great country of
ours . . .' He talked and talked and talked . . . and what
Cassidy thought of it all remained a secret between him
and his Maker.

But – I must be honest – under all the windy rhetoric
there was a genuine emotion, an affirmation of essential
brotherhood between the cleric and the politician. They
had been friends a long time, hammered out hard bargains
together. They were both Irish by origin, both absolutists
by nature, both caught in the same dilemma: that whatever
the rules or the dogmas, you had to bend them to make
the social contract work. If you didn't, you got blood in
the streets.

As I nodded off into reverie, with the eulogy only half
done, I remembered the tale Cassidy had told at his last
dinner in my house.

'The Cardinal's a shrewd old humbug. He tells me what
I ought to do. I tell him what I can do. He huffs and puffs
a bit and gives me a few quotes from Augustine or Aquinas.
I make a bad joke and leave with the confessional vote in
my pocket. It's not as big as it used to be, but it's still
there, a negotiable bill like the hard core Marxists and the
Total Disarmers. Fact is, sonny boy, I admire folk who
have convictions – but they're dangerous tools at best. The
only thing I'm sure of is that man is a mad animal and you
only make him madder by backing him into a corner.
You've got to give him space and sexual release and enough
of whatever drug he's prone to, so he can work off the
fury in safety . . .'

The choir intoned the ancient versicle, 'Eternal rest give
to him, O Lord, and let perpetual light shine upon him.
May he rest in peace.' Then abruptly it was over and I was
one of six men, marching in slow lockstep down the nave
with Cassidy's coffin perched precariously on our

shoulders. Even then I felt no grief, no prickling of unbidden tears. It was only when I stood in the cemetery, shaking hands, murmuring ritual thanks for the condolences, that I felt a sudden onrush of shame and remorse. This wasn't all panoply and political humbug. Cassidy had been a big man. He had left a large space and the two clowns I had dined with last night were not half big enough to fill it. I wasn't big enough either. I had neither grace enough to forgive him, nor generosity enough even to embrace him on his first and last night in my house.

It was then that the tears came and with them a terrible sense of solitude. I was the outlander now. People were kind, but they didn't quite know how to deal with this hybrid with his English clothes and his formal speech, and the tears rolling down his cheeks.

The Premier and Loomis drove me back to the hotel. It was their show and they'd stage-managed it pretty well. I thanked them on behalf of the family.

'Our pleasure,' said Loomis with a shrug. 'He deserved a good send-off.' He handed me a sealed envelope. 'That's the material you asked for. Keep it in a safe place.' Then, with unexpected grace, he offered a compliment: 'You gave a good performance today. I didn't know you were hurting so much. A solo performance like that – it's rough.'

'Tomorrow, it will get rougher.' The Premier was gloomy. 'We were warned a long time ago: "After Cassidy, the bloody deluge!"'

5

Before the first rains came, I hoped to be long gone. I knew, too well, the whole sorry routine of a witch-hunt. The press shouted the scandal. The public was roused to self-righteous fury. The Government instituted a Royal Commission with power to call sworn evidence from all and sundry. The Commission dragged on until the last juice had been squeezed from the scandal – and the last drop of passion drained from the argument. Indictments were filed against the readiest scapegoats. Then, with the public bored into silence, it was business as usual for the wide boys.

The last thing I wanted was a summons to appear before Her Majesty's Commissioners to testify on oath about Charles Parnell Cassidy. So, every day was precious to me. At three in the afternoon, before the flowers had begun to wilt on Cassidy's grave, I went to Micky Gorman's office for a preliminary conference about the estate.

Gorman – he who handled the affairs of the press baron – was a big, florid fellow with a jolly laugh and a shrewd eye and a fund of drolleries to divert the unwary. I knew him from my salad days and had a healthy respect for his skill. I showed him the copy of the will and the trust deeds. He gave them a cursory glance and told me: 'I drew the documents. I can act on them if you want.'

I told him of my dinner with the Premier and the Attorney-General. He groaned.

'Loomis is a fat bully. I can handle him. There'll be no

delay in probate. All the properties in the schedule are clean and taxes are paid up to date.'

'Loomis was suggesting there are other interests – not clean.'

'Did he offer any proof?'

'He gave me what appears to be a list of foreign corporations and trusts. He claims Cassidy was connected with them, and that they in turn are connected with criminal operations. He demanded that I hand over to him any of Cassidy's papers relating to names on that list.'

'Do you have the list with you?'

I passed him the envelope Loomis had given to me. He scanned the contents quickly. It seemed he was not happy about what he read. He handed it back and asked, 'Do you, in fact, have any of Cassidy's papers?'

'None at all, other than those on your desk.'

It was a careful piece of casuistry. Microfiche records are not papers. They are photographic copies. Gorman seemed relieved.

'That lets you out.'

'Not quite.'

'Oh?'

'As executor. I'm charged to assemble and dispose of the estate. Cassidy's papers are part of it. So I need to know who's holding them and where. You must have some in this office.'

'Some, yes.'

'Where are the rest?'

'First,' said Micky Gorman, 'I'd better tell you about the birds and the bees. You've been away a long time. You and Cassidy were sworn enemies. What could you know?'

'What indeed?' Ignorance was my strongest shield. Micky Gorman doled out his next words like gold dust.

'In politics and in law, Cassidy was a natural. He understood governance – every goddamned nuance of the game!

When you saw him in action it was like watching a great tennis player – mind, muscle and emotion perfectly harmonised and driving towards the kill.' He grinned and gave a small, embarrassed shrug. 'Forgive me. I'm not usually so eloquent. But I admired the bastard – envied him too. He seemed to do everything so easily – even the bullshit and the blarney, which is the hardest act of all for an intelligent man. Well, he had a very simple theory of Government: the ruler ruled; the Premier was what his title said – top man on the totem pole; the democratic process was just that, a process by which power was attained. He applied the notion right down the line. He was the one who called the shots. Look! My biggest client, Gerry Downs, runs a nationwide chain of newspapers and TV stations. He's spent millions over the past decade trying to nail Charlie Cassidy. He's never managed to do it. Now, of course, he'll destroy the underlings, and the local machine – but Charlie's dead and home free! How did Charlie manage it? He used every ploy in the book: bribery, blackmail, patronage – assassination too, if you come right down to it! – but his hands were always clean. When I was offered Gerry Downs' work, the whole climate of the situation was, to say the least, unusual. Cassidy had sold out of our partnership, but he was still our client. Downs was offering me, in fees and retainers, more money than you could poke a stick at. I went to Cassidy. I told him I was concerned about conflict of interests. Cassidy shrugged the whole thing off with a grin. I remember word for word what he told me: "Micky, I couldn't give a hoot in hell what you do. I'll lay you long odds I sleep more soundly than Gerry Downs. If he wants to wean you away from me, that's fine. There's not a document in your hands that won't stand up to scrutiny in open court. If Gerry Downs ever asks you – which he won't – you tell him what I said."'

Gorman broke off and sat slumped in his chair, toying with a paperknife. I prompted him.

'And that's what you're telling me? By all your records, Charlie Cassidy was clean?'

'Whiter than white.'

'But you're also telling me he was guilty of bribery, blackmail, murder . . . Do you know that – or are you guessing?'

'I know it.'

'How?'

'Don't ask me. But once I did know, I bought Cassidy out of the partnership. I paid twice the face value of his holding. That ought to tell you something.'

'I'm not trying to make trouble. I simply want to know whether anyone can prove charges against Cassidy.'

'They don't have to be proven now. Imputation, association, inference – that's all that's needed to discredit his memory. But there is tangible evidence against many of Charlie's people; bribery, conspiracy to pervert the course of justice, intimidation – that sort of thing. Gerry Downs will be publishing a pretty formidable series which will be enough to bring down the Government at election time. The opinion polls run heavily against them even now.'

'You still haven't told me how Charlie managed to stay safe for so long.'

'Are you sure you want to know?'

'I have to know. I'm married to his daughter. My kids are his grandchildren. They'll never forgive me if I start hedging on history.'

'You want it. You get it.' Gorman's tone was suddenly curt. 'Every novel you've ever read runs to the classic pattern. The criminals are the corruptors. They buy the cops. They blackmail the legislators. They terrorise the innocent. The Mafia, the Camorra, the Triads, that's how they work. Right?'

'Yes.'

'Charlie Cassidy did exactly the opposite. He ran the villains. He was the Godfather, the Lord High-Bloody-Panjandrum of the underworld. He was a power-broker, born to the role. He started rich, you see. He didn't have to sell himself for money. There was enough Irish Catholic in him to keep him out of messy sexual situations. Oh, there were women in his life, plenty of 'em, but he never got caught with his pants off, looking ridiculous. He was what my Irish grandmother called a *steady* man. He could pay his way into any alliance; but the ones he made were all offshore. That was his secret, don't you see? Offshore money, offshore power. Hong Kong, Macau, Singapore, India, the Bahamas, Florida. You stick a pin in the map, Cassidy had a man there. And he had respect. That was the key to it. He had respect. If he needed a killer or an intimidator, he flew one in from outside; so he never had to depend on the local police or the local thugs. If he needed more capital he had offshore money to back him.'

'But what was he offering in return? No individual can match the resources of the international crime syndicates.'

Gorman brooded over the question for a moment then, sombrely, he gave me the answer.

'Patronage! That's what he offered. Grace and favour from King Charlie Cassidy! He could pledge this whole bloody State – the unions, the clubs, the rackets, the building permits, control of the transport lines, the ports and airfields. He dispensed the goodwill of the Federal Government, too; because Federal members depended on Charlie's safe voters to win their own seats . . . That's a hell of a lot of security, Martin. In the end, however, it wasn't quite enough. These last three years Charlie was running downhill. He was losing ground every day.'

'To what? To whom?'

'Age . . . mortality. He didn't have the heart or the muscle any more. The other thing, well . . .'

'Let's have it, Micky, please!'

'The other thing was drugs. He always said: "If you can't beat 'em, join 'em." You couldn't wipe out the traffic but you could regulate it and limit its consequences. He was wrong. He couldn't control the flow of narcotics. He couldn't contain the marauders in the market or match the flow of new money they created . . . So his negotiable security was eroded. Sad, when you come to think of it.'

Micky Gorman heaved himself out of his chair, walked to the window and stood staring out at the blue water framed between the skyscrapers. After a long moment of silence, he told me: 'Martin, I'm having second thoughts. It will make a cleaner situation, all around, if you get someone else to handle Cassidy's probate.'

I felt a sudden surge of anger, but I managed to choke it back.

'Just as you like. Bundle up the files you have. Prepare a final account. I'll be back at midday tomorrow to settle up and take delivery of the documents.'

'Thank you. No hard feelings?'

'None at all, Micky. I'll even bring a basin of water, so you can wash your hands!'

'You go to hell!'

'Where are the rest of Cassidy's papers?'

'I don't know. At his house. At his bank. He hasn't confided in me for a long time.'

'I don't blame him, Micky. Do you?'

He didn't answer. I didn't press the point. Three minutes later I was in a taxi, driven by a Viet with an angelic smile and madness in his eyes, on my way to Cassidy's harbourside home.

6

I had always remembered Cassidy in an Edwardian setting of walnut and mahogany and studded leather, of Waterford crystal and antique cutlery, of genre pictures in baroque frames and family photographs in silver ones. His whiskey was always poured from heavy square decanters, his wine dispensed from beakers with gilded lips. His favourite books were bound in tooled Morocco, with markers of watered silk. He opened his mail with an agate paper-knife. At ease in his study, he wore a velvet smoking jacket and monogrammed slippers. Clare used to call it his 'Trinity-squireen-look', which was intended to convey an impression of ripe scholarship and material well-being and political wisdom.

This house, however, was the habitat of a quite different man: a youthful, modern, ebullient fellow, who loved the sun and the dazzle of bright water and cool colours in his drapes and simple lines in his furniture and pictures pulsing with light. It was a three-storeyed town house built from road-level to the water's edge, angled to the north-east with a breathtaking view of Sydney harbour and its traffic of shipping and pleasure-craft. The rooms were large and airy, the bookshelves and cupboards were all recessed into the walls, so that one moved freely from the mobile present of harbour traffic to a visionary past, captured and framed on every available wall space. I wondered which of his women had persuaded him to change his image and his life-style.

Cassidy's resident staff – Elena and Marco Cubeddu – received me into the house. He was immigrant Sardinian, very formal, very correct. She was a girl from Lazio, inclined to be voluble until she was hushed by a low-spoken word from her husband. They had come to pay their respects at the funeral, so they knew I was family. They seemed a little unclear as to my function as executor; but once they had grasped the fact that I was an *avvocato* as well as a son-in-law they were more at ease.

While Elena went to make me coffee, I had a private talk with Marco. I told him first of Cassidy's bequest to

him and his wife – a hundred and fifty thousand dollars.
Clearly, he had not expected so much but, a true Sardo,
he still maintained a dignified reserve.

'He was a great gentleman. It was an honour to serve
him. We shall have Masses said for his soul.'

'How did you come to him, Marco?'

'Mr. Melville recommended us.'

'You mean Mr. Marius Melville?'

'Yes. I had worked for him in Milan. Then, when we
decided to emigrate, he wrote to Mr. Cassidy, seeking a
post for us.'

'Will you go back to Mr. Melville?'

'I don't know. One waits to be invited.'

'Marco,' I chose the next words carefully, 'Mr. Cassidy
explained to me before he died that you were a man of
trust. I need your help.'

'In what particular, sir?' He was a man of caution as
well as confidence.

'Like all politicians, Mr. Cassidy made enemies as well
as friends. Now that he is dead, his enemies will try to
blacken his reputation for political reasons.'

'Sadly, that is normal in my country also.'

'May I count upon your discretion not to discuss with
anybody your period of service with Mr. Cassidy?'

'I have already had approaches, sir. Visits from journal-
ists, telephone calls from newspapers. I have given them
all the same answer. He is dead. He has a right to decent
silence.'

'Thank you, Marco. My family and I are grateful for
that, too. Another matter: no one is to be admitted to the
house without my permission. No tradesmen, no repair-
men . . . no one!'

'That may be a little difficult, sir.'

'Oh?'

'The signorina has a key. She comes and goes. She sleeps
here when she chooses.'

'And who is the signorina?'

'Mr. Cassidy told us to call her Miss Pat. Her real name is difficult to pronounce.'

'But who is she?'

Marco coughed discreetly and chose his words with care. 'She is – how do you say it? – Mr. Cassidy's *donna di confidenza*. She works on his private business. Sometimes she acts as his hostess with people from overseas.' He picked up a silver-framed photograph from the coffee table. '*Eccolà!* There she is.'

There were two figures in the photograph. They looked like a mother and daughter, both dressed in traditional costume, posed in a tropic garden outside a beautiful old Thai house, elaborately carved and gilded. The daughter looked about sixteen years old, the woman somewhere in her mid-thirties. Both had that strange placid beauty which haunts the memory like a Buddha smile.

Marco said quietly, 'The older one is Miss Pat.'

'And the younger . . .?'

He answered with cool respect. 'I have never enquired, sir.'

There was a dedication in the lower right hand corner of the picture, but it was written in Thai so I could not read it.

I asked, 'Do you have an address, a telephone number for Miss Pat?'

'Yes, sir. When Mr. Cassidy began to be ill she gave it to me. She said I must call her whenever Mr. Cassidy was unwell. It's in the kitchen. One moment please.'

A moment later he was back with a tray of coffee and sweet biscuits and a scrap of paper on which was written a Thai name, Pornsri Rhana, and a Sydney telephone number. I thanked him and folded the paper into my pocket-book. I handed him my card and told him: 'For the moment, leave things as they are with Miss Pat. I shall try to telephone her. If she comes here before I've made contact, give her my card and ask her to telephone me at the Town House. Now, if you will excuse me, I must go through the house and inspect everything – especially Mr. Cassidy's papers.'

'All his papers are in the safe, which is in one section of the wardrobe in Mr. Cassidy's bedroom. He stored them there before he left for America. Unfortunately, I do not have the combination or the key.'

'I have them. Is there another set?'

'I do not know, sir.'

'Who else might know?'

'For his personal affairs, he used only Miss Pat. For his official work he brought someone from Parliament . . . Please sir, drink your coffee before it gets cold. If you need anything else, just dial zero on the house phones – the green ones.'

He bowed himself out and left me to my coffee and my puzzlement.

Charles Parnell Cassidy was too clever a man to receive a known spy into his household. So, clearly, his relationship with Marius Melville was one of openness and mutual trust. Whether I should trust him was not half so clear. Pornsri Rhana was yet another problem. I felt an instant resentment against her because Cassidy had given her the name of the daughter he had thrust out of his life. And if she was, as Marco had seemed to suggest, something more than a business aide, then there was real perversity in giving a mistress the name of his own daughter. But then, the Cassidy I knew was a perverse son-of-a-bitch with a wide streak of cruelty in his make-up. I asked myself why I cared so much and why I was taking so much trouble to protect his memory. I tried to thrust him out of my mind and concentrate on my inspection of his house.

For the moment, I was not interested in his possessions – pictures, jade, exotic and valuable curiosities from all over the world. These would be listed and valued for probate by professionals. I was concerned only with documents. I wanted every scrap of Cassidy paper under my control. Later I would decide what to do with it.

Cassidy

There was nothing to inhibit my search. Cassidy's keys, his wallet, his folder of credit cards, his pocket diary, had all been handed to me at the hospital on the night of his death. The diary was the most useful item and might in the end prove the most revealing. It was the usual vademecum of a busy man. It contained the combination of his safe, the numbers of his bank accounts and insurance policies, addresses and telephone numbers of doctors, dentists, lawyers, friends male and female. Pornsri Rhana was among them, listed as a resident in a very expensive apartment hotel.

My search was thorough. I opened every cupboard, rummaged in every drawer, checked every pocket in every suit. Nothing. Apart from the photographs – Cassidy with the plebs, Cassidy with the nabobs, Cassidy with the royals – the place was as bare of personal history as a public art gallery. Finally, I came to the safe, a big commercial affair nearly six feet high, hidden behind a sliding door and set on a concrete block over one of the steel bearer beams of the structure. They must have used a crane to get it in. They would need another one to get it out – and a laser drill with a charge of explosive to force it. Before opening it, I locked the bedroom door and closed the drapes over the French windows that led to the balcony. It seemed a panicky paranoid precaution – until I saw the contents of the safe. The two upper shelves were stacked solid with currency: American hundred-dollar bills, Swiss francs, Deutschmarks, sterling pounds in high and low denominations, gold ingots of various weights, Kruger-rands, Mexican, Russian and British gold pieces. I did not attempt to count it but clearly it added up to a tidy fortune.

The next shelf was occupied by stacks of photograph albums of uniform size and shape. I opened three of them at random. Most of the exhibits were pornographic shots taken on brothel premises or at orgies in private houses. Neatly typed labels identified the place, the date and the participants. Others, taken with telephoto lenses, recorded furtive meetings on street corners, in automobiles, in public parks.

Charles Parnell Cassidy was a twentieth-century man, exercising the most primitive magic of all – once you possessed the images of men and women engaged in the sexual act, you held their souls in bondage.

The remaining space in the safe was stuffed tight with papers: legal briefs tied with pink tape, bundles of letters, ledgers, notebooks large and small. I had neither energy nor inclination to read them now, but I had no doubt they would fit with the rest of the hoard, as instruments of power, recording debts to be called in, services to be exacted when the need arose.

Here was the proof of Gorman's accusations that Cassidy had engaged in bribery and blackmail. Murder? Given the nature of the material, murder was a daily possibility.

It was obvious that Cassidy thought so too. Laid on top of the albums was a .38 automatic. The safety catch was on but there was a magazine in the chamber. I left the weapon untouched. Immediately I saw the shape of the problem. Sooner or later, people would come looking for this material. If I were Loomis, I would find cause to swear out a search warrant. If I were a villain, I would send in the best safe crackers money could buy – and a pair of Italian domestics wouldn't worry me at all. So, interesting and urgent question: What was I, Martin Gregory, executor, going to do about it? For tonight, nothing.

I felt suddenly bone-weary and nauseous. I locked the safe and shoved the key in my pocket. The time was five-thirty. I would have loved a stiff Scotch, but the thought of drinking in Cassidy's house with his ghost grinning over my shoulder appalled me.

Instead, I used his telephone to call Pat in London. She was delighted to hear from me and eager to talk, but she sounded frayed and fretful.

'I hate your being away, darling! I don't know what's come over me. I snap at Clare and the children. I'm having recurrent nightmares. I'm a little girl lost in a dark forest. I hear Daddy calling, but I can't make him hear me . . .'

'Perhaps you ought to see a doctor. Call Peter Maxwell.'

'I went to him yesterday. He was kind and understanding. He explained that the death of a parent is often a bigger shock than we expect – and that my – our – estrangement only made things worse. He wants me to get away for a while. Clare suggests we take a chalet in Klosters and do some skiing. The children have a half-term coming up; they'd enjoy the snow. What do you think, darling?'

'Go, by all means. I can't see myself getting out of here for at least three weeks. You might as well relax and enjoy yourselves.'

'I wish you could be with us. I miss you very much . . . How did it go today?'

'The ceremony went off well. The Cardinal gave a most friendly eulogy. All the top brass turned out, the Governor-General, the Prime Minister . . .'

'And what happens now?'

'Some scandal-mongering, I'm afraid. Possibly a Royal Commission into your father's administration.'

'Why can't they let him rest in peace?'

'There's no mercy in politics. If you're contacted by the Australian press, tell them you have no comment. You've been living abroad for many years. You have no information on your father's career or his private life. Give Clare the same warning.'

'Are you sure you're all right, Martin?'

'A bit frayed, that's all. I've had a long day. The funeral this morning, lawyers this afternoon. I'm at your father's house now. There's a whole mess of papers to wade through – days of work, in fact. I can use a good night's sleep. Any other news?'

'Not much. People have been very kind. There are telegrams from folk we haven't heard from in years. Mr. Melville has been especially kind. He's called several times from Zurich.'

Once again I felt a prickle of fear, but it seemed that fear made me skilful in duplicity. I asked, 'And who, pray, is Mr. Melville?'

'You know! The one Daddy mentioned in his last letter to you. I forget what he said exactly. I'm still vague about all that happened that night. But apparently they were good friends who did a lot of business together over the years. Mother remembers the name, but she can't recall ever meeting him. However, he's been very solicitous, a telegram first, then flowers, then a very sweet letter of condolence. He said he would get his people in Australia to make contact with you and help you in every way possible.'

'That's kind, but please tell Clare not to cultivate the man. Just stay formal and polite.'

'Why do you say that?'

'It's difficult to explain on an open line. Your father made good friends and bad enemies. I've hardly begun to sort out one from the other. So, the less you're involved with any of his old associates the better.'

'Oh, Martin! That's awkward.'

'What's awkward?'

'Our holiday. Mr. Melville offered us the use of his chalet in Klosters. I accepted.'

'Then turn it down! Think up some excuse.'

'What excuse can I possibly offer? The man's just trying to be kind. Why insult him?'

Why indeed? Once again, I heard Charlie Cassidy's ghostly voice: 'Show respect. He merits it. He keeps iron faith with his friends.' Pat's anxious voice stirred me out of the brief reverie.

'Martin? Are you still there?'

'I'm here. I'm sorry if I barked at you, sweetheart. Let the arrangement stand. Go to Klosters, enjoy yourselves.'

'Thank you, darling. And you take care too! Look up some of your old colleagues. See if you can get yourself a game of golf and a weekend sail.'

'I'll try. I promise. Give the children a kiss. My love to Clare – and a special loving to you.'

'We all miss you very much. God bless, sweetheart.'

And thus, thought I in my innocence, thus endeth the funeral day of Charles Parnell Cassidy. Here am I, the man he hated, sitting in his empty house, with a couple of million worth of fine art on the walls and a safe full of explosive secrets, waiting for the big blow-up!

7

I walked from Cassidy's house back to my hotel. It was a stiff hike around the hilly promontories of the harbour, but I needed the exercise. More, I had to escape from the suffocating sub-world into which Cassidy had seduced me. I wanted to enjoy, however briefly, the simple anonymous commerce of the streets.

I was scared now. I knew too little and too much. Under all its up-to-the-minute gloss, Sydney was a rough, tough town, with a deep harbour and hundreds of square miles of virgin bush around it. Lots of people turned up dead. Some didn't turn up at all. I was under threat, because I could threaten others.

If I wanted to survive, I would have to turn horse-trader, blackmailer too, if necessary, as Cassidy had done in his time. To do that I had to take physical possession of all the contents of Cassidy's safe, before the villains sent in a safe-cracker or the Attorney-General decided to swear out a search warrant. If I were in his shoes I could find a dozen pretexts to do it. My guess was that he was waiting until the newspaper stories gave him the excuse, or I decided to dump the whole mess in his lap and head for home. I had the uneasy feeling that I had already lost that option and that I should even now be preparing for enemy action.

But who were my enemies? Who would make the first sorties against me? Loomis and the Premier had made no secret of their hostility. My old colleague Micky Gorman had abdicated from Cassidy's affairs. Marius Melville – whoever he was! – wanted to stay very close; but he at least was ready to trade. The rest was a blur of faces, a babble of voices heard at a funeral, winks and whispers and threats disguised as compliments – and, in the distance, thunder and the gleam of weapons in the dark.

All the mathematics worked against me. I could not begin to number my enemies; but where did I turn for friends? Pat had suggested blithely 'get some golf and some sailing'. It was not half so easy as it sounded. I had been away too long. The break with home-folk and homeland had been too brusque, too final, to be mended by a phone call or a surprise appearance at the Squadron or on the first tee at Royal Sydney. My face would be splashed all over tomorrow's press as Cassidy's son-in-law and executor. A sail on the harbour or eighteen holes of golf wouldn't be worth the explanations I should have to give. So, stinking of fatigue and suppressed anger, with a black devil perched on my shoulder, I came back to the Town House.

There was a note in my box: 'Please call me between seven and eight. Urgent . . . Laura Larsen.' I shoved the message slip in my pocket and headed for the elevator. My suite was on the eighth floor, a two-roomed apartment with a view across the rooftops to a small segment of the harbour. I shaved, showered, put on a track suit and slippers and poured myself the long-awaited drink. I was just beginning to unwind, when there was a knock at the door. Thinking it was the night maid, I called 'Come in!' The knock was repeated.

I opened the door to find Pornsri Rhana standing in the hallway. She was dressed in shirt and jeans and for an instant I thought she was one of the stewardesses from Thai Airlines, who overnighted at the Town House. Then I remembered her from the photograph I had seen in Cassidy's house.

She was a classic type: pure Siamese from the central provinces, small, honey-skinned, placid and perfect as a porcelain doll. She joined her hands and bowed her head in the traditional *wai*. Her English was faultless. Only the formality was exotic.

'I am Pornsri. You are Martin Gregory. I had a message that you wanted to see me.'

'Thank you for answering so promptly. Please come in. Do sit down . . . May I offer you a drink?'

'Fruit juice, if you have it, please.'

My hand trembled as I poured the drink. She was so calm, so completely at ease, that I felt like a fumbling lout, all thumbs and hobnails. I tried to explain my embarrassment.

'Until this afternoon, I didn't know you existed. I saw your photograph in Cassidy's lounge. Marco explained you in Italian. He called you "*donna di confidenza*". I presume he meant "confidential secretary".'

'Marco is always very discreet.' She gave a small pout of displeasure. 'Charles Cassidy and I were lovers. My daughter is his child.'

'The one in the photograph?'

'Yes. She is in school in Switzerland.'

'I presume you know who I am and what I am charged to do?'

For the first time she smiled, the tolerant evanescent smile of a Bodhisattra.

'I know much more than that. You were like a jungle ghost in our lives. Nothing I could do would appease you. I could never persuade Charles to drive you out. There was so much anger between you. I can feel it now, even as I sit here.'

'Then why did he ask me to act for him after his death?'

'I tried to dissuade him, believe me. But he would hear no argument. He said, "Martin will be doubly honest. He hates me so much that he'll have to prove to himself and my daughter that he's virgin pure. Apart from that, he's the only man I know who can control our partners and hold the enterprise together."'

'What enterprise was he talking about?'

'You don't know?' There was surprise and fear in her voice. 'He had a briefcase full of material to give you. I helped him assemble it.'

'I have the briefcase. It's lodged in my bank. I begin to study the microfiches tomorrow.'

'Then, until you have finished your study and made your decision, nothing that I can say will make much sense.'

'Would you answer some questions for me, please?'

'If I can.'

'Do you have a key to Cassidy's safe?'

'No.'

'Do you know what's in it?'

'Some – not all. Charles always referred to it as his insurance policy. I do know that most of the essential material is duplicated in what you have.'

'Are you aware that Cassidy made no provision for you and your daughter in his will?'

'We agreed that long ago. Charles provided for us in other ways. I hold a substantial interest in his Asian ventures.'

'I am told the newspapers are mounting an attack on Cassidy's administration. Will that cause you embarrassment?'

'No. I shall not be here. I leave in a few days for Bangkok. Besides, how much can the papers write about a man and a woman making love?'

'More than you might believe! . . . Are you aware that Cassidy is alleged to have connections with criminal elements, here and abroad?'

'I'm aware that he dealt with a lot of strange people in

politics and in business. I'm not sure that I judge them in the same way as you do. We are another people. We do not expect perfection from those who are bound with us to the wheel of life . . . My father was a political General; my mother was his favourite concubine. He bought her out of the dance troupe of Prince Pramoj. Each of them taught me to understand how life is lived in politics and in the Palace. You bargain; you compromise; you survive . . . But you never compromise, do you, Mr. Gregory? You never take off that mask of legal virtue. Charles Cassidy ate up life as if it were a mango – but he was never a hypocrite. He drove hard bargains with hard men. He made no secret that there were other women in his life. He knew that I had another existence, too. We could be happy because we accepted the terms of the contract.'

This was will-o'-the-wisp country and I was not going to be enticed into it. I continued to thrust questions at her.

'What is your position in Cassidy's business affairs?'

'I represent him in Thailand, Malaya, Laos and Vietnam.'

'Do you – did Cassidy – traffic in drugs?'

'We had, and still have, large interests in pharmaceutical manufacture, from the raw materials to the finished products. This is an international industry. I am not familiar with all of it – only my territories. I do know that what is legal in one country may be illegal in another.'

It was a hedged answer, but I let it pass.

'Do you know a man called Marius Melville?'

'Yes.'

'What can you tell me about him?'

'Only that he and Charles were very close. And that you cannot fail to meet him.' Her manner changed abruptly. Now she was angry and imperious. 'Mr. Gregory, you are interrogating me like a country policeman. I am not some ignorant peasant. I came here because you asked me to come.'

She stood up and made as if to leave. I was shamed into an apology.

'Please! I beg your pardon. I'm bad-tempered because I'm tired and I'm doing something I hate – cleaning up Cassidy's messes, when I'd like to be rubbing his nose in them. I'm angry with you, too – though it's not your fault.'

'With me? Why?'

'Because . . .' I knew I was making a fool of myself, but I had to get it out. 'Because Marco told me Cassidy used to call you Miss Pat. That's the name of his daughter, my wife. I found that . . . a kind of insult. It's crazy I know, but –'

'No, not crazy. Names are important. They grow to us like hair and limbs. But you must let me try to explain something . . .'

Now, suddenly she was in control and I was enveloped in a leaden cope of fatigue that held me down, pressed all the strength out of me. She squatted on her heels in front of me. As she spoke her hands made little fluttering gestures as if she were talking to the deaf.

'Charles was obsessed by his past, haunted in a way that I would not have believed possible for so positive and ruthless a man. His wife and his child had left him. You, whom he regarded as a son, had stolen them. You had violated the relationships on which he had totally depended. He was an old-fashioned man. He could not beg for loyalties he thought were his by right. And let me be honest, Martin Gregory, your women were not educated to handle such a man. He and I met first in Bangkok, at a reception given by my father at the Oriental Hotel. We were immediately interested in each other. My father fostered the friendship. Cassidy was valuable to him, for politics and for international business. I was a surprise to Cassidy. My mother, who had been educated in a princely household, had taught me about men and their needs and all the demands they can make on one woman.' She laughed, a small, mocking sound. 'Charles Cassidy had so much to prove that he needed a whole dictionary of women. I was at least a condensed version. Of course in the end he knew that he was being manipulated, but he liked it. He began to understand the Asian way – that the bamboo bends to the wind and the falcon soars on it . . . So while we were together I was any woman Cassidy wanted me to be – wife, mother, sister, child. It was a game, a happy game, like dressing up in clothes from someone else's cabinet. It certainly wasn't an insult to you. Besides, my name is hard to say in English . . . Do you understand?'

'I think so. I'm very sorry I was rude. What can I do to make amends?'

'Just talk to me again, when you have studied the documents. Then, when you have finished in Australia, come to Bangkok and see what needs to be done with that part of the estate.'

'What do you think it needs?'

'A strong man to control it – to scare off the bandits.'

'I'm Cassidy's executor, not his heir.'

'You could be his successor. He hoped you would. You will see that he left the way open.'

'No thanks. I struck off his shackles when he was alive. I'm damned if I'll wear them after his death.'

'Don't be too hasty, Mr. Gregory. Take a good look at the kingdom before you abdicate the throne.' She offered her hand. Her touch was cool and smooth as satin. 'I must go now. Call me when you want to talk again.'

A moment later she was gone and I was left cursing my tactless tongue. It was as if a bright bird had perched on my window-sill and I had frightened it away with my lumbering stupidity. Then I had a second thought, more base but probably closer to the truth: if Cassidy had in truth left me the keys to a kingdom, had he left me his consort and his child as well? I had never been in love with an Asian woman, but I could spot an Irish horse-coper a mile away.

8

At five past seven I called Laura Larsen at the Melmar Hotel. She was brusque and businesslike, quite unlike my Lady Owl-Eyes.

'We have to talk. Things are happening faster than we expected. I had a man on your tail all day today. He called to say there's a police surveillance group working on you as well. They were watching Cassidy's house. They followed you back to the hotel. In addition to that, I've got a copy of the first piece Gerry Downs is running on Cassidy this weekend. It's a shocker. The Government will be forced to take action. The action will have to include you as custodian and administrator of the estate . . .'

'So where do we meet?'

'I'll call for you at the Town House in fifteen minutes. Dress very casually. Don't use the elevators. Walk down the fire stairs to the basement car park. I'll pick you up there. Don't leave anything of importance in your room . . .'

It seemed an absurd piece of melodrama and I felt very resentful about playing it. I was, after all, a servant of the law on a legal errand in my homeland. The notion of police or private surveillance was repugnant to me. I was still stubborn enough to believe that righteousness was my strongest armour and the letter of the law my sharpest sword; but the conviction was getting blurred now. If Cassidy had indeed been engaged in criminal activities – and even Loomis and the Premier claimed to know that he had been – then I had no place to stand. I was not his lawyer. I was, as any layman might be, simply the executor of a deceased estate. I was not entitled to privileged custody of information or documents.

That, too, brought its own problems, since monies or possessions traceable to drug trafficking could, under recent legislation, be confiscated. Cassidy had claimed in his last letter to me that all the monies in his bequest to Clare were clean. Nonetheless, I might still be required to prove them so in court. Common sense told me that I had to lay hands on the documents in Cassidy's safe while it was still legal for me to do so. I had to know what was in them before I was forced to surrender them to the police. But if his house were still under surveillance – as I seemed to be – certain difficulties presented themselves. I picked up the telephone and dialled Cassidy's house. Marco Cubeddu answered.

'Marco, I need to call on you again tonight. It may be late, but it is important.'

'No matter, sir. I am at your disposal.'

'Did you know the house is being watched?'

'I did not know. I thought it might be. No one has attempted to enter.'

'Is there a rear entrance?'

'Only from the water. There is the boatshed where Mr. Cassidy's speedboat is kept. Next to that there is a small jetty without lights. You would find it hard to identify at night.'

'Is the boat in running order?'

'Always. I service it myself. All you have to do is run it down the slipway on the cable.'

'So I could come by the front way and leave by sea?'

'Of course. What time may I expect you?'

'Between ten and midnight. That's the closest I can get at this moment.'

'I shall be waiting. Did Miss Pat call you?'

'She did. Thank you.'

'Until later then, sir.'

I still had time for one more call, this time to Paul Henri Langlois of the Banque de Paris. He was dressing to go out to dinner. I told him my problem.

'Paul, I'm in a jam. Late tonight I'm taking possession of some very hot documents, plus a sizeable amount of currency and bullion. I don't want to hold them longer than I can help.'

'How big is the package?'

'It's not a package. It's more like three or four pillow-cases full of stuff. Can you keep them at your place overnight and have them lodged in your safe deposit first thing in the morning? I want a seal on each bag and your signed receipt. Sorry to put this on you, but I'm swimming in rather deep waters.'

'I guessed you might be.' Paul Langlois had a fine Gallic taste for intrigue. 'One of the problems of marriage is that we get the bride's family as well as the bride . . . Come to my house, say at half past twelve tonight. I'll take possession of the items and give you an interim receipt. In the morning I'll have our security people pick them up and transfer them to the bank. Can you organise it?'

'I can. Thanks, Paul. I owe you a big one. See you in the small hours.'

'Swim very carefully, my friend. Sydney harbour has some of the biggest sharks in the world!'

The phrase haunted me as I made my furtive way down the fire stairs. I had been away so long I had forgotten the underlay of violence in the Australian character, the deep respect for roguery in the national ethos. Our founding fathers had ruled by the triangle and the lash. We had a century and a half of legal genocide to our credit. Powerful sections of our union movement were run by criminals, adept in the arts of rabble-rousing, intimidation and viol-ence. Our police and our penal custodians had a reputation for brutality, venality and occasional murder – and my own colleagues, servants of the law like Loomis and Micky

Gorman, were living on a diminishing capital of principle and an increasing contempt for due process.

The stereotypes of the 'lucky country' – the easy-going, sun worshipping, 'ow-are-yer-mate' Australian, friend of all the world – were fictions. We had our underworld chieftains – rich, well organised and well groomed. They could have you spiked with heroin, shot in an alley, chained and dumped in the deeps off the coast. No one would know and surprisingly few would care. Inquests could be delayed indefinitely for want of a body. Verdicts could be determined by perjured police testimony.

We had our narcotics empires, which stretched from Florida to Pakistan and Turkey. We had a whole hierarchy of pimps and panders, running a girl racket through Bangkok, Manila, Taiwan and Hong Kong. We had the Mafia controlling our country towns, where a post-war migrant population now owned orchards and vineyards and wineries, and greenhouses full of illegal grass. We were the fifth largest legal producer of opium in the world. With our tiny population of fifteen million we were one of the largest per capita consumers of illegal heroin. The alleys of Kings Cross and the lanes of our country towns were littered with syringes and glassine sachets.

Now I – Martin the Righteous, God help me! – was being seduced little by little into the fringes of this criminal empire. I had done nothing wrong, but already I was involved with the casuistries of the trade.

Already I was beginning to circumvent the law by the deliberate concealment of documents, which in my heart of hearts I knew to be connected with criminal conspiracies. But since no one – not even Loomis – could read my heart of hearts, I could hold up clean hands and cross my breast and swear: No, your Honour, at the time I moved the said documents, I had not read them; ergo, I had no knowledge of their contents; ergo, I am not in misprision of a felony. Though I may be a liar damned and double-damned, it's sucks to you until you can prove it in this court . . . Besides, your Honour, I'm not sure that due process works any more in this country. I begin to wonder whether Cassidy may not have had the right idea. You must know the great Charles Parnell Cassidy. He appointed you to the bench. You may even have heard him say these selfsame words, because he did on occasion repeat himself:

'"I learnt it at my father's knee, sonny boy! And he learnt it from his father, who laid the foundations of the Cassidy fortune by selling grog after hours, and running a two-up school in the barn at Widows' Peak. Always pay the policeman to look the other way, and pay double to the girl who can get him to bed and swear she'd seen the strawberry mark on his backside! Criminal law's a farce, sonny boy. You can plant evidence and suborn witnesses and make sweetheart deals with the prosecution. The only laws we're really interested in making stick are the laws of contract – because if commerce doesn't work we're eating tree bark instead of bread!"'

I swear I could hear his rich actor's voice echoing round the concrete caverns of the car-park as I waited in a shadowy corner for Laura Larsen to show up. She was ten minutes late. which I didn't expect from her.

She arrived in a big steel-grey Mercedes, which she slalomed dangerously through the concrete pillars of the parking lot. Dressed in slacks and blouse, with a red band round her hair, she looked like any young hostess from the Eastern suburbs. She was flushed and talkative.

'Sorry I'm late! The bloody manager buttonholed me just as I was leaving the hotel. We've got a Japanese delegation arriving on an early flight tomorrow and our best interpreter is sick . . . I didn't want to drag you out like this, but Mr. Melville called from Zurich. He insisted I meet you. There's a little hole in the wall called Da Stefano, down by Circular Quay. The food's good and there's a private corner where we can talk . . . How are you, anyway? You've been a busy, busy boy! What do you think of your old home town? It's grown up now – rich, rough and randy! I gather you didn't make yourself too popular with Loomis and the Premier . . . Don't look so surprised! That's what I'm about – Little Miss Listening Post . . . Oh hell! Why am I rattling on like this? Because I'm scared, that's why! Gerry Downs plays dirty pool – and I'm not sure I know how to handle you either, Martin Gregory!'

'Forget about me and concentrate on your driving. Otherwise we'll both end up in hospital.'

She gave a small strained laugh and patted my knee, which was meant to be encouraging, but was downright dangerous with the peak-hour traffic of Kings Cross.

'Relax! I've got a clean licence and I've never lost a lawyer in my life . . . By the way, you and your wife feature prominently in Gerry Downs' revelations. She begins as the victim of "brutal domestic tyranny in a typical Irish Catholic marriage of convenience". You enter as the "courageous kid from nowhere, putting his career on the line for love. And likely to collect a fortune at the end of it!" How does that go for openers? You can read the first article over dinner.'

'And how did it come into your hands?'

'I told you. That's what I'm about – tourism and entertainment and all the promotion dollars that go with them. The Melmar Marquis pays a lot of heavy retainers.'

'Miss Larsen, I'm getting very tired of people mucking about with my life – especially people I've never met!'

'You've met me.'

'I have. And, would you believe, I like you. You know I'm married and I know I'm married, but I'm glad you called. Dinner with you is the best offer I've had these last three days. But Marius Melville, Gerry Downs – I don't know them from a hole in the ground. And I don't want to!'

'Let's do each other a favour.'

'Fine. What's the favour?'

'Christian names. I'm Laura, you're Martin. You sound

so bloody British when you say Miss Larsen. It's like . . . like going to bed with your socks on!'

I laughed. I laughed loudly, uncontrollably, until the tears rolled down my cheeks. All my memories of Britain in summer came crowding back in a rustic comedy: fat ladies in deckchairs; grandfathers with long trousers rolled up their shanks, paddling in grey water; young lovers, fish-belly white, nuzzling uncomfortably on a pebbly beach . . . And there was I in the middle of them, ridiculous in baggy underpants and ankle socks . . .

Laura Larsen seemed puzzled by my laughter.

'I didn't think it was that funny!'

'Laura, my love, I can't tell you how funny it really was!'

'So you're going to enjoy your dinner.'

'Enjoy it and pay for it.'

'Now there's a generous man!'

'Think you . . .'

'Think I what?'

'Think you, if Laura had been Petrarch's wife, he would have written sonnets all his life.'

'Now what sort of question is that?'

'It's not a question. It's a quotation from Byron. And since I'm in the mood, here's another one: "Laura was blooming still, had made the best of time, and time returned the compliment."'

'I think . . . I really think I'm beginning to like you, Martin.'

'I think I'm beginning to like me too . . . God Almighty, woman! You just ran through a red light!'

'Poetry always did send me crazy. Recite some more, please!'

Four off-colour limericks and ten stanzas of *The Lady of Shalott* brought us to the door of Da Stefano, a seedy shopfront that opened into a tiny trattoria, with immaculate linen, summer flowers, candlelight, good crystal; and Stefano himself, a young man handsome as a grand opera brigand. He welcomed us with a flourish, offered us his own special apéritif, then informed us that there were no choices. We would eat what he served, we would savour every mouthful, we would be grateful to the good God for leading us to his table.

We were grateful indeed. We ate well and drank better. We swopped travellers' tales and silly jokes. We flirted recklessly, knowing that we were safe in the small circle of candlelight. We were like folk in the plague time, heedless of the rattle of the death-carts and the chant of the hired mourners in the alley. But with the coffee came the reckoning – the bill to be paid, the truth to be told. Laura fished in her handbag and brought out an envelope full of folded newsprint.

She told me: 'That's the first salvo from Gerry Downs. It publishes on Saturday in their weekend supplement. Don't wave it about here. Take it back to your hotel and study it in private . . . It's all bad news, because it will force the Government to bring on a Royal Commission. The police will be tramping round in big circles to cover their own earlier footprints . . . Which brings me to the next piece of bad news. Mr. Melville says he has an offer on the table for something you've got. He says it's a fair offer, but it won't last for ever. If what you've got is compromised – I'm using his own words – it becomes valueless and the offer's withdrawn. He says you'll know exactly what he means.'

'Do you know what he means, Laura?'

Her answer was cryptic, to say the least.

'He didn't tell me. I didn't ask. I'm paid to pass messages, not to make explanations.'

'Do you write shorthand?'

'Yes.'

'Good! Jot this down. It's a message from me to Marius Melville. Transmit it by telex. Send a confirming copy to my hotel. Quote: First, I didn't solicit the offer. I was simply made aware that it exists. Second, I am taking the materials in question under immediate study to determine their nature and their future disposition. Third, I do not like dealing through intermediaries on matters of importance. I need a face-to-face meeting with you. I tender my thanks for your kindness in offering your chalet to my wife and family. Had the offer been made to me, I should have felt obliged to decline it; but since my wife accepted, I am grateful for your consideration. I cannot, however, permit my position as executor to be compromised. Signed, Martin Gregory. Unquote.'

She finished writing and stared at me for a long moment. She shook her head in disapproval.

'My God, Martin, you're a hard-nosed bastard!'

'I hope Marius Melville knows that too.'

'He does. I'll see he gets your message.' She gave me a small regretful smile. 'Well, that rather takes the edge off our dinner party, doesn't it?'

'Not for me. I'd like to do it again – without Marius Melville at the other corner of the triangle. Now, would you do me a favour, please?'

'If I can, sure.'

'Do you have a reliable limousine service at the Melmar Marquis?'

She gave a mocking grin.

'Naturally, we have the best.'

'Would you call them and ask for someone to pick me up here? I'll want him on call until one or two in the morning.'

'Why spend the money? I'll be happy to drive you – unless you're going girl-chasing, of course.'

'I'm very happy with the girl I've got, thank you.'

'So why not let me drive you? Or are you doing your happily-married-man act and backing off before bedtime?'

What could I say? I was light-headed and a little drunk. I rose to the challenge like a trout to a fly.

'Two conditions: you ask no questions; you do exactly as you're told.'

'Agreed.'

'You're hired.'

'Now tell me what I do.'

'You drive me to a cab rank. You lose yourself until exactly twelve-thirty, when you drive up to the jetty at Rose Bay. I'll arrive at the same time by motor boat, unload some gear and stow it in the car. Then you'll drive me to an address I'll give you. The important thing is that you time it exactly. Don't hang around, otherwise you'll attract a prowler or a police patrol. If I'm delayed – God forbid! – drive away and come back. If you are questioned by the police, tell 'em the truth. You're waiting for a friend who's returning from a cruise. He's bringing gear ashore.'

'Do I get paid for all this?'

'You're doing it for love!'

'Good! You can write me a sonnet.'

'Let's get out of here.'

We walked out of the candlelight into the dingy street. As I held the car door open for her, Laura Larsen kissed me lightly on the lips.

'Thank you for a pleasant dinner, Mr. Petrarch.'

It was a small, agreeable gesture, nothing to presume on, nothing to build a scandal on; yet it made me feel intolerably lonely, isolated and vulnerable, in this rough and randy town on the last continent before the ice-packs.

9

I knew that, sooner or later, I could be questioned about my actions that night; so I decided to memorise and record the time sequence. We left the restaurant at ten-thirty-eight. At ten-fifty I picked up a taxi on the rank at Circular

Quay. At eleven-ten I was dropped at the gate of Cassidy's house. There were no pedestrians in sight. The only vehicles were a red station wagon parked about fifty yards down the street and a cream combi van directly opposite the gate. I could see no light or movement within the van; but it was the most obvious spot for a surveillance team.

Marco Cubeddu opened the gate and bolted it behind me. Once inside the house, I explained my mission: to clear out Cassidy's safe and deposit the contents in a bank safe-deposit. I would need pillowcases to pack the stuff and transport it to Rose Bay on Cassidy's speedboat. Marco had a better idea. There were several old sail-bags in Cassidy's boathouse, relics of the days when he had sailed with the Squadron. They were larger, stouter and more natural-looking than pillowcases. After all, I didn't want to look like an amateur house-breaker carrying his loot.

Marco would not witness my access to the safe. He would not see the contents. He would simply accept a note of instruction in my handwriting. He would drive me to Rose Bay in the speedboat, help me to unload, then drive back and winch the craft into Cassidy's boathouse. Thereafter, anyone who wanted access to Cassidy's papers would have to come to me. Marco Cubeddu and his wife would remain as custodians of the property and its remaining contents. It was a simple operation, almost risk-free.

Marco brought me the sail-bags—big, heavy sacks of green oilcloth, closed by drawstrings. He lined each one with a sheet and showed me how to draw the corners together at the top so that at first glance the fabric would look like crumpled sailcloth; then he went off to winch down the speedboat and make her ready for a swift departure.

Once again I locked myself in Cassidy's bedroom, opened the safe and began emptying the contents, shelf by shelf. I worked fast but carefully, glancing briefly at each pile of documents as I stacked it into the sail-bag. My finical lawyer's conscience kept reminding me that if ever

I were examined on the transactions of this night, the first questions asked would be what had I abstracted and what had I finally delivered to the officers of the court? The proper practice was to have a witness, who listed every item at the moment of transfer. There was no time for such nicety, I had to be packed and gone by midnight.

One item did give me pause: Cassidy's pistol. I was just about to pick it up when I remembered one of my elementary lessons in forensic law: weapons, like people, have criminal histories; make sure you don't muddle the history by indiscreet handling. I picked up the gun with a pencil, wrapped it carefully in one of Cassidy's handkerchiefs and stowed it on top of an album of pornographic pictures.

On the lowest tier of the safe there were two locked drawers, one large and one small. I fumbled through Cassidy's keys until I found the two that fitted. The small drawer was full of jewellers' packages of precious stones: diamonds, emeralds, sapphires and rubies. I did not need the handwritten weights and descriptions to assure myself that these were fine-quality gems, worth a great deal of money. I folded the packages into another of Cassidy's handkerchiefs and wedged them between two bundles of letters.

The larger drawer contained the real surprise packet: two flat envelopes of transparent plastic, heat-sealed and full of white crystalline powder. Each envelope was stamped with an elephant, which I seemed to remember signified heroin, and the symbol K.50, which had to be half a kilogram. I had no means of proving what the powder was unless I opened the envelopes, but if it were pure heroin its street value was astronomical. But for Cassidy to have held it here in his own house seemed, at first blush, a madness beyond belief. However, it was a madness that put me, too, in instant jeopardy. I could justify my possession of documents for at least as long as it took me to list and study them. There was no way in the world I could justify the unreported possession of a kilo of scheduled narcotics. Loomis would have me handcuffed and charged before I could say Charles Parnell Cassidy.

So, it seemed I had Hobson's choice: leave the stuff for someone else to find, or hand it over first thing in the morning, with loud protestations of ignorance and virtue. Loomis would be very happy about that. He would pat me on the head, give me a big rosy apple and sit me at the top of the class. Then, on clear evidence of a drug connection, he would swear out a warrant for the seizure and delivery of every scrap of paper in my possession – right down to the toilet rolls – and there wouldn't be a damn thing I could do about it.

Then a new thought hit me. Perhaps he wouldn't do that at all. He was a very downy bird, our 'Call-me-Rafe' Loomis. He might be quite happy to bury the plastic bags six feet deep with Cassidy himself, and even happier to embroil me in a little game of now-you-see-it, now-you-don't.

Conclusion? Not to rush to any conclusion. Every damned item in those sail-bags was tainted anyway. So I borrowed some more of Cassidy's handkerchiefs, wiped my fingerprints off the envelopes, packed them into the sail-bags and locked the empty safe. Then, on Cassidy's notepaper, I wrote a note for Marco Cubeddu:

To Whom It May Concern

On the evening of the 18th February, in my capacity as executor of the estate of the late Charles Parnell Cassidy, I visited his residence, opened his safe with the keys which had been given to me in London and took possession of documents and other items. All these items have been transferred to the custody of a bank, pending probate of Mr. Cassidy's will. Marco Cubeddu and his wife remain, until my further instructions, legal custodians of the premises and their contents.

Martin Gregory

93

I explained to Marco that he should not present the note unless he were asked for it and that he should not volunteer any information beyond what was requested by a police officer. Marco reminded me stiffly that he was a man from the Barbagia, the high secret country of Sardinia, where a stranger is hard put to prise even the time of day out of the locals.

I apologised for my lack of politeness and commended him for his discretion. We drank a Scotch together and then lugged four bulging sail-bags down to the boathouse. As we unshackled the slipway cable and let the big Riva slide the last metre into the water, my watch showed five minutes before midnight.

The Riva is a beautiful craft, a highly polished wooden speedboat, with a lethally large engine under the hatch. It is built in Italy and is rarely seen in Australia because of the high import duties levied on it. It starts with a roar, takes off and guzzles fuel like a jet aircraft. Marco told me this one was a gift from Marius Melville to Charles Cassidy – taxes and duties all prepaid of course.

Rose Bay was just around the corner. We had at least thirty minutes to kill before our rendezvous with Laura Larsen. Marco asked whether I would like a quick run around the southern fringes of the harbour. I told him I would like nothing better. He headed out into the channel and opened the throttle.

I watched him as he drove the sleek, beautiful craft through the choppy water. He was another man; tall, defiant, a black Ulyssean silhouette against the moon. He took us at a fast run past the Opera House and under the span of the Harbour Bridge. As we came about I asked him to slow down so that I could watch the lights on the shoreline. We could talk then, too.

I asked him: 'You're a mountain-man from the Barbagia. Where did you learn to handle a boat so well?'

'On the waterfront in Cagliari.' He was flattered by my

interest. 'I had an uncle there who ran a couple of tuna
boats. Then I got a job on a smuggling run to Tunis – twice
a week; cigarettes, watches, whatever was going. She was
big and fast – thirty knots – and she was owned by a *grosso
pezzo* in Palermo. You had to have good nerves for that
game. Then somehow Mr. Melville heard of me and asked
me to skipper his boat, the *Serpente d'Oro*, which was
berthed in Porto Cervo. She was a fast machine, too; four
crew, eight passengers, twenty-five knots. We cruised
her in the summer and chartered her in the off months
between Tunis, Morocco, the Balearics, Corsica and
Sicily . . .'

'What sort of charter?' I tried to make the question
sound ingenuous. He shrugged and gestured widely.

'Anybody and everything! Runaway lovers, Friends of
the Friends, political agents, cigarettes, guns. It wasn't
my business to ask. I made the rendezvous. I picked up
passengers and consignments. I delivered them – sometimes at sea, sometimes at out-of-the-way ports. I paid
cash. I collected cash. It was a good life; because Mr.
Melville's arrangements always worked. I never once ran
into the Guardia di Finanza. I never once heard a shot
fired – not in three whole years. That's how I was able to
emigrate to Australia. No convictions, no black marks
from the police. I love the sea. You are not hemmed in.
You can always disappear over the horizon.'

'Did you enjoy working for Mr. Cassidy?'

'At first, yes. He was very like Mr. Melville. They
thought the same way, talked the same way. But later,
when he became ill . . . Boh! He changed. He began to
lose vigour. He tried to balance things. He would not
plunge forward any more. I should not say this perhaps;
but he needed a son. He needed you, *Dottore*. It is sad
that you were separated so long.'

'Yes. It was sad. But he was very attached to Miss Pat.
Apparently she was a great help to him.'

He cut the throttle and let the nose of the craft settle in

the slack water. Clearly he was ready to talk. It was as if our conspiratorial act had given me a new status in his eyes.

'. . . I mean no disrespect to the dead; but I never understood what Mr. Cassidy saw in that one. She is beautiful, of course, like a doll. She is graceful and clinging.' He made a faintly sexual gesture as he searched for the word. 'She is *sinuosa*, like a vine twisting and turning round a tree. She must have satisfied him in bed, because Mr. Cassidy was a potent man who needed much sex. But – she didn't belong. She brought strange people to the house. Chinese, Japanese, Koreans, types like that . . .'

'Did you know she had a child by Mr. Cassidy?'

He hesitated over the answer. At our first meeting he had denied all knowledge of the relationship. Finally he said, 'I thought it possible. It was not my business to discuss it, outside the family. Now, of course, you are family. So we can talk openly.'

'Yes, I am family. So, it would seem, are Miss Pat and her daughter.'

'Boh!' The exclamation was full of contempt. Marco was old Europe. Whatever was done outside the matrimonial bed was a trifle. Whatever was born outside of it had no legal existence. 'They are connected, yes, but they are not family. Oil and water don't mix.'

'But Mr. Cassidy obviously trusted her.'

'Too much, I think.'

'Why do you say that, Marco?'

'Before he went away, he decided to leave the keys of his safe with her. When he told me of it I was offended and angry. I told him that if he could not trust me, his man of confidence, he should not trust a foreign woman. Besides, I could not control what she brought in or what she took out. I was not prepared to remain in his service if anyone else had access to the safe during his absence. Mr. Cassidy understood my anger and agreed. So the safe remained locked until you arrived.'

'But Miss Pat came and went at will during that time?'

'Yes.'

'She slept where?'

'In Mr. Cassidy's room.'

'In spite of his promise to you, he could have left her a key.'

'Nevertheless, I can swear she did not open the safe.'

'How can you be sure?'

'I had glued four hairs around the door of the safe. They were almost invisible. One might have been noticed, but not all. They remained unbroken until you yourself opened the safe. So Mr. Cassidy did keep faith with me . . . But why are you worried? Is something missing that should be there?'

'I have no way of knowing, Marco. I'm just a cautious man.'

'Better so,' said Marco drily. 'One lives longer.' He looked at his watch. 'Twenty-five minutes past twelve. Time to go in.'

He gunned the engine, swung us round in a wide, foaming arc and headed in towards the Rose Bay jetty. As we neared the shoreline he trained the spotlight on the parking lot behind the jetty. I could see the grey Mercedes, parked with its nose towards the sea. Its lights flicked on and off three times. Marco tossed the fenders overside and eased the Riva against the landing stage with scarcely a creak of the pilings. We moored her briskly, fore and aft, then hefted the heavy sail-bags and set off down the jetty. It was as well there were no witnesses, because paper weighs a lot more than nylon; and, with one bag over each shoulder, we were staggering rather than walking.

By the time we reached the car Laura had the boot open and was sitting at the wheel with the engine running. She did not get out. She was simply a vague profile behind the heavily tinted glass. Marco and I stowed the bags in the boot. I slammed the lid. We exchanged a brief handshake.

He set off at a brisk trot down the jetty. I got into the car. Laura Larsen had it moving instantly.

Just before we pulled out into New South Head Road, she asked, 'Where to?'

I gave her Paul Langlois' address. She nodded curtly and moved into the traffic lane.

I asked her: 'Any problems?'

'None.' She was terse and withdrawn. 'After I left you, I called Mr. Melville in Zurich. I gave him your message.'

'I asked you to telex. I have reasons for wanting a record of the communication.'

'My shorthand was confused. It was easier to report verbally. However, I told him what you wanted. He did send a telex in reply.'

She thrust a folded paper at me and switched on the dashboard light so that I could read it.

'For Gregory. Your position as executor clear and unprejudiced. Your personal position more complicated. A good hotel has a Gideon Bible in every room. Read and ponder Genesis 2, verses 16 and 17. Until we meet, as now we must – Melville.'

'Satisfied, Martin?'

'You kept your promise. Thank you.'

'You'll notice I'm still keeping it – not asking any questions.'

'Thank you for that, too.'

Those were the last words we exchanged until we had delivered the sail-bags at Paul Langlois' house. She did not come inside with me, but waited in the car until I had seen the bags sealed and accepted a receipt. Then, as we drove off, she asked the very reasonable question: 'What do you want to do now?'

If I had given her a straight answer I would have said: 'I'm as lonely as a shag on a black rock. I'm dog-tired and deep-down scared. I want to forget what I am and who I am, take you back to my room and make love to you.' Instead I told her: 'I'd like you to drop me off at the Town

House. Then I'm going to pour myself a large drink and read Gerry Downs' article – and, of course, Genesis 2!'

'The Town House. Very good, sir!'

'Why are you angry with me, Laura?'

'Because you're a fool – a stiffnecked, wooden-headed, bloody fool!'

'Why do you say that?'

'You rifled Cassidy's safe tonight. That's a statement, not a question.'

'You're guessing.'

'No. You had Marco Cubeddu with you. I've known him for years.'

'I've placed Cassidy's papers in custody of a bank. I had a right and a duty to do that. Where's the problem?'

'You've opened the door to Bluebeard's chamber. Now you know what's inside it. Soon, other people will know that you know. What do you think that buys you? A lot of enemies and maybe a bullet in the head. You're an innocent abroad, Martin! You don't know a fraction of what goes on in this State. You know even less about Cassidy's private and business life.'

'But you know all about it!' I was angry now. My patience was rubbed raw. 'Who the hell are you, anyway? Who's your boss and why doesn't he mind his own business?'

She didn't answer. She turned the car off the main road into a tree-lined street, parked in a pool of shadow, then slewed round in her seat to face me. When, finally, she spoke, her voice was tinged with weary sadness.

'The stuff you brought ashore tonight and whatever else Cassidy put in your hands before he died could get you killed. It could get your family threatened or kidnapped. That's why Marius Melville has taken them under his protection in London and Switzerland.'

'You call it protection. Couldn't it equally be a threat, a kind of custody?'

'It could be. It isn't.'

'Prove it.'

'I know him like the palm of my hand: how he thinks, how he works, how he waits, yes, even how he strikes. I'm probably the only one in the world who knows him like that – and manages to retain his trust.'

'Then you've been lying to me, haven't you?' Angrily I began to mimic her: '"Mr. Melville didn't tell me. I didn't ask. I'm paid to pass messages . . ." Now you tell me you're the one in all the world who knows him best. So what does that make you?'

'His daughter,' said Laura Larsen flatly. 'His only daughter, his only child.'

The blandness of the admission shocked me more than the fact itself. I asked a simple, silly question: 'Your name – Larsen . . .?'

'I was married and divorced. It suited me to have another name than my father's.'

'And what is his real name?'

'Melitense. The name signifies "a man from Malta"; in fact, he was born in Palermo. When he became an American citizen he changed it to Melville.'

'Why are you telling me this, at one-thirty in the morning?'

'Because you're going to find it out anyway from Cassidy's files. Because it's important that you trust me.'

'And because, suddenly, I'm a threat to your father and he wants to buy my silence!'

'You'd be very wise to sell it, Martin! For your family's sake, if not your own.'

'Don't you see – can't he see – that I have nothing to sell? I don't own those documents. They're part of a deceased estate. I have to dispose of them in accordance with the wishes of the testator.'

'Cassidy gave you the option to sell –'

'Only the microfiches. And how would you know that anyway?'

'He wrote to my father and told him.'

'He left me free to sell or hold. Whichever I do, there are legal consequences.'

'Martin, Martin!' She reached out and grasped my hands. 'You're still not hearing me! You're talking the language of the law!'

'It's the only one I know, goddammit!'

'Then, goddammit, you'd better learn a few others very fast! Street talk! Triad talk! *Il gergo dei bassifondi* . . . That's where Cassidy operated: the low quarters, the other side of the river. That's where your paperchase is going to lead you. And if you don't learn how to survive there, you're dead!'

'Is your father threatening me?'

'No. As of now, you're still family.'

'That's nice!'

'I'm talking about the others, the rival groups: Chinese, Vietnamese, Japanese Yakuza, the political terrorists, Irish and Arab, the rogue unions, the big international traders who dealt with Cassidy. For all of them now, you're a walking disaster. The threat you represent will be doubled when they read Gerry Downs' newspaper. Do you think the Government or the police are going to protect you? The hell they are! Who's left, Martin? Only Marius Melville, Mario Melitense.'

It was then that I understood quite clearly that I had crossed the Rubicon. I was in barbarian country. All the rules of peace and war had changed. The language was gibberish. Even the gods were alien.

I don't know how long I sat, in silence, staring out at the tufted blossom-trees, with starlight shining through their branches and deep pools of shadow lying beneath them. I saw a cat slinking past, a small feral creature in the jungle of suburbia. I heard a mopoke, making his lonely, two-note call above the distant hum of traffic. He was a real bush creature, surviving precariously a long way from home. Then a human sound woke me out of my reverie. Apropos of nothing at all, Laura Larsen said softly, 'With the shadow on your face, you look just like Charlie Cassidy.'

'So . . .?'

'Nothing. For a while, just a little while, I thought I was in love with him.'

'Was he in love with you?'

She smiled then and I remembered Miss Owl-Eyes, whom I had met a thousand years ago on Flight QF2. London, Bahrain, Singapore, Sydney.

'No, he wasn't in love, but he could give you the wonderful illusion that he was. And when you found he wasn't, you still didn't mind.'

'That's a nice epitaph for any man.'

'I hope I don't have to write one for you, Martin.'

She looked so sombre and woebegone that I couldn't be angry any more. I reached out and drew her towards me and kissed her. She responded eagerly and we sat, clinging together awkwardly, like adolescent lovers, in the front seat of the car. Then, abruptly, she thrust me away.

'Enough, please! We're not children any more. You've got the police in your hotel. I've got my father's security staff in mine. Call me in daylight and tell me you trust me and you still want me in bed and I'll tell you how I feel . . . Fair?'

'Fair enough! But don't blame me if I remember I'm a married man with a wife and family at risk. I'm sorry I stepped out of line.'

'I'm glad you did. It proves you haven't been writing sonnets all your life, or legal briefs either. Shall we go, Mr. Petrarch?'

And so, as Sam Pepys might have put it, I came solitary to bed in the Town House. Before I slept I skimmed through 'Call-me-Rafe' Loomis' list of suspect companies and Gerry Downs' scandal piece. I confess they made insipid reading for one who, tomorrow, would read the naked truth in the secret memorials of Charles Parnell Cassidy.

Then, as any Christian gentleman should when over-nighting in a sinful city, I opened my Gideon Bible and read Genesis 2, verses 16 and 17:

'And this was the command which the Lord God gave the man: Thou mayest eat thy fill of all the trees in the garden except the tree which brings knowledge of good and evil. If ever thou eatest of this thou art doomed to death . . .'

10

Charles Parnell Cassidy had always been a tidy worker. His briefs were beautifully drafted, his case-references meticulously indexed. He diarised every exchange, con-firmed every instruction in writing. His accounts were accurate to the last cent. At the end of the day he destroyed every scrap of superfluous paper and ticked off the day's business like an aircraft check-list.

'Organise yourselves!' he would thunder at us. 'Thus, and only thus, can you be sure you've opened every avenue of relief to your client and raised every possible obstacle against his adversaries. I will not brief untidy silks. I mistrust eccentric geniuses at the Bar. Generally they're delivering a performance instead of a plea and our clients are paying through the nose for it. Above all, I loathe, hate and detest sloppy juniors!' Thus the great man before he took to the hustings and made his reputation as the most successful local ham since Billy Hughes or Robert Gordon Menzies, Warden of the Cinque Ports – God save the Queen!

So, when I locked myself in my office at the Banque de

Paris, with Cassidy's briefcase and a microfiche scanner, I was not surprised to find that what he had called 'a rag-bag' was, in fact, a carefully ordered and indexed record of his works and days. I decided to address myself to this record first. Once I had mastered the plan, I could use it as a grid for a study of the material I had removed from his safe. Without such a guide, I could flounder for weeks through the miscellany of material.

In the beginning I had difficulty assimilating the texts thrown up on the small screen. They were illusions, not reality. I was accustomed to paper – the texture of it, the weight of it, the colour, the imprint of type upon its surface. I needed something that could be tagged and numbered as an exhibit in evidence . . . Then, slowly, I settled down. What I had here was information, the real foundation of power. I had not yet to present it in court, only to judge its authenticity and its value.

The first microfiches dealt with Cassidy's selection as a Labor candidate for election to the State Parliament in the mid-sixties. They consisted of diary entries in Cassidy's emphatic hand:

Jan.15th. Stinking hot. Tempers frayed. Send the staff home early. Joe Mullins calls. He's the sitting member for Waterside. He tells me he has cancer and expects to die before Easter. I commiserate. He curses me out. He needs my attention, not my sympathy. Then he informs me that he's recommended me for preselection to contest his seat in the by-election after his death. He tells me it's a safe constituency but the local Party is split between mid-line moderates, the Far Left and the bare-knuckle boys from the waterfront and the metal trades. If I'm endorsed on the split vote they'll make my life hell. If I get a unanimous endorsement, I'm safe for twenty years. I tell him I'm not sure I want to muddy my shoes in politics. He abuses me to hell and back . . .
'Your old man made his fortune selling liquor and bet-

ting slips to the workers. It's time you paid your dues. Call me Monday and let me know your decision.' Next, the Cardinal's on the line. He mourns like a cooing dove over Joe's impending demise. Then he reads me his favourite sermon about Christian democracy and the apostolate of the work-place. The which, translated into basic English, means 'The British sent the Irish out in chains with the First Fleet. We've dragged ourselves up by our bootstraps until we're one-third of the population, with a stranglehold on the Public Service and a good part of the Labor Party in our pockets – and by God we're not letting go one toehold of our gains!'

What the hell! He's right. I wasn't flogged through High School by the Christian Brothers and booted through Law by my old man, just to surrender the rewards to some nobody with a First Fleet name and a Public School tie . . .

Now, dead on five-thirty, when I'm locking away my papers, in walks Baldy McCubbin. Baldy is the left hand of God in the Labor Party of New South Wales. He's a bruiser, but he's very bright. His nose is broken. His face is scarred by a razor cut. His flinty eyes mirror the grudges of a lifetime. His voice sounds like gravel running down a metal chute. He sits down without being asked, spreads his two ham fists on my polished desk-top and tells me: 'You're recommended for preselection when Jack Mullins dies. If I approve, you're in. When you're in, you pay dues. I'm here to read you the rate card.'

I toy with the ebony ruler, which is a useful weapon and legal as well. Very quietly, I give Baldy the facts of life:

'I'm not for sale. If you want dead meat, go to a butcher's shop. I hate bullies and blackmailers and I can fight just as dirty as any of your boys in the Painters and Dockers. If you want legal advice, you ask politely and pay promptly. If you want service in Parliament, you elect me and you get it for free. But I don't pay, not now, not ever, not one goddamn brass razoo! . . . Have I made myself clear, Mr. McCubbin?'

'You have,' he says and walks out. I'm hot and tired and angry. I hope to Christ Clare isn't in one of her moods when I get home. I need a quiet drink and a long swim and, for a change, some happy sex . . .

The next item was dated January 25. The script was curiously laboured, as if the writer were forcing himself to achieve a clerkly hand.

Dear Cassidy,

The way you handled the preselection committee was a joy to watch – and to get Baldy's vote was a bloody miracle! Now, if you can run a half-way decent campaign, if you don't commit murder or rape the Secretary's girlfriend, you've got the seat in your pocket.

Question is, what will you do after that? Your bum's too broad and your brain's too good for the back benches. This Parliament has a year to run. I don't think we can win the next election. We're too divided. We've had too many strikes to be popular. And, besides, we don't want to be seen helping to run the war in Vietnam. So for you it's twelve months on the back benches, then a term in Opposition as a member of the Shadow Cabinet. After that, I think you'd be ready to take a crack at the Premier's job.

Think about it carefully. Start building a patronage list. Start getting your funds together, because it's an expensive exercise if you want to stay in control and not go on anybody's payroll. Start making friends in big business and in the unions. We need the middle-class vote. So you've got to be seen as an honest broker, with friends in capital and labour.

But get moving now. Five years isn't very long to

build an empire. You'll find time runs away from you very quickly.

When I die, the Cardinal will hand you a sealed envelope. It's my legacy to you. Use it wisely. Have to stop now. I'm hurting more and more each day. Death begins to look like a friend.

Good luck, brother.

Joe Mullins

The nature of Joe Mullins' legacy was not revealed immediately. I had first to deal with a series of letters, documents and commentaries on senior members of the Labor Party, union officials and high members of the public service. Cassidy was a great admirer of the French method: the dossier into which you fed every scrap of information, however trivial, about an individual, until you could draw his portrait blindfold.

About this time, too, he was beginning to dispense favours – mostly in the form of unsecured loans at very reasonable rates of interest. These loans came, not from the trust funds of the partnership, but from a small finance company called Clarevale Finance, of which Micky Gorman was the titular head and whose funds were provided from Cassidy's private purse. Cassidy approved the candidates, but it was Micky who authorised the loans, signed the receipts for interest and kept the books. The client list contained some surprisingly prominent names; and a large number of foreign ones: Chinese, Lebanese, Italian, Greek. Even though his political career had hardly begun, Charles Parnell Cassidy was acting like a true evangelist and converting the migrant tribes along with the local ungodly.

Joe Mullins died on Good Friday that year. Three months later, Charles Parnell Cassidy made his maiden speech in the Legislative Assembly. There was no copy of the text on microfilm, but there was a full copy of Joe Mullins' legacy: a complete diagram of the patronage system of the existing Government and its connections with the criminal community.

It was by now a very dated document. Some of the people named in it were dead – of natural or unnatural causes. Some had aged into respectability or impotence. But there were others, ringed in red, who were still riding high and mighty in their hierarchies. Cassidy's footnote was illuminating:

> . . . The more it changes, the more it's the same. You work with the tools you've got. You live in the house you inherit. If you make a frontal attack on an institution, whether it's criminal or legal, you'll break your heart and your head. You have to infiltrate it, suborn the guards, seduce the secretaries, bribe the underlings, scare the high ones . . . In Australia you can never win an election on a reform ticket. We love our little villainies. We vote for the candidate who can maintain them at an acceptable level . . .

This was Vintage Cassidy. He was a born sceptic. He had breathed in doubt with the incense at Sunday Mass. As to his tactic of infiltration, a note from his Parliamentary Leader was instructive:

> . . . I note and approve your desire to maintain a low profile during your first year or two in the House. However, I can't have you dissipating your talents on the back benches. I have therefore secured Caucus approval for your appointment as my personal counsellor and my liaison officer with the Shadow Ministries. This will give you access to all the information at our disposal and the chance to build some alliances among your colleagues. No need to tell you they'll be testing you at every step. You're the new boy and you're rich – and we take delight in slashing down the tall poppies . . .

Cassidy's reply was brief and to the point:

. . . I accept. It's a role I'm used to Queen's Counsel lets off the big fireworks in court. I'm the man who briefs him. Just for your future guidance: I'm especially interested in Industrial Development and the functioning of the Police Department. The present Government has misfired on the one and studiously corrupted the other. We have to produce a blueprint for change . . .

At first blush, neither was a very promising department for a rising politician; but at this early stage of his career Cassidy was more concerned with staying out of the limelight than getting into it. Besides, he always worked by contraries. Industrial Development was a catch-all portfolio, properly called Industrial Development and Decentralisation. Its long-term aim was to spread industrial enterprises around the country instead of concentrating them along the overcrowded seaboard. It dealt with growth areas, new technology, small businesses, pockets of unemployment, foreign investment. It was rich in talking points and the Minister in charge of it was a most eloquent talker.

Cassidy, who could have beaten him hollow in any debate, refused to engage him. Instead, he set up a series of conferences – all carefully minuted – with Baldy McCubbin and the principal union leaders in the State. His message was simple: 'You want high employment and a solid industrial base. That means foreign investment. I'll get it for you. However, there's a price tag. I have to guarantee industrial peace on the work sites. Can you give me that?'

They couldn't and they wouldn't. He was asking them to castrate themselves, make a pact with the devil, turn themselves into running dogs of the Capitalists. Cassidy shrugged it off with relaxed good humour. 'The essence of democracy is the right to cut your own throat with your own razor. I'm taking a trip abroad in fourteen days. If you change your minds before then, let me know; but I'm damned if I'm going to compromise my credit for a bunch of numbskulls who are still back in the days of Keir Hardie!'

A week later, Baldy McCubbin came to him with a draft document which could, he said, be negotiated between the unions and any overseas investor. Cassidy's comment was scrawled across the microfiche image: 'We could have done this on day one. Why did he have to waste so much energy?' However, his real feelings were expressed in a memorandum to Marius Melville in Florida:

. . . With this agreement now established in principle, we are in an ideal position. There is no doubt in my mind that Labor will win the next election. There is no doubt that so long as Baldy McCubbin is alive the union pledge will hold. After the election, I become the official broker. Pass the word to the boys not to play games with me . . .

Melville's reply was terse:

. . . No games. You deliver; we deliver.

M.M.

Cassidy's attitude to the police force was curious. The fortune he had inherited from his father had been made in part from 'sly grog', the illegal, after-hours trading in liquor. This trade was the natural adjunct of all the others; gambling, prostitution and the drug traffic which, during and after the Vietnam war, had grown to epidemic proportions. In a sense, Cassidy was born into the family, that tenuous but durable network of pimps, bookies, loan sharks, smugglers, thugs and assassins who pandered to the pleasures of John and Jill Public. He was a lawyer. He knew how the system worked. He understood the macabre symbiosis between the policeman and the criminal: how neither could subsist without the other, how neither would be necessary if John and Jill Public were not such erratic animals – greedy, gullible, violent, scared; and still stupid enough to believe in Santa Claus and the free lunch.

It was a memo from the Leader which forced him to define his position in a form suitable for the record. The memo read:

> . . . The present Government has extended patronage and protection to wealthy criminals and their associates. Senior police officers administer that patronage and provide the protection, at a high price. They are therefore accomplices in criminal acts. We will inherit that same police force. What shall we do with it or about it? Your opinion, please? . . .

Cassidy's answer was dated two days later:

> . . . We'll inherit the police, just as we'll inherit the villains and the good, honest citizenry who only want a call girl, or a drink after licensed hours, or a hand of poker, or a roll of the dice, or a jolt of heroin. We dare not disrupt the system by staging a Night of the Long Knives. That could bring on a police strike with looting, violence and blood in the streets. Neither can we afford the collapse of public confidence which would follow an indictment of the present Premier, certain of his Cabinet members and senior officers of the police force. Besides, in a mud-slinging contest, our side isn't going to come out squeaky-clean either . . . So let me try to work up a scenario for you. I don't want to put it into the record system, because it leaks like a string bag. When it's ready, I'll call you and we'll talk at my place. But I give you fair warning. Don't expect a rigorist document. I was bred under the shadow of Cromwell on the one hand and the Grand Inquisitor on the other. You can't induce virtue by the rack. If you can't enforce the law you become a laughing stock. If you don't enforce it you become a criminal. This is a traders' town, with three million inhabitants and a torrent of transients looking

for fun after dark. So it really isn't a question of virtue, but of an acceptable incidence of vice – yours, mine and the visiting firemen's included . . .

The next item, number 24, was a receipt for five thousand dollars, identified as 'the purchase price of fifty glossy prints and fifty negatives, the property of our client, the undersigned Isobel Albeniz.' The signature was a bold, squarish backhand. A typewritten statement indicated that the prints were held in Cassidy's safe and that the negatives were deposited outside Australia with instructions for their publication in certain circumstances. Clearly this was the pornographic material still sealed in the sail-bags and lodged in the strongroom.

Item 25 was a press clipping which recorded the discovery, in a Brisbane apartment, of the body of Isobel Albeniz, 38, one-time prostitute and madam of several expensive Sydney brothels. The coroner's verdict was suicide by an overdose of barbiturates.

Item 26 was a photograph; a smiling, handsome fellow called John Augustus Ranke, Detective-Inspector in the New South Wales Police Force. A note in Cassidy's handwriting declared: 'This man is an extortionist and a professional assassin. He is responsible, to my certain knowledge, for the deaths of Isobel Albeniz and at least two other people.' A later postscript noted that Detective-Inspector Ranke died in an automobile accident while holidaying in Manila in 1978.

I looked at my watch. It was after midday. I called Paul Henri Langlois and suggested we lunch together. With infinite Gallic regret, he declined. He was entertaining Le Nickel from New Caledonia on their half-yearly junket in Sydney. Tomorrow perhaps? Of course tomorrow! I should be there for a whole series of tomorrows, feeling more and more like some grubby little voyeur peering through a tenement keyhole.

What the hell! If I had to eat alone I might just as well

work. I asked one of the secretaries to send out for coffee and sandwiches, then settled back at the screen.

The new cassettes of microfiches dealt with Cassidy's offshore business arrangements. They began with a diary note dated June 1968:

. . . The only way to make money and keep it is to operate transnationally. The only way for me to do this legally is through discretionary trust arrangements of which I am not the beneficiary. Marius Melville has been most helpful in this matter. He suggests a worldwide chain of autonomous companies, each in a tax haven, with the shares owned by a central trust in a secure location, the company funds being exported to the same trust. He has recommended a firm of Swiss lawyers skilled in this kind of operation . . . The longer I stay in the political arena, the more clearly I see that money is the only shield and the sharpest sword. If a man is rich, he can't be bought with money. If the funds lie outside his visible control, he can't be bullied, black-mailed or seduced into parting with them; besides, the traditional trust is still the best defence against fiscal invasion . . .

The next item was a letter from Horstman and Preysing, Attorneys at Law in Zurich. They were pleased to inform their distinguished colleague that the Rotdrache trust deeds had been signed and commercial companies in the Rotdrache series had been set up in Liechtenstein, Monte Carlo, Panama, the Bahamas, Hong Kong and Bangkok. All funds, other than those required for day-to-day opera-tions, would be transmitted back to the trust account at U.B.S. Zurich. Access to funds and information was by a common code as previously designated and known only to the trustees and their lawful delegate. Once again, Cassidy had added a recent footnote:

113

. . . The code consists of Latin literals, a five-figure sequential numeration based on the first group, then Latin literals again. Even you should be able to work that one out, sonny boy. If you can't, the answer's in cassette number 10, item eight. But try, just for the hell of it. Pity is, I won't be around to time you! . . .

It wasn't too complicated. Most operators of trans-national companies run them in series – Bluebird Canada, Bluebird Switzerland, and so on. In this case the series name was Rotdrache – Red Dragon. In Latin it became Draco Ruber. Sequential numeration worked thus:

3 5 1 2 4
D R A C O

So the access code became: DRACO – 35124 – RUBER.

I checked my answer against cassette number 10. I felt a childish triumph when I found it was right. Then the triumph turned to anger. Here I was, twelve thousand miles from home, still being manipulated by Charles Parnell Cassidy – and him, in the best Irish fashion, six feet under the sod! I was only at the beginning of his records, but already the highlights of his activities were becoming clearer and the shadows in the corners were deepening.

Cassidy had been an empire-builder and sooner or later one would expect to stumble on human bones beside the caravan tracks or around the outpost fortresses. Detective-Inspector Ranke had been a very nasty piece of goods – but I wondered who had paid the driver of the car that killed him in Manila. If, as the Gerry Downs' article claimed, Charlie Cassidy had a stake in the Manila girl-gambling-and-drug rackets, then it was as easy for him to hire a hit-man as to sell a ten-year-old girl in a bar. Cassidy's note to Marius Melville and Melville's curt reply had been couched in the lingo of the Brotherhood – more binding than any contract. So, with the Brotherhood behind me and the Attorney-General in front, I was truly beleaguered. I was also sitting on four sail-bags containing evidentiary material, a pistol and a quantity of heroin, for possession of which I was now answerable at law.

Enough was enough! The microfiche material I could handle. The rest was a timebomb – and I had to get rid of it. I packed up all the materials and put them back in the safe deposit. I left the sandwiches and coffee untouched and walked out into the gaggle of Sydney's lunchtime streets and a pall of midsummer heat.

After two minutes' walking I was drenched with perspiration. I flagged down a taxi to take me to the Melmar Marquis. I told myself I needed a pleasant lunch in air-conditioned comfort. I was lying in my own teeth. I wanted to see Miss Owl-Eyes, to eat and talk and touch body to body with her. I was lonely and beginning to be as scared as she had warned I should be.

The foyer of the Melmar Marquis was vast, cool and murmurous. The front of house staff were all beautiful girls or handsome boys, who wore midnight blue blazers with the double-M monogram on the pocket. They smiled readily and offered eager help. I addressed myself to a Taiwanese charmer at the information desk who offered to page Miss Laura Larsen for me. Three minutes later the lady came swaying down the staircase, fresh as a summer flower – and formal as the Court Circular!

'Mr. Gregory! How nice to see you. I'm running late, I'm afraid. We have a convention of Japanese communication engineers. Their inaugural luncheon begins in fifteen minutes. If you don't mind waiting at the bar, Leon will take care of you, then I'll show you the accommodation we discussed for your people.'

As she steered me away from the desk I asked, 'Why the pantomime?'

'Because I'm on duty – and I wasn't prepared for a casual visit.'

'Shall I leave?'

'No, for God's sake! I'll order lunch in my suite. I'll fetch you when it's ready. You look worn around the edges. Is anything the matter?'

'I've started going through Cassidy's files.'

'Have you learnt anything?'

'More than I want. Less than I need.'

She touched my arm lightly, steering me over to the bar.

'Leon, this is one of our new clients, Mr. Gregory. We're lunching upstairs, but I'm running late. I'll call down as soon as I'm free. Mr. Gregory, may I recommend one of Leon's Margaritas – out of this world!'

It was a good exit and it cut me down to junior size. Leon, mannerly as a marquis himself, asked me: 'What's your pleasure, Mr. Gregory?'

'What the lady recommended – a Margarita.'

He mixed the drink with a flourish and it tasted good. He asked me: 'Will you be staying with us, Mr. Gregory?'

'Probably. I'm discussing the possibility of an international legal convention.'

'If Miss Larsen arranges it, you can count on success. She's a wonder, that girl. Always cheerful, always on the move – and she knows the hotel business inside out. Already we're up to eighty per cent occupancy, which is great. We've got class and comfort, if you see what I mean.'

It felt comfortable to me too until, half way through my drink, 'Call-me-Rafe' Loomis hoisted his pudgy body on to the next bar stool and gave me his furtive, jowly grin.

'Well, look who's here! Martin Gregory. This is a surprise.'

'You're a long way from Parliament House, Mr. Loomis.'

'But never far from you, Mr. Gregory.'

'Would you like a drink?'

116

'Never known to refuse. What are you having?'

'A Margarita.'

'I'll try one.'

He waited until the drink was served and Leon had drifted away to another customer, then he said, 'You foxed my boys last night. You went to Cassidy's house in a taxi. But you never came out. We didn't solve the mystery until this morning. You left by boat.'

'Something illegal in that?'

'No. Sneaky perhaps. Smartass perhaps. But certainly not illegal.'

'So why the surveillance and the harassment?'

'Not harassment, Mr. Gregory – security. This is a rough town. You're an important man with distinguished connections. We don't want anything to happen to you. So we provide police protection. Free of charge, you'll notice.'

'According to Gerry Downs, free police service is getting rarer and rarer.'

'Ah! So you've seen the first piece. It doesn't publish until Saturday.'

'Someone gave me an advance copy.'

'And . . . ?'

'Clearly, you, as Attorney-General, will have to make some response.'

'Any suggestions?'

'Some. But I'd rather not discuss them in a public bar.'

'Name the time and place. I'll be there.'

'The Premier's office, Parliament House, at a time convenient to you both.'

'Why the Premier? You and I can handle this.'

'I think the Premier will want to attend.'

'He's a busy man.'

'I'm trying to save him trouble. You, too, for that matter.'

'Where do I contact you?'

'You know where I am every moment.'

'Almost every moment.'

'I'll call you at five this evening, at your office.'

'What do I tell the Premier?'

'Tell him the end is nigh – and the executor of the deceased estate would like to talk to him.'

'Very funny!'

'Not funny at all, I'm afraid. When we first met, you tried to bully me out of my proper functions as executor. You were having – what did you call it? – "forensic fun". Now, the fun's over. I wish to open legal communications with Cassidy's successor and his Attorney-General. A conference is the first step.'

'Which means that you've got something to give us.'

'It means that if and when I have something to give you, it's recorded, certified and I get a receipt for every item.'

'I told you at the time – that's standard procedure.'

'Good.'

'Let me make a guess at what you've got.'

'No guesses. I'll call you at five.'

The telephone buzzed behind the bar. Leon answered it. I prayed he was as well trained as he looked. He put down the receiver and announced, 'They're ready for you now, Mr. Gregory. Tenth floor, someone will meet you at the elevator.'

I thanked him and slid a ten-dollar note across the bar. He made no move to pick it up.

'The drinks come with the compliments of the house, sir.'

'Just saying thank you for the service, Leon.'

'My pleasure, Mr. Gregory,' said Leon. He picked up the note and began wiping the bar near Loomis' elbow. Loomis sat, hang-jowled and unhappy, staring into his liquor.

Laura Larsen was waiting for me outside the elevator on the tenth floor. Her smile was warm.

'Good afternoon, Martin.'

I bent to kiss her. She offered her lips, but there was no

passion in the brushing contact. I apologised for coming unannounced. I thanked her for inviting me to lunch. She chided me lightly.

'I told you last night. You're still family. You're welcome.'

Her hand was cool as she led me along the corridor to her suite, a large three-roomed apartment with an office, a sitting room and, I presumed, a bedroom beyond. Luncheon was set in the sitting-room; chilled soup, cold cuts, salad and cheese, with a bottle of Chablis cooling in the ice-bucket. For a moment I felt an oaf, shambling and tongue-tied. Then I managed to get the words out.

'You told me to call you in daylight . . . you wanted the answers to two questions. The first is "yes, I trust you". The second –'

She laid a cautionary finger against my lips.

'The second lands us both in trouble. Let's save it for another time, eh?'

'Just so you know –'

'Just so we both know we're walking tip-toe through a minefield . . . I'm hungry. Let's eat. Will you pour the wine please, darling?'

Because I had either to make talk or make an adolescent fool of myself, I asked, 'When is your father coming to Sydney?'

'He's not. If you want to see him, it will have to be somewhere else.'

'Where, for instance?'

'Hong Kong, Bangkok, Hawaii –'

'He said he wanted to see me.'

'Not exactly that. He said, "Until we meet, as now we must".'

'Is there a difference?'

'Yes. He's waiting for you to make the first move; which is what Cassidy provided in his will.'

'Then could you get in touch with him and ask him when and where a meeting could be arranged?'

'Certainly. Is there any other message?'

'Tell him I've read Genesis 2. I have eaten of the tree of knowledge – and I'm suffering from acute indigestion.'

'Not at my table, Martin Gregory! Wipe that grim look off your face and enjoy your lunch!'

I did enjoy it. I enjoyed the easy talk we made, the cautious affection we exchanged. Of course it was a pretending game: let's pretend there isn't any time but now, that we can be just good friends, that I don't have a wife and two children and that, here in this room, I can hardly remember their faces. I remembered something else, however. An old uncle, who was very kind to me, made one day a strange kind of confession: 'Martin, I've been lucky. I've never met a woman I wanted more than my wife. I've often wondered what would have happened if I had.' Something of what I was thinking must have shown in my face, because, quite abruptly, Laura asked the question: 'What really brought you here, Martin?'

I had said I trusted her. Now I was being asked to prove it.

'I needed to borrow some courage. I'm scared.'

'You should be. I told you that last night.'

'The stuff I took from Cassidy's safe . . . I've decided it's too hot to handle.'

'Why so?'

'There are albums of porno pictures of prominent cit'-zens, bought by Cassidy from a woman who was later murdered. There's a kilo of heroin, a pistol that could be hot, a lot of assorted currency, gold bars and some very precious stones. There are also reams of paper I haven't even glanced at.'

'What are you going to do with the stuff?'

'Declare its existence first; have an official inventory made and certified; then sort out what belongs on my desk and what the Government has to handle.'

'Does that include the material my father wants to buy?'

'No. That's a briefcase full of microfiche records. I'm

only at the beginning, but my guess is that it duplicates all the material in the safe, but includes a great deal more.'

'Are you prepared to sell it to my father?'

'I can't answer that question yet.'

'I should tell you, Martin, my father won't bargain.'

'I'm not concerned with the price. I'm concerned about the ultimate disposition and use of the records. So, until I've spoken with your father, I'll retain my option to sell or hold.'

'Martin . . .' She held out her glass to be refilled. 'I have to explain something to you.'

'No, you don't.'

'Yes – yes, I must. We're not children. That's the only reason we're sitting here at this table instead of being in bed together on the other side of that door. We fit, you and I. The chemistry works for us. We both know it. But we're not halfway people. It's all or nothing. So we've still got our clothes on and you can face your wife without lying and I can face my father and tell him I've done what he asked – kept a check on you. He's an old-fashioned man. I'm an old-fashioned woman. But if you were my husband, I'd tell my father to go to hell and follow you to the world's end. Your wife did that years ago. She walked away from Cassidy and went with you. You couldn't get so lucky twice in a row. Not even if you wanted to.'

'Don't you think you'd better tell me the rest of it?'

'If you fall out with my father, I stand with him, not with you.'

'I understand.'

'No, Martin, you don't. We're talking about another world – Cassidy's, my father's, mine. You've strayed into it or, rather, Cassidy dragged you into it as his final joke. But nothing here works by the rules you've learned . . . Take this hotel, all the Melmar hotels. We do well, because we're known as safe houses. Every room is swept every day for bugs and surveillance mechanisms. Our security system is the best in the world. It filters out not only criminals, but the police, industrial spies, any category we choose to exclude. We have bodyguards, escorts, lawyers, doctors and any other service you want . . . If you wanted, you could live here for a month and nobody would know you existed. When you went to another Melmar hotel, your requirements would be known and respected to the letter . . .'

'Why are you telling me all this?'

'I'm afraid for you. You know too much and too little. I can't help you because you don't belong to me . . . and you're not sure where you do belong anyway. Forgive me! I didn't mean that the way it came out.'

'Then what do you mean?'

'Martin, you can't see this; but I can. The centre of your life is not your wife, not your family – it's Charlie Cassidy. Oh, I'm not saying you don't love them, of course you do – otherwise I'd have picked you off the tree like a ripe apple. But ask yourself: why did you make a runaway marriage? Cassidy! Why did you settle in Europe? Cassidy! Why are you here with me in this room? Because you're retracing Cassidy's steps and trying to sort out the mess he's left . . . Don't tell me it's the inheritance, I wouldn't believe you. Any lawyer in the world can handle a probate job. No! This is something different. It's a grudge fight – or a love game; but one of the players is dead and the other is matched with a ghost!'

She was near to tears and I could not find it in my heart to be angry with her. I went to her and took her hands and squatted in front of her and tried to put a smile into the question: 'So you want me to break off play, is that it?'

'Yes.'

'And how exactly do I do that?'

'Make your peace with the Government, if you must. Apply for probate on Cassidy's will. Sell the briefcase to my father – and take the first plane home!'

'All the wise monkeys rolled into one. See nothing, hear nothing, say nothing.'

'Yes!'

'Take the money and run.'

'Yes.'

'That's the third warning you've given me.'

'It's the last, Martin, absolutely the last.'

'And what do I say when I look at myself in the mirror?'

'You say: "I'm rich. My wife is beautiful. My kids are healthy. And thank God I'm alive to enjoy it all!" . . . Now kiss me and go before I make a damn fool of myself and hate you for it!'

11

Outside the hotel, the air was oven-hot and laden with exhaust fumes. For a moment I stood irresolute on the kerbside, debating whether to give the rest of the day a miss and take myself surfing for the afternoon. Then I heard two businessmen behind me discussing the bank rate, which had risen half a per cent that morning. I looked at my watch. It was twenty minutes to three. I went back into the hotel and asked the concierge to find me the address of the Sydney office of U.B.S. – the Union Bank of Switzerland. The doorman whistled a taxi to get me there.

I was lucky. The manager, punctiliously Swiss, was back from lunch. My card gained me entrance, my driver's licence confirmed my identity, the name of Paul Henri Langlois lent me added grace. Thus prepared, the manager was only a little frigid when I asked whether he would access me to his headquarters in Zurich. He could, of course – in principle! In fact, he would need more information than I had so far given him. On the back of another visiting card I wrote in German 'coded access' and handed him the card.

He warmed noticeably as he read it. He composed his own access code on the desk computer, then turned the instrument towards me. I punched in the code from Cassidy's files – DRACO 35124 RUBER. I waited in silence until the great brain had done its work.

The manager asked politely: 'Have you found what you wanted, Mr. Gregory?'

I took time to answer him. It is never a good idea to be too complaisant with the custodians of money. You pay their salaries. You must make them aware they are as liable as you to misfeasance, malfeasance and simple human error.

Finally, I nodded and told him: 'Thank you. This is what I wanted.'

The luminous symbols told a fantastic story. The Rotdrache trust had, in short-term deposits, in bonds, in gilt-edged equities, in metals, in prime real estate, a net asset value of 584 million US dollars. The Rotdrache series of companies showed an additional net worth, reported daily, of another 150 million. The details were displayed on five ensuing frames. On no frame was there any mention of liabilities, either actual or contingent. What I was viewing was a vast repository of wealth, daily augmented, hourly augmenting itself.

The manager prompted me gently: 'There is no problem, I trust, Mr. Gregory?'

'No problem.'

'If there is any transaction you wish us to execute . . .'

'For the moment there is none.'

'We are at your service at all times.'

'Thank you. I'll be in touch.'

'Before you cancel the access, would you like to make a print-out?'

'No.'

The manager permitted himself a small nod of approval. 'Then you simply press "Cancel".'

I waited until the screen was blank again, thanked the manager for his courtesy and walked out again into the oven-heat of Sydney. For one dizzy moment I wondered if I were going mad or whether I were anchored in some interminable nightmare, enveloped by a thousand cobwebs.

A passerby jostled me back to sanity. I began walking swiftly back to the Banque de Paris. Now it was absolutely imperative that I finish my first scan of the microfiches in Cassidy's briefcase. Then, please God, I might begin to have some clue to what were, on the face of it, the crazed caprices of a dying man. Then, as I walked, I recalled phrases from Cassidy's last handwritten note to me:

. . . given that infamy is always predicated of politicians, I decided long ago to come to terms with ill-repute and, wherever possible, turn it into profit . . .
. . . let me give you fair warning. All of it is dangerous, some of it lethal, material . . .

God knows, the figures I had just seen were lethal enough, a high temptation to terrorists, extortionists, blackmailers! Then he had offered me options:

. . . get rid of the stuff, at a nice profit . . . deliver all the material to the Attorney-General of New South Wales . . . make your own decision as to its use or its destruction. You'll be the potent one then . . . You'll be the rich one – if you want to be . . .

By the time I reached the Banque de Paris I had convinced myself that Charlie Cassidy had been acting with total, if tortuous, rationality. He had made a fortune out of the ungodly. There was no joy in the possession if he had no heir. There was no point in having an heir who was not prepared to defend his possession. Which brought me bang up against Cassidy's valediction: 'That's why I've made you a backhanded gift of the worst side of myself.'

Then I remembered another Sibylline saying, this time from Pornsri Rhana, mistress, confidante, mother of Cassidy's child:

'Don't be too hasty, Mr. Gregory. Take a good look at the kingdom before you abdicate the throne.'

Where better to study the kingdom than in Charles Parnell Cassidy's Doomsday Book, a briefcase full of microfiches? The trick was to discover how to read the book to best effect. The root document, which I had not yet found, was the deed establishing the Rotdrache trust. This would name the trustees, the beneficiaries and the conditions under which assets would be administered and benefits would flow. After that, I had to find the chain of command which held the hugely profitable network together. I could not imagine that the mere possession of an access cipher would put me in possession of an Aladdin's cave of treasures.

However, the manager of U.B.S. had clearly presumed that it did. He had offered to honour any transaction I cared to make; but I could not believe in any arrangement so simple and vulnerable. On the other hand, Cassidy, the most convoluted of men, had a saying: 'Dazzle 'em with flashing lights, all around the horizon. While they're waiting for Moses to appear with the tablets of stone, they'll miss the key inscription right under their noses.' All in all, I could never say I hadn't been warned.

My most important find during the rest of the afternoon was a memorandum headed simply 'Schedule of Requirements, C.P.C. to M.M.' It was, on the face of it, as arid as a shopping list:

Transmission of information: Telephones can be tapped, documents lost or stolen, speech distorted or misunderstood. Codes can be deciphered, meetings monitored. Cut-outs for casual employees are needed in the style of intelligence operations. Training in information security is necessary for permanent personnel.

Transport of commodities: We buy into the container business. We buy into road transport and shipping agencies. We set up deals with maritime, road haulier and airport unions.

Banking services: Should be handled only through large international institutions. In high finance, fringe dwellers are dangerous.

Travel agents: We will look to purchase established agencies.

Customs and Excise clearance: Again, we buy our own Customs agency, which cultivates its own contacts in the service.

Accommodation for personnel: You're the hotel man. This is your business!

Legal and fiscal counsel in all jurisdictions: These are my pigeon, at home, in South-East Asia and in the United Kingdom.

Relations with law enforcement agencies: We should exchange experience on this matter.

Buffer zones: We have to establish need-to-know rules, a code of discretion and a mechanism of enforcement.

To this he had added a postscript:

. . . I can set up the Australian organisations with affiliates in New Zealand. In Manila we have in place an organisation of expatriates with established connections. In Indonesia we have some skills and contacts. Thailand, Hong Kong and Malaysia are good for us. Singapore is tight as a drum and dangerous for the outsider. The same applies to Japan. Deals can be done, but only through a local entrepreneur. In any case, my notion is to build a secure commercial base to confirm the confidence of our suppliers and our clients . . .

It was all as bland as butter. You could cite the documents in any court and argue them as the proper guidelines for a sound international commercial enterprise, working in a variety of jurisdictions. The most interesting piece of information was contained in a later memo from Marius Melville, easily identified as a reply to Cassidy's comments:

M.M. to C.P.C.: Agree general lines your thinking. Agree also your efficacy for Australia and New Zealand. Our criteria for other territories are simple: who can best establish a local corporation; who has best access to appropriate staff; who has best mechanism of control? Since we are dividing our net down the middle, I don't have a problem with any management that delivers an acceptable profit.

The last missive seemed to indicate that the companies in the Red Dragon chain were controlled jointly by Cassidy and Marius Melville, but that the trust was Cassidy's personal base. It would also explain Melville's need to remove the microfiche collection from public circulation. If, on the other hand, I were to take Cassidy's place in the enterprise, then clearly I would have to prove myself an acceptable partner – or be eliminated. By now, it was nearly five o'clock; time to call Loomis at the Attorney-General's office. He sounded frayed and short-tempered.

'The Premier has to leave here dead on six-fifteen. He can take us both at five-thirty, O.K.?'

'By me, splendid.'

'Can you bring any material with you?'

'No. This is procedure, remember? What happens if and when . . .'

'I remember. Don't be late. The Premier has a busy night.'

It seemed I was going to be busy myself. I dialled the number of Pornsri Rhana. She seemed pleased, but hardly surprised, to hear from me.

'Thank you for calling, Mr. Gregory. What can I do for you?'

'I think we should meet again, as quickly as possible. Are you free for dinner this evening?'

'I can make myself free – if you'll let me provide the dinner at my house. We need to talk. It is private here.'

'I didn't mean to put you to trouble.'

'On the contrary. It will be a pleasure. Oh, and dress very casually please. It's much too hot for collar and tie.'

'What time would you like me there?'

'Eight o'clock.'

I had to deal with one other matter. On the bank notepaper I wrote out a certificate, to be signed by Paul Henri Langlois, that, just after midnight on the date specified, he had received from Martin Gregory four large canvas sacks for deposit in his strongroom. He had not inspected the contents. He had closed the bags with the bank seal and had them transported the following morning by security truck to the bank. They would be held there pending instructions from Martin Gregory or his lawful delegate.

Paul gave me a quizzical Gallic look and remarked, 'You seem to be under great pressure, Martin.'

'I am. I'm trying to cover myself across a very big board.'

'It is not always possible. Sometimes it is not even advisable.'

'I'm listening, Paul.'

'You've been away a long time. You have learned to think and work like a European – everything by legal definition, options under different jurisdictions, case-histories, precedents . . . If ever you are challenged in court, you have chain-mail defence, beginning with a clear intent to act within the law. In this country, in this State, it doesn't work like that. Oh, the foundations of law, the

129

precedents and the principles are the same as in England – but the respect for them, the insistence on them? No! There is too much careless drafting, too much flippancy about consequences. What is the Australian phrase? – "she'll be right, mate!" Unfortunately, things are not always right or rightly done. There is still the outlaw complex, the worship of the successful rogue . . . So you may find that, instead of covering yourself, you are leaving yourself wide open to attack . . . the enemy walks around the Maginot Line and mounts a blitzkrieg from the air . . . Forgive me, I am intruding into your family affairs.'

'Not at all. I'm grateful. I'm feeling very isolated just now.'

'Any time you need to talk, I am here. If you want a safe place to hide, the bank keeps a couple of apartments for visiting officials . . . Also I have a holiday house at Whale Beach . . .'

'You're a good friend, Paul. Thank you.'

'For nothing. I hate bullies and intimidators. There are too many in this great country – too many by half.' He signed the certificate and handed it back to me. 'Walk warily, Martin.'

Fifteen minutes later I was face to face with the Premier and Rafe Loomis, the two likely lads who had inherited the mantle of Charles Parnell Cassidy. Loomis seemed sour and a little drunk. The Premier was at pains to be cordial.

'I'm delighted you've decided to trust us, Martin.'

'Has Mr. Loomis outlined the conditions?'

'A certification of all documents in your presence. A clear agreement on which are Government property and which a part of Cassidy's estate. An official receipt for all articles of which we take delivery.'

'And you both agree, Mr. Premier?'

'Yes.'

'Very well. Last night I went to Cassidy's house and opened his safe. I put the contents in four sail-bags and

130

delivered them immediately, by sea and motor transport, to Paul Henri Langlois, of the Banque de Paris in Sydney. He sealed them in my presence and had them taken next morning to his bank, where they now rest, still sealed, in the strongroom.'

'Any witness to the act? Any inventory?'

'No. I left a receipt with Marco Cubeddu, the houseman. I also have a receipt from the Banque de Paris.'

'Did you examine the contents of the safe?'

'Only in the most cursory fashion, as I packed them.'

'But now you volunteer to display them, on request, to authorised officials of the Government.'

'Yes.'

'Then, for the present, we are happy to leave them in your custody. Thank you for your co-operation, Mr. Gregory.'

I felt like a gape-mouthed idiot. I must have looked it, too; because Loomis gave me a jowly grin and said, 'You see? It didn't hurt a bit!'

I put the question to the Premier. 'Only three days ago Loomis here was screaming for possession, talking misprision of felony if I concealed as much as a laundry list. What's changed his mind?'

'I have.' The Premier seemed somehow a little taller. 'I've convinced him that while we're wading through the surf that Gerry Downs is kicking up, unknowing may be better than knowing. If we don't know we don't have to hedge or lie. We just promise a full enquiry. If we're asked about documents, we say that Cassidy's private papers are in the hands of his executor, who has promised full co-operation in uncovering all matters relevant to our investigations.'

'It seems I could have saved myself the bother of this visit.'

'On the contrary,' said Loomis blandly. 'You've just won yourself a whole column of commendations.'

'So now, perhaps you'll take your policemen off my tail.'

'I'm not sure that's such a good idea.'

'Do it, Rafe!' The Premier was testy. 'Do it now!'

Loomis picked up the telephone, punched out a number and ordered someone called Batterbee to 'call off the bloodhounds and assign 'em to normal duty'. Then he put down the phone and said, with a shrug, 'You're on your own now, lover-boy. If I were you, I'd stay away from dark alleys and dark women!'

The Premier stood up and offered his hand. I had the odd feeling that if I kissed it he wouldn't take it amiss. He said, with seemly gravity, 'Thank you for your confidence in us, Martin. I hope we'll meet again before you leave for England. Rafe, why don't you offer Martin a drink?'

Loomis waited until the Premier's footsteps had receded down the long corridor. Then he burst out: 'God! He's a pompous bastard! Give him three months in office and he'll be acting like bloody Napoleon! You don't really believe he worked out this afternoon's ploy, all by his little self?'

'What should I believe?'

'That I'm a little brighter than I look . . . What will you drink?'

'Scotch, please. A light one. I can't stay long.'

As he poured the liquor, he asked, 'When you opened Cassidy's safe, did anything jump out and bite you?'

'Like what?'

'Like items of special interest?'

'I told you. There's a whole mess of stuff to be examined. I couldn't spare the time. I wanted to get it packed and out of the house.'

'Now you can have all the time you need,' said Loomis agreeably. 'Take a long cruise and work on board ship . . . By the way, I hear you sacked Micky Gorman.'

'You heard wrong. I offered him the probate job. He declined, on the grounds of conflict of interest. Gerry Downs retains him now.'

'Is he still holding any of Cassidy's papers?'

'None. I've collected them all and paid his bill. It was routine stuff: title deeds, stock certificates and the like.'

'That's a relief.'

'Gorman and Downs – they make a very odd couple.'

'Did Micky tell you what brought 'em together?'

'No.'

'Ask him – or, better still, ask Gerry Downs.'

'I've never met the man.'

'Don't you think you should, seeing he's about to smear your family across the front page of his weekend magazine?'

'I've never thought of Cassidy as my family.'

'That's the joke, isn't it? Living, you were sworn enemies. He wouldn't even acknowledge his own grandchildren. Dead, he's hung round your neck like a bloody albatross.'

He tossed down his drink at a gulp and poured himself another four fingers of raw spirit. He took another large swallow and then rounded on me again.

'You're a wasted man, Martin Gregory!' He was spoiling for an argument. I was determined not to give him one. I shrugged and grinned and sipped my drink and let him rant on. 'You've got brains and guts and you can design a tiger-trap with the best of us. But you're cold. You've got no fire; you've spent it all hating Charlie Cassidy . . . I admired him. He was a big man. He ran the Party like a racing machine. His only mistake was that he never groomed a successor. You could have been the one. You know that, don't you? Even now, you could nominate for his seat and win it at the by-election – not on your name, but on Charlie's, no matter what muck Gerry Downs prints about him! But . . . oh, shit! What's the use? You've got a bellyful of bile and you've still got "Made in England" stamped on your backside, like Grandma's chamberpot . . . Here, have another drink.'

'No thanks. I've got a dinner date.'

133

'I hope she's pretty. I'll have my driver take you to your hotel.'

'Thank you.'

He fixed me with a red and rheumy stare.

'A couple of questions before you go. That list of companies I gave you. Have you turned up any references to them in Cassidy's papers?'

The question concealed a snare and I spotted it just in time.

'Not yet. I'm still working through the formal documents: the will, the trust deeds, and so on. The rest of the stuff will have to wait. Besides, now that you've decided that ignorance is bliss, there's no hurry, is there? What was your other question?'

'How are you going to handle Cassidy's creditors?'

It seemed a stupid question for a lawyer to ask. I shrugged it off.

'The normal routine. We advertise the settlement of the estate. Creditors render claims. If they prove valid, we pay.'

'I used the wrong word,' said Loomis, with a grin. 'I told you from the start, Cassidy was the paymaster for the machine. He kept the books. He held the funds.'

'Where?'

'I should have thought under his own hand, in safe-deposit perhaps.'

'Whom did he pay?'

'I've never asked. Sometimes we made suggestions for special patronage. But Charlie kept the full list to himself.'

'How did he pay?'

'Cash, gold, stones, sometimes drugs. That's why I asked whether anything jumped out and bit you.'

'I'll check and let you know what I find.'

'Don't bother.' Loomis took another mouthful of liquor 'You're the one who'll have to answer when the monthly payroll falls due . . . And before you start telling me about legal debts and illegal graft, let me tell you something.

These boys break legs and stick bombs under cars and kick you about in dark lanes . . . You didn't want to trust me. You didn't want police protection. Fine! You're on your own, Mr. Gregory. And the best of British luck! . . . I'll call the car pool and tell them you're on your way down.'

He looked like a basset hound and dressed like a tailor's nightmare, but, my God, he was bright! The Premier might pretend to be Napoleon; but Loomis was Fouché in the flesh; supple, complaisant, all-seeing, all-knowing – and absolutely implacable.

I got back to the hotel at a quarter to seven. In London it was a quarter to eight in the morning. I called Pat. The call was switched through to our answering service, where the duty operator told me that the family was already *en route* to Heathrow to catch an early morning flight to Switzerland. They would be in Klosters by mid-afternoon. The address there was Haus Melmont. There were two telephone numbers and a telex code. There would be no problem communicating with them. The difficulty would be to explain all that was happening to me.

It was the word 'happening' that stuck in my gullet. I was not in control of my life any longer. I was simply responding to events arranged by others. I was being manipulated by people who a week ago were as alien to me as little green men from Mars. Cassidy himself was determining my destiny from whatever lodging he had found himself on the other side of the grave.

Each day I was becoming more isolated, more impotent for lack of information and allies. It could take me weeks to master the details of Cassidy's Byzantine activities. It could take double the time to make contact with half the shadowy personages involved. I needed help. I needed legal support, constitutional advice. Most of all, I needed a safe guide through the nether world of State politics.

Suddenly I was enveloped in a wave of weariness, a near-nausea that made me feel drained and dizzy. I stretched out on the bed, closed my eyes and lay quiet until the nausea subsided. It was a trifling incident, the natural by-product of fatigue, frustration and the tension of a fear that I was unwilling to call by its real name. But it did make me see the loom of another problem. What if I fell ill or met with an accident or fell victim to thuggery on a dark night? Who then would deal with the mess of pottage Cassidy had left me and my family?

First thing tomorrow morning I had to find myself a replacement for Micky Gorman, someone to handle the probate of the will and the disposition of the trusts. Tomorrow? Why not now? I leafed through my address book and found the address of a man whom I admired more than any other in the law: Julian Steiner, Professor Emeritus of Constitutional Law, scholar, humanist and mentor of some of the best men in the profession. Thank God, he was at home, spry and rasping as ever. He said: 'Martin! I heard you were in town. I thought of sending condolences. Then I wasn't sure they'd be appropriate. I'm delighted to hear from you.'

'I need help, Professor. Help and advice.'

'What sort of help?'

'I need a bright and honest lawyer to handle the probate of Charlie Cassidy's will.'

'That's a tall order. You could start, like Diogenes, by buying a barrel and a storm lantern. On the other hand, you could call Arthur Rebus, of Fitch, Rebus and Landsberg. Mention my name.'

'Thank you. I'll do it first thing in the morning.'

'I'll see if I can contact him tonight to put him on notice. A question, though – how complicated is the job likely to be?'

'So far as the will and the trusts are concerned – and so far as I've been able to determine – everything's straight-forward, clean and unencumbered.'

'Good.'

'As for the rest – what you used to call the ambient

areas – that's where I need advice. Could you possibly give me an hour of your time?'

'My house. Ten-thirty tomorrow morning.'

'Thank you, Professor.'

'You sound a little fatigued.'

'I'm suffering from a bad case of culture shock.'

'It's like clap. You get it by keeping the wrong company. Be consoled. It's an uncomfortable illness, but not fatal.'

'How right you are, Professor! I'll see you in the morning – and thank you.'

Half an hour later, shaved, showered and dressed in cotton slacks, sports shirt and espadrilles, I was on my way to dinner with Pornsri Rhana. Her apartment was in a new tower block, with a northward aspect and a panoramic view of the harbour from the Heads to the Harbour Bridge. I had made fantasies about how it would be decorated – traditional Thai, with gilt carving and silks and brocades, and she herself in the formal costume of a woman of quality. Instead, I found the same cool colour scheme which prevailed at Cassidy's place, the same open, uncluttered look to the furnishings and a matching collection of local paintings. The only reminders of her origins were a beautiful bronze Buddha, with a bowl of rose petals in front of it, and the brocaded robe and slippers which my hostess was wearing. We exchanged the traditional salute, hands joined, palm to palm, the head bowed in respect. She called me Mr. Gregory as she had done at our first meeting. I called her Madam, because I was afraid of stumbling on her name. Then I asked, 'Please, will you call me Martin?'

'And will you call me Pornsri.'

She stretched out a hand to draw me across the threshold, then led me through the lounge and out onto the terrace to see the lights of the harbour and the glow of the city.

She said simply, 'I love this place. It's like living on a mountain. You can't imagine what that's like for a woman

137

like me, born and brought up in the flatlands of the delta. When I go home, I have to rearrange my mind completely.'

'Does your daughter like it here too?'

'She prefers Europe. She feels less conspicuous than she does here. Thailand makes her uneasy. There is much of her father in her. She will never be the subject woman.'

'Was Cassidy fond of her?'

'When she was little, he doted on her. When she began to be a woman, he wanted to take control of her life, determine her education and her friends. I had to explain to him that she was an exotic and that I was the only one who could teach her both Asia and Europe. What she needed from him was love and protection.'

'And he gave both.'

'Oh yes! He was a good father – perhaps because he had learned from his first failures. By the way, have you told your wife that she has a sister?'

'Not yet.'

'You should think about it. It would not be good if she heard the news from someone else.'

'Knowing Pat, she may ask to meet your daughter.'

'If she wants, we can arrange an encounter. For my daughter it would not present a big problem. In Thailand there are many polygamous families, children of different mothers by one father . . .'

There was a flurry of cold wind out of the south. She shivered and drew me inside, closing the doors against the chill. She made me sit down in what she called 'the comfort hole' – a sunken area surrounded by low cushioned steps, with a large square table in the centre. She served drinks and a dish of spiced lobster pieces, then sat crosslegged in front of me while we chatted in desultory fashion about everything except the man who had brought us together. It was easy talk, so easy that I missed the subtlety of it, the unspoken presumption that Cassidy had created, willy-nilly, a web of relationships in which we were all bound together by gossamer threads.

It is a notion which to us in the West has become alien but which, in Asia, has long and subtle consequences. The man you help after a car accident has claims on you. You are in debt to him, not he to you. You have intervened in his life. You are responsible for the consequences of that intervention.

All this, of course, is hindsight. All I knew then was that for the first time in days I felt rested and at ease. There was none of the sexual tension that had marked every exchange between Laura Larsen and myself. It was like drifting on placid waters, over shallow pools where there were no deeps, no hazards, no sinister caverns in the banks.

The meal fitted the mood: a succession of small dishes, spiced or bland, sweet or sour, fish and fowl and beef. There were hot towels for the hands and a sorbet to cool the palate after the hot sauces. Pornsri served the meal Thai style, kneeling at the low table. She explained the dishes and talked of her childhood in her father's big house, with the gilded spirit-dwelling at the entrance and the lilyponds inhabited by great golden carp. She talked of her mother, the dancing beauty whose fingers were so supple that she could bend them backwards to touch her wrist. It was like listening to a fairytale or a chapter from Marco Polo's voyages – until the table was cleared and fresh tea was served and she faced me with the blunt question: 'I have to know, Martin – are you willing to help me?'

'Willing, yes. Whether I'm able is another matter. I need much more information than I've got at this moment. I'm not half way through Cassidy's records. I know nothing at all about your affairs. I can't jump in blindfold.'

'You don't trust me?'

'I don't know. You have to be open with me before I counsel you.'

She gave me a long, searching look and then began a brusque, concise narration.

139

'I am a one-third shareholder in the Chao Phraya Trading Company, which has its headquarters in Bangkok and either agents or affiliates in Malaya, Laos, Kampuchea and Vietnam. The other shareholders are The Melmar Hotel Company, Bangkok, and Rotdrache Bangkok who are, among other things, merchant bankers with European affiliations. They are also nominees for Charles Cassidy's holdings. The company therefore conforms to Government regulations about ownership by Thai nationals or Thai corporations.'

'And what does the company do?'

'It imports foreign goods, exports local products. It represents foreign firms; Japanese, Chinese, Korean, American. It manufactures under licence from a Swiss pharmaceutical company. In short, it's a cover-all enterprise.'

'Who runs it?'

'My father is President. I am Vice-President, because it looks better that way. Our General Manager is Chinese but a Thai citizen. Our staff are recruited locally.'

'And the other board members?'

'A director of the Melmar Hotel, a Swiss gentleman from Rotdrache and a member of the Royal Household.'

'They all seem very respectable people.'

'Respectable!' The word seemed to irritate her. 'I don't know what that means. They are traders. They make money where and how they can. So far, they have done well for themselves and for Chao Phraya. They knew that I had Cassidy behind me and that I voted his shares. But . . . now that Cassidy is gone, I am a minority and I am a woman in this traders' world. So things are beginning to change. Our General Manager is making demands – a seat on the board, a substantial block of shares. If we don't satisfy him, he will leave and take a lot of business with him. The Melmar people – that is the man you asked about, Marius Melville – would like to buy me out altogether; but behind this offer is another person, high at the Royal

Court. My father is afraid of him. He advises me to sell.'

'But surely all this must have been brewing while Cassidy was alive?'

'No!' The denial was emphatic. 'You don't know the power that man had – the respect in which he was held. They had a name for him in Thai, it means a warrior who laughs at armies. He never raised his voice. He never argued over trifles. But when he had made up his mind, he was like a pillar of iron. Nothing would shake him. Now that he is gone, there is no one . . .'

'There is still Marius Melville.'

'He is a different man altogether – powerful, yes, but one who makes a trade of mystery and who serves not only his personal interests, but those of much larger foreign groups. He will not hurt me. He will give me a fair price for my shares, but if I refuse the offer he will never forgive me. He needs to control the votes, you see. Cassidy and he were friends, they worked well together, so Melville was content. But he would not be happy with a stranger in the group. However, if you were to come in and pick up Cassidy's shares, I do not think he would disagree.'

'I don't see how I can do that. I don't know enough. I don't even know yet who has legal control of Cassidy's interests outside this country.'

'Surely that's in the files he left you.'

'I haven't found it yet.'

'I need help now!' Suddenly she was angry and imperious, forgetting all caution as she counted off her bill of complaints. 'Every day my father and I are being squeezed a little more: protection money so no one burns our go-downs; extra guards on the trucks so they don't get hijacked; bigger bribes for the police and the Customs men and the shipping clerks who book space for our merchandise. It's an old game in Asia; but this time the stakes are very high . . . Cassidy knew how to play it from the beginning and everybody knew that he knew: the Palace folk, the police, the generals, the old Chinese families –

even the caravan masters who brought opium down from the high valleys. Now we are isolated. There is only Marius Melville, whom I have never met, and you, the man who hated Cassidy.'

'I hold no malice against you or his child. I'll help where I can. But I'm not the man you need. Besides, I have another life to live.'

'Are you happy in it – now that you have no one to hate?'

'I think it's time I left.'

I heaved myself out of the lounging place and made for the door. She made no apology, no move to stay me. She walked ahead of me to the entrance door and opened it. She shook her head in a kind of ironic puzzlement.

'If I'd said anything like that to Charles he would have slapped me across the room.'

'I don't doubt it.'

'You disappointed me, Martin.'

'My apologies, Madam. Cassidy was always a hard act to follow. Thank you for dinner. Good night.'

As I headed for the elevator, I heard the door slam violently and the chainbolt rattle into place. I found myself palming my eyelids, brushing my face with my hands, as if I had walked through a tangle of cobwebs.

12

Professor Julian Steiner had aged twenty years since our last meeting. His lion's mane had thinned to white cotton wool. His high-domed forehead was ruled like a musical stave. His great nose had become pinched and sharp like an eagle's beak. His finger-joints were swollen and arthritic. But there was still that wonderful light in his smile, that impish twinkle in his dark eyes. He measured me head to toe, then sat me down with a brusque: 'Well then! Let's take it from the top!'

The awe of my student days overwhelmed me again. It was as if I were back in his lecture-hall, struggling desperately to 'state the facts, state them concisely, in chronological order, with only the relevant circumstantial details'. He listened, as he always did, in silence, lying back in his armchair with his feet on the desk, his fingertips making a small spire just under his nose.

I told him everything, from my first breach with Cassidy, up to and including last night's dinner with Pornsri Rhana. It was a long story and one not easy to tell. When I had finished the narration, he sat in silence for nearly a minute. I remembered his silences better than his utterances. It was more than a student's life was worth to break them. Finally, he faced me with an unexpected proposition.

'Abdicate! Give Arthur Rebus power of attorney, dump everything in his lap and go home.' He sprawled again in his chair, grinning at me quizzically behind his joined palms. 'You don't like the idea?'

'I'm not sure it can work.'

'Why not! There are twenty-three partners in Arthur Rebus' outfit. They have excellent offshore connections and they've been briefed in several Royal Commissions on organised crime and the drug traffic. Rebus is highly efficient, totally honest – and he doesn't scare easily.'

'Certainly I'd like to appoint Rebus to handle the probate.'

'He's already agreed to that. He's awaiting your call. But Martin, you have to be absolutely open with him. The fiscal authorities will try, as they always do, to inglobate all assets. They will want to examine all available documents. Rebus can handle them very well. But you cannot exclude him arbitrarily from any sources of information.'

'What about Cassidy's other activities and associations – with Marius Melville, for instance? With political graft and organised crime?'

'Do you have any proof that he was so engaged?'

'Lots of indications, much hearsay. Enough to provoke an investigation. Not yet legal proof.'

'Two points then: in default of proof, you are not obliged to take any action. In any case, you are not required to judge the morals of a dead man. So why bother? So long as the heirs get their legal entitlement from the estate, your duty is discharged . . . Or is there something else you haven't told me?'

'There is; but I'm not sure I can put it into words.'

'Let me try then. You fought him, but you could never beat him. Even at the end he escaped you. He made you custodian of his affairs, then killed himself in your presence. You can't forgive him and you can't forget him. So you want to unravel his life and see what he was made of. It won't work, Martin. You'll end up with a big pile of coloured wool with no human shape to it at all.'

'But if I do it your way?'

'It's exorcism – bell, book and candle! The demon departs. The angels appear on a cloud of incense. Unless . . .' He lapsed again into silence, weighing the words. 'Unless, like Faustus, you have sold him your soul and he will not give up his claim. Am I insulting you, Martin?'

'No, sir.' I tried to make a joke of it. 'But the fact is I haven't made the deal yet. I'm still studying the terms and conditions.'

Steiner was not amused. He said gravely, 'Be careful. Mephisto is a very persuasive salesman. I think I should tell you that I knew Charles Cassidy very well. I liked him. I respected him. He was, to use a biblical phrase, 'learned in the law'. When he began to engage himself in politics he came to me for a private refresher course in Constitutional Law – especially in the areas of State and Federal sovereignties. For nearly six months we spent three hours a week together and I have to tell you he worked me as hard as I worked him. One day, during a particularly complicated discussion on anomalies in jurisdiction, I asked him what he was really digging for. His answer came fast as a gunshot: "The roots of power, Julie – the taproot and every goddamn fibre. There's no point in winning power at an election unless you understand the biological functions of it . . ." The subject became an obsession with him. It was the axis around which all his thinking revolved: the power to withdraw labour, the power to manipulate money, to impose order by force, to suppress information, to monitor communications – all of it within the existing constitutional framework. I found it a fascinating exercise in the grey areas of the law . . . But, towards the end of it, I found I had lost Cassidy – or he had lost me. We were no longer talking the same language. I was concerned with principles, he with situations. I was dealing with the ethics of the social contract, he with its manipulation. He was dedicated to pure pragmatism, based on the ugly proposition that the human animal was infinitely corruptible . . . This was about the time you married his daughter and the fabric of his domestic life began to tear apart; so I was inclined to be tolerant of his aberration. There are ugly periods in all our lives. I should have known better. I should have recognised the old ecclesiastical paternalism under which he was nurtured. As a Jew, I should have recognised the *Führer-prinzip* even when it was enunciated in an Irish-Australian brogue . . . But that's what it turned out to be. He was the arch-corruptor, the supreme manipulator, Mephisto to the life . . .' He thrust a long, bony finger at me across the table. 'That's what worries me, Martin. At every step you're acting and thinking exactly as Cassidy planned. You've come to me for advice, as Cassidy did. I've offered you a counsellor and a colleague to keep you honest. You still haven't accepted him. You're tempted, aren't you, Martin? There's at least half a billion dollars in trust; there's all the mystery of an underground empire through whose frontiers you have a passport, to which it seems you could be the heir apparent . . . So tell me, Martin, do you want Arthur Rebus or not? If you do, pick up the phone and call him. There's the number . . .'

Now it was my turn to be silent. Julian Steiner waited, calm and watchful as an old eagle. Finally, I found the words I needed.

'I won't abdicate. I can't. I have to finish what I've begun. I will, however, brief Arthur Rebus – and I'll give him full access to everything I've got.'

'Good!' said Julian Steiner with a grin. 'Then at least you'll have a conscience to tell you when you're about to become a crook!'

So, at midday that same day, on the premises of the Banque de Paris, with a cheque of five thousand dollars, I bought myself a conscience. I also executed a power of attorney and an act of delegation of my powers and duties as executor of the Cassidy estate. Paul Langlois witnessed the documents and took copies for his files. I went through the whole transaction with as much enthusiasm as if I were buying a wooden leg.

My new acquisition, Arthur Arnold Rebus, was as non-descript a man as you would meet and ignore in a month of Sundays. He looked thirty-five but was probably ten years older. He had sandy hair, sandy eyes, a freckled horse face, hands and feet too big for a thin, flailing body and a voice deep enough to sing bass in *Boris Godonov*. He wasted no time on courtesies and was as sharp as a butcher's carver.

'. . . I'll deal with the routine stuff first: the will, the trust deeds, valuations of property and chattels. You'd better run me over to the house and introduce me to the custodian – what's his name? – Cubeddu. We'll need to arrange inventories, valuations, and so on. That's routine. You can leave it to us, we're good at it . . . For the rest, I'll work with you every day for as long as is necessary to

146

get the hang of the microfiche stuff and the materials from the safe. I've got some specialised knowledge which will help you to round out the picture. Oh . . . the Thai lady needs some attention. You'd better arrange for her to meet me. I don't want any skeletons rattling in unopened cupboards. One other thing . . . you and I . . .'

'Yes?'

'You're the client. I need full confidence and complete information. I take instructions and give advice. If I don't agree with the instructions, I'll say so. If you don't agree with the advice, we argue it. If we can't work harmoniously, we call it a day. Clear?'

'Clear. How much do you charge?'

'Here's the rate card. It's steep, but you get the best value in town. Also you get a free education in backstairs politics.'

'In which I'm lamentably deficient.'

'You'll learn fast. Next week, we should go to Canberra together.'

'Why Canberra?'

'The Federal capital. Home of the Federal Police, whose Commissioner is an old friend of mine. You need him. He needs you; you can give him access to Cassidy's records. So it's a constructive situation. I'll make the arrangements. Also I want to dedicate a couple of nights to showing you the underside of the city – and how Cassidy's fiefdom works. I promise you won't find it boring . . . Now, let's talk about Mr. Marius Melville. You say you've never met him.'

'That's right. I've spoken to him once.'

'Yet your wife and family are guests in his house at Klosters.'

'Right. The arrangement was made without my knowledge. I didn't want to make an enemy by cancelling it.'

'But that puts you in Melville's debt?'

'To a limited degree, yes.'

'Debts have to be paid – old custom in the Honourable Society. And his daughter, this Miss . . . ?'

'Laura Larsen.'

'Miss Larsen is your official minder.'

'According to Melville, yes.'

'And according to Martin Gregory?'

'Do you want it straight?'

'How else?'

'We make sparks together. I could happily fall into bed with her.'

'Have you done it yet?'

'No.'

'Keep it that way – otherwise you'll be up to your neck in trouble. How do you and your wife get along?'

'I love her. I love my family. There was a certain amount of stress before I left; but that's hardly surprising in the circumstances.'

'So you're vulnerable – sexually, I mean?'

'Damn it, man, do you have to spell all the bloody words?'

'Today, yes. Tomorrow we take 'em as read. If you need a little sexual exercise I can steer you in safe directions. But you don't want to end up baretailed and rampant in someone's photo album.'

'Anything else?'

'Yes. I'd like to buy you lunch out of this retainer.'

'I'll accept.'

'Let's go to my club. It'll be good for your image to be seen in reputable company.'

'To hell with you, Mr. Rebus!'

'And to hell with you, Mr. Gregory!'

For the first time I heard him laugh: a deep, rumbling sound like an underground train. It seemed to take an age for the sound to reach the surface; then he gurgled and spluttered and mopped at his face with a handkerchief.

When the spasm was over he announced, 'I like you. I

think we'll do well in harness – provided I can keep you alive!'

Once inside the portals of his club – one of the more hallowed shrines of the Australian Establishment – my shambling, freckle-faced conscience became another being. His clothes seemed to fit better. He stood taller. His hair was sleeker, his manners more polished, his whole persona more dignified and daunting. Everyone greeted him – judges, knights of commerce, bankers, a stray general, a Privy Councillor or two, the Leader of the Opposition in the Federal Parliament. He returned every salute according to a rigid protocol of whose rules I was ignorant: a nod here, there a smile and an off-hand gesture, for this one a hand's clasp, for that other a murmured aside, for some a studied surprise as though they had just been dredged up from a sludge of old memories.

Those to whom he introduced me were obviously the privileged. Even then the presentation was brief, the name always mumbled thus: 'Mr. . . . arrumph . . .' The description emphasised '. . . client of mine from London.'

Further conversation was discouraged. He declined several offers of drinks at the bar and led me straight to a table for two in a shadowy corner. When we were seated, I paid him a compliment on his very fancy footwork. He shrugged and grinned.

'We're right in the heartland here, Mr. Gregory – old money, new power structures, oligarchies that reach round the continent and across the oceans: banking, insurance, oil, metals and – always and everywhere – the law; you and I and the silks and the judges . . . So, as you have observed, one has to learn some pretty nifty jigs and reels.'

'Charlie Cassidy must have been in his element here.'

'He was, though God knows how he got past the committee in those days. The old rules used to be: no Catholics, no Irish, no Jews need apply.'

'If I know the old bastard, he dealt his way in.'

'I'm sure. More deals have been set in this dining-room than the chef has set jellies.'

'What sort of deals?'

'You name it: development permits, mineral leases, Government supply contracts, how much it would cost for an advance look at the prosecution case and how much for a *nolle prosequi* from the Crown, the going rate for a knighthood when knighthood was in flower.'

'And the public wears it like a clean shirt!'

'Because, my dear Mr. Gregory, there's no such animal as the public. There's only Tom and Jane and Dick and Mary. So long as they're nuzzling in the food trough, or getting laid, or trying to win a fortune at the races, they couldn't give a damn – until, of course, one of their kids gets busted for drugs or dies of an overdose or tries to make an easy five thousand on the mule run to Bangkok and cops twenty years in a Thai prison! Then they scream blue murder; but the screaming stops long before election time, when the Government pumps money into housing or mounts a purge of the police force, which will halt the day it disappears from the front page. Here, take a look at the menu.'

It wasn't hard to choose: Sydney rock oysters, a salad of lobster tail, a superfine Chardonnay to help it down. Flushed with the comfort of the meal, I made bold to offer a criticism of his thesis.

'We all know what's happening. I'm far enough into Cassidy's files to have some idea of the scale. But just suppose you or I were elected Premier of this State tomorrow on a reform ticket. Where and how would we start to clean house?'

'Fair question, my friend. But naïve, terribly naïve.' He took his time disposing of an oyster and a sip or two of Chardonnay. 'The answer is simple. You don't start anything, anywhere, until you're forced to it. The first priority is to pay your debts: Cabinet appointments, jobs for friends and friends of the friends. You have to get them in place first, otherwise you're out there naked and shaggy as a cormorant on a rock! Then, just as you're feeling safe, you become aware that the distance between you and the Tom, Dick and Mary who voted you into office is longer than a trip to the moon. You also become aware of a vast army of bureaucrats whose sole function is to be sure you don't do anything rash – or, preferably, anything at all. Think of the inertia in that vast mass of people and paper. Think of the force necessary to budge it even one centimetre. Take an example: you know your Police Commissioner is bent. You really would like to get rid of him. The first thing you need is evidence. You don't call for it yourself. Protocol – and animal cunning – say you call for it from the Minister for Police. He doesn't have it; he'd be nuts if he did; but he promises to see what's in the file. Then he discovers the file is in circulation. When he gets it back it's mysteriously incomplete. He promises an immediate investigation to find the missing items . . . Do I go on?'

'No. I get the picture.'

'That's just the inertia element. What about the other elements: the collusive, the conspiratorial, the venal, the threatening? You have to deal with them all, while you open fêtes and make policy statements about health, education, cost of living, drunken driving, the plight of the farmers . . . until the day comes when you realise that that's the only way the game can be played. You let the cancer run its course while you're scratching the itch in the crotch of society.'

'Counsels of despair, Mr. Rebus?'

'No, Mr. Gregory. A lesson in *realpolitik*. You see that whitehaired gentleman in the corner, with the three younger men? That's Gerry Downs. The one on his right is his Editor-in-Chief. The one on the left is his in-house counsel. The fourth is . . .'

'Micky Gorman, by God! Isn't this rather a public place

for a conference? Doesn't Downs have a private dining-room at his newspaper?'

'Of course, but he likes to be public from time to time.'

'Did you know he'd be here today?'

'How could I? Pure chance. But it might be fun to say hullo to them on the way out. Micky doesn't like me very much – and I took a million and a half from Gerry Downs in an out-of-court libel settlement last year. It's on appeal, but he hasn't a hope in hell of winning . . . By the way, how's the lobster?'

The lobster was tasting better with every mouthful. I liked this Arthur Rebus and his chameleon personality and his bristling, prickly humour. For the first time since my return to my homeland, I began to feel less lonely and more relaxed. I said as much to Rebus. He grinned and raised his glass.

'Relax – that's the magic word. What's Cassidy to you or you to Cassidy any more? He's left your family a tidy fortune, which may turn out bigger than you think. You're not responsible for his misdeeds. You don't have to write apologies for the man – though a hundred words of protest against Gerry Downs mightn't go amiss. You know: "*De mortiis nil nisi bonum* – and respect the privacy of the family." That sort of thing. I'd say two weeks will see me ready to take over the estate. Then you can go home.'

'I'm not sure it's going to be as simple as that.'

'Why not? I have your power of attorney. I can do whatever is needed.'

'I was thinking of Marius Melville.'

'Ah yes!' said Arthur Rebus. 'Ah yes! I had rather left him out of my calculations. He's a horse of a different colour – and he could be a Trojan nag full of nasty surprises. Certainly you have to meet Melville before you can decide anything about the offshore holdings. I'd like to meet him, too, if it seems appropriate. But if the offshore situation looks messy, I don't want to know about it, much less touch it . . . Now, let's have coffee and then we'll go pass the time of day with Gerry Downs and Micky Gorman.'

It was a brief but edgy little ceremony. Arthur Rebus said, 'Hullo, Gerry. Hullo, Micky.'

Gerry Downs said, 'Hullo, Arthur.'

Micky Gorman flushed and said, 'Hullo, Arthur. Hullo, Martin. This is a surprise.'

Arthur Rebus said, 'Gerry, I thought you should meet our new client, Martin Gregory, married to Charlie Cassidy's daughter. Martin, this is our great press baron, Gerry Downs.'

Gerry Downs' greeting was cool: 'I heard you were in town, Mr. Gregory.'

Arthur Rebus said genially, 'I'm handling the probate arrangements and, of course, representing the general interests of Cassidy's legatees.'

Gerry Downs took the point. He said to me: 'We're doing a four-part series in our weekend magazine on Charlie's career. It starts next Saturday. It's not exactly a hymn of praise, but I'd be happy to send you advance proofs – in case you'd like to check the family background material for accuracy.'

Rebus grinned and shook his head.'I couldn't advise my client to accept the offer. You have your own editors, your own legal advisers. Micky here knows the family background inside out, don't you, Micky? I'm sure you'll be very careful about what you print. But we have to preserve the position of the family, especially Cassidy's daughter and the minor children.'

'Sure you do,' said Gerry Downs easily.

'However, we appreciate the offer.' Rebus added an amiable afterthought. 'I'd like to return the favour. If I were you, Gerry, I'd give up Chinese Checkers for a while. I hear the game could get rough, very quickly.'

'Thanks, I'll remember it,' said Gerry Downs. 'Nice to meet you, Mr. Gregory.'

As we walked out into the sunshine I asked Rebus the

meaning of the last cryptic exchange. He explained, a little ruefully: 'Like a lot of public moralists, Gerry Downs is embarrassed by his private vices. Gambling's one of them. Heavy games with heavy players. One of his cronies is Harry Yip Soong, who is being shaken down by a rival triad. Harry won't pay – so he's liable to get a bomb under his car or a fire in his basement. I'd rather Gerry Downs didn't get hit before I collect for my client. Besides . . .' he said it with a laugh, 'he's a fellow club-man.'

'So was Charlie Cassidy.'

'Death cancels all debts – and most loyalties.'

'You're a portentous bastard, Mr. Rebus.'

'I've just fed you a good lunch, Mr. Gregory. At least you can be polite to me.'

Our next call was at Cassidy's house. Marco Cubeddu received us with cautious formality. He loosened up a little when I explained that the Signor Rebus was a colleague whom I had appointed to deal with the formalities in respect of his legacy. Arthur Rebus completed the seduction by explaining, in very passable Italian, the procedures involved and by copying into his notebook the personal details of Marco and his wife. Marco, who had the Italians' awe of advocates and medicos, was much impressed and confided to me that 'this one seems a good type – a man of trust'.

Finally, we were at the butt-end of a long, talky day. We arranged to meet on the morrow to work through Cassidy's file; then Rebus went back to his office while I returned to the Town House to make my call to Pat and the family in Klosters. It was breakfast time for them.

'We're sitting here like royalty,' Pat told me, 'with a cook and two other servants and a big Mercedes in the garage. Provisions are delivered. We have a number to ring in Zurich in case of emergency. I've booked the kids and myself into ski-school. Mother's American scholar has turned up and is lodged in the guest chalet . . . and I'm missing you very, very much, darling. When do you expect to come home?'

'Very soon. Old Julian Steiner has found me a good man to handle the probate details . . . There are, however, some other matters I don't want to discuss on the telephone. Before they can be settled I have to meet with Marius Melville. After that, please God, I'll be on the next flight home. Where I'm sitting now it's lonely and draughty . . . By the way, there's something you should know. Your father had a mistress.'

'That's no news. He had quite a few over the years. Who's this one?'

'A Thai lady. Cassidy made her a partner in one of his offshore enterprises.'

'You've met her then. What's she like?'

'Good looking, well educated, well connected in her homeland. She'll present no problem as far as your legacies are concerned. But she has a child by Cassidy, a daughter about sixteen, who's being educated in Switzerland.'

There was a moment's silence; then she laughed a little unsteadily.

'Well! That's a good item for the breakfast session.'

'I didn't want to tell you until I got home; but, equally, I didn't want you to get it second-hand. I don't know whether the press has it or not. It's a bit of a shock, but . . .'

'Not at all, darling!' She was in control again now. 'I have a Siamese sister. What's surprising in that? Is she prettier than I am?'

'I've only seen a photograph – and you're much the prettier.'

'Well, what can I say? Daddy was always full of surprises. Clare will be interested, but I doubt she'll lose any sleep over it . . . Just make sure you don't develop a taste for Thai ladies!'

'Don't tell me you're jealous.'

'You'd better believe it, Martin Gregory. A wandering

daddy was bad enough. I couldn't wear a playboy husband. Come home soon, please!'

'As soon as I can.'

'You haven't told me anything about what you're doing.'

'I don't want to discuss it on an open line.'

'You sound troubled.'

'I'm feeling my way through a maze, not knowing who or what is going to pop out of the bushes around the next corner . . . Yes, you could say I'm troubled.'

'Please darling, do try to relax a little. Call some of our old friends . . .'

'I'll get round to it . . . Let me talk to the kids, then I'll come back to you.'

It was pleasant to talk to the children, comforting to know that the family circle was still unbroken and that, so far, no malign influence had invaded it. But the comfort was brief and when I put down the receiver I felt more isolated than ever before. The evening stretched before me, bleak and barren as a desert. Then the telephone rang, startling in the silence. When I picked up the receiver, a woman's voice said, 'Hold a moment, please. Mr. Erhardt Möller is calling from Manila.'

The name meant nothing to me. The voice that spoke was heavily accented – perhaps too accented to be genuine.

'Mr. Gregory, you don't know me. My name is Erhardt Möller. I am a business associate of the late Charles Cassidy.'

'Yes?'

'We had regular transactions which are on record in Mr. Cassidy's files.'

'I am not aware of such transactions – at least, I have not yet come across them.'

'You will. This call is to put you on notice that you are holding to my account a certain quantity of chemical products, stones to a high value, an assortment of currencies. I shall call on you within ten days to take delivery.'

'I'm afraid I can't . . .'

'I'm sure you can, Mr. Gregory. I'm sure you will . . . You have ten days to check the records and establish my entitlement. Remember the name: Erhardt Möller, from Manila. Goodnight.'

That was the last jolt I needed, at the end of a long day. Arthur Rebus was still working at his office. I gave him the news and suggested we fly the next morning to Canberra to see the Federal Police Commissioner. He promised to call the man and get back to me within half an hour. If we were going he would book the tickets. Then I called Miss Larsen at the Melmar Marquis and waited an age while they sounded her bleeper through the marble halls.

I told her: 'Things are happening fast. Tell your father I need an immediate meeting. I'm choosing the place: the Oriental Hotel, Bangkok. Ask him what he knows about one Erhardt Möller, who has just called me from Manila, claiming that I'm holding money and valuables to his account. He'll be here to collect in ten days . . .'

'I'll call Father right away.' She was terse and business-like but there was an edge of anxiety to her voice. 'I also think you should move here, tonight. I'll book you a suite with a harbour view – at concession rates! Our limousine will call for you at eight-thirty.'

It was a tempting offer and I was almost ready to accept when the phone in my bedroom rang. I asked Laura to hold while I took the call. Arthur Rebus was on the line.

'We're booked on the eight a.m. flight to Canberra. A police car will meet us at the airport. The Commissioner is eager to talk. He knows Mr. Erhardt Möller, who it seems is a very nasty customer. He thinks you need protection, which he's happy to offer.'

I told him Laura Larsen was on the other line with a similar proposal. He said curtly, 'Stay on your own turf. No more favours from Melville or his daughter. Insist on the meeting with Melville by all means. And Bangkok is a good place, because the Federal Police have a strong contingent of narcotics people working there. But I repeat:

157

no more favours and no more footsies with the Lady Laura. I'll pick you up at the hotel at seven in the morning.'

He hung up and I went back to Laura Larsen. I saw no reason to lie to her, so I told her half the truth.

'I'm in discussions with a new law firm who I think can handle the probate of Cassidy's will. That was one of the senior partners. I'm flying to Canberra with him in the morning. When I come back, we'll talk about a change of lodging. Meantime, how soon can you get in touch with your father?'

'Right away if I'm lucky. It's mid-morning in Zurich. Stay by the phone.'

'And don't forget to ask him about Erhardt Möller.'

'I won't. But Martin . . .?'

'Yes?'

'Father may suggest some other meeting place. What do I tell him?'

'Tell him as politely as you can that he's the buyer and I'm a very reluctant seller, and I'm sick of dancing to other people's music. It's the Oriental Hotel, Bangkok.'

'You have had a bad day, haven't you?' She was very quiet.

'I've known better.'

'We could have dinner, if you like.'

'I like. I like very much and I thank you for the sweet thought; but until your father and I have met, we won't know whether we're allies or enemies, will we?'

'Now you sound exactly like Charlie Cassidy.'

'Some people seem to think I'm already wearing his shoes.'

'If you are, be sure you're big enough to fill them . . . Stay in your room. I'll call you back.'

She didn't call. She came an hour later in person. She brought a telexed confirmation of my flight to Bangkok on Thai Airways and the reservation of the Graham Greene suite, four days hence. She also informed me that her father had never had any dealings with Erhardt Möller who, as he put it, 'belonged on Cassidy's side of the wire'. By easy inference, he was my pigeon and I had to eat him or choke on the feathers. By an even easier deduction, I owed the lady a dinner and an apology for my ill-temper. She refused the one and shrugged off the other with a wry grin.

'I don't blame you, Martin. I'm sorry for you. You're swimming between the rock and the whirlpool – and you can't trust the lights or the landmarks or the voices . . . But I beg you to believe I've been honest with you.'

'I do believe that.'

'So try to understand this: the only picture my father has of you is the one Cassidy gave him. I've tried to add my own touches to the portrait. I haven't been very successful, because women's comments on family business are not very welcome. However, I was able to explain the pressure you're under. You've won your point; my father agrees to the meeting in Bangkok. But he'll make you pay for the concession. So be very careful, Martin, very watchful . . . And try to make some gesture of respect . . .'

And there it was again, Cassidy's warning: 'If ever you meet him, show respect. He merits it. And never forget that while he keeps iron faith with his friends, he's as ruthless as Caligula to his enemies.'

'A penny for your thoughts,' said Laura Larsen.

I told her I thought we could both use a drink; what I really thought was that neither of us would be satisfied until we had made trial of each other in bed – and that to make the trial under the shadow of Marius Melville was a recipe for disaster. Laura Larsen raised her glass in a toast.

'I give you hope, Martin: that we can both lay the ghosts in our lives.'

After she had left I ate a tasteless meal in the restaurant and then sat watching a tasteless comedy on the television in my room. I also drank two glasses of port, which I knew would give me a foul headache in the morning. It was the port, more than sound reason, that made me call Pornsri Rhana. She sounded sleepy and a little testy.

'Who is this?'

'Martin Gregory.'

'It's very late.'

'I know. When are you leaving for Bangkok?'

'The day after tomorrow.'

'I'll be there myself in five days' time. Call me . . . let me see . . . call me next Thursday morning at the Oriental Hotel.'

'Does this mean you're willing to help me?'

'It means I'm willing to see what your needs are and then decide whether I can help.'

Now she was wide awake and friendly as a kitten.

'Martin! . . . And after I was so rude to you the other evening. I was so ashamed of myself. In Bangkok, I promise I shall make amends –'

'Please! There's no need. Mr. Marius Melville will be with me. Between us, we should be able to make some sense of your problems.'

'I hope so, Martin. I do truly hope so. But you won't be selling out, will you?'

'That's not my intention at this moment.'

'Good! There is too much at stake. And when I fight I am very strong, Martin – you will find I am a great help to you.'

'I have no doubt of it . . . Goodnight.'

'Goodnight, my dear, dear man!'

When I slept I heard the sound of temple gongs and the jingle of golden bells. I dreamed a wild, erotic Technicolor dream in which Pornsri Rhana was a dancer with a jewelled cap and fingers that curved back to touch her slim wrists. I woke at three in the morning with a splitting head and a mouth like the bottom of a bird cage. It was the perfect coda to a very messy day.

13

'He's a military man,' said Arthur Rebus, 'which doesn't
endear him to the ordinary race of coppers or politicians.
He's got a ramrod for a backbone and you can use his
shoes for a mirror and he addresses his staff, men and
women, as if they were all, and always, on ceremonial
parade. He hates slackers and despises fools and a bent
copper goes straight to the guillotine. But he's bright, make
no mistake. He got his intelligence training in London and
the US and did his fieldwork in Vietnam and Laos . . . If
he trusts you, he'll go through fire, water and the rages of
God to protect you . . . If you let him down he'll hound
you to extinction . . .'

We were bucketing through a summer storm on the
forty-minute milk run from Sydney to Canberra, which is
the Federal Capital of Australia. Rebus seemed concerned
about possible friction between the Commissioner and
myself. I couldn't see why he was making such a mouthful
of it.

'I'll tell you why,' said Rebus. 'This Commissioner has
been pressing for legislation enabling the State to distrain
all proceeds of criminal activities, especially those arising
out of the drug traffic. He's been dealing with Mafia
"families" up and down Australia. He'll have his own
dossier as thick as your arm on Cassidy and his associates
in New South Wales. So he's not going to take you at face
value. Even if he did, your face value isn't so great.'

'Why not, for Christ's sake?'

'First, you're the executor of a very suspect estate. Your

161

wife and family are big beneficiaries. You yourself are the legal possessor of documents on which there's a standing offer of five million – and you've already discovered they may be the key to half a billion . . . So, first up, the Commissioner's going to treat you with very healthy suspicion. You could be rich enough to buy and sell a small empire. You might even be bidding for him.'

'My God, you've got a dirty mind, Mr. Rebus!'

'It gets dirtier, Mr. Gregory. Your wife and family are lodged with one Marius Melville. You're supposed to be paymaster to one Erhardt Möller. You're certainly holding heroin, diamonds and money. You've got a yen for Melville's daughter and a link with Cassidy's Thai mistress . . . The Commissioner's not your run-of-the-mill copper. He's an intelligence man. He's trained to think of connections and consequences beyond his own bailiwick. He's going to take you apart and put you together again like a watchmaker before he's prepared to trust you. So listen up like a good fellow . . . We've got to cope with a natural antagonism between the species. We're lawyers. The Commissioner is a policeman. He's plagued to death by people like us. He's the custodian of the law. We make our money by exploiting its defects. He makes a watertight case, we punch a hole in it. He arrests the criminal, we spring him. So let's have a little loving kindness! Put a bridle on that tongue of yours and think before you speak. Better still, let me speak for you. That's what you're paying me for, after all!'

So, it was small wonder that by the time I walked into the Commissioner's office, I was as nervous as a schoolboy at his first encounter with the headmaster. The man who greeted me was as slim, trim and dapper as regular exercise and a good military tailor could make him. His hands were manicured, his cheeks freshly barbered. His grip was firm and welcoming. His smile was open and his eyes lively with curiosity. He announced cheerfully: 'You've made my week, gentlemen. Until this morning it's been a series of disasters. We bungled a big bust in Queensland. We lost our extradition case in Eire. One of our star informers was roasted in the trunk of his car in Frenchs Forest last night. And the press has just announced what we've been telling the Minister for months – that Australian airports are wide open to terrorist attack, because we have neither the manpower nor the weapons to protect them. Now, would you like to˙ bring a little cheer into my life? Mr. Gregory . . .?'

'My learned friend Mr. Rebus has given me a warning. He tells me I might be a suspect witness and that I've got a short fuse which could put you and me at odds. So I'm going to let him lead for me. Then I'll answer any questions you like to put to me.'

'Then you have the floor, Mr. Rebus.'

I had to dip my hat to the man. He delivered the whole story in twenty minutes flat – from Cassidy's last night in London to my upcoming appointment with Marius Melville in Bangkok.

The Commissioner listened in silence, making an occasional cryptic notation on a yellow pad. When Rebus had finished, he said simply, 'So, in the five days – four really – before you leave for Bangkok, you have to finish your study of the microfiches and decide whether you want to sell them to Marius Melville.'

'That's right.'

'And you also have to determine who really controls that half-billion offshore trust fund.'

'Yes.'

'Then you have to make some decisions about yourself: like every man has his price and what's yours, or money has no smell and it buys an awful lot of service. That sort of thing.'

'That sort of thing. Yes, Commissioner. And I'd like your help to reach the right decision.'

'I'm a policeman, Mr. Gregory, not a Father Confessor.'

'Then, as a policeman, you'll understand the importance

163

of the information in my possession. You'll be able to explain to me the strange behaviour of certain State officials – and how Charles Parnell Cassidy, as Premier of the State, could have built up a worldwide connection with criminal elements. If you can't, we're wasting each other's time.'

The Commissioner grinned and turned to Arthur Rebus. 'He does have a short fuse, doesn't he?'

'Mark of an honest man, Commissioner,' said Arthur Rebus cheerfully. 'What you see is what you get. If you don't like it you lump it . . .' He turned to me. 'Cool down, Martin. There's a long march ahead of us all. Why don't you try to answer Martin's question, Commissioner?'

'About Charlie Cassidy . . .' The Commissioner took time to compose his thoughts. 'I had a number of meetings with him during his term as Premier. Most of them were in the presence of his Minister of Police and other members of his Cabinet, but two or three times we were alone. The last one was about a month before he left Australia. He sat where you are now and we talked more frankly than we'd ever done before. The subject – for the record at least – was the creation of a National Crimes Authority which could co-ordinate the efforts both of the Federal Police and the law enforcement agencies in each State . . . Charlie Cassidy hated the idea, root and branch. I thought I understood the reason: he himself was up to his neck in illegalities; but I have to say his reasoning surprised me. He said, "Listen, Commissioner! Every time we pass a new piece of legislation, we create a new class of criminals. It's automatic, like a curfew in wartime. Anyone who misses the last bus home is liable to be shot. My father made a fortune out of legislation that closed the pubs at six. He did a back-door trade with anyone who had a thirst after that time. Prostitution? The same thing. Drugs? We've criminalised the addiction and let the traders have a field day. Do you know how many respectable lawyers – friends of mine among 'em – are financing, out of their trust funds, syndicates for heroin purchase? It's the best investment there is, because the security is a courier's life. The interest rates for the client are the highest, because the increase in product value from source to consumer is exponential. Gambling? The same thing. The Government collects a tax on every gaming transaction, so every bet with a corner bookie is an illegal act. And, talking of taxation, we've criminalised that too: notional assessments, retrospective legislation, onus of proof on the taxpayer and not on the Department. It's a long list, Commissioner; but if you like to think about it, part of your job is to enforce injustice . . ."'

The Commissioner picked up a paper knife, a miniature Gurkha kukri, and began toying with it. After a while he went on.

'. . . I didn't try to argue the proposition. Charlie had a taste for paradox and he could dazzle you with heady rhetoric. I wanted to hear the point he was trying to make. He took a little time to get to it. ". . . Symbiosis, Commissioner. Living together from a shared resource. The mistletoe on the tree trunk, the bee that pollinates the flower, the predators who cull the forest animals. Without criminals, you have no reason for existence. Your men can't function without informants. They have to have allies and friends in the criminal community. They offer protection, they make deals . . . You agree to shut your eyes to a lot of indictable offences in the hope of making one big bust. It's normal. It's the human compromise. Without it, you get the police state: order in the streets and a blackshirt on every corner and presumption of guilt and no habeas corpus. After that, of course, you get bloody revolution; which is the way the terror game develops . . . Do you see where I'm walking you, Commissioner?"'

The Commissioner slashed the air with the miniature kukri. 'I could see it all right, like a big black hole in the ground, but I wasn't going to give Cassidy the satisfaction of admitting it. He sat there with that crooked Irish grin, enjoying my discomfiture. Then he went on: ". . . The old-fashioned anarchists weren't too far wrong. They wanted the minimum of law, the freest possible play for the natural forces in society. Our problem is that we've inherited the British tradition: great respect for property, small regard for human life or the quality of it. There's no room for compassion in case-law . . . So what I'm telling you is that we're not British any more. We're a polyglot country; Italians, Greeks, Croats, Turks, Viets, Chinese, Japanese, Taiwanese – you name it! And if we try to put that society into a strait-jacket we'll have a whole sack of troubles . . . I know you don't like me, Commissioner. You think I'm a rogue Irishman who'd sell his sister for a dram of whiskey. Maybe you're right. But I'm a lot more than that. I'm the fellow who slips through the lines and parleys with both sides. I'm the deal-maker, the man they trust because he holds the purse and pays out fairly on the bets. I take a fat percentage for the house, but that's known and accepted, because I keep the peace. The problem is, Commissioner, I'm a temporary phenomenon. I'm mortal. I'm not going to be around too long . . . and so far there's no successor in sight. So I'm giving you fair notice; though I don't know what you can do about it either. The country's too big, the population's too small, the ethnic mix is too complex . . . Never forget it was the Irish who civilised the Germanic barbarians – at least we like to think we did! But hell, who was the last great Irishman you could put a name to – except Jack Kennedy and Charlie Cassidy . . . !"' He put down the kukri, joined his finger-tips as if in prayer and quizzed me over the top of them. 'Would you say, Mr. Gregory, that was an authentic rendering of your father-in-law?'

'Right down to the grace-notes, Commissioner. My compliments.'

'If you were sitting where I am, would you have believed it?'

'Up to a point, yes. Before I stole his daughter, Charlie

used to talk to me about the Kennedy clan. whom he'd known quite well. He used to say that, apart from the dates, he could have written their biographies without a note or a reference, they ran so close to primal pattern. He used to say politics was a power game, no more, no less – but you had to know where the wild pieces were on the board.'

'Did he always have criminal associations?'

'Depending on what you mean by the word, yes. You can't be in the liquor business, or the law business, or the tax business and expect to consort with virgins twenty-four hours a day.'

'Interesting you should say that, Mr. Gregory. What do you think Cassidy expected of you?'

There was a barb under the question and I wanted the Commissioner to know I'd seen it. I told him: 'Cassidy used to call me Martin the Righteous – and he didn't mean it as a compliment. He knew he'd get an efficient administrator of his daughter's estate. For the rest, he had put a burr under my tail and died laughing at my discomfort.'

'As you see, Commissioner,' said Arthur Rebus drily, 'there was a real bond of Christian charity between 'em!'

'Question time, Mr. Gregory.' The Commissioner was suddenly brusque.

'Go ahead.'

'Why did you refuse access to Cassidy's documents to the Attorney-General of New South Wales?'

'Because Cassidy had warned me they could be dissipated or conjured into confusion. Besides, I did not refuse access, I deferred it until I, as executor, had examined them.'

'Will you offer access to my people?'

'Yes. *In situ* and under my supervision or Arthur Rebus'.'

'Who is Marius Melville?'

'I don't know. I've never met him. Clearly a friend and associate of Cassidy. Indications are that he is Mafia-connected.'

'What do you propose to do about Cassidy's offshore trusts?'

'Since I don't know either the trustees or the beneficiaries, I can't answer that question yet. I'm making it my first business to find out.'

'However,' said Arthur Rebus, 'the man has problems. He's been away too long. He doesn't know how the system works any more.'

'Example, Mr. Gregory?'

'When I opened Cassidy's safe, I found, among other things, a kilo of heroin, several packets of very fancy stones and a mixed bag of high-value currencies. Loomis the Attorney-General obviously knew of, or guessed at, their existence, but he didn't want to touch them with a ten-foot pole. Then, out of the blue, some goon called Erhardt Möller telephones from Manila and says he'll be down to collect . . . Over to you, Commissioner.'

'Erhardt Möller. Heavy muscle in the Painters and Dockers Union – which, in case you don't read the reports of our Royal Commissions, controls every tonne of container traffic passing through Australian ports. The organisation has a history of violence, intimidation and murder. Some of its members left the country and went to the Philippines, where they dug themselves into the girl traffic, gambling, low-class terrorism, high-class piracy, gun-running and go-go bars . . . You should go up there some time and take a look. You can get a bet on any race in Australia or the US. You can marry a local girl, turn her automatically into an Australian citizen, bring her home to Sydney and put her on the game, which is what some of our likely lads have been doing. You can buy a container-load of small arms, with an end-user certificate, and have the container re-routed to anywhere in the world. That, more or less, is Erhardt Möller.'

'It doesn't explain why Charlie Cassidy was his pay-master.'

'Put it this way, Mr. Gregory. If you want peace and free trade on the waterfront, someone has to pay for it. Otherwise you've got a million tons of container shipping anchored off the Continental Shelf. If, on the other hand, you're buying and selling, someone has to put up the working capital. Charlie was the boss, in politics and in trade. Charlie paid the score. Simple.'

'Maybe not so simple,' said Arthur Rebus mildly. 'The whole question of the contents of Charlie's safe bothers the hell out of me. Look! He knew before he left Australia he was gravely ill and probably dying. Why would he leave a load of dynamite in his private safe, in his private house? Didn't that thought occur to you, Martin?'

'I confess it didn't. The sheer size of the damn thing distracted me. It was installed, on specially laid girders, when the house was built. You'd have to pull the place down to remove it – and you'd need a thermic lance to get into it . . . On balance, with Cubeddu and the State police as watchdogs, I'd have said Cassidy could have felt fairly secure. Besides, once he knew that hc was dying, what did he care? Still . . . let's leave the possibility open. I've got another, more urgent question. What do I do when Mr. Erhardt Möller knocks on my door?'

'He won't, because he doesn't dare set foot in Australia,' said the Commissioner. 'He'll send a couple of his collec-tors.'

'And what am I supposed to do?'

'Nothing. You're giving me access to Cassidy's records. I'm giving you a day and night minder. Agreed?'

'Agreed – and thank you. Now tell me about Marius Melville. My wife and family are his guests. I'm friendly with his daughter. I'm meeting him in Bangkok – and I know damn-all about him.'

'Ah! Well . . .' The Commissioner warmed to this sub-ject, like a don delivering his favourite discourse. 'Marius

Melville, . . . formerly Mario Melitense. Old Palermo family with connections in Malta, small but ancient nobility, men of trust for generations. Melville himself is a phenomenon. He has degrees in architecture, structural engineering and business administration. He has also studied hotel administration in Switzerland. He has no criminal convictions. F.B.I. files record that he has connections with all the big Mafia families but that he does not belong exclusively to any. It's the historic pattern again. The noble is a man of trust to all but exclusive to none. He seems to have established himself as chief laundry-man, washing hot money and investing it in legitimate enterprises, of which the Melmar hotel chain is the principal one. It's a brilliant conception. Melville holds twenty per cent of the shares. He farms the rest out among the families in equal shares, while he remains the arbiter of policy. He has no direct association with low-life activities, gambling, drugs or prostitution, but he supplies lodging, facilitates travel and moves funds for mobsters. That's what he offers, you see – facilitation – and there's nothing criminal in the service *per se*. Allied with the travel business there's transport. trucking, materials supply, international transmission of monies, you name it. No country excludes him, because he's a big developer and investor. Also he's a very good diplomat. So he keeps the peace between the racial groups. He understands that everyone needs a slice of the pie. When he's here, for instance, I monitor his movements and his contacts, but none of our villains get near enough to taint him. Everything's done at arm's length. He even snubbed Gerry Downs because of his gambling connections with Harry Yip Soong . . . That, in brief, is the man you'll be dealing with in Bangkok. You won't be able to bluff him. You'll have to treat with him eyeball to eyeball. So you'd better be fully briefed before you leave.'

'Can you help with that, Commissioner?'

'I can give you my best man: between him, you and Arthur here, you should be able to make sense of the documents. After that, of course, you have to make your own decisions, which will have longer consequences than you imagine at this moment.'

'Pay me a courtesy, Commissioner. Concede I may be an honest man. Say, straight out, what's on your mind!'

He hesitated a moment, obviously reluctant to show his hand. Finally, he consented.

'Very well. This is my opinion, for what it's worth. Cassidy was a brilliant rogue who died before his villainies caught up with him. He saw you as his natural heir. In a strange way, your defection confirmed him in that idea. You challenged him and beat him at his own game. So now he's put his empire – most of which is offshore – within your grasp . . . But first you have to want it enough, and then you have to be strong enough, to reach out and take it. It's a classic psychodrama, part revenge and part amends. His Thai mistress is yours for the taking – though my guess is that if she'd borne him a son, you'd have been out of the picture altogether . . . Then there's Marius Melville. He has no son, so his daughter's on offer for a traditional family alliance. Your wife and children are rich enough now so that you won't feel too guilty about leaving them . . . If you do, that settles another score for Cassidy. His daughter finally realises she left a good father for a faithless husband . . . How do you like my scenario so far, Mr. Gregory?'

I hated every line of it and said so. But I had to admit that it was vintage Cassidy. The old bastard knew me better than I knew myself, and I had already felt the prickling of the sexual temptation. The other had not touched me yet and I could not judge how potent it might be. It was then that the Commissioner showed what sort of an intelligence man he really was. He spelt out the rest of the scenario for me.

'There's a half-billion trust fund, already in place. There are company structures to feed it. But even if those structures are criminal, the fund is already laundered into respectability. So you could get rid of the criminal elements and function as a potent but respectable businessman. Of course, if you wanted to go further and actually reverse Cassidy's villainies, you could retain everything, but make an alliance with us and with other enforcement agencies and literally put a large part of an enemy empire in our hands. It would be an intelligence coup of the first magnitude . . . and we wouldn't grudge you a cent of what you made out of the operation. Think about it for a moment, Mr. Gregory.'

'It sounds like a prescription for instant suicide.'

The Commissioner shrugged off the objection.

'High risk, big profits. It's the name of the game.'

'Your game, Commissioner. Not mine.'

'Not yet,' said the Commissioner calmly, 'and of course it may never be; but I'd be delinquent if I didn't explain the opportunities it offers.'

'I'd like you to explain something else. How come you can operate on this global scale and you can't do anything about that little nest of vipers in Macquarie Street, Sydney, in the State of New South Wales?'

That touched a raw spot. He flushed, sat bolt upright in his chair and picked up the kukri again. Arthur Rebus became suddenly absorbed in a speck of lint on his lapel.

'I am doing something – but it's obviously not half enough. There are three reasons. First: I'm dealing with elected members of Government and high civil servants in a sovereign state. That state has its own police force. I cannot invade its jurisdiction. Second: I'm a public servant, limited by the policies and the funds given me by my masters here. Third: I was a soldier before I became a policeman. I learned very early that you don't win a war simply by killing the enemy's soldiers. You win it by cutting off his access to food, water, fuel and ammunition, by restricting his movements, blockading his forage routes – until you can starve him into surrender. I've learned the same lesson as a policeman. Our prisons are full to bursting – with petty recidivists, one-time felons, crazies, three-time losers. Things are so bad that it pays a State Government to wink at parole rackets, just to provide space in the cells. But the big boys – Arthur can list 'em for you – the big boys are still free and piling up the loot. I can't touch 'em until I can cut off their supplies, break into their communications systems, access their bank accounts and distrain their criminal profits.' He grinned and spread his hands in deprecation. 'That's why I'm being so nice to you, Mr. Gregory. You can key me into their system at a new point. So which is it to be, yes or no?'

'Don't rush the man, Commissioner.' Arthur Rebus raised a warning hand. 'Let's take this very gently. Let's look at worst and best cases. The worst is that Martin here has no access to the trust at all. The trustees are in place. It's a watertight administration now and for ever more. Then my advice would be that he follow the implied intent of the testator and sell the microfiches to Marius Melville. You will have had all the access you need, so Martin will have done his duty as a citizen and earned his right to a legitimate profit . . . Are you reading me?'

'Loud and clear,' said the Commissioner. 'Now I'd like to hear good news. What's the best case?'

'That Martin has access to and authority over the trust fund.'

I said I couldn't for the life of me see how I could have such authority. The trustees were in place. The trust deed was a frozen document. Arthur Rebus chided me like a benevolent schoolmaster.

'. . . You're not thinking straight, Martin. Let's get back to basics. What is a trustee?'

'One to whom property is entrusted for the benefit of another.'

'How is such property administered?'

'With such due and proper care as the trustees would devote to their own interests and affairs.'

'Next question. The trustees may choose to administer the property directly or . . .?'

'Or by delegation to fit and proper persons or institutions.'

'Good man! Now, so far you've discovered from the microfiches that you have access to the accounts of the trust. My guess is that as we go further into Cassidy's records, we'll find that there's a document of delegation to you from the trustees.'

'Why should there be?'

'Because, if my guess is right, Charlie Cassidy himself held the original delegation, and you, as his executor, are the natural successor.'

'You've lost me, I'm afraid.' It was the first time I had heard the Commissioner admit to human frailty. 'Charlie Cassidy set the whole thing up. How could he be a delegate in his own interest?'

'My dear Commissioner . . .' Arthur Rebus jumped at the chance to deliver a little homily. 'Let me try to make amends for all the damage I've inflicted on a whole army of Crown prosecutors . . . The purpose of a trust is to protect the interests of the beneficiaries and especially to protect them against the gatherers of taxes. So someone, not Charlie Cassidy, settles a trust, not to Charlie's benefit, but to the ultimate benefit of his grandchildren, or a home for delinquent women or destitute alcoholics. Charlie can swear on a stack of Bibles he doesn't own or control the trust funds. He can't be taxed on them. He can't be called to account for them. The trustees are responsible . . . But there's nothing to stop the trustees delegating Charlie to perform any act on behalf of the trustees. He's using their authority, not his own. He's subject to their direction, like any servant. If there are queries about his actions, he simply refers them to the trustees . . . Meantime, of course, he can milk the thing dry if he chooses, because the trustees have given him the key to the milking machine.'

'Beautiful!' said the Commissioner softly. 'A sweet,

sweet fiddle! Why didn't someone tell me all this years ago?'

'It's never too late,' said Arthur Rebus in his amiable fashion. 'I'm sure Martin would cut you in for a share of the loot.'

The Commissioner was not amused.

'I'm not sure that's a very good joke, Mr. Rebus.'

I wasn't amused either. These were two very bright fellows and they were working me, like a pair of sheepdogs, into a very tight corner. I decided it was time to do some manipulation of my own. I told them: 'Let's talk plain business, Arthur, and cut the jokes. The Commissioner wants his man to access Cassidy's files, with us. I agree that. I agree to the copying of any and all relevant microfiche material. I make a point here: I have already been warned by Marius Melville that if, in his view, the value of the material is debased by premature circulation, the deal is off. So, by going this far, I am putting five million at risk.'

'Point taken,' said the Commissioner. 'But why tell him?'

'Because I don't like dealing under false pretences.'

'Very laudable,' said the Commissioner drily.

'What other help can you offer him?' asked Arthur Rebus blandly. 'He's more at risk than I expected.'

The Commissioner thought for a moment before he answered.

'I think he should be armed. I can get him a licence to carry a pistol, provided he knows how to use the weapon. I can give him contact numbers in Sydney, Bangkok and other places. I could, if a sufficient degree of mutual trust existed, swear him in as a special constable under the Act and endow him with limited police powers. That, however, would place him squarely under my jurisdiction and I'd have his head on a dish if he fouled up. I have to point out, however, that there's no way I can cover him while he's abroad. I can give him local contacts among our foreign staff. I can suggest a couple of reliable minders who do freelance work; but he pays 'em and briefs 'em himself.'

Arthur Rebus pursed his lips and shook his head slowly from side to side in theatrical disapproval.

'It's not really very much, is it, Commissioner? He's got his own life and the lives of his family on the line now.'

'What is he?' asked the Commissioner curtly. 'Honest John Citizen or a bounty hunter? We're talking about international crime, not a dingo shoot on a sheep run. You have to tell me, Mr. Gregory, do you feel you have any entitlements other than those we've agreed?'

'There's one – straight answers to straight questions.'

'You'll get them, Mr. Gregory. Let's hear the questions.'

'Do you trust me, Commissioner?'

'Not completely.'

'Why?'

'I don't know how you'll react when you know for certain you're worth half a billion dollars. I don't know either how far I can bet on your sexual morals. Straight enough for you?'

'Yes, thank you. Next question: Cassidy had a pistol in his safe. What do I do with it?'

'Give it to my man. He'll arrange ballistic tests to see if the weapon is linked with any crimes. Then he'll give it back to you.'

'I'm staying at the Town House. Melville's daughter has suggested I move to the Melmar Marquis. She says it's more secure. What's your advice?'

'If you can stay out of her bed, by all means move to the Melmar. The Town House is harder to police. It caters to show business folk, so there's a lot of coming and going. At the Melmar you'll have house security as well as ours. But don't leave any significant papers lying around; keep them at the bank. Next question?'

'Cassidy's mistress, Pornsri Rhana.'

'Ah!' The Commissioner beamed satisfaction across the table. 'I was beginning to wonder why we hadn't talked about her. Her father's a general. She's well connected to the Embassy here and obviously to high circles in Thailand. She runs a company called Chao Phraya Trading Company, in which she is a substantial shareholder. That company interests us, principally because, among its activities, is the manufacture and distribution of pharmaceutical products in South-East Asia. This means it is legally entitled to buy and process raw opium for medical use. More importantly, however, there is an increasing exploitation of synthetic substitutes, compounds quite legal in themselves, by illegal drug traders right around the world. The only way we can trace this kind of activity is when local agents for legitimate companies begin importing large quantities of certain products like barbiturates, psychotropic compounds and so on . . . Any increase in this traffic means that there's a glut of raw opium in the producing countries, which is snapped up cheaply by the criminal trade. So Pornsri Rhana interests us . . . In this connection, does the name Red Dragon mean anything to you, Mr. Gregory?'

It gave me great satisfaction to spell out the connection for him.

'Red Dragon, English translation of the German Rotdrache, which is the name of the trust we've been talking about. That trust holds one-third of the Chao Phraya shares. The other third is held by Marius Melville.'

'How come you didn't tell me that?' Arthur Rebus sounded aggrieved. 'We've been talking about the god-damned trust for half an hour.'

'Sorry, Arthur, but that's the silly thing that happens. We get so absorbed in the substance of an argument that we forget the significant details.'

'Thank you, anyway,' said the Commissioner. 'Now things begin to make sense. Red Dragon has shown up in other areas too. We may be able to correlate these with the information in Cassidy's files.'

'Take note of something else, Commissioner. I'm meeting Pornsri Rhana in Bangkok. Apparently her interests in Chao Phraya are being threatened. She wants me to help her defend them.'

'Which you've promised to do?'

'Not yet. I've promised only to assess the situation and then make a decision.'

'Chivalry is not yet dead,' said Arthur Rebus. 'But may I suggest that this is a very dry argument. I'm hungry and thirsty.'

'I'll lunch you at the Commonwealth Club,' said the Commissioner.

'Are you sure you want to risk your reputation by being seen with us?'

'No problem at all.' The Commissioner rose happily to the lure. 'We've got a slush fund for the entertainment of likely informants. You two come in the category of supergrasses. I'm happy to lay out the money.'

Which seemed to me to make game, set and match for the Commissioner. I liked him; he had a solid, gritty granite feel about him. I resented the fact that he could not, or would not, express a full trust in me. It reminded me of the small but threatening shadow that, ever since the night of her father's death, had lain across my relationship with Pat. I was Martin the Righteous. I would settle for nothing but the whole loaf and the best love and the completest trust. The thought that I mightn't merit any of it was galling as a pebble in my shoe.

'You're sore,' said Arthur Rebus, as we washed up in the men's room at the Commonwealth Club. 'I warned you he'd put you through the wringer.'

'I'm not sore at him, for Christ's sake! I'm sore at me for letting myself get embroiled in this whole lousy game. I should have shut my ears to everyone and gone about the straightforward business of being an executor according to the rules.'

'No way you could have done that, sweetheart,' said Arthur Rebus, as he ran a comb through his unruly hair.

178

'This is war. Big men in white hats, big men in black hats, all the villains and suckers in between. They all want what you've got and if they can't shill you into handing it over, they hang you up by the thumbs until you change your mind. By me, the Commissioner's your best bet.'

'I'd just like to hear that he trusted me.'

'I'd like to hear it, too – just for the record.' He patted an errant hair into place. 'But it wouldn't mean very much, would it? After all, you're not sure you can trust yourself . . . Come on, little brother! Why be a super-grass if you can't enjoy the goodies you get from the coppers!'

Be it marked to his credit, the Commissioner lunched us well, and relaxed enough to let us enjoy it. He also answered two questions I had forgotten to put to him earlier.

'. . . Micky Gorman? You've probably forgotten – or it may have happened after you left – that he was handling the trust funds for the partnership. He felt Cassidy was sailing too close to the wind with certain investments. There were, and still are, strict guidelines. So he complained to Charlie. Charlie didn't bat an eyelid. He said, in effect, "Good! Let's have an audit and a guidelines check by the Bar Council." They got it. Charlie came out smelling of roses. Micky Gorman got his knuckles rapped for sloppy record keeping! He never forgave Cassidy and from that day on he bent every effort towards breaking up the partnership and pulling Cassidy down . . . Gerry Downs? Well, he's another kettle of fish altogether. He's rich as Croesus. He runs a media empire. He loves to gamble. If you're a gambler, on cards or horses or the tables, you rub shoulders with big-time crooks. That lays you open to guilt by association, but it doesn't make you a criminal. Gerry's slept with a lot of women, but that doesn't make him a criminal either – though it has put some strain on his health! I've checked through a lot of information about him. He's like a pointer, he tells you when there's hot money around. But at the end of the day all I can prove is that he's a larrikin who likes living in the fast lane . . . As to what was the quarrel between him and Cassidy, that's a confused issue. They were at odds over newspaper lotteries – and I understand that was settled at a very high figure in Cassidy's favour. There were other things, too. For a while, they were both competing for the same woman. Even as I say it, I wonder if Gerry shows up in any of your porno photographs?'

'No way!' said Arthur Rebus emphatically. 'That's not Gerry's style. He likes the best of everything and he demands exclusive possession! I even doubt there's too much malice in his campaign to blacken Cassidy's memory. He wants Labor out and the Liberals in. This is one way to make it happen.'

'Don't let's make it too simple.' The Commissioner wiped a fleck of gravy from his lips. 'Gambling means big money to be laundered. Gambling means loan-sharking and intimidation and occasionally murder. I still watch the players to lead me to the operators, especially now when the triads are moving into Chinatown and the local boys are getting ready for war . . . Which reminds me, Mr. Gregory . . .'

'Yes, Commissioner?'

'A word of advice for Thailand. I've got staff there working closely with the office of the Narcotics Control Board. I've got constant telex links and radio contact. But none of it is too secure, because the Palace insists on access to the communications system. In short, you'll have friends, but you'll be very vulnerable. My advice is not to go wandering the town, or accepting social invitations from Miss Rhana. Stay in the hotel compound and do your entertaining in your own suite or, better still, in the public areas.'

The lunch had mellowed me somewhat, so I challenged him with a laugh.

'You still don't trust me, eh Commissioner?'

He responded agreeably enough, but he still wouldn't yield me an inch.

'It's not a matter of trust, Mr. Gregory. It's common sense. You're valuable to me now. I want to keep you alive as long as I can.'

And that, as Arthur Rebus aptly remarked, was pure cliché. It proved that the Federal Police Commissioner himself was not safe from the corruption of Gerry Downs' television serials. It also gave us the first real laugh we had had all day.

14

The return flight to Sydney landed at twenty minutes to six. Arthur Rebus and I took a cab back to the city. Rebus wanted half an hour with me at the hotel before he went home. Ever since we had left the Commissioner's office, he had been preoccupied and taciturn. I was bone-tired, so I didn't mind the silences. In spite of the abrasions of our day's discussions, I felt at the end curiously reassured. As from the following day, I should be shadowed day and night by guardian angels and stayed up by the presence of a police expert who would help me to make sense of Cassidy's documents. I had a pistol licence in my pocket and the name of a reliable gunsmith. At least I was no longer alone, a floating particle in a hostile atmosphere.

Rebus, however, took a different view. Sitting in my room at the Town House with a large whiskey clamped in his fist, he told me, moodily: '. . . I'm more worried now than I was this morning. You don't see it, Martin, but I do. These are war-games. You're important because you're sitting on Cassidy's files; but for the rest, you're an expendable element. The Commissioner will sacrifice you with as little compunction as he would a decoy platoon in a field operation . . .'

'I can't blame him for that, Arthur. He made it very clear. My options are still open – most of them, anyway.'

'No, Martin! Listen to me and try to understand. This whole melodrama of rogue unions, rogue cops, rogue politicians, drug runners and their ilk is about one thing – power! If a maritime union controls the waterfront, it controls the trade of the nation. If a building union can hold up the construction of silos, the wheat rots and the rats eat it. So deals have to be made – big deals, legal and illegal: an investigation dropped, a claim settled, a felon given an early release . . . The real problem of drugs is not the casualties, tragic and all as they are, but the fact that narcotics have become a world currency, a black-market coinage which will buy anything anywhere, whose value is increased by shortage, whose movement is impossible to monitor . . . Look at the coastline of this continent. How the hell do you patrol it? Impossible. You could land a goddamn army anywhere from Normanton to Derby and the only ones who'd know about it would be the kangaroos! . . . The Commissioner's right. You're valuable to him because you can key him in to a new grid in the underground system. But once he's in, you're no longer important to him, because you have no political or executive power. He won't be indifferent to what happens to you. He's too moral a man for that; but he won't give all his blood to keep you alive – and he won't weep too long at your grave . . .' He sipped meditatively at his liquor. 'I guess what I'm really trying to say is that this, at root, is a moral matter. It involves a moral commitment, which I believe the Commissioner has. He really hates the corruptors and the intimidators. Between him and them it's war to the knife. All through today he was looking for the same commitment from you. He didn't get it. Neither did I, for that matter. Maybe we're both misreading you, but it seems to me you're still doing a teeter-totter act on the tightrope. Which being said, you're welcome to spit in my eye . . .'

There was a knock at the door – a bell boy with a large manila envelope. I borrowed a two-dollar bill from Rebus, to tip him. The envelope carried the sender's name: Standish and Waring, Solicitors. Inside was a letter and a sheaf of documents. The letter read:

Dear Mr. Gregory,
We act for the Macupan Pharmaceutical Company Ltd. of Manila. We understand that you are the executor of the late Charles Cassidy's will and that you have taken legal custody of his estate.

In October last year, Miss Pornsri Rhana, of the Chao Phraya Trading Company, Bangkok, applied to purchase at par one million five hundred thousand one dollar shares of Macupan Pharmaceutical, promising to pay upon issue of the shares.

A copy of the share application and a photostat of the share certificate is enclosed. Also enclosed is our client's agreement to accept payment in any country of the world, such payment to be made in a mixture of currencies, a consignment of precious stones of agreed and certified value and a consignment of pharmaceutical products whose value is similarly certified.

Copies of the certifications are attached. Miss Rhana informs us the currency and other items required for the settlement had been held for her by the late Charles Cassidy and that they would probably now be in your possession as executor. We would point out that the payments do not attract tax or require tax clearance, since they are considerations passing between two foreign entities, using an Australian entity only as the medium of exchange. Neither is there any probate problem, since the items in question are not part of the estate of the late Charles Cassidy.

May we ask you, therefore, to communicate with us as soon as possible, so that a date and time may be set for the payment of the consideration and the delivery of the share certificate?

Sincerely yours,
Gordon Standish

I flipped through the documents and handed them without comment to Arthur Rebus. He read them slowly, nodding his head like one of those old-fashioned porcelain Buddhas. Finally, he looked up and said, 'Now that's what I call real style! No threats. A nice, courtly letter from one legal colleague to another! I wonder what the Commissioner will make of this one.'

'Standish and Waring . . . The Premier recommended I use them for Cassidy's probate.'

'You could have done a lot worse. They're old line, stuffy, desperately slow – and completely reliable.'

'So why would Erhardt Möller use them as his collectors?'

'Precisely for that reason. Given these documents, they wouldn't think of questioning the instructions of their client. If the client tells them that a kilo of heroin is a pharmaceutical product or a new line of baking powder, they'll accept it as fact. Why should they do otherwise? They'll expect a similarly courteous and uncomplicated response from you. If they get it, the matter's closed. But I'd like to hear first from Miss Pornsri Rhana. Either she's been set up, or she's setting you up for Mr. Erhardt Möller, or this is standard pattern for transactions between Cassidy and the boys in Manila.'

'I'd like to hear what the Commissioner advises.'

'Why don't you leave the lady and the Commissioner to me? I have your power of attorney. No sense to keep a dog and bark yourself. I'll drop in to see the lady on my way home and phone the Commissioner tonight. In the morning, I'll call Standish and Waring and let them know I'll be handling the matter under your power of attorney. We'll meet at the bank in the morning.'

I was glad when he left. He could be a diverting character, but he had all sorts of unexpected edges to bruise one's self-esteem. I needed some balm for my wounded feelings. So, good and faithful husband, I telephoned my wife in Klosters.

It was Clare who answered the phone. She told me Pat and the children were already out on the slopes. Pat had found this marvellous ski instructor who was bringing them along at an enormous rate.

'. . . They're having a wonderful time, Martin. It would do your heart good to see them.'

'I'm delighted. And what about you, Clare? How's the big romance?'

'Coming along very nicely. He's kind and considerate. Terribly absentminded, but I can cope with that. He's working on his book. I'm working on him. It's a very comfortable situation. How are you holding up, Martin?'

'I'm holding up. Your old man left a tidy estate to the family – and a bloody minefield for me. I'm picking my way through the middle of it now.'

'Pat told me about the Thai mistress and the daughter she bore to Charlie.'

'That's only the half of it. I've spent today in Canberra with the Federal Police. I have to go up to Bangkok in three days' time. Also, for security reasons, I'm changing hotels. I'm moving tonight to the Melmar Marquis. Write it down – the Melmar Marquis. In Bangkok, I'll be at the Oriental.'

'I know, dear.'

'How do you know?'

'Mr. Melville called last night to say he'd be meeting you there. He kindly offered to carry any letters or messages.

Would you like me to have Pat call you when she gets back?'

'What time will that be?'

'It's normally quite late – three, four in the afternoon. They're doing the long runs now, stopping at the halfway hut for lunch, then skiing the last leg to be home before dark. But I guess that'll be the wee, small hours for you.'

'It will indeed. Just give her my love and kiss the kids for me. I'll call as soon as I'm installed in the Melmar. Lots of love, Clare. And good luck with your scholar. By the way, what's his name?'

'Leonidas Farkis . . . and if you say it's a funny name, I'll kill you! He's a Greek-American, a great scholar who . . .'

'Hey, hey, hey, relax, Clare! This is son-in-law Martin, remember? I'm on your side. Always have been.'

'I know!' She gave a little, unsteady laugh. 'It's just that I'm very, very fond of him and Pat and the children don't always understand his funny ways . . . I'm sorry you're having such a bad time with Charles' affairs. Do be careful. He could be such a monster; he probably left booby traps everywhere. Try to come home soon. The children miss you terribly and Pat gets very restless without you . . . Goodbye, my dear!'

When I put down the receiver I felt a sudden pang of jealousy and resentment. Pat was restless! Pat had found a new ski instructor who kept her out on the slopes until dark. Splendid! This is the day the Lord hath made, Alleluia! Meantime, dutiful husband, I, Martin Gregory the Righteous, had just been licensed to carry a firearm, warned that he was an expendable element in a war-game and that people didn't trust him because he had lust and greed written all over his face!

I called the Melmar Marquis and asked to speak to Laura Larsen. This time they found her within thirty seconds. I told her that if she still had room I'd love to come and stay at her place.

She said, 'Good! I think it's wise . . . and I'll be glad to have you near anyway. When you arrive, ask for Peters at reception. He'll take you up to the suite, register you there and explain the house procedures to maintain your privacy and at the same time keep your communications open. I won't see you tonight, because I'm hostess to a group of travel agents who are very important to us. But I'll come and have breakfast with you at eight in the morning. How was Canberra?'

'Busy.'

'And your new probate lawyers?'

'I'm impressed. They're very efficient. I'll tell you about them when I see you. *Ciao*.'

That made me feel a little better and if it added a line or two of lechery to my public face, then too bad. I shaved, showered, put on fresh linen and a fresh summer suit and poured myself a drink to farewell the Town House. I was just beginning to enjoy it when the telephone rang. Mr. Erhardt Möller was on the line from Manila.

'Good evening, Mr. Gregory. You should by now have received a set of documents from our solicitors, Standish and Waring.'

'They arrived, yes.'

'And you will deal with them promptly?'

'I have already begun to do so, Mr. Möller. I handed them immediately to the solicitor I have appointed to deal with the Cassidy estate and asked him to expedite the matter.'

'But as the documents clearly indicate, this has nothing to do with the Cassidy estate.'

'Precisely what I have asked him to verify, Mr. Möller. Once that is done, completion can take place immediately.'

'I hope you understand that there is a certain pressure.'

'I do indeed, Mr. Möller. I, too, am under pressure to divest myself of Cassidy's affairs and get home. So there are no problems on our side, as I am sure there are none on yours. Standish and Waring are very reputable people. One relies on their documents.'

187

'Of course. May I have the name of the man who is acting for you?'

'Certainly. His name is Arthur Rebus, spelt REBUS . . . That's right, a picture puzzle. How clever of you! Yes, he is very well known and highly respected in the profession. His firm is called Fitch, Rebus and Landsberg. I'm sure he'll do an excellent job . . . Yes, of course, it would be entirely proper for you to communicate with him directly. I'll give you his address and office telephone number . . . My pleasure, Mr. Möller.'

When I put the phone down I didn't feel half as chirpy as I sounded. These people were hardline professionals. Their timing was impeccable, their urbanity more menacing than any overt violence. I found myself hoping that the Commissioner would let the payment go through so that I could get at least this bunch of villains off my back. Then, as an additional precaution, I called Pornsri Rhana's number. She was at home. Arthur Rebus was with her. I asked to speak with him. When I told him of the call from Möller, he lapsed into double-talk. I found he was very good at it.

'. . . Yes, that's an entirely expected development. My present reading is that we are faced with option three – standard offshore procedure. It also answers my question about the materials in the coffer deposit. It was a temporary measure, complicated by the premature exit of the depositor.'

'Would the Commissioner let this deal go through?'

'I think he might, especially if it worked like a tracer dye in a water system.'

'I take your meaning. Will you check it out with him?'

'Naturally. That's what you pay me for.'

'How's the lady?'

'Happy, I think. Why don't I let her tell you herself?'

A moment later, Pornsri herself came on. She was bubbling with satisfaction.

'I have to thank you, Martin. Your Mr. Rebus is most

helpful. The papers are in order, of course. I can explain the whole background to you in Bangkok. Thank you again, my dear.'

And that, it seemed, was that. It was time to move on. I called for a bell-boy to pick up my bags, walked out of the room and headed for the elevator.

The Melmar Marquis wrapped itself around me like a security blanket. Mr. Peters from reception conducted me to my suite, a pair of magnificent chambers with an eastward view of the harbour. He filled in my card with as much care as if he were inscribing the details in the Book of Kells. He explained the system by which all calls were diverted through a monitor before being put through to me, how visitors were dealt with at reception and packages for special guests screened by the bell-captain. Then he presented Mr. Paul, butler to V.I.P.'s like me. Mr. Paul or his assistant would be at call day or night. His minions delivered champagne, fruit in a silver epergne, a silver bucket of ice, a silver dish of chocolates and a leather-bound menu card embossed in silver. Mr. Andrew, the night valet, appeared to ask if I needed any suits pressed or shoes cleaned. In short, I was cosseted like a chief of chiefs; and when I wondered whether the room was bugged or the bed scanned by a hidden camera, it was almost as if I were entertaining obscene thoughts. For a final touch, there was a bracket of the latest bestsellers on the bedside table, so I read myself to sleep and woke to a fine, clear summer morning with the sunlight dancing on the wake of the ferries criss-crossing the harbour.

Punctually at eight, Laura Larsen joined me for break-fast in the suite. We kissed chastely and talked self-consciously for the opening gambits. Then she said brusquely, 'Let's stop this silly game, Martin. We know what we feel for each other. Let's be open about it. Let's admit that we don't want to add new complications to our lives . . .'

'I admit. You admit. So where does that take us?'

'To Bangkok first, and your meeting with my father. You've got to understand how important that first encounter is going to be.'

'Laura, my love! How can I understand it? I've never met your father. I have only the sketchiest idea of his relations with Cassidy. As to his personal activities . . . what can I possibly know? On the other hand, all these years I've meant nothing in his life. Why am I suddenly so important?'

'Martin, you said you trusted me.'

'I do.'

'Then why do you lie to me? You said you were going to Canberra to confer with a lawyer. That was perhaps not a lie, but it certainly wasn't the whole truth. You were picked up at the airport by a Federal Police driver. You spent the morning at police headquarters. You lunched with the Commissioner at the Commonwealth Club, you went back to headquarters and were driven in a police car to catch the 5.05 flight to Sydney. Last night, just after you arrived, two new guests checked in. My security staff thought they might be police officers. They're usually right about such things. Well?'

'In other words, you've been having me shadowed.'

'I told you from the beginning. You've got my father and you've got me, whether you want us or not.'

'Is your father a criminal, Laura?'

'What did the Commissioner tell you when you asked him that question?'

'Your father provides services for criminal elements. He has never been convicted of a crime.'

'Everyone provides services for criminal elements – the builder, the baker, the shoemaker, the cab-driver, the hotel-keeper. So what?'

'As you say, my love, so what? But I think you'll agree my position is somewhat special. A long time ago, I walked out of Cassidy's life and took his daughter with me. From that time on there was a blood-feud between us. Then a couple of weeks ago he turns up on my doorstep in London a dying man. He asks me to be his executor. I accept. It's a formality, a routine service . . . Like hell it is! I'm not half way through his papers and I realise that Cassidy's set me up. I've got all his records. So either I'm the new king of the castle, or I'm the pretender who has to be knocked off before a new king takes over. Either way, your father's got a vested interest in my fate. My prime interest is in staying alive, which is why I went to talk to the Federal police. I don't feel half so secure with the local boys who were running things in Cassidy's time.'

'Will you tell my father that?'

'Yes.'

'Will you tell him what you disclosed to the police?'

'Yes – and I hope he'll be equally direct with me.'

'He will. Be sure of it. That's why he and Charlie Cassidy got along so well. They both knew exactly where the bottom line was – though they often disagreed on how to get to it.'

'What's the bottom line now, for your father?'

'I am,' said Laura Larsen.

Demure as a Dresden shepherdess, she waited for my reaction. I wasn't impressed. Daddy was solicitous for his little girl's future. I was solicitous for my daughter, too. Wasn't everyone? The melody was simple, if not without charm. I told her it needed some orchestration to lift it out of the commonplace.

'You're not a very friendly audience.'

'Try to remember I'm sitting in the middle of the theatre, right under the big chandelier. If it drops, it falls on my head. I'm not hostile, just wary.'

As she talked, haltingly at first, then eloquently, I began to see another woman altogether, more subtle, more versed in history and its consequences than the little Miss Owl-Eyes who had snared me between London and Bahrain and held fast to me ever since.

'. . . My father is a dynast, pure and simple. He is the

191

summary of all his past. His future is without meaning unless there is a successor to whom he can transmit the tribal tradition. He is proud of his nobility – even though it is only a petty title. He is descended from some obscure Knight of the Order of Malta, but, because he's Sicilian born, he is rooted in that tradition as well: the old inbred pride, the hatred of the foreign oppressor, the suspicion of the central Government, the conviction that the rogueries of one's own folk are more easy to cope with than the virtues of the outsider . . . That's what he built on, you see. That's why the Mafia families in America accepted him and kept faith with him. He was above them, but not against them. He was bound by the same code as they. He might not approve them; he would never betray them. They could live together in trust . . .'

I was reminded vividly of Cassidy's apologia to the Commissioner . . . 'Symbiosis, living together from a shared resource . . . It's the human compromise. Without it you get the Police State: order in the streets and a blackshirt on every corner!' I was tempted to tell her the thought, but I said nothing. She was plunging ahead with her own case for the defence.

'. . . That was Cassidy's tradition, too. I remember the long nights in our house in Connecticut when he expounded it to my father – Cromwell's sack of Ireland, to hell or Connaught, the great extirpation, the great famine, the coffin ships, the Black and Tans, the Easter Rising, the bloody tyrannies of Norfolk Island and Van Diemen's Land – all of it strung together like a bard's song in that winning brogue he could turn on or off like a wine-spigot . . . Father and he were like brothers together, laughing, quarrelling, chasing women, talking up great plans and how to make them come true. Which they did, by God! . . . But the sadness was the same for both: there was no son in the house. Cassidy felt that you and his daughter had betrayed him. I'm an only child. I'm divorced. There's no grandson in prospect either. So you see

I really am the last of the line for my father. He's built an empire, but there's no one except me to take it over and run it. Left to themselves, without my father's arbitration, the Families will rip it apart within two years . . . Are you answered, Martin Gregory?'

'Almost. I'd like to ask you one more question. Clearly, after your father dies you'll be rich and well cared for. How much do you really care what happens to his empire?'

'Oh, I care!' She was deadly serious now. 'I'm a dynast too, you see. In a way you probably can't understand, I'm ashamed of being childless – more ashamed because my father's want is so great. But I'm old country, as he is. I want to end up a matriarch with my sons kissing my cheeks and my daughters bringing their boys home for my approval . . . So make no mistake, I care! And you, Martin? . . . You've talked to the politicians, you've talked to the police and the lawyers and me and Cassidy's mistress – but where do you stand? What do you want? What will you say to my father when he offers you five million dollars for Cassidy's records?'

'I'll tell him he can have them; but they won't be exclusive any more. I've already opened them to the Federal Police. So they're probably worthless to your father.'

'He'll appreciate your frankness. He'll hardly commend your wisdom.'

'Other climates, other customs. I owe your father no debts. He was Cassidy's friend, not mine.'

'Are you my friend, Martin?'

'Yes, I am.'

'Then what will you do when . . .'

I leaned across the table and sealed her lips with my fingertips.

'Please, my sweet! Because I am your friend, don't try to commit me to decisions on "ifs" and "maybes". As a lawyer, that's repugnant to me. As a man, I hate being jockeyed into promises I can't keep. Let your father tell me what he wants. I'll reason with him about it. If it makes

193

good sense to both of us – fine! – we're in business. If it doesn't, one of us walks away, with no hard feelings. It's as simple as that.'

'No, it isn't.' Her denial was emphatic. 'My father is a very complicated man. I cannot explain to you how meticulously he measures his relationships with other people: his praise, his blame, his gratitude, his disapproval, the punishment he metes out for delinquency . . .'

'Punishment! Who does he think he is – God?'

'Sometimes, yes.' She gave me an uncertain little smile and told me: 'All right then. No "ifs". No "maybes". Just so we stay friends. What are your plans today?'

'I'm at the bank all day with Arthur Rebus.'

'Dinner tonight?'

'I'm not sure. There's a lot to do before I leave for Bangkok. May I call you later?'

'Of course. Have a good day.'

She kissed me lightly on the lips and was gone. I called for Mr. Paul the butler to remove the breakfast things while I made ready for my session at the bank.

The man the Commissioner had sent us to study the Cassidy files was a pink-cheeked, baby-faced fellow, with an alto voice and a mind like a mantrap. His name was Donohue, his rank was Detective-Sergeant. His first act was to take possession of the pistol I had found in Cassidy's safe. He put it in a cellophane bag which he tagged and sealed and shoved in his briefcase. Next, he produced two bags of glucose powder, identical in size, weight and marking with those which contained the heroin. Having switched the bags, he turned his attention to the stones, which he examined one by one with a jeweller's loupe, checking the description of each one against the notations on the packets. Finally, he announced the Commissioner's decision that the monies, stones and glucose could be handed over to Standish and Waring in settlement of the share transaction with the Macupan Pharmaceutical Company in Manila. The stones and the currency were traceable elements; but the Commissioner had had a crisis of conscience – political and personal – about releasing a kilo of heroin onto the open market. He added an off-hand postscript.

'Of course, Mr. Möller's going to be hopping mad when he discovers the switch. So watch your back, Mr. Gregory.'

'I hope you fellows are watching it for me.'

'If that's what the Commissioner promised, I'm sure we are.'

'And what about the lady?' asked Arthur Rebus. 'She's at risk too, isn't she?'

'Possibly. But she leaves the country on Saturday. Möller won't get the stuff until she's gone . . . Anyway, the Commissioner's not really interested.'

The way he said it wasn't encouraging. Our lives were the Commissioner's pigeon. They were a matter of supreme indifference to Baby-Face.

After that, the three of us settled down to view the remaining microfiches in Cassidy's briefcase and the papers I had removed from his safe. Both Donohue and Rebus were goggle-eyed at the variety of information available: extracts from share registers, confidential reports on senior police officers, depositions from the divorce cases of Cabinet ministers, bank statements, copies of betting slips, patronage lists, a suicide note, transcripts of telephone conversations, reports of Shire Council meetings, a list of brothels in the metropolitan area, each classified for cleanliness, security, entertainment value; a similar list of gambling establishments with the ownership of each, nominal and actual.

For my part, I was beginning to be wearied by the stuff. Important as it might be to the mechanics of venal government, or as an ultimate weapon in the fight for reform, it was becoming less and less relevant to me, because I could not act on it. My power, if indeed I had any, lay elsewhere, in the manipulation of money. So the only thing I was looking for now was a document, if such existed, that appointed me delegate of the Rotdrache trustees. Finally, towards the end of the afternoon, we came upon a single microfiche headed:

ROTDRACHE TRUST
EXTRACT OF INFORMATION

The extracts were set down thus:

Settlor of Trust	Marius Melville
Date of Determination	Ten years from date of settlement
Trustees	Horstman and Preysing, Zurich
Beneficiaries	As listed in Deed of Trust
Delegate of Trustees	Martin Gregory (upon decease of C. P. Cassidy)
Documents	All documents are held in the offices of Horstman and Preysing, Zurich

'Bingo!' said Arthur Rebus softly. 'You're in!'

'I wouldn't advertise it,' said Sergeant Donohue. 'We worry about people with high financial profiles. When do you go to Bangkok?'

'Sunday. Why do you ask?'

'I'd hold up delivery of this stuff to Mr. Möller until after you've left.'

'I have a suggestion, too,' said Arthur Rebus. 'Today's Thursday. I'd like to get you out of town first thing tomorrow morning, take you cruising on Pittwater for a couple of days and then deliver you straight to the plane on Sunday.'

'But we haven't finished with the microfiches yet. There's at least another day's work.'

'You've lost interest,' said Sergeant Donohue coolly. 'Your judgement's not reliable any more. We're the people who'll be using the material. Leave me to finish the run through and I'll deliver the briefcase to your plane on Sunday.'

'He's right,' said Arthur Rebus, in his amiable but acid fashion. 'Now that I'm sure you've got the key to the milking machine, I want to keep you close to me – at least until I've collected my fees!'

Suddenly I felt humiliated by their bland assumptions. Suddenly I remembered Cassidy's last letter to me:

'. . . Material will be abstracted, key documents will be lost until the whole potent pattern is destroyed. You, of course, won't have to worry. You'll be Martin the Righteous, sleeping the sleep of the just with the receipt for a failed reformation tucked under your pillow.'

I remembered something else, too, much further in the past, when he came into the office waving a copy of Moss Hart's *Act One*. He perched himself on the edge of my desk and read out one sentence. 'In theatre, the greatest enemy is fatigue.' Then he launched into one of his famous monologues. 'It's the same in the law. We wilt under the pressure of detail. We are smothered by verbiage. Whole passages in a brief become a blur . . . That's when we're most vulnerable and our clients most at risk! . . .'

I was not only wilting, I was beginning to lose even my anger. I looked from Rebus to Donohue and then told them flatly, 'You're patronising me, gentlemen. I don't like it. We're going to finish this job together. I couldn't bear it if either of you knew more than I did. I'd hate to think I knew less than Rafe Loomis.'

'That's a sudden change of heart.' Arthur Rebus pricked up his ears at the reference. 'Thinking of going into State politics, are we?'

'It's been suggested – by the same Rafe Loomis, no less.'

'Well, at least you could afford it . . . You two start work. I'm going to send out for some drops. This scanner is making my eyes hurt.'

We worked right up to closing time. Donohue had filled a notebook with ciphered references. We all agreed that one more day should see us through. Rebus invited us to his club for drinks. Donohue declined. He wanted to call the Commissioner and then get home to his wife, who was expecting a baby. Before he left, however, he presented me with a small problem of protocol, which might blow up into a large problem of jurisdiction.

'. . . You've already discussed this material with the Premier and the Attorney-General of New South Wales. You agreed to make whatever is relevant to criminal matters available for inspection by the State police. Now you've come over their heads to us . . . And you're about to dispose of certain items like money, jewellery and drugs which the Attorney-General thinks or knows you have. How do you propose to handle the situation; because, while you can defer it, you can't duck it.'

It gave me a perverted pleasure to hand the question straight to Arthur Rebus.

'. . . Now that your fees are guaranteed, Arthur, let's have full opinion.'

'With pleasure,' said Arthur Rebus. 'The situation appeals to my sense of irony . . . We haven't gone over anyone's head. Your first recourse was to the State authorities. Then we decided it was desirable to seek advice at Federal level . . . All protocols have been observed. Sunday you'll be gone, taking Cassidy's briefcase with you. Miss Rhana will also have left town. Which leaves me sitting here, pretty as a picture, with four bags of documents and porno pictures from Cassidy's safe, plus a consignment of glucose powder – which still bothers me, by the way – precious stones and currency which, *prima facie*, are consideration for an offshore transaction. On Monday I call on Loomis, display my power of attorney and ask him how he'd like to handle the whole business. You're in the clear, I'm your noble and true servant at law. If Loomis is as cute as I think he is, he'll thank me and send me home while he thinks out a position. If he claims that he's been denied access to any documents, then I'll suggest that he ask the Commissioner to make the Sergeant's transcripts available . . . You'd be happy about that, wouldn't you, Sergeant?'

'The Commissioner is God!' said Baby-Face piously. 'Whatever he says, I do.' To me he said with a grin, 'Be careful in Thailand, Mr. Gregory. I spent a year on assignment there. It used to be a fun place. Now it's almost as dangerous as Sydney. See you in the morning, gentlemen!'

When he had gone, Rebus helped me lock the documents in the safe, then walked me down to his club for a drink. He repeated an earlier proposition.

'I told you I'd show you the underside of the town. Why not tonight?'

'Why not? Let me call Laura and tell her I won't be back this evening. What about your wife?'

'I don't have a wife,' said Arthur Rebus. 'She died five years ago. Since then I've been a freelance. Besides, there's nothing too glamorous in what I want to show you.' He signalled the waiter for another round of drinks. 'Of course, nothing exists here on the scale of crime in the United States: the drug traffic in Florida and the West Coast, the power of the Syndicates; but for a new, young country, with only fifteen million people in it, we've got more than our share of very shrewd criminals. I'd like to have your reaction to what you've seen since you've been back – and what I want to show you tonight . . . You're a real chameleon. Just when I think I've got you measured and colour-graded, you change.'

'No mystery, Mr. Rebus. Protective pigmentation, that's all.'

'I wish I could believe it, Mr. Gregory. One moment you flare up like a furnace. The next you're pissing ice-water. It bothers me. I like to have a consistent reading on my clients.'

I knew what he was driving at. I was hard put to explain it.

'. . . The problem is that I'm not sure whether I belong here any more. I've been in exile a long time. I'm not sure how much I'm prepared to commit to the country. I've developed a very comfortable sense of detachment. I'm in the banking business and money knows no frontiers. I'm angry that Cassidy dragged me back and embroiled me so deeply with people and matters I'd prefer to ignore. Then I ease down and think: "Take the money and run. What's Hecuba to him or he to Hecuba?" When I wake next morning and look across the water, I'm mad again, because this beautiful bloody country is being made a prey to crooks.'

'But you're not sure you want to do anything about it?'

'Not yet. No.'

'Well . . .' said Arthur Rebus softly. 'Well, well, well! Let's finish our drinks and start our little tour. My driver's waiting for us in the car park.'

As a tour guide, Arthur Rebus was original, not to say eccentric. It was six-thirty when we left the club. Homing traffic was still thick on all the arteries, but Rebus had his driver take a long swing through the densest areas, while he regaled me with a list of Sydney's more recent murders.

'See that pond in the park? They've fished two bodies out of there in the last few months. One was a man. He'd been shot once in the back of the head. The other was a woman slated as a witness in an upcoming drug case. She was spiked with an overdose of heroin . . . That hotel on the corner, the big Edwardian building . . . Fellow who owned it was a local identity, hail-fellow-well-met, president of the football club, clean record. One day a group of Vietnamese approached him. They'd like to run a restaurant upstairs in the old dining-room. He refused. They pressured him some more. He still refused. They shot him and dumped his body in the street. That's just a symptom of the rise of Asian standover crime . . .' In the next suburb the driver slowed down at the corner of a cul-de-sac. Rebus rolled down the window. 'Look to your left. You can see stains on the roadway. A car was burned out there a couple of weeks ago. A charred body was found in the trunk. That was a race-fixing job. The Commissioner mentioned a similar case in Frenchs Forest. Same method, different reason . . . That house over there, impressive isn't it? Built like a fortress, with every security device known to man. The owner's a professional assassin, a hit man; but he hasn't been seen for months. Hot rumour says he's dead . . . These are all recent happenings, indirectly connected with the fact that Cassidy was losing his grip. He couldn't hold the lid on the pot . . .'

'That surprises me. He told me in London that his illness attacked fairly suddenly. Until then he was functioning pretty well.'

'It wasn't his health,' said Arthur Rebus flatly. 'The game had got too big. I never quite understood how big until I started working through those files with you . . . You'd think that anyone who controlled half a billion in liquid funds, as Cassidy did, could call his own tune in any market . . . For a while, obviously that's what he did in Thailand. With Marius Melville as an ally, secure sources of supply and safe transport routes, he was top of the heap. But he couldn't stay there. There was too much junk in the market. It was coming in from all over the place and suddenly there were more chiefs than Indians – Pakistanis, Lebanese, Turks, Viets and, of course, the Chinese. Cassidy's deal – limited supply, high returns, monopoly market – just wouldn't stick any more. A bent cop could shop around the gangs for the best retainer. Cassidy's control of the lawmen started slipping too . . . So the gang bosses started their own campaign of enforcement, with the same ritual elements – the shot to the back of the head, small-calibre weapon or, with the women, the spike, a lethal overdose of heroin . . . Over there, by the way, is our best known brothel. High-profile advertising, aimed at the visiting firemen. It's also where a lot of pretty girls get started on the drug habit – and end up a few years later on the street, peddling themselves for a fix.'

'The way you describe them, things are completely out of hand.'

'Not quite,' said Arthur Rebus calmly. 'The game's getting rough, but violence tends to be self-limiting. Big criminals are realists. They know the public and the press will only take so much disorder . . . They want to damp it down.'

'And what will the new Government do about it?'

'Let's be precise.' Rebus made the point with some emphasis. 'It's not a new Government. It's the same one – with a new Premier and a new Cabinet. They're all Cassidy minions, of course; but if they can live down their past, they may make some changes for the better. Loomis can be as slippery as an eel, but he's tough too. Rumour has it that he's already looking for a reformer to head up the police force. He's got pressure from all sides: the churches, community groups, the wiser heads in the Party . . . We'll stop here and take a stroll . . .'

The stroll took us through a series of alleys and arcades, just off the main thoroughfare of Kings Cross, which is the most densely populated square mile in the southern hemisphere. In contrast with the bustle and the bright lights a few paces away, the alleys had a furtive and defeatist air and the young or nearly young who congregated there were, for the most part, addicts or peddlers on the prowl.

Arthur Rebus said quietly, '. . . This is Desperation Street, cheapest place in town to buy a body, male or female. You'll notice there's not a policeman in sight. What good would they do? They could make twenty busts an hour and fill the holding cells with kids who'll be screaming their heads off for a fix before midnight. They could pick up the peddlers and sweat 'em for information on their sources; but the peddlers know that they'll end

up with a bullet in their heads if they open their mouths –
and sometimes the man who shops them is a police officer
who gets paid in cash and powder. You think this is
bad . . .' he kicked an empty syringe into the gutter, 'but
there's a corner like this in every big country town. In
every suburb there's a milk bar or a pizza joint that peddles
the hard stuff. As for marijuana, God knows how many
acres there are under cultivation in agricultural areas and
in clearings in the rain forests . . . Enough, anyway, to
prove that Cassidy's theory of an acceptable balance of
natural forces was a nonsense, . . . though I'd agree that,
at one time, he might have believed it . . . Seen enough?
Then let's walk a couple more blocks and have dinner at
Rosa's. The food's great. I hope all this hasn't spoiled your
appetite.'

I was already engulfed in a black depression and it took
a hefty martini to jolt me out of it. The ambience helped
too; spotless linen, low lights, fine crystal and a smiling
padrona who had once been a film star in Rome and who
cosseted Arthur Rebus as if he were her new leading man.
She was amiable to me also and she walked us through the
menu like a tour guide in love with her territory.

By the time we were wined and fed, we were both
agreeably mellow. Arthur Rebus said, '. . . I was going to
take you round to a few late-night joints; a gambling club,
a disco where, if you're a cash client and kosher, you can
buy any narcotic you name . . . But hell, it's just more of
the same. You can do the essential mathematics in your
head. Crime in this country is a multi-billion dollar industry
that touches everyone's life . . . even mine, Mr. Gregory!'

'I quote your words to the Commissioner, Mr. Rebus.
In the law, you can't expect to deal all the time with
virgins.'

He gave me a long, hostile look and then said coldly,
'Five years ago, my wife was shot dead in our own house
by an intruder. He was sixteen years old, strung out and
crazy for a fix.'

'Oh Christ! I'm sorry!'

'It's all right. I'm over it now. It only hurts when it rains . . . But that's why I took you on, Martin Gregory – to see if I could seduce you onto the side of the angels.'

'Do you think I need to be seduced?'

'Yes.'

'Thank you. Are you going to tell me more about this seduction business? Once you got me into bed with the angels, what exactly would you expect me to do?'

'Start thinking about other people instead of yourself and this . . . this shabby vendetta with a dead man!'

'For instance . . .?'

'For instance, this afternoon. Sergeant Donohue warned you that Möller might come gunning for you, once he discovered he'd got glucose instead of heroin.'

'So?'

'You're protected. The woman's not. Is that fair?'

'The decision was taken out of my hands.'

'She trusted us. We put her at risk. How will you feel if she turns up dead in Bangkok?'

'Why should she?'

'Because that's the way the game is played. You default, you die.'

'I'll call the Commissioner in the morning and argue it out with him. After all, nothing irrevocable will have been done until you deliver the stuff to Standish and Waring.'

'And if he still makes difficulties?'

'I'll take a trade. He wants me to deliver Cassidy's network. My price is Pornsri Rhana.'

'Why not call him now?' said Arthur Rebus. 'I've got his private number. Rosa will let you use the phone in her office.'

'You had this all set up for me, didn't you?'

'In a manner of speaking, yes.'

'Then forget the brandy and order me some coffee in the office. I'm going to need a clear head for this one.'

The Commissioner was in bed when I called. He was

brusque and not at all disposed to change his mind. He pointed out that to traffic in hard drugs was a felony, that the street value of a kilo of pure heroin was astronomical and that Pornsri Rhana was in fact a trafficker who was getting away scot-free. Once she was out of his jurisdiction it was good riddance to bad rubbish . . .

That set me back on my heels for a few moments and I regretted the good wine I had drunk. Then the adrenalin started to flow and I gave him my argument. He wanted Cassidy's trading network. Pornsri Rhana was the key to it. She was the lynchpin that held the Europeans and the Asians together. We needed her alive. The only way to ensure that was to make the full delivery to Erhardt Möller, by way of Standish and Waring. It should not be beyond the skill of the Federal Police to monitor the transmission of the material from lawyer to client.

It took me fifteen minutes of steady argument to convince him: but it was by no means an unconditional surrender. He told me flatly, 'You owe me, Mr. Gregory. I'll want payment in full – with interest.'

'You'll get it, Commissioner. God knows how, but you'll get it.'

When I returned to the table, Arthur Rebus was nursing another large brandy. When I told him the news he grinned at me like a Cheshire cat and said a little thickly, 'You see. You've really got a good heart, Martin. The problem is to get you mad enough at someone else besides Cassidy.'

When I got back to the hotel at twenty after midnight, the concierge handed me a telex:

LEONIDAS AND I TAKING CHILDREN BACK TO LONDON TO BEGIN SCHOOL ON MONDAY. PAT STAYING ANOTHER WEEK IN KLOSTERS. PLEASE GET HOME AS SOON AS YOU CAN. WE ALL MISS YOU.
LOVE, CLARE.

In Klosters it was twenty after two in the afternoon. I called the house. It was the cook who answered. Her English was heavily accented but quite intelligible. Mrs. Gregory was out skiing. She was not expected back until late afternoon.

15

I spent a miserable night, kept awake by an overdose of coffee and alcohol, plagued by fits of jealousy and anger, sweating through patches of haunted sleep. At five in the morning I got up, put on a track suit and set out to jog a three-mile circuit round the harbour fringe and back, through the quiet suburban streets to the Melmar. At seven-thirty I rang Klosters again. It was nine-thirty in the evening there. A manservant answered. Mrs. Gregory was dining out. She was not expected back until midnight. I left a message asking her to call me at the bank, no matter what hour she came in.

By the time Laura Larsen arrived for breakfast I was shaved, showered and half way human. I was also determined to discharge Cassidy's business in short order and go home. Clare Cassidy was a clever woman. She had put out the warning flags and I would be a fool not to respond to them.

I asked Laura: 'When is your father expected in Bangkok?'

'Today, I believe.'

'Can you get your travel people to switch my air and hotel bookings from Sunday to Saturday, then telex your father and tell him my change of plans?'

'I'll do it, of course; but why the hurry?'

'Something's come up. I need to get back to London as quickly as possible.'

She set down her coffee cup, called the travel desk and asked for immediate action on my request. Then she sat down and reached out to touch my cheek. She said, gently, 'You're very sombre this morning. Is something wrong?'

'I had a bad night – too much wine, too much coffee and a rather depressing evening with Arthur Rebus.'

When I told her about it she was angry and scornful.

'. . . So what was he trying to prove? Sydney's a rough and raunchy town? There are wild women and nasty men and the crime bosses run the mobs by their own rules? So what's new? What about New York, Miami, Naples, Houston, Texas, for God's sake? He's brainwashing you! They all are! It's the elementary technique – make the victim feel shame and guilt. A little way down the track they'll have you believing you spiked the girl in the pond . . . or dealt with junk in Kings Cross. Come on, Martin, this is too much already! You've got to make your own decisions, do things because you want them.'

Whereupon I did just that. I got up, lifted her to her feet and kissed her, long and hard. She surrendered slowly, then the kissing went on for a long time.

Then, very gently, she pushed me away and said, 'I wonder what brought that on?'

'I hate scolding women – especially at breakfast.'

'Ah!' She gave me a little crooked smile. 'And I hate to catch a man on the rebound from a wife.'

'What's that supposed to mean?'

'I was in the telex room when the message came in addressed to you. I'm a nosey bitch. I read it. I'd have been angry, too, if it had been addressed to me.'

'So now what?'

'I'd like to even the score and kiss you.' This time the kiss lasted longer, but some of the magic was gone and what was left was a heady mixture of desire and calculation and the bitter-sweet revenges of jealousy. While she was rearranging her hair and putting on fresh lipstick, she gave me another surprise.

'I've decided to come to Bangkok with you. After all, I have a big stake in what's decided between you and my father.'

'Does your father know this?'

'I'll tell him when I telex your new arrival time.'

'And he'll approve?'

'Why should he not? He made me your guardian angel. And I have been an angel, Martin, haven't I? Much more than I wanted to be . . . No! No! No more games. I've got to meet a conference planner from a big insurance group, punctually at nine. But tonight we do have dinner, yes?'

It was only after she had gone that I remembered. Pornsri Rhana was leaving for Bangkok on Saturday. There was only one flight on that day, so it would be impossible for the two women not to meet. I wondered whether I should give them both fair warning. On second thoughts, I decided against it. A little black comedy might enliven the life of Martin the Righteous.

Half an hour later, at the bank, I told Arthur Rebus about the message from Klosters and my decision to leave early for Thailand and afterwards head back to Europe. From the moment of my departure he would be in full charge of the probate decisions, the disposition of all Cassidy's records, with the exception of the microfiches which I was taking with me. He was not a happy man . . .

'. . . The probate is routine. We're well advanced with inventory. My people have checked through the documents annexed to the will and the Australian trust deeds. There's no real problem. The tax people will have to be satisfied, of course, but I don't foresee too many hitches. Cassidy was, after all, a very tidy lawyer. The stuff from the safe is a different matter. There's a stack of gold bars, all the account books, the porno photographs and a miscellany of hot documents. I can see an unholy row brewing between the State and Federal authorities about possession of all that stuff. With Gerry Downs' articles in publication, any leak could bring down the Government. So I'll have to sort out that little mess the best way I know how. It's the situation in Switzerland that concerns me.'

'It bothers the hell out of me, Arthur.'

'Because you think your wife's having an affair?'

'Because she's never done anything like this before. She's always made a big event of getting the kids back to school. Why didn't she call me? Why did she leave it to Clare to send the telex?'

'Perhaps she tried to call but missed you.'

'There were no messages at the hotel. She's meticulous about communications, always has been. Besides, the security aspect is dangerously messy – the kids in England, she in Switzerland. Nothing's happened yet, but if anything blows before I get home, everyone's terribly vulnerable.'

'Perhaps Mr. Marius Melville has persuaded her otherwise: a powerful man, a lifetime friend of her father, connections everywhere. I imagine he could be very persuasive . . . about anything.' He broke off for a moment and then, a trifle uncertainly, broached a new argument. 'I'm more worried about you. You're being forced to rush through a critical confrontation with Marius Melville because you're worried about a domestic situation. You're resentful about it, too, which makes you vulnerable in other ways. I can't help wondering . . .'

'Whether Marius Melville is setting me up.'

'Or simply softening you up. You and I have both done that with legal adversaries. You're quite a prize for any marauder. You've got to expect rough tactics.'

'So what do you advise?'

'Talk to your wife first. I presume she will call as you asked. Suggest, very gently, that there are certain risks and you'd prefer she were home with the children. If she doesn't buy that, don't fight. Arrange to meet her in Zurich. There's a regular Swissair flight from Bangkok.

I've used it several times . . . Old and simple counsel, Martin: never fight over the telephone. One of you is sure to slam down the receiver. Then there's hell to pay afterwards . . . What else can I say? Let's get back to work. We've got a lot to get through today.'

We went to join Sergeant Donohue at the scanner. I told him of my conversation with the Commissioner. He was very offhanded about it.

'Then he'll instruct me in due course. That's his way. I'll get a phone call or a telex or a letter in the daily bag. Relax, Mr. Gregory. The Commissioner works strictly by the book. I'm surprised he gave way on this one . . .'

Ten minutes later, while we were trying to make sense out of a complicated but badly drawn diagram on the banking connections of certain casino owners, Pat called from Switzerland. I asked the switchboard to give me the call in an interview room two doors down the corridor. Pat was composed and cordial.

'Martin! I'm sorry we've been missing each other. You got Clare's telex?'

'I got it. I'm not sure I understand it.'

'It's simple really. I've been working very hard at *langlaufen*. That's –'

'I know what *langlaufen* is, darling.'

'Well then, you'll understand. There's a big competition at the end of this week. My instructor thinks I'm good enough to enter the women's section. I don't expect to win, but I could manage a place . . . I put all this in a letter. Mr. Melville's bringing it out to you in Bangkok. He's been very kind. He's letting me have the house for the extra time. You sound very grumpy. Is something the matter?'

'Yes. I don't like the family being split up at this time. There are certain risks . . .'

'I know. I talked about those with Mr. Melville. He told me he'd have people on watch day and night at the kids' schools and at our house. He says you're very valuable to him and he wants to make things as easy as possible for us all. So I'm not really a neglectful mother, darling. Truly I'm not . . .'

Had I let it lie there, things might, just might, have been different. I didn't. I had to hammer the nail right into the wood. I said, 'Listen, love! I told you from the beginning I didn't want you to accept favours from Marius Melville. You did, so that's water over the dam. But now, any day, I can find myself in an adversary position with him – and you're asking his advice on your life as if I don't exist. It isn't good enough, sweetheart. He's not your husband, I am. At least you owe me the courtesy of a call before you make a decision like this . . .'

Then, with an almighty crash, the heavens fell in.

'Courtesy! My god, Martin Gregory, you're a fine one to talk of courtesy. Did you ask my permission before you started catting around Sydney!'

'What the hell do you mean, catting!'

'You know damn well what I mean, Martin! I was prepared to wear it, because I knew you were working for us and I knew the stress you were under. But not now, Martin . . . not ever again . . .'

And then, as Arthur Rebus had warned, the receiver was slammed down and I had only myself and my ill-humour to blame. Or did I, by Christ? Someone had done a very good job of traducing me to my own wife. It was a real Cassidy ploy – convoluted, paradoxical, full of nasty little ironies – except that Cassidy was dead and buried and the piping of his ghost was getting thinner and thinner. Rebus counselled, as all lawyers do, a cooling-off period. He drafted a telex to Pat and handed it himself to the operator at the bank:

I DO NOT KNOW WHAT YOU HAVE HEARD SO I CANNOT AND WILL NOT DEFEND MYSELF AGAINST ANONYMOUS CALUMNY. I WILL BE PASSING THROUGH ZURICH ON MY WAY

HOME TO LONDON. WILL TELEX YOU AR-
RIVAL TIME AND ASK YOU TO MEET ME. IF
WE CAN MAKE SENSE TO EACH OTHER, LET'S
GO HOME TOGETHER TO OUR CHILDREN. I
LOVE YOU.

MARTIN

I told him I didn't believe it would do much good. Pat
was her father's daughter. Once an idea was fixed in a
Cassidy head you had to use a jackhammer to ream it out.
Rebus did not argue. He sat me down in front of the
scanner and ordered me to concentrate.

'. . . It's your last chance. You have to know the issues
that will be decided by a sale or no-sale of our information
to Marius Melville. You have to guess what more he's
going to ask of you and how you're going to respond.
We've got to discuss worst cases, best cases, all the options
in between – including, very possibly, a bullet in your
head. Are you ready now, Mr. Gregory?'

'I'm ready, Mr. Rebus.'

'Then switch on, Sergeant Donohue, and let's see how
we arrange the rape of the ungodly.'

Half an hour later we struck gold: a whole series of
diagrams of the organisation and shareholdings of Cassidy's trading companies in the Far East. They followed
an identical pattern. One-third share held by a local – like
Pornsri Rhana in Thailand – one-third by Melville through
his Melmar group, one-third by Cassidy through the
Rotdrache trust. Since the local shareholder was always
a Cassidy nominee, the assumption was that policy would
be determined in Cassidy's favour.

These organisation plans were followed by schematic
diagrams, showing the acquisition of products, their distribution and the transmission of funds from their trading
transactions. These diagrams made it clear that Australia,
as a stable, British-style democracy in the South Pacific,
was emerging more and more as a clearing house for

financial transactions, container shipping and bonded air-courier services. Money was washed through under a variety of business names. Goods were held in bond, free from Customs checks, and onforwarded by container ship or aircraft. Given the proliferation of trading in arms, drugs and classified strategic materials, given the shortage of trainee Customs officers and the venality of some local staff, it was an almost foolproof system.

Finally, there was an outline, less easy to follow, of the connection between Cassidy's Far Eastern operations and groups on the mainland United States, in the Bahamas, Europe and the Mediterranean Basin. Sergeant Donohue was hopping with excitement. He was insistent that all the diagrams had to be copied before the briefcase left the country. The schematic material was too valuable to risk. It was, like the Enigma cypher during the war, the key to a huge sector of criminal operations. Once again, it was Arthur Rebus who issued the caveats.

'. . . First question: how much does Marius Melville know about the actual contents of the briefcase?'

'He must know a hell of a lot.' Sergeant Donohue was emphatic about it. 'Otherwise, why would he offer five million for it?'

'If he knows,' said Rebus amiably, 'why pay anything?'

'To remove the thing from circulation.'

'Not good enough, Sergeant. Every villain knows that you buy nothing in a blackmail situation. You can copy anything ad infinitum. What say you, Martin?'

'I'm trying to read what was in Cassidy's mind when he put together this little box of tricks . . . He never did anything simply. His whole career was an elaborate series of moves and counter-moves, designed to confuse his friends as much as his enemies. Laura Larsen was telling me the other day that Cassidy and her father were like brothers. I believed her; but I'm sure it was like the Brotherhood of the South – full of reservations, open always to conflict of interest and the suspicion of treachery.

Cassidy was comfortable with that. He understood it. So my guess is that, in all his dealings with Melville, the information we have in this briefcase was his insurance policy. He let Melville know just enough so that he realised the insurance policy was in force and that Melville might be able to cash it in after Cassidy's death . . . Now I'm not sure that situation obtains any more.'

'Why not?' It was Sergeant Donohue who asked the question.

'Because by now Melville knows we've been in contact with the Federal Police.'

'How would he know that?'

'His daughter has been having me watched. She was able to give me a full account of our movements and contacts in Canberra.'

'So you've got nothing to sell,' said Rebus flatly. 'The material has been exposed. It's worthless.'

'Except that Melville doesn't know what the material is.'

'You think he won't guess?'

'It doesn't matter what he guesses. He doesn't know. He won't know until the material is actually in his hands.'

'Why should it ever get there?' asked Donohue. 'You leave the briefcase here, locked up in the vault of the Banque de Paris. Rebus has access to it. So have we. You go to Bangkok and simply tell Melville, very courteously, that there's no deal.'

'And,' said Arthur Rebus, 'that the briefcase material is compromised. What does he do then?'

'Then he has to present a new deal. I'm still sitting as delegate of a half-billion trust fund which is also the effective owner of one-third of all the Oriental enterprises and has a stake in some of Melville's as well.'

'On the other hand,' said Donohue pleasantly, 'he might decide to take you out – permanently!'

'I don't see what that buys him.'

'An empty space on the board.'

We were just mulling over this pleasant proposition when the telephone rang. The switchgirl asked me to hold for a call from Parliament House. A few moments later, Rafe Loomis came on the line.

'Martin?'

'What can I do for you, Mr. Loomis?'

'You remember our last meeting?'

'I do.'

'My driver drove you to a dinner date.'

'Not exactly. I told you I had a dinner date. Your driver took me back to my hotel. I went out later to keep the date.'

'Whatever you say, Martin. The police would like to talk to you about your date.'

'Why?'

'Best we don't discuss it on the phone. Detective-Inspector Nichols is on his way to see you now. Is it convenient?'

'As it happens, yes. Arthur Rebus, my lawyer, is with me – and Sergeant Donohue of the Federal Police.'

'Oh! Well, in that case . . .'

'Inspector Nichols will be very welcome. Once I know what he wants, I'll give him all the help I can. There's only one problem. I leave tomorrow for Bangkok.'

'I know,' said Rafe Loomis. 'I hope the Inspector will have finished with you by flight time.'

When I put down the phone and told them what Loomis had said, Sergeant Donohue offered the happy thought that this was where the dreck was about to hit the fan. Arthur Rebus regretted that he had not made the handover to Standish and Waring and taken delivery of the share certificate. Donohue then began to debate whether he shouldn't call the Commissioner and seek some direction on the matter. He finally decided against it on the grounds that he couldn't yet define the matter in terms the Commissioner would accept. Which was just as well, because

215

the matter which Detective-Inspector Nichols wanted to discuss was something quite different.

At seven in the morning, a neighbour going to work noticed that the front door of Pornsri Rhana's apartment was ajar. She rang the bell. There was no answer. She pushed open the door and called. Then she went downstairs and asked the doorman to investigate. He found Pornsri lying on the bed. She was heavily bruised on the neck, face and arms. An empty syringe was lying on the floor. The body was cold. She had obviously been dead for at least an hour. All the evidence suggested that she had been forcibly subdued and injected with a massive overdose of narcotics.

My first reaction was numbness. It was as though I had been struck by a bullet and was still walking. Then I felt violently ill. I rushed to the toilet and vomited into the pan. When I came back, the Inspector began his questioning.

'We know from our surveillance reports and from our questioning of Marco Cubeddu that you had contact with the lady. So we'd like to ask you some questions – in private, if possible.'

'Not possible,' said Arthur Rebus quickly. 'My client will respond here and now, in the presence of his solicitor and an officer of the Federal Police.'

'So be it,' said Inspector Nichols wearily. 'Had you in fact met the lady, Mr. Gregory?'

'Yes. On two occasions. The first was on the evening after Charles Cassidy's funeral. She came to my hotel. We had a brief conversation about her connection with the deceased and her involvement with his affairs abroad. The second was on the day of my last meeting with the Attorney-General. I went to her house for dinner and was back at my hotel before midnight.'

'Where were you last night?'

'With me,' said Arthur Rebus. 'We dined at Rosa's in Kings Cross. I dropped him back at his hotel about half an hour after midnight.'

'You didn't go out again?'

'No. I telephoned Klosters in Switzerland. Then I went to bed.'

'Alone?'

'Regrettably, yes.'

'No other communication with the lady other than on the two occasions mentioned?'

'Yes. A telephone call to her house.'

'I was there when the call came through,' said Arthur Rebus. 'I was conferring with her about some documents.'

'This would be when?'

'The night before last.'

'What documents were you conferring about, Mr. Rebus?'

'A share certificate in a Philippines company and the consideration that was to be paid for it. The transaction was being handled through Standish and Waring, who represent the Macupan Pharmaceutical Company in Manila.'

'Was there anything abnormal about that transaction, Mr. Rebus?'

'Quite a lot,' said Rebus. 'And Sergeant Donohue here will be able to communicate it to you. Before we get to it, however, I'd like to establish some groundwork.'

'What sort of groundwork?'

'Are you aware that the deceased was the mistress of the late Premier, Charles Cassidy, and that she had borne him a child?'

'Yes, we were aware of that.'

'It was common knowledge?'

'In certain circles, yes sir. On the whole, though, it was what you might call a discreet situation.'

'You were aware of the fact that she was a major shareholder and director of the Chao Phraya Trading Company, Bangkok? Are you also aware that the Macupan Pharmaceutical Company of Manila is run by Erhardt

217

Möller, a former member of the Painters and Dockers Union, who has heavy form here and big criminal connections abroad?'

The Inspector was uneasy about both questions. He stumbled a little over his answer.

'I'm sure both pieces of information are in my files, Mr. Rebus, but I'll have to check. I've come straight from the scene of the crime to you.'

'Furthermore – and you'll note that all this information is volunteered – Mr. Gregory as executor and I as his local solicitor are engaged to settle Mr. Cassidy's estate. We have still to establish what provisions Cassidy made for his mistress and her daughter – and, indeed, what happens to the girl now. This is one of the reasons which takes Mr. Gregory to Bangkok tomorrow and was taking Miss Rhana there on the same flight.'

'All this is very helpful, sir; but what we're really looking for is a motive for the murder. Can you help us there, Mr. Gregory?'

'Not very much, I'm afraid. From the start, I found myself in an embarrassing situation with the lady. She was the mistress of my wife's father. Her child, therefore, is my wife's half-sister.'

'They could therefore be rival claimants to an estate.'

'Not possible, Inspector,' Arthur Rebus intervened swiftly. 'You'll see that when I demonstrate Cassidy's will and trust deeds, which I am sure Mr. Gregory will want me to do.'

'I can confirm, Inspector, that Miss Rhana told me that Cassidy had made adequate provision for her and for their child. It was he who established her interest in the Chao Phraya Trading Company. I am not yet clear on the details. We were to discuss them in Bangkok.'

'Thank you, gentlemen. This brings me to Sergeant Donohue and this – this abnormal share transaction. What can you tell me about it, Sergeant?'

'Not a lot,' said Donohue cheerfully. 'I'll have to clear

with my Commissioner first. Do you mind if I make a phone call from another office?'

He walked jauntily out of the office, secure in his own righteousness and the protection of his own Service. Inspector Nichols was less happy.

'I might have to take some new instructions myself. I'm not sure you're going to make that plane tomorrow, Mr. Gregory.'

'I'm quite sure he will.' Arthur Rebus was bland as honey. 'You'd have to show cause to hold him and impound his passport. If there were any fear of that I'm sure the Federal Commissioner would have him sworn in immediately as a Special Constable under the Act and pack him off on assignment to Thailand. Besides, I have all the available information, all the relevant documents and Mr. Gregory's power of attorney as well. Never put the frighteners on a good witness, Inspector. You lose him before you get to court. By the way, what arrangements have been made about informing the victim's relatives – her father and her daughter? The father's an important man, a general in the army. The daughter's at school in Switzerland.'

'I'm not sure that anything's been done yet, sir. We only found the body a couple of hours ago.'

'You got here very fast.'

'That was Mr. Loomis. He suggested Mr. Gregory might be our best informant.'

'I was wondering how the report got so quickly to the Attorney-General's office. That's hardly normal, is it?'

'No, sir. But the victim's relationship with Mr. Cassidy put her in a special category – if you know what I mean.'

'Has the press got the story?'

'The place is swarming with 'em . . . reporters, photographers, TV crews . . . Gerry Downs' people are going to have a field day with this one.'

At that moment, Sergeant Donohue came back with an announcement.

'My Commissioner's on the line, Inspector. He'd like to speak to you personally.'

As soon as Nichols had left the room, Donohue said hastily, 'Word from the Commissioner. No transaction took place. No money passed, no diamonds, no drugs. What we were discussing are demands to Mr. Gregory for a handover of substantial funds under pretext of a share transaction. We were investigating the situation, but we hadn't come to any conclusion about it. We let Standish and Waring carry the bag. Clear?'

'Very clear.' Arthur Rebus was frowning now. 'What now becomes even clearer is that Pornsri Rhana was not killed by Möller's people. Her death puts them out of pocket for big money . . . After the pay-off, yes, I might have understood it; but not now.'

'Don't be too sure,' Donohue uttered a respectful warning. 'Mr. Gregory was the real paymaster. This could be a warning to him . . . On the other hand, there is your earlier suggestion, Mr. Rebus . . .'

'Which one, Sergeant?'

'Marius Melville – and an empty seat on the board of Chao Phraya. When it's two seats to one, it doesn't matter to him which of the two falls vacant, does it? Provided he's got the new nominee in his pocket.'

'Which in this case, Melville may have.' The words were out before I had time to weigh them. 'Pornsri told me she and her father were under pressure from someone at the Palace. What if that someone were in league with Marius Melville?'

'Let's dream on that awhile,' said Arthur Rebus hastily. 'The Inspector's coming back.'

Nichols was in pensive mood now. He said, 'The two Commissioners will be talking. I'd better get back to brief my men. Thank you for your help. I look to you to provide all necessary depositions, Mr. Rebus.'

'The moment you ask for them, Inspector. Needless to say, I'll be in constant touch with my client.'

'Good day, gentlemen.'

'And that,' said Sergeant Donohue, 'is the best double-shuffle I've seen. My old man is very quick on his feet.'

'Let's get some coffee,' said Arthur Rebus. 'You look like hell, Martin.'

'I'm scared. It's as simple as that. I'm scared for my wife, my family, myself. What sort of people are we dealing with?'

'Nice people,' said Arthur Rebus. 'People who are photographed at the Black and White ball and get their daughters' weddings in the social columns. People with million-dollar houses and stunning city offices and a private army of thugs and assassins. So let's reason about this killing. Who arranged it – Möller or Marius Melville?'

'Möller had no reason to believe we weren't paying off. We went through all the right motions. Now he doesn't get a cent . . .'

'Which means either way that he goes after Mr. Gregory – or his family.' Thus Donohue, as he walked out to order coffee.

'Can he reach my family, Arthur?'

'These people can reach anywhere, Martin. What's the price of an air ticket and a killer's fee against a kilo of uncut heroin and all that loot from Cassidy's safe? . . . But I don't think we should put Marius Melville out of court, either. His motive is even stronger . . .'

It was only then that I remembered Laura Larsen. I told Rebus I had to ring her. He nodded agreement, but stopped me before I had finished dialling.

'Hold it a moment. It's a rough way to pass bad news. Why not ask her to come round here? It's ten minutes in a taxi. Besides, I'd like to meet her, see how she reacts.'

It made sense. I called the Melmar Marquis. Miss Larsen was in conference with clients and could not be disturbed. I asked to speak with the Duty Manager. He was persuaded, with difficulty, to call Miss Larsen out of her meeting.

I told her: 'I have bad news. I don't want to give it to

221

you over the phone. Can you grab a cab immediately and come to the Banque de Paris? I'm on the third floor, working with Arthur Rebus.'

She didn't argue. She didn't question. She was with us in eleven minutes flat. When I told her of Pornsri's death she went white as chalk. She clasped her hands to stop them trembling. Rebus brought her a mug of coffee and held it to her lips. His bedside manner was impeccable.

'. . . Violence is always a shock when it strikes so close to home . . . We thought it best you should hear the news from friends . . . Sergeant Donohue is dealing with certain aspects of the matter which fall within Commonwealth jurisdiction. The murder itself is a matter for the State police. The chief investigating officer, Detective-Inspector Nichols, has just left . . . The press boys are swarming like bees. We want to protect you and Martin until your flight time tomorrow . . .'

'I can arrange that, at least.' She said it with a sudden surge of determination.

'Did you know,' asked Sergeant Donohue quietly, 'that Pornsri Rhana was a partner with your father and Cassidy in the Chao Phraya Trading Company?'

'I was aware of it, yes. I was not concerned in the activities of the company.' She turned to me. 'If this is going to turn into an interrogation, Martin, I shall need legal representation.'

'That wasn't the intention. I wanted to spare you the shock of a bald announcement on the phone. Sergeant Donohue is not the investigating officer; this is not his jurisdiction. He's interested in certain dealings between Chao Phraya and a company in the Philippines.'

'Then you shouldn't discuss them with me.' She was fully in control of herself now. 'They are my father's affairs. He's in the air now, on the way to Bangkok. There's no way I can contact him. Besides, Martin holds Cassidy's vote . . .'

'Are you sure of that, my dear?' There was a subtle

change in Rebus' attitude. 'It would help us a great deal if you were. We're going through Cassidy's records. We haven't come across that item yet.'

'I . . . I don't know. I just presumed that, as Cassidy's executor . . .'

'Of course.' Rebus was his old bland self again. 'Most natural thing in the world. But you do see that we're all on the brink of a very messy scandal. There's no way now that Cassidy's love affair and his love-child can be kept secret. No way, either, that the press won't call this a drug-related killing.'

'Was the woman an addict?'

'No; but the method is almost ritual for women who fall foul of the drug barons.'

'I repeat. I know nothing of these things. I'm in the hotel business.'

'I'd stick to that,' Sergeant Donohue approved. 'Just keep saying it over and over.'

She gave him a quick, suspicious glare.

'That's an odd thing for a policeman to say.'

'I'm an odd sort of policeman,' said Sergeant Donohue cheerfully.

'I should get back to work,' said Laura Larsen. 'I think you need more protection from the press than I do, Martin. I'll have someone pack your bags and shift them into one of our company suites. Come to my room when you get back. I'll be holding the key. And don't come through the foyer entrance, use the public bar. The front office and the switchboard will inform all callers that you've checked out.' She stood up. 'Thank you all for taking this trouble. It was a kind thought.'

I offered to take her downstairs to find her a taxi. She refused. I obviously had work to do. She would be glad of the walk back to the hotel. Arthur Rebus watched every step of her exit and then nodded his approval.

'That's quite a woman, Martin. I hope to God she's on your side!'

'Now!' said Sergeant Donohue briskly. 'Decision time. Action time. What are you taking to Bangkok, Mr. Gregory?'

'Clothes, personal documents, travellers' cheques. Three items from the file: the access code to the trust and the two sets of the organisation plans we've just been looking at. You'll make your copies here.'

'Good! All the other records will remain here at the bank.'

'Under my authority,' said Arthur Rebus.

'The Commissioner suggests we put 'em under Federal Seal – just in case Inspector Nichols decides to move in with a State warrant.'

'Clever!' said Rebus with genuine admiration. 'But I still want the Commissioner's written agreement on access.'

'You'll get it. Mr. Rebus. Now, Mr. Gregory, you have a pistol licence, but no weapon. Right?'

'Right.'

'Then before you leave this afternoon I'm going to make you a personal gift – a souvenir of this happy occasion. It's a pocket pen and pencil set. Both are lethal weapons and quite illegal – but since you'll be out of our jurisdiction, who's going to know? Next question. What are you going to tell Marius Melville?'

'No sale on Cassidy's records. And I'm taking over Cassidy's interests.'

'And you think he'll buy that story?'

'It isn't a story. This is a power game. How can I play it if I give up the only base I hold?'

'You could leave it to the professionals,' said Arthur Rebus.

'They've done a hell of a job so far! My marriage is poisoned. My kids are under threat. Pornsri is dead. Cassidy's boyos are still trampling all over my life. It's enough. I'm in the game now, for keeps!'

'Nothing we'd want to do to stop you,' said Donohue mildly, 'unless you start playing on our turf; then we grab you by the short and curlies and shove you in the lock-up.'

'And you lose a good lawyer,' said Arthur Rebus. 'However, that being said, I do admire a slugger, don't you, Sergeant!'

'Not much,' said Donohue drily. 'A slugger is usually a bonehead. I prefer a brainy fighter who doesn't get marked up.'

'Suggestions, Sergeant?' I had to ask the question.

'Two, Mr. Gregory. Meet the victim's father. Assuage his grief. Offer help with his granddaughter in Zurich. The Thai set great store by such human gestures. He's a general in the army; he should have high friends. Next, I'd enquire whether Mr. Melville is negotiating to build a hotel in Bangkok. If so, he has to choose a Thai partner. That makes him both friends and enemies. Money talks. You've got enough to buy yourself some beautiful conversation . . . Now, may I suggest we call in Mr. Paul Langlois and see how we can seal up this stuff without discommoding him too much.'

An hour later I was sitting with Arthur Rebus over a very late lunch in Rosa's restaurant. I had eaten little and drunk only a glass of wine, but I felt strangely detached from my surroundings, utterly devoid of any emotion. I asked Rebus if he thought there was anything more I should do before I left. Should I call Marco Cubeddu, talk to Rafe Loomis or the Premier? Should I write my note of protest to Gerry Downs?

'There's nothing, Martin. I'm your other self now – your doppel-ganger. Forget everything here. Go and do what lies ahead of you.'

'It's funny! The night Cassidy died, everything changed – even my wife. It was like the onset of an ice-age, with people and animals and plants freezing into grotesque shapes, and yet I didn't feel anything. It's like that now.'

'You need a woman tonight,' said Rebus, 'a nice, warm, friendly woman, first names only, no questions asked, all laughs and no tears afterwards.'

'I've got a woman, Arthur.'

'I was afraid of that.'

'I'm not. If she's all the things you say, I'll bless her and be grateful. Even if she's not, she's a passport into Marius Melville's domain.'

'And you don't feel badly about that?'

'I told you. I don't feel anything. That's the magic – Cassidy's special malignant magic . . . a spell for all sexes and seasons . . . Cassidy on woman! Now there's a whole book still to be written. "Woman," he used to say, "woman, sonny boy, is a compendium of wonders. The one thing you must never expect her to be is a gentleman!"'

It was nearly six in the evening when I got back to the Melmar Marquis. The public bar was noisy. The foyer was crowded with incoming guests and end-of-day drinkers, men and women, from the neighbouring office blocks. So I was able to move without attracting the attention of the cameramen and reporters waiting by the entrance. As I passed the newsstand, I caught a glimpse of the banner headline, 'Cassidy's Mistress Murdered'. I didn't pause to buy a copy, but hurried across to the elevators and rode up to Laura's room.

My arrival interrupted a telephone call. She gave me a quick kiss, pointed to the drinks and hurried back to the phone. I poured myself a very stiff whiskey and sat down to wait. The conversation with a travel agent seemed to last an age. By the time it was over, all the emotion had drained out of our meeting. Laura poured herself a drink and then perched in the armchair opposite me, kicking off her shoes and tucking her legs beneath her. It was as if she needed to maintain an airspace between us. She said gravely, 'You scare me, Martin. I've never seen any man so angry – not even my father.'

'I don't feel angry.'

'I believe you. That's what makes it so terrible. Did you know this woman very well?'

'Not well at all. I had dinner with her. I found her very

attractive. She asked me for advice and help in her affairs. I promised to look into them . . . I told my wife about her. We had to face the ironic situation that her daughter is my wife's half-sister . . . What gets to me is the sheer, gratuitous inhumanity of the act. Out of the blue, a faceless, nameless someone invades a house and snuffs out a woman's life. They've invaded my life, too . . . Someone's told my wife I've been playing around in Sydney. She's sent our children back to school and is working out her resentments on the ski-slopes. Your father's had his part in that little drama . . . But we're not at the end of it yet. Whoever killed Pornsri Rhana is going to take a crack at me or my family . . . I'm not angry, because I can't afford to be when I step onto the killing ground.'

'Obviously you believe my father's involved in all this.'

'Directly or indirectly, he has to be, because his affairs and Cassidy's are connected, right across the board.'

'So why are you confiding in me? You know I'm his daughter. I've told you I have to stand with him.'

'Because murder has been done. Murder will be done again. I'm near enough to loving you to give you fair warning . . .'

'About my father?'

'About me, Laura. Cassidy trained me in the law. He taught me to love it and respect it as the last bastion against barbarism. Then he turned traitor and sold the gates and now the barbarians are pouring in. So there's nothing left but to throw away the book and pick up the sword – live or die!'

For a long, long moment she sat, with downcast eyes, picking at a thread of fabric on the arm of the chair. Finally, she raised her head and faced me. Her eyes were full of tears but her voice was steady.

'It's sad, Martin. I don't belong to you. You don't belong to me. Tomorrow's a big, big question mark. Surely we can afford to lend each other one night from a lifetime.'

16

Shielded by a screen of Melmar staff, we left the hotel at
eleven, to catch the one o'clock flight to Bangkok. Sergeant
Donohue rode with us. He stood watch over us in the
diplomatic lounge, while an airline officer processed our
tickets and our luggage. When Laura went to the powder-
room, he gave me the address of General Rhana and the
names and telephone numbers of my contacts on the staff
of the Australian Federal Police stationed in Bangkok. He
also gave me a hurried update on the murder.

'. . . It's a dressed-up killing. The post mortem shows
she wasn't spiked but strangled. Now that the press has
put out the drug story, the killer's purpose is served . . .
Our man in Manila has interviewed Erhardt Möller, with
a Filipino officer in attendance. Möller says yes to everything. It was a legitimate share deal. He did telephone
you – no threatening intent, of course. Yes, a quantity of
chemical was involved – a new compound still under test
for the treatment of schizophrenia. It's very scarce and
very costly. A check with our drug companies reveals that
such a product does exist, is available in small quantities
at an exorbitant price . . . One more thing. The share
register of Macupan Pharmaceutical shows the holdings
as follows: one-third Austral Enterprises, Manila – that's
Erhardt Möller and his bunch – one-third Rotdrache and
one-third Melmar Corporation, Manila.'

'So whose shares was Pornsri supposed to be buying?'

'I don't think she was buying shares at all. The stock
certificate has to be phoney paper . . .'

'So why were they calling in funds?'

'Our man says there's a Liberian freighter broken down and waiting for repairs off Luzon. They can't pay the demurrage, so the cargo is up for sale to the highest bidder.'

'What's the cargo?'

'Small arms, grenades, bazookas and anti-personnel mines – and an end-user certificate for – would you believe? – Chile?'

'And who's the highest bidder?'

'Macupan Pharmaceutical. But settlement is fourteen days from now.'

'So why, Sergeant, would they kill off their banker, Pornsri Rhana?'

'I can't answer that yet,' said Donohue with a shrug. 'We set up the skittles and knock 'em down, until one day there's a skittle that nobody can knock down . . .'

Then Laura came back. Our flight was called. Donohue spread his protecting wings over us until we were seated, slap in front of the bulkhead in first class. Then he left us, locked in our capsule to enjoy our last eight hours of privacy.

There was little we could do, except hold hands. There was little left to say after the long night when what we had agreed to lend had become a gift that neither of us wanted ever to take back. Yet we were not desperate any more. We were very quiet, floating on a swift current over which we had no control, which was whirling us inexorably towards a dark, uncharted sea. 'When we arrive,' Laura had said, 'we must be formal with each other. We must be seen to be separate. My father is very astute. He is also very jealous, bred to the notion that the strongest of men is vulnerable through his women. You must make your decisions as if I did not exist, because I shall no longer be the woman you held in your arms last night. Do you understand what I'm saying, Martin?'

Strangely enough, I did understand it. The gift we had

exchanged was a freedom and not a bondage. The sweet sadness of the aftermath was an absolution from whatever might be done when we came, captives to circumstance, into Bangkok.

The first few hours of the flight took us away from the lush coastal fringe and right across the arid heart of the continent. Looking down at the raw earth-colours of the land, furrowed by ancient cataclysms, scored by millennia of wind, and drought, and rare floods that turned it once again into an inland sea, I felt a sudden, piercing pang of loss.

This was my land and I knew it hardly at all. This was my land and I had exiled myself from it, exiled my children from it – for what? A vendetta against a man now discredited as a rogue? A marriage that was already in peril? Hung like the Prophet in his coffin, between heaven and earth, I could see all the follies of my past, all the simple pleasures I had missed. What I could not see, as the desert unrolled itself like a prayer carpet towards the sunset, was the shape of the future – for me, for Pat, for the children. Everything was in confusion now. Everything was at risk.

The steward brought us a menu. Then he brought us drinks and canapés. We toasted each other . . . 'I wish you the best of everything, my love . . .'

'And I you . . .'

I asked, 'Does your father travel with an entourage?'

'Well, I wouldn't call it anything so grand. He has a secretary, a masseur who is also a bodyguard, and that's it.'

'He has no woman friend?'

'Many, but no permanent lover. What makes you ask?'

'I'm trying to build up a picture of the man I'm going to meet.'

'Don't. You'll be creating an illusion. My father is not a simple man, but he works to one simple rule: always tell the truth; you can be sure most people won't believe you.'

'You're saying I should believe him.'

'Believe him, yes. Not necessarily like him or agree with him. I tell you this because I won't be present when you meet. He will insist on a face-to-face encounter, alone in his suite.'

'And what do I insist on?'

'Nothing. You listen. He likes people who listen. You ask questions, if you want. Then you tell him you need time to think. He won't object to that either. But when you come back, he will expect an answer, yea, nay or on specific conditions. He deals all the time with hard men. He despises weak ones . . .'

Then lunch was served and, after lunch, a mindless police film with banging guns and maniac car chases and gutter dialogue. I listened to Mozart on the sound system. Laura dozed, with her head on my shoulder. I felt very tender towards her, grateful beyond words for the liberation of our night together. I felt as if the ice around my heart had suddenly splintered away and I was able to feel again, laugh and cry and lust and be afraid again – for Pat, for my children, for the small white vagrant spirit that was all I had left of Martin the Righteous.

We touched down at Don Muang airport an hour before midnight. The stink of the delta and the fumes of a million trucks and cars lay over the city like a pall. The Thai officials passed us through with a smile. A driver in spotless white, with the insignia of the Oriental Hotel embroidered on his pocket, led us to an air-conditioned Mercedes and, with patriarchal caution, drove us at high speed along the military road into the city where, in the press of buses, taxis, farm trucks, samlors and a whole mobile junkyard of vehicles, he turned into a suicidal maniac.

As we swung into the narrow alleyway that led to the entrance of the hotel, Laura leaned across and kissed me. We clung together for a moment. She told me: 'Father doesn't get up until eight-thirty. I swim every morning at seven. That would be a good time for us to meet. Good luck!'

We walked into the hotel together; but immediately an unspoken protocol separated us. The Duty Manager took charge of Laura and whisked her towards the elevator.

'Your father is waiting for you, Miss Larsen – in the Royal suite. This way please. Your luggage will follow.'

His assistant was only a shade less courtly to me.

'You have the Graham Greene suite, Mr. Gregory. It has a beautiful view right down the river. We hope you'll enjoy your stay with us.'

Let me say it now. The Oriental Hotel, Bangkok, is one of the great hotels of the world – an oasis of civilised comfort in a ramshackle delta city built on mud, hopelessly overpopulated, awash with stinking water in monsoon time, heavy with polluted air in the dry. If you could afford it, you could live and die there and never believe that such squalor existed. I stood on my balcony and looked up and down the river with its firefly traffic of small boats, and across the dark water to the godowns and teak barges on the further shore. The godowns had always been there, since the Chinese came, carrying porcelain and silk to trade for long-grained delta rice, the best in Asia. But behind the godowns, where once Conrad and Maugham and Noël Coward had seen palm groves and paddy fields, now there were the yellow lights of an urban sprawl, so dense that they had filled in the canals to accommodate it. Still, below me in the gardens of the Oriental there were palms and hibiscus and plumeria trees and bird of paradise flowers and small, perfect women who made their Western sisters look large and awkward, like farm horses among the fillies in a race of champions.

The porter arrived with my luggage. A bell-boy came with him to present a peremptory message from Mr. Marius Melville: 'Ten tomorrow morning, in my suite – M.M.' Hard on their heels came a waiter to offer me a welcoming cup – a compound of rum and exotic fruit juices. He was followed by a chambermaid to unpack my clothes and take away any travel-stained linen. At one-thirty in the morning, still wakeful, I was sipping my drink and leafing through an early edition of *Stamboul Train*, when the telephone rang.

'Mr. Gregory.' The voice had a long Queensland drawl. 'This is John Marley, Federal Police. The Commissioner sent us a message about you. Just checking in.'

'That's a kind thought. Thank you.'

'He also said to warn you that Möller has people here. They've got a dive they call an office down in Patpong Road. They send Filipino bands and singers up here – other things, too. If you get any funny calls or messages, please let us know.'

'Happily, Mr. Marley. And thanks again.'

'One thing more. General Rhana knows that you are in Bangkok. He has been told through the Thai Embassy that you wish to pay your respects. He has agreed to receive you. I suggest you call him early in the morning – nineish.'

'Any briefing?'

'His rank says most of it. He's not in the top echelon of the power structure, but he's got a lot of clout just the same.'

'How is he taking his daughter's death?'

'We have no word on that. He's dealt only through the Embassy. He asked for the body to be shipped home and, so far as we know, the granddaughter is remaining at school in Switzerland. If I get anything else I'll let you know . . . Sleep well, Mr. Gregory.'

'You too, Mr. Marley.'

'Fat chance, I'm afraid. The Thai police have just arrested two Sydney girls at the airport. They had two kilos of heroin each. They were going back on the plane you came in on. Silly little bitches never learn . . . My guess is they were just mules making a cover run for something much bigger. But the Thais have got their bust, so they're happy. I'm going to be up all night.'

It was then that I remembered Sergeant Donohue's

parting gift – a pocket pen and a pocket pencil, each of which fired a bullet, lethal at short range. As I laid them side by side on the table, they looked pitifully inadequate. Neither would stop a charging man unless the bullet hit him in the heart or the head. Essentially they were tools for an assassin, not for a man defending his life against assault. Still, they were all I had. I had best be grateful.

Suddenly I felt deathly tired. I put the chain on the door, locked the French windows that opened onto the terrace, asked for a wake-up call, made my last ablutions, tumbled into bed and slept like the dead until the telephone jangled in my ear at six-forty-five.

Laura was at the pool before me, swimming steady laps, breast-stroke, on the sunny side of the water. I dived in and fell into rhythm beside her.

She said, '. . . Father's in a strange mood. He doesn't look well. He says the journey from Zurich exhausted him; but I think it's something more than simple fatigue . . . I told him about the murder. He seemed very distressed. He said it could have profound effects upon his dealings here. He's negotiated to build a new hotel on the far west coast, near Phuket, between Malaysia and Burma. It's a big project that involves feeder air services, from Malaysia as well as Bangkok . . . So he's most sensitive to public and political relations. He wanted to know what I thought of you. I didn't tell him you'd shown Cassidy's documents to the Federal Police. I'm relying on you to do that, as you promised.'

'I'll do it. What else did he ask?'

'He wanted to know how you felt about Cassidy and what effect, if any, his death had had on your marriage. I told him I didn't know, hadn't asked and it wasn't my business anyway. He accepted that; but grumbled that everything was important in business and women never seemed to understand that fact . . . Finally, he got around to the real question: could I work with you in a commercial enterprise?'

'And you told him?'

'I wouldn't know until I tried. Then he asked who I thought would be the boss if we joined forces.'

'And what was your answer to that one, Laura Larsen?'

'I told him we wouldn't know that either, until we had our first fight.'

'In short, he's thinking about an alliance. With me running Cassidy's interest?'

'He's thinking about it. He won't propose it until he's met you and tested you.'

'But you've met me and you've tested me.'

'Only the love, Martin. The rest of you is still a mystery to me . . . You should go in now. Father's terrace overlooks the pool. He'll be stirring shortly.'

Back in my room, I ordered breakfast to be sent up and then telephoned General Rhana. His English was fluent, if exotic, his manner reserved but meticulously polite. I told him I wanted to meet him, offer my condolences and give him whatever information he wanted about my brief association with his daughter. His response was more eager than I expected: he lived quite close, he could be with me in twenty minutes. He was punctual to the minute, a small, dapper man, immaculately tailored, with fine-boned features and sombre dark eyes. He joined his hands and bowed in greeting. He refused coffee, but accepted a glass of mineral water. He acknowledged my sympathies with grave dignity and then prompted me: 'I should like to know, please, who you are, how you became connected with my daughter's life and what you know of her very terrible death.'

I told him everything I knew – which, even as I laid it out for him, seemed pitifully little. He listened carefully, asking only an occasional question; but the questions revealed a precise knowledge of his daughter's affairs, of her relations with Cassidy and with the Melmar interests in Thailand. I ended by offering to visit his granddaughter in Switzerland and providing her with such family support as she would like to accept. Then I waited. He excused himself and went out to pace up and down the terrace. When he came back, I poured him another glass of mineral water and waited again. Finally he managed to set his thoughts to my alien language.

'. . . I believe what you have told me, Mr. Gregory . . . it fits with what I know from my long association with Charles Cassidy and as a director of the Chao Phraya Trading Company . . . He and I got along well together. We were never close friends. What father can be a close friend of his daughter's lover? But I liked him and respected him. He did not think in black and white, as so many westerners do. He understood that what appears to be one colour is a combination of many. He understood that what is good for one man is poison for another. The hill folk will die without the poppy harvest; addicts in other countries die because of it . . . We trade guns to the Chinese war lords in the triangle because we would rather have them as uncertain friends than certain enemies. Our country is a monarchy, modified by the army, modified by an electoral system and a precarious balance of commercial progress and social discontents. Cassidy understood these things. He never drove too hard a bargain. He didn't mind paying squeeze provided he was not squeezed too hard. So, he got the protection he paid for. In the beginning, it was the same with Marius Melville. He let himself be guided by Cassidy. He let my daughter and me deal in our way with our own people . . . Am I explaining myself properly? This is not easy for me.'

I told him he was explaining himself very well. I begged him to continue.

'However, as Cassidy declined in health Mr. Melville changed, little by little. It was not so much a personal thing, you understand. It was all the changes that are taking place right across South-East Asia. The economic balance has shifted. Singapore can no longer compete with Taiwan. China is opening her frontiers to trade and

tourism – and what will all her millions do to the manufac-
turing market and what kind of a consumer market will
they become! Vietnam is now the occupying power in
Kampuchea, so we are threatened on our north-eastern
frontiers . . . Indonesia makes ready for a push into
Papua-New Guinea. Marcos is gone; the Philippines are
in new ferment . . . All these changes, Mr. Gregory, challenge the Americans who control the capital necessary
for adaptation and survival. Mr. Melville represents that
capital – at least, a very special and powerful section of it.
So he is under big pressure. When he acts, it is not with
the subtlety of Cassidy, because he does not control his
own destiny as Cassidy did . . . He is much harsher, much
more demanding. He has found friends here who approve
that, because he has enabled them to shift a large part of
their capital out of Thailand and into the United States . . .
So, Mr. Gregory, Cassidy was your enemy, but you tried
to be a friend to my daughter. I will try to be a friend to
you . . . my daughter was not killed for drugs or money,
but for more complicated reasons. Your police are investigating. I shall make my own enquiries. You may learn
something from Mr. Melville. Whichever of us is the first
to find out the truth will tell the other. Yes?'

'Yes, General. And what happens then?'

'The question is premature, my friend. There is a saying
in the Ramayana . . . "A good hunter never shoots at a
bird-cry. He waits until the bird is in full view." . . .You
have done me a great service, Mr. Gregory. Please call on
me at any time.'

Again, the joined hands and the bow and he was gone.
I looked at my watch. Nine-thirty. I still had half an hour
to spare before my meeting with Marius Melville. I took
out the organisation plans of the Cassidy/Melville enterprise which Donohue had enlarged from the microfiches
and tried to fix them, as visual entities, in my memory. If
Melville and I were going to talk turkey, this was the bird
we would be talking about, a big, plump bird with a lot of

meat on it for the folk at the High Table – and generous pickings for the underlings below the salt.

Cassidy's side of the diagram was clear and simple. All the dividends from all his interests flowed back to the Rotdrache trust in Switzerland. His organisation was vulnerable principally in its local partners – Thai, Korean, Filipino, Taiwanese, Indonesian. Melville's organisation was much less easy to decipher. The lines of communication were much longer. They bent through more cities. Most of them ended in a box called, cryptically, 'Holders unspecified'. Cassidy's empire was smaller, more controllable. I guessed, from my experience of the US fiscal system and the practice of US laywers, that there were many more shifts, stratagems and treacherous byways in the domains which Melville shared with the Honourable Society. I knew in my bones that, once Melville was gone, Laura would have no hope of controlling the ramshackle system. Her safest move would be to get out rich and let the vultures pick the corpse down to the bones. But this was her business and Melville's, not mine. I was as well briefed now as I would ever be. I ran a comb through my hair, straightened my tie, clipped the pen and pencil into my inside breast pocket and rode upstairs to the Royal suite.

The man who met me at the door of the elevator was young, well groomed, hard of eye and muscle and studiously polite.

'You'd be Mr. Gregory. Welcome, sir. I hope you'll forgive me, but I have to search you. It's an inflexible rule, a built-in condition of Mr. Melville's life assurance policies.' He ran expert hands round my body and up and down my legs. 'Thank you for your courtesy. If you'll go straight ahead, sir, Miz Burton will take care of you.'

Miz Burton, a well groomed woman in her late thirties, gave me a dazzling smile and led me into a large chamber walled in tinted glass, with a panoramic view of the delta.

She offered me coffee, which I refused. She apologised profusely because Mr. Melville had been detained by an unexpected call from California. Then she left me to solace myself with a distant glimpse of Wat Arun, the Temple of Dawn, shining in the morning light.

I waited perhaps five minutes, then the doors to the bedroom opened and Marius Melville stepped into the room.

The effect of his sudden presence was strange. The air in the room was charged with electricity, as if a storm was about to break. Yet around the man himself there was an aura of stillness and singular repose. He was tall, lean almost to frailness, but he held himself straight as a guardsman. He must have been well into his sixties; his hair and his imperial beard were snow white. His skin, the colour of old walnut, contrasted vividly with the immaculate whiteness of his tropical suit. His hands and feet were small as a woman's. His eyes were black as jet. His nose was a hawk's beak above a mouth thin and scarlet as a knife-cut. Yet, when he smiled, his whole face lit up and you felt warmed as if by an embrace. He came towards me and held out a welcoming hand.

'Mr. Gregory. A great pleasure to meet you.'

'The pleasure is mutual, Mr. Melville.'

'Please, sit down. We have much to discuss.'

I took a high chair. He sat on the settee, with the coffee table in front of him.

'First, if you will permit me, I should like to thank you for your care of my wife and family in Klosters.'

'Please! It was the least I could do for the daughter of an old and dear friend . . . I always felt sad that he had been estranged so long from his family. As one gets older, one has great need of continuities. But,' he shrugged eloquently, 'our destiny is written on the palms of our hands. Most of us learn too late to read it . . . You are a lawyer, I understand?'

'Yes.'

'And you specialise in corporation law, banking and international tax matters.'

'That's right.'

'Cassidy always spoke very highly of your talents.'

'He was praising his own handiwork.'

'Which he was sometimes disposed to do, eh?' Melville gave a small, good-humoured laugh. I smiled and slid away from the contentious subject.

'Sometimes.'

'Well now, to business, Mr. Gregory. I have an offer on the table: five million dollars for a briefcase full of the microfiche records of the late Charles Cassidy. Are you willing to sell?'

'I'm afraid not.'

He took it quite calmly. He studied the backs of his hands for a moment, then he asked, 'The price is too low, perhaps.'

'The price is not an issue, Mr. Melville. Cassidy left me free to decide on the disposition of the documents. My decision is not to sell them.'

'Then of course I accept that. I confess I am not too surprised. My offer was made when Cassidy first told me he was terminally ill. At that stage he had no means of knowing whether you would accept to be his executor . . . However, there are certain other options which I should like to discuss with you, if you are so disposed.'

'I'm a good listener, Mr. Melville.'

He gave me a swift, appraising glance and a smile that had very little humour in it.

'I believe you are, Mr. Gregory. Yes, I believe you are. Well then . . . Charles Cassidy and I were friends. We were also associated in business and therefore, sometimes, our interests were in conflict. Most of the time we managed to resolve that conflict by friendly negotiation. Occasionally, we had sessions of very hard dealing, in which one of us came out the loser. For this reason, and by mutual and open understanding' . . . He made a large, Latin gesture of opening his heart to me and to the world, 'each of us preserved certain areas of privacy in our business affairs. We did not disclose everything to each other . . . One of the reasons I was prepared to buy Cassidy's records from you for so high a price was precisely that. Once he was dead, there was no one else who could profit from his secrets. Unless . . .' He lapsed into a small, carefully contrived, silence . . . 'unless you yourself decided to take over his interests. He hoped you would. He told me he was going to discuss it with you in London. I presume he did so?'

'He did.'

'And your decision?'

'To take the matter in stages. First, to study the basic documents. Second, to establish the exact relationship between the Melville enterprises and Cassidy's. Third, to ascertain your future intentions and, finally, to decide if, when and how I step into the enterprise.'

'Very prudent,' said Melville drily. 'Very logical and lawyer-like. Cassidy trained you well. No wonder he hated your guts. Now, may I ask to what stage you are now arrived?'

'Stage one is completed. I have studied what Cassidy left me. I have arranged for further research to be done on certain areas of obscurity. Now I am part way through stage two. I have an outline knowledge of the connections between Cassidy and yourself.'

'Would you mind describing them to me – as you see them?'

'Better still, Mr. Melville, let me show you a copy of my diagrams. You will be able to correct any obvious errors.'

I took out the microfiche blowups and laid them in sequence on the table in front of him. He pored over them for nearly a minute, his eyes downcast, his face immobile as a wooden mask. Finally, he put the cards together in a neat stack and handed them back to me with a smile.

'Very good, Mr. Gregory. Acceptably accurate. A few

minor changes would bring them right up to date. I begin
to wonder if you are not almost as formidable as Charlie
himself – a strong ally, a dangerous enemy. So, if you
accept my assurance that you are at the end of stage
two . . .'

'I do.'

'Then I should like to hear your assessment of both
businesses.'

'I'm not an accountant. Even if I were, I do not have
enough figures to make a financial judgment. But in general terms . . .'

'That's what I'm anxious to hear: the general terms.'

'Very well.' I spread the cards again and, using Donohue's pencil as a pointer, began an elementary analysis.
'There's Cassidy – there's Melville. Leaving aside the questions of gross income and net worth, because I know
Cassidy's but I don't know yours, I'd say Cassidy's in a
much sounder position than you.'

'You intrigue me, Mr. Gregory! Please go on.'

'Item one. All Cassidy's income flows back to a single
trust in a secure tax haven. The trust is very rich; so you
can cut off all the trading companies and sink 'em in the
ocean, but the trust remains a solid financial institution in
its own right. I know that for various reasons the companies
are vulnerable, and we should talk about that, but in a
final analysis they are dispensable. Now, let's take you.
Your revenues are not shown as flowing back to a single
source. Just as the lines of control do not lead back to one
institution . . . in short, Mr. Melville, you are a very rich
man but, if my guess is right, you are not your own master.
These people,' I pointed the lethal pencil at the card, 'these
"unspecified holders" could, in the last resort, unite against
you and bring you down. Equally, they and you could
mount an assault against Cassidy's interests and bring those
down. But the core asset would still remain untouched . . .
End of commentary. If I have seemed impertinent you
must forgive me. You did ask.'

'On the contrary, my friend. I find your candour refresh-
ing and your logic sound. I am vulnerable – as vulnerable
as Cassidy when he came to you the night he died and
begged you to take over the administration of his affairs.
I am older than he was; though, thank God, I am in better
health. Still, I am daily aware that I am living on borrowed
time. Like my friend Cassidy, I have a daughter, but no
son . . .' He gave a small dry laugh and made a fluttery
gesture of deprecation. 'God knows why I tell you this,
but in the early days, before you ran off with his daughter,
Cassidy and I used to say that you and Laura would make
a good match. We even made plans to arrange it. Then
she married this fellow Larsen, you and Cassidy became
enemies and all our plans came to nothing. However, in
the weeks since Cassidy's death I have thought that another
kind of alliance might be possible – an alliance of interest
which is often more permanent than marriage. That's your
third point, Mr. Gregory. Where do we both go from here?
I need a man to protect my daughter and her interests.'

'Against Friends of the Friends?'

For the first time, I had touched a nerve. A slow flush
of anger showed under the dark skin. A moment later he
was in control of himself. He said coolly, 'Against the
intrigues normal to every large institution.'

'Before I could make any comment on that, I would
have to know whom I was getting into bed with.'

'In a business sense, of course.'

'Of course.'

'That might be difficult, not to say dangerous. The whole
point about corporate structures is that they create new
legal persons, untainted by history. A corporation cannot
commit adultery. It cannot go to gaol. It cannot be indicted
for murder. All the entities we are talking about –
Cassidy's, mine, the Friends' – are such corporate bodies.
But in the end there has to be a strong man to run them.'

'And what makes you believe I am that man?'

'Cassidy thought you could be. My daughter says you

243

are. Each minute that we talk brings me closer to the same opinion.'

'Then perhaps you will allow me to ask you some questions.'

'Go ahead.'

'Why have you invaded my family life?'

His head came up with a jerk. His mouth tightened into that thin red line. He looked like a snake reared and ready to strike.

'Invaded? That's an ugly word, Mr. Gregory.'

'Ugly things have happened. My family were invited to Switzerland without reference to me. While you were there, someone did a very good job of convincing my wife I was playing around in Sydney. Someone clearly encouraged her to do a little playing of her own and to split the family at a critical time while she remained to take part in some damned amateur ski championships.'

'I don't understand a word of this,' said Melville coldly. 'You insult me, Mr. Gregory.'

'I haven't finished yet. You set your daughter to watch me or have me watched from the moment I left London. The fact that we have become friends as a result of the encounter is no thanks to you. Finally, the day before yesterday, Pornsri Rhana, one of our fellow shareholders in Chao Phraya Trading, was found murdered in her Sydney apartment – and you haven't said one goddamned word about it since I entered this room!'

'And you think I engineered all this.'

'You certainly engineered my family's visit to Klosters and your daughter's surveillance of me. I'd be happy to hear your explanation of the rest of it . . . After all, if we're going to work together we'd better start with a clean deck, hadn't we?'

That surprised him, as I had hoped it might. He stared at me for a long moment, trying to read in my face how much I really knew and how far I was bluffing.

With obvious reluctance, he began to explain himself.

'. . . You know as well as I that Cassidy disapproved of your marriage to his daughter. It was against his wishes; it was against the Church. I don't think he believed too much in God, but, like all the Irish, like all the Sicilians and the Maltese, the Church was where he was born, the Church was where he wanted to die. He used to say to me often: "It's no marriage, Mario. It's a sacrilege. If I could break it up, I would. That way they'd both get a fresh chance; and if Martin decided to marry your daughter – which she'd be free to do, because she was married outside the fold, too – then I'd happily give him the blessing I refused him in the first place!" Do you believe what I'm telling you, Mr. Gregory?'

I shrugged and told him that if it wasn't true it was at least *ben trovato*. I could almost hear Cassidy saying the words.

He went on: '. . . So after Cassidy's death and your departure for Australia, I decided to see for myself how things lay between you and your wife. I was not in Klosters, but I have many friends there. It was simple enough to plant a rumour or two, gossip heard from Australian visitors, a letter displayed at a party . . . It soon became clear that you had parted under strained circumstances, that your wife was uncertain and suggestible. She is also of a certain age, when the attentions of a young and handsome ski instructor are at least flattering. To the best of my knowledge, nothing has happened; but if it had, I should have been very happy to foster a match between you and my daughter. There now! What have I done that is so terrible? If you and your wife still love each other, I have brought you closer together. If you don't – then you are both rich, free and happy . . .'

Once again I was caught, snap-frozen, in that ice-age of irredeemable malice. I couldn't be angry with him. I believed every word he said; about Cassidy, about Pat, about himself. In the same mood of utter detachment, I

245

asked him to give his version of the murder of Pornsri Rhana. He shook his head emphatically.

'For this I have no explanation. She was Cassidy's mistress, Cassidy's choice to run Chao Phraya Trading. She voted with Cassidy on the board of directors. I met her a few times. She was very beautiful, but I have small taste for Thai women. I find them full of sweetness but without fire. However, that is a personal taste . . . Regretfully, Mr. Gregory, I cannot help you.'

'Then perhaps you would be willing to check a line of reasoning that has been put up to me.'

'By whom?'

'By two people – my lawyer and a very experienced police officer.'

'You mean you've been to the police about this?' He seemed genuinely shocked.

'Other way round. The police have been to see me.'

'Of course. Forgive my stupidity. Go on.'

'The police know the woman was Cassidy's mistress. They know she worked for Chao Phraya. They know that company's connection with the pharmaceutical business . . . All this and some more, including the existence of a trust called in German Red Dragon, and the existence of a Melmar subsidiary which holds one-third of the issued stock . . . Now, they come to me and say, "Martin Gregory, you're a lawyer. We're going to read you a scenario and you're going to give us an opinion on it . . ." Here's the story they read me . . . Marius Melville is an international developer with no criminal convictions but a lot of criminal connections. Cassidy was a brilliant crook who managed to stay out of gaol. He has set up a chain of companies in South-East Asia in which Melville controls one-third of the shares. Cassidy's dead, Melville wants to take over. Easiest way is to grab another third of the votes, leaving the Cassidy interest isolated and outvoted . . . You see how they're reasoning, Mr. Melville?'

'I do.' He seemed very calm about it. 'It's called a hypothesis, a "let's suppose", an unproven assumption.'

'I told them the same thing, almost in the same words. But they went a little further.'

'Oh?'

'They suggested that the killing may have been arranged by one Erhardt Möller, an expatriate criminal who is a one-third shareholder in Cassidy's Manila operation. If you had him on your side that would give you control of two companies instead of one . . . That's the police theory, of course.'

'It has one fatal flaw, I'm afraid. The woman's share reverts to her father, General Rhana. How can I possibly get him to sell out?'

'A little more pressure would do it. Pressure from the personage at the Palace who can say yea or nay to your hotel permit, who would love to get his hands on the very substantial reserves of Chao Phraya. Pressure from below – from the police, the customs men and the shipping clerks, who are already putting the bite on . . . That's the reading I got. What do you think of it?'

'Ingenious, but a fairytale.'

'Except for one fact. Möller was waiting for a remittance from Pornsri to buy a cargo of arms under demurrage in Luzon. The remittance was never sent. My lawyer was dealing with it and the police intervened. But some time yesterday Möller bought his cargo. I wonder where he got the money from?'

'You must know,' said Marius Melville softly, 'that you have just committed a dangerous indiscretion.'

'What's indiscreet about it? We're private. We're talking deals. You have to know the kind of partner you'd be getting. I have to know that I'm not in business with a man who's getting so short-sighted he can't see the snipers in the trees . . . Oh, and that's another thing, Mr. Melville. Please never, never meddle in my private life again.'

'Is that a threat?'

'No. It's a polite request.'

'I'm happy to grant it . . . Now, may I take it you are willing to join forces with me to protect our joint interests and, in due course, those of my daughter?'

'I'm willing to discuss such an arrangement; heads of agreement first, details in due course. I have to tell you that's going to involve some disclosures about who controls what on the Melville side . . . There are a lot of nasty diseases about and I want to know whom I'm getting into bed with.'

'I repeat, Mr. Gregory – I'd like to see you bedded and wedded with my daughter. She likes you very much – and she comes with a hell of a dowry!'

'That's a poor joke, Mr. Melville.'

'It wasn't intended as a joke. There'd be fewer divorces if people ran their marriages as a business partnership! May I suggest we meet at five this afternoon to discuss heads of agreement. I'm bidden with Laura to lunch at the Palace . . . Which reminds me: we needn't make a big song and dance over the General's interest in Chao Phraya Trading. I'm sure we can offer a very generous buyout. Why don't you call him and talk to him? You're a very persuasive advocate!'

17

As he walked me courteously to the door, I knew beyond a shadow of a doubt that I had just heard the reading of my own death warrant. The sentence would be executed as soon as a deal had been arranged for the merger of our two interests. My only hope of reprieve was a marriage with Laura Larsen and a formal act of fealty to the code of the Friends which lay behind all the courtly phrases of the dialogue: 'There is no halfway house, Martin Gregory. You are with us or against us. If you are against us, there is no place on the planet where you can feel safe again!'

The only weapon I had – and that would soon be denied me – was time. Marius Melville would not move against me until he was sure I had delivered every scrap of information and provided him with full access to Cassidy's trust funds in the event of my death. That was the code of the Honourable Society: no leaks, no loose ends. Marius Melville would neither report to the Friends nor call in the executioners until he was sure he had a tidy and controllable situation.

That was the real purport of the 'heads of agreement' discussion. My best, my only, hope of survival was to string out that debate as long as possible. Melville would expect no less. I was a hard-headed lawyer, trained by Cassidy. I had been at pains to appear arrogant and all-knowing, absolutely confident of my tenure over Cassidy's trust funds.

So, time! I hurried to my room and set down the crucial figures. In Bangkok it was coming up midday. In Sydney and the other eastern cities of Australia it was three in the afternoon. In London it was six in the morning. In Zurich seven . . .

My first call was to the Commissioner in Canberra. He was out; he was not expected back for two hours. I left a message telling him to expect a fixed-time call from me. Then I called Arthur Rebus. He was in the middle of a clients' conference. I pleaded with his secretary to drag him out of it, by the scruff of the neck if necessary. I gave him a hurried rundown on my conversation with the General and with Marius Melville. He was almost as worried as I was. We discussed moves and strategies and arranged that he would double up on all calls and contacts, in case my own communication system broke down. He uttered one final caution:

'. . . You can't make any agreements without appropriate documents. We're holding everything here. When it comes to the final crunch, tell Melville you'll have me bring them up to Bangkok. I'll arrive with a clerk, who I hope will be lent to me by the Commissioner . . . So keep talking, Martin, and try to keep it as friendly as you can. Good luck!'

Next I called John Marley of the Australian Federal Police in Bangkok and invited him to lunch with me in my suite. Then I called Klosters. My palms were sweating and my mouth was dry as the ringing went on and on. Finally, the housekeeper answered and reluctantly agreed to wake Mrs. Gregory. When she came on the line I talked in a desperate rush of words.

'Listen, darling! I beg you not to hang up on me this time . . . Don't talk, just hear what I have to say. There's been a murder . . . yes, a murder. Your father's mistress, the Thai woman. It happened in Sydney. I'm here in Bangkok to see her father and Marius Melville. It's a long story that I can't tell you now; but this is a time of great danger for everybody – for me, for you, for the children . . . No, I'm not exaggerating; it's a simple, brutal fact. I'm in touch with the Federal Police, but I'm out of their jurisdiction. So are you and the children . . . I want you to pack your bags now. Get a car or a train to Zurich and take the first available plane to London . . . Don't make any farewells, please, please, just go!'

'Martin, if this is some kind of trick to get me home, I'll never forgive you.'

'It's not a trick. You're the one who's been tricked. This is murder – the mother of your half-sister, strangled in her apartment. It wasn't rape, or robbery. It was a cold-blooded criminal conspiracy that began with your father and now touches all our lives. I can't say anything more.

250

I'm here, trying to hold back an avalanche, and I can't do it much longer. Now, will you do as I ask? Whatever you think I've done, whatever you're involved with, don't fight me now. If you don't believe me, think of the kids . . . Now tell me you'll do as I ask!'

There was a long pause, then finally she said, 'All right, Martin. I'll go. When will you be back?'

'As soon as I can. Four, five days at the outside. I have to call into Zurich on the way back.'

'Couldn't I wait for you there? That was your first suggestion, remember.'

'No! Everything's changed. I want you home, with Clare and the children.'

'What has Mr. Melville got to do with all this?'

'Don't ask me. I can't talk about it. And please don't you talk about it either, especially not to the servants there. Just tell them there's a family crisis. Anything . . .'

'Martin?'

'Yes?'

'Do you really care for me any more?'

There was a whole tirade of anger, love and resentment ready to my tongue, but I couldn't utter it. Suddenly I understood how much malignant damage had been done to us both. I said very gently, 'Yes, my love. I care. I care enough to kill for you – and I may have to do it. Now please, pack and go home!'

'I will. I promise. I'm so sorry . . . I'll try to make it up to you.'

After that, I needed a drink. I made myself a long vodka and tonic and sipped it, standing on the terrace, watching the daytime traffic on the swirling brown waters of the Chao Phraya River. Time was when I could have woven a fantasy about every pagoda and every ramshackle go-down. I could have read you the course of the great rice boats and the logging barges and the narrow-gutted vegetable boats with their outboard motors trailing on the end of a long spindle. Not now. All I felt was a sense of utter solitude and alienation, of murderous indifference and the relentless creaking of the wheel of life.

I went inside and called General Rhana. I wanted another meeting as soon as possible. This time he suggested we meet at his house on Soi Kasemsarn, near the old Jim Thompson estate. He would send his car for me at two o'clock and have me back in good time for my meeting with Marius Melville at five. He had come to a conclusion: 'Things begin to make sense – not good, but unhappy sense. I am not content to be pushed from one side to the other like the beads on an abacus . . .'

I wasn't content either. I had to hold his confidence. He was my only conduit into the complex, contradictory market-place of Asia, where now I was an unwilling specu-lator. I had hardly put down the phone when it rang again. Laura was on the line, pleasant but formal.

'Martin, a request from father. Would you mind if he deferred the meeting until tomorrow morning at ten? Apparently the Palace lunch is going to be a long one. The discussions may extend themselves afterwards. After that, he simply must rest. I don't want him to overtax himself.'

'That's fine. I'll be able to spend some time by the pool . . .'

'I may see you there, if we get back early enough.'

'Have a pleasant lunch.'

I had my own lunch date with John Marley of the Federal Police, a gangling fellow in his mid-forties, who looked like an attentuated basset-hound and talked in the long, flat twang of an outback farmer. He turned out to be much brighter than he looked.

'. . . Things you have to know, Mr. Gregory . . . We have no general policing authority in Bangkok. We're part of an international anti-drug force. I couldn't do anything for those two silly girls last night except take information and make sure the Consul-General was informed. So, if you create an affray or get mugged in an alley, it's the Thais who'll deal with you – and none too gently at that.

Next . . . Nothing is simple in Asia. Ethical judgements are based on different premises. Prostitution, the girlie bars, the liquor traffic are concessions run by the army and the police. Nobody talks about that because it comes up as a Human Rights question at United Nations. Drugs? They're a multi-level operation. If you're on the high level, you stay clear and make millions. If you're low-level, you get busted and go down for twenty years – unless you can raise a hefty bail, when they let you skip the country . . . Now, your Möller from the Philippines. He's legitimate here. Import, export, mostly through Chinese houses. Entertainment too – bands, singles, club acts. With those kinds of connections, you can front anything . . . Have you thought where that puts you, if you're acting for the late Mr. Cassidy's interests . . .?'

'I've thought about it. I don't like it. I don't know quite what to do about it.'

Marley popped a spicy shrimp into his mouth and then grimaced as the hot sauce seared his tongue.

'. . . That's our problem, too. How do you pick the grass seeds out of a sack of wheat? How do you tell clean money from dirty in your own wallet? You can't. In a democracy, you have to make a case before you can convict a villain and take him off the streets. You're a lawyer. You know how long that takes. So we concentrate on the possible – which is two silly girls with glassine bags taped round their navels . . . I guess my message is, Mr. Gregory, that on us you shouldn't depend – not for your life, anyway!'

'What can you tell me about General Rhana?'

'Not much. That's Thai politics, out of my line of business. The significant thing is that there's been nothing in the Thai press but a four-line obituary for his daughter. That's bad image, bad luck.'

'Marius Melville?'

'Again, what would I know? Hotel magnate, questionable financial connections; but who gets a look at a bank account in Thailand – even if you could read the damn thing, which I can't. One of the biggest financial institutions in the country is run by the army. So what does that tell you? Where does Cassidy's company fit, Mr. Gregory?'

I had to tell him I didn't know. That simple admission was the measure of my ignorance and naïveté in this intricate international power game. One thing, however, was becoming clearer and clearer: that the simple rules of moral, social and political judgement became quickly obscured. Pragmatic judgments had to be made at short notice. Absolutes were impossible to discern. Relatives were the rule – the possible good, the avoidable evil, the acceptable compromise. All in all, it was an informative but depressing lunch, and I was glad when it was over.

General Rhana was hardly more informative. His residence was a beautiful old Thai house, in the middle of a large compound enclosed by a high brick wall, topped with coils of sharp-bladed anti-personnel wire. The garden was a riot of tropical plants. Big golden carp cruised slowly around the pond. The portals were guarded by gilded demons. Our drinks were presented by kneeling servants. The General himself seemed to be endowed with some antique splendour of authority.

He listened in silence when I told him of my meeting with Marius Melville. Then he began to question me. His manner was quite different: firm, full of power, sceptical as a judge.

'You are convinced, Mr. Gregory, that Melville was responsible for the death of my daughter?'

'I have to be very precise about this, General. You must not put words into my mouth, especially since they are words from another language . . .'

'Please!' He made a small apologetic bow. 'It is important that you be precise. Go on.'

'I believe, though I cannot prove, that Melville conspired in the murder of your daughter. He admits the motive. He wishes to take control of Chao Phraya Trading and the other companies which Cassidy formed throughout South-

East Asia. He has suggested that we buy out your shares and Pornsri's at a very generous figure. I believe also that he wanted to teach me a lesson – that if I stood in the way of his ambition I, too, would be eliminated . . . Life is very cheap to people like him.'

'It has always been cheap in Asia, too,' said the General. 'However, one thing does concern me. You have not at any stage said how you yourself intend to act. Indeed, a few moments ago, when you were talking of buying me out, you used the word "we", as if you and Melville were still acting in concert, singing a duet as it were.'

'I have to maintain that impression with Melville – and indeed I have to maintain my situation of control as Cassidy's nominee, until I can decide what to do.'

'Meantime, what are you advising me to do, Mr. Gregory?'

'I'm advising you to sell your shares – no, let me be exact. I am advising you to say that you will consent to sell, provided the price is right. If Melville plays tricks, I personally will arrange to purchase the shares.'

'Which,' said the General coolly, 'would then put you in control of the company; which might then raise the reasonable question whether you and not Melville arranged my daughter's murder!'

His dark eyes never left my face. I had the absolute conviction that, if I gave him the wrong answer, he himself would have me killed quicker than Marius Melville. I pointed to the phone on his desk.

'Can you dial an international call on that?'

'I can, yes.'

'Then I'm going to give you a number. You will dial it yourself. You will find yourself connected to the Commissioner of the Australian Federal Police in Canberra. I will introduce you. You will ask him any questions you choose to verify my good faith. Here is the number.' I scribbled it on his desk pad and pushed it across to him. He lifted the receiver and dialled. There was the usual pause, then I heard the number ringing and an indistinguishable voice responding.

The General said, 'Mr. Gregory would like to speak with the Commissioner. He is calling from Bangkok.' He handed me the receiver.

When the Commissioner answered, I told him: 'Commissioner, I am with General Rhana. I want you to explain to him as concisely as possible my relations with your department . . . No, you and I can talk at another time.' I handed the receiver to Rhana and waited out a long, one-sided conversation.

Finally, the General put down the receiver. He said quietly, 'I have insulted you, Mr. Gregory. I beg your pardon.'

'There is no insult. You'd the right to prove me out. You have just done so. Now, let me tell you two things. First, you should sell the shares, because it is I and not Melville who is going to take control of those companies and I am either going to purge them of criminal activities or destroy them. That is the bargain which I have made with the Police Commissioner. Second, I am at war with Melville. He has invaded my life, as he has yours. He will not scruple to kill me if it suits him. So this is a war, General. I'm not sure I can win it, but I have to fight it. However, I am not at war with Melville's daughter. She has done me no harm, only good. I want no harm to come to her.'

'Cobras hatch cobras,' said the General flatly.

'You and your daughter engaged with Cassidy in a criminal enterprise. Does this mean your granddaughter must share the responsibility? There has to be some hope of a new beginning.'

He looked at me with something like pity in his dark eyes.

'There is no new beginning, Mr. Gregory, only the slow extinction of desire. For most of us there are many more incarnations, before we arrive at Nirvana . . . Now, let me explain how we should handle this matter. I agree to sell you the Chao Phraya shares. You agree to sell them to the man who really wants them, Melville's friend at the Palace, the one who can clear the way for his hotel project. Two things happen: I am reconciled with a man who could otherwise do me much harm; I am also reasonably rewarded. Melville's project is approved. You are, for the moment, reprieved, because he believes that you have become a willing tool in his hands. After that, there will be much business to discuss, but you must first go home and visit your family . . . The rest you leave to me . . .'

Let me say it plainly, once and for all. I knew exactly what he was proposing and how I had led him to it. I had judged Marius Melville on circumstantial evidence and my own interpretation of it. I had communicated that judgement to a powerful man whose daughter had been murdered. I had exposed Melville to the same threat that he was holding over my head: the tribal executioner, the legendary sacred man who suddenly came and purged out the traitor and disappeared as suddenly into the crowd.

I remembered what Marley had confessed to me of the impotence of the police. I remembered what Arthur Rebus had said of our friend the Commissioner: 'He won't give all his blood to keep you alive. He won't weep too long at your grave.' The conclusion was all too obvious. In outlaw country you look after your own skin, otherwise someone's going to nail it up on the wall of the barn . . . And yet, and yet . . . was not this the whole sum and substance of Cassidy's philosophy: 'the minimum of law, the fullest possible play for the natural forces of society'? What else was General Rhana telling me in his carefully modulated English?

'. . . This is my country. We have never been colonised. We have learned from the "farangi", the foreigners; but we have never been directed by them. So, you ask no questions. You let me handle this business in my own way.

You stay only as long as I tell you. When I say it is time to go home, you go. Understand?'

'I understand, General. But there are people in Bangkok who are connected with the man who arranged your daughter's murder.'

'Who are these people?'

I told him what Marley had passed onto me about Erhardt Möller's office in Patpong Road and my own guess that Möller himself might visit Bangkok.

He made a note on his pad and said grimly, 'If he comes, he will never leave. As for the others, they will find life so uncomfortable, they will have no time at all to think of you. Is there anything else, Mr. Gregory?'

'I am still waiting for your answer on Melville's daughter.'

'He robbed me of mine, Mr. Gregory.'

'One for one, General. It's enough.'

'And if I say it is not?'

'May I borrow a sheet of paper?'

As he fished in the drawer of his desk, I took the lethal pen out of my pocket. When he lifted his head it was pointing at his forehead.

I told him very slowly, 'General, this is a killing weapon. I'm sure you've seen others like it in your military career. I have only to press the trigger mechanism and you are a dead man. This is how much I care that nothing should happen to Laura Larsen.'

He did not flinch. He smiled.

'This is the first time I have been threatened in my own house.'

I put the pen back in my pocket.

'That's the illusion, I'm afraid. We're all under threat, every day. The barbarians are at the gates.'

'Perhaps we are less afraid of them than you are, Mr. Gregory. You have my word . . . no harm will come to the woman.'

'Thank you, General.'

'Let me walk you out to the car.'

In the garden, he plucked a bloom from the frangipani tree and handed it to me. As I inhaled the heavy sweet perfume, he said, 'That's how I remember my daughter best: a little girl sitting by the fishpond, making garlands of flowers . . . I must visit my granddaughter as soon as I can face her without shame. At present she is staying with a relative of mine in our embassy . . . If you would call to see her it would be a great kindness. She knows only that her mother is dead. The circumstances are being kept from her . . . Strange! She and my daughter loved Cassidy so much. I wonder if he knows how much grief he left behind!'

I wanted to tell him that I didn't believe Cassidy gave a hoot in hell. What kept me silent was the unbidden thought that I was living Cassidy's gospel to the letter: 'Never get mad, get even. A man can smile and smile and still be the son-of-a-bitch he wants to be.'

When I got back I was numb with fatigue and half stifled by the lethal smog of the city. I went down to the pool, which was crowded with guests, found myself a lounger on the shady side, ordered a Planter's Punch and settled down to watch the passing beauties: Thai, Chinese, Japanese, American, Australian, Burmese, Indian, and all the flavours in between. The embarrassment of riches overwhelmed me very quickly, because the next thing I remembered was Laura prodding me awake and telling me I was snoring my head off and disturbing the other guests.

I ordered another drink to celebrate her arrival. She talked about the luncheon in one of the dependencies at the Palace and the long tour of inspection on which she had been taken while her father was discussing business with the Air Marshal who was to be his principal associate. Everything seemed to have gone well, although there were one or two crucial questions to be decided. I guessed that I might have the answer to one of them, so I asked the pool steward to bring me a telephone and called Melville in his suite. The masseur answered. I asked if I could interrupt his ministrations long enough to convey some important information to Mr. Melville. When I told him I had seen the General and that he had agreed to sell his and his daughter's shares, Melville gave a small bark of approval.

'Good! Very good! You work like Cassidy. Tic-tac! The matter is settled . . . Did you discuss a price?'

'It wasn't appropriate. I told him, as you had told me, the buy-out would be generous. We should demonstrate that.'

'We shall, we shall! It sounds as though you are talking from the pool.'

'I am.'

'Is Laura with you?'

'She's just arrived. Do you want to speak with her?'

'No. You can pass the message. Tell her I'm calling the Air Marshal now to see if we can arrange a visit to the hotel site tomorrow. That means putting off our meeting; but it seems we're on the same wavelength now, so there's no real hurry, is there? You might care to fly down with us to Phuket . . . Think about it. Talk to Laura.'

When I passed her the message, she gave me a long, questioning look. Then she asked bluntly, 'Am I hearing right? I expected fireworks between you and father. He told me your talk this morning was very abrasive. What's happened to change things?'

'Nothing. I did what I promised: offered to buy out the Rhana shares. The General agreed. That obviously has cleared an obstacle from your father's path. He's happy. For today, I'm his white-haired boy.'

'And tomorrow?'

I looked around. The bathers were drifting away. The seats left and right of us were empty. So I told her the truth.

'Tomorrow or the next day, or the day after, he'll have me killed. Unless, of course . . .'

'Unless what?'

'Unless I dump my wife and family and marry you!'

I knew what she wanted to say: that it was all a paranoid fiction and she didn't, couldn't, wouldn't believe one crazy word of it. Instead, she sat, dumb and dejected, shaking her head from side to side as if to clear away the vestiges of a nightmare.

Finally, she found voice. 'I know at least part of that is true, because he put the same thing to me in a different way. He said: "If you're fond of this Gregory, grab him and take him to bed and keep him happy there. If you can't, the boys are going to drop him off the deep end of the pier, because he's dangerous. Cassidy was dangerous too, but he was dancing to the same music as we were. Not this one! We're in waltz-time, he's doing a barn dance. So see what you can do, like a good girl!"'

'And what did you say?'

'Like a good girl, I said I'd try. I want to keep you alive, Martin.'

'Did your father tell you what he had done with my wife?'

'More than he told you, I think, Martin.'

'Then I want to hear the rest of it.'

'Once he'd got her thoroughly upset with rumours of your fictitious escapades – Pornsri was one of the names mentioned, by the way; I was another; God knows who else was on the list – then he paid a very handsome *ski-meister* to seduce her into a love affair. She was angry enough and enough of her father's daughter to say to hell with you and toss her cap over the windmill.'

'Just like we did – borrowing a little fun out of a lousy lifetime. I can't say I blame her! . . . But, by the living God, I hate your father's guts!'

'How do you think I feel? I used to think there was something wonderful and sacred about being old-country, old-family. Now I know what it really means. I feel like –

like a she-camel, up for barter in the bazaar. Order me another drink, will you? I want to get drunk!'

I couldn't afford her drunk, or talkative, or betrayed by self-pity, so I made her dive into the pool with me and we swam, up and down, until the anger in us both was damped to a dull glow. Then we made a pact of silence – our own *omertà* – and sealed it with a long and very public kiss under the frangipani trees.

I hoped Marius Melville saw the kiss from his eyrie in the Royal suite. I hoped and prayed that what I had learned of his daughter in bed was the truth and that I could trust her to play out her part of our comedy of surrender, even though she didn't know the end of it, and my guess was a mile wide of the mark.

My first act when I got back to my room was to call General Rhana. My next was to have the concierge book me a limousine and a reliable driver. Then I telephoned Melville's suite and, with old-country formality, asked permission to take his daughter out for the evening. He consented, with old-country grace.

So, in mutual desperation, we hit every night spot in town and I delivered her back to the Royal suite at four in the morning. If that meant anything to Mr. Marius Melville, it had to mean that I was family now – that I belonged to him, body, soul and breeches.

Our night's carouse was a mistake. At seven I was wakened by a call from Melville's masseur. We would leave at nine for the military airfield at Don Muang. He would be down at seven-thirty to help me to recovery. I told him to go to hell. I would recover in my own time. By eight I was regretting my refusal of a healing service. By nine, hidden behind dark glasses, primed with a litre of black coffee, bilious with resentment, I was downstairs waiting for Laura and Marius Melville.

As we climbed into the big limousine, Laura and her father sitting together in the rear seat, I perched on the jump seat, Laura made a theatrical virtue of fragility and announced: 'My God, Martin, I'm sorry! Father's just impossible! He insisted we both come along on this god-damned excursion. I don't know why he needs us, for Christ's sake! Half the Thai army and air force and Cabinet seem to be invited, not to mention the press . . . Three military jets. I've told him there's no way you and I are going with his party. We're going where the drinks are and we don't have to talk politics or money.'

Melville listened to her tirade with amused tolerance. He seemed happier to have me as courting lover for his daughter than a sour-faced lawyer with a chip on his shoulder. However, he was too good a businessman to pass up a chance in the money-market.

'. . . It wouldn't hurt, Martin, to plant the information that you're in the banking business in London and that you have access to the Rotdrache trust. We've got a lot of our friends' money in this project, but a London cachet never hurts – or a Swiss one, either. I'll mention it to the Air Marshal and . . .'

I thought it was time to call a halt and let him know that I wasn't yet wholly shackled to his interests.

'You're pushing me, Mario! Don't do that! I took your daughter out on the town last night. I'm in no shape to talk money with the armed forces' bank. That way, you and I will both get screwed. You carry on with your programme. Laura and I will tag along with the press and stay out of sight until we've recovered.'

He didn't like it, but he bought it. After all, I had made the whole thing possible and, in spite of his irritation, he had put up with this pair of casualties. He even praised my usefulness.

'. . . Everything fell into place the moment I told the Air Marshal he could have the company shares. I'd better tell you we're selling them to him at market value and I'm picking up the difference myself. Even if we pay double the market price to Rhana, it's a good deal . . . It also heals a long-standing breach between him and the Air

Marshal. So we get ourselves two friends in the high echelons of the armed forces. Rhana's been invited to come along today. He won't be travelling with the Air Marshal and me, so perhaps you and Laura wouldn't mind looking after him.'

To which Laura, not unreasonably, made answer that if we survived the run to the airport and an hour's flight to Phuket and ninety degrees of heat and a Thai luncheon, we might – just might – be able to spare a thought for General Rhana.

Melville, flushed with yet another victory, laughed and patted her hand and urged me: 'You have to work on her, Martin. She has so much to learn about this financial world of ours.'

Then he launched himself into a lecture on the Palace and its hierarchies and all the whirlpool currents that coursed about the throne, as the great-grandchildren of the Chulalongkorn dynasty still jockeyed for preferment and influence.

'. . . This is the sort of thing you have to learn, Martin. Cassidy and I absorbed it with our mother's milk. We never escape our past. It is mirrored in our present. It repeats itself in our future. Those who understand that will be the new oligarchs. Those who ignore it will be swept away in the wreckage . . .'

'Father dear,' said Laura desperately, 'you are becoming a bore. It's too early, and too hot. Be grateful that I'm your daughter and Martin is too polite to quarrel with you. Cassidy wouldn't have stood this for two minutes.'

'I've thought often,' said Melville. 'We should dedicate a memorial to Cassidy . . . Nothing grandiose. He would have hated that. A bust, perhaps – or, even better, a priapic figure with a real goat's grin! – where people could come and leave their complaints and their satires as they do on Pasquino in Rome.'

For a moment, I lost control and let the truth slip out.

'I'd be happy to subsidise the priapic figure. It would be the perfect answer for Charles Parnell Cassidy.'

It was admittedly an arcane joke for a smoggy morning in Bangkok and it hung in the air for a long moment. Laura got it first and burst into immoderate laughter. Melville caught it just before it fell to earth and was not amused. He told me so curtly.

'Cassidy was my dear friend.'

'He was my sworn enemy. That's a difference you have to wear.'

Instantly the knife was out, thumb on the blade and striking upwards.

'He was once my daughter's lover also.'

'Stop it, Father!'

'Take it easy, Laura. I'll deal with this.' Suddenly I was talking like a husband and the illusion I had sought to create was almost complete. 'I told you yesterday, Melville, never again to interfere in my private life. You're doing it now. You're putting horns on me before I'm even betrothed to your daughter. I won't stand for it, not now, not ever.'

'And what the hell do you think you can do about it, Mr. Martin Gregory?'

Very slowly, I reached into my jacket pocket, brought out the pencil, pointed it into the upholstery of the seat an inch from his head and pressed the release. There was a crack like a snapping pencil, a puff of vapour and a neat round hole appeared in the fabric. Laura gave a stifled cry. Melville's thin body contracted in a spasm of fear. Behind his plate-glass screen, the driver heard nothing. Finally, Melville managed to find the words he needed to patch up his pride.

'It seems I have not too much to teach you, Martin Gregory.'

'It seems all you have to learn, Mr. Melville, are better manners.'

He did not answer me, but addressed the question to

Laura: 'Are you sure, my dear, you want this dangerous man? If you don't, I can always dispose of him.'

'I would like to keep you both,' said Laura, and – God bless her heart! – the fiction was complete. Melville reached out and drew me into a paternal embrace. He kissed me on both cheeks and muttered what might have been an apology. I was happy he didn't kiss me on the lips. It seemed my death was to be deferred, at least for a little while.

In the military area of the Don Muang airport, there were three executive jets drawn up on the tarmac. Inside the air-conditioned staff room, tea, coffee and iced drinks were being dispensed to a small army of dignitaries and guests. There were the Air Marshal and his staff, members of the Palace household, the chief architect, the chief engineer, the contractor, a couple of bankers, a gaggle of people with clipboards, the air crews, a small contingent of press and, slightly separate and a trifle forlorn, General Rhana and his aide-de-camp. He gave us a brief, formal greeting and then stood aside while we were presented to the others in descending order of magnitude.

Mindful of the role we had agreed to play, Laura and I behaved like lovers, anxious to be together. In spite of the protest I had made in the car, Melville still tried to manoeuvre me into discussions with the Air Marshal.

'. . . Mr. Gregory is senior counsel to an important banking group in London. He could be a strong ally in our projects here . . .'

The Air Marshal was properly impressed and anxious to talk, but I begged off. I never liked to talk without an adequate briefing. Naturally, the project would merit serious consideration. Given Mr. Melville's connection, it would be given priority in the discussion of my bank and of the Rotdrache trustees . . . Meantime, I was squiring a beautiful woman. We had both had a very late night. The Air Marshal would surely understand . . .

He did. He assured me he, too, had once been young

and devoted to women. Now he was no longer young but still devoted. I laughed dutifully and he waved me away and devoted himself to serious talk with Melville and the Palace people.

Laura and I fell into talk with our pilot, a handsome young man, nephew of the Air Marshal, who had trained with the US Air Force and was obviously slated for a brilliant career under his uncle's patronage. He showed us our route on the chart: down the river to the Gulf of Thailand, then south by east over Hua Hin, along the Burmese border to Ranong, then down the shore of the Andaman Sea to the island of Phuket. We would be there in an hour, drive to the site, have lunch with the air force and be back in Bangkok for cocktails and dinner.

It was just after ten-thirty when we were called for boarding; the Air Marshal, the Palace people and Marius Melville in the lead aircraft, the General and the minor functionaries in the second, Laura and I happily tucked in with the junior officers and the press men. Five minutes later we were airborne, climbing in wide spirals eastwards, in the wake of the Air Marshal's plane, then levelling out for the sweep over the lower reaches of the river, the paddies and salt-pans of the delta, and the beaches of the eastern gulf.

The pilot did his best with a dutiful commentary on the route; but I dozed through most of it while Laura, with intermittent groans, nursed a canned Bloody Mary and a hangover headache. We were about two hundred miles south of Bangkok, just skirting the bulge of the Burma border, when it happened.

The pilot yelled and banked steeply to the left. We felt a single, sudden jolt as though we had hit an air pocket, then the aircraft levelled out and we saw far below us a fireball and a scatter of debris tumbling down towards the grey sea. We were all silent, listening to the hurried chatter from the open cockpit.

Then the pilot announced shakily, first in Thai and then

in English: 'Ladies and gentlemen. An accident has taken place. The Air Marshal's plane has blown up in mid-air. There is nothing we can do. I am ordered to return to base.'

Laura gave a single choked cry and hid her face against my breast like a terrified animal. I held her there all the way back to Bangkok. I felt the silent sobs that racked her; I felt the pulse racing in her white throat; apart from that, I felt nothing.

18

'Bite your tongue,' said Arthur Rebus, in his crisp, no-nonsense fashion. 'Comfort the lady and, for Christ's sake, stop scratching your conscience or it will never get better. I'll be with you at midnight tomorrow, Bangkok time. Send a car to meet me at the airport. Don't bother to wait up. I'll come to your room for breakfast . . .'

I was calling him from my bedroom. General Rhana was waiting in the sitting-room reading the headline reports of yesterday's accident. Laura, heavily sedated, was asleep in the Royal suite, with the masseur and Miz Burton keeping vigil. Arthur Rebus was still talking.

'Have you spoken with your wife?'

'Yes. She's home, as promised.'

'How does she sound?'

'Not hostile. Very subdued.'

'That's hopeful.'

'I'm not sure I know how to handle it from here, Arthur.'

'I've just told you. Bite your tongue and forget about rights and wrongs.'

'Easy to say.'

'If it works, you've got a lot of life ahead of you. If it doesn't, call it quits and go live happily apart on Cassidy's legacy. Don't argue the case. You'll end up with a mouthful of ashes . . . By the way, Loomis sends his love.'

'What do I do now? Go dance in the streets?'

'He also sends a suggestion. If you want to contest Cassidy's seat at the by-election, you've still got time to nominate. He'd almost guarantee preselection.'

'Not interested.'

'Why not? Do you want to be an expatriate all your life?'

'I wouldn't want to end up like Cassidy.'

'Cassidy made one big mistake – he never got the gall out of his system.'

'Drop it, Arthur, please!'

'Just as you like. Don't forget the car. See you!'

I put down the receiver and went in to see the General. He folded the newspaper carefully and then announced with equal care: 'I came to offer my profound sympathies to Miss Larsen and to yourself. A terrible affair. It robs her of a father. It robs the country of one of our most brilliant military men. Not to mention the other distinguished citizens.'

I thanked him and told him I would convey his sympathies to Laura, who was still in shock and under medical care. Then he reminded me of my promise.

'You did say, Mr. Gregory, that you would stand behind the share purchase offered by the late Mr. Melville.'

'I did, General, and I shall be happy to honour that promise. However, I should like you to consider another suggestion. I have decided to dispose of all the Cassidy interests in Chao Phraya Trading and eventually in all other South-East Asia trading companies. I am advising Miss Larsen to do the same with the Melville interests. It is clear that these enterprises are best managed by indigenous shareholders. As you know, all of them are very profitable – and all of them could do with some drastic housecleaning to purge out criminal activity. So, if you are interested, I should be prepared to offer you all our shares at book value. You could buy them on margin and pay for them over a period of, say, five years, out of the profits of the company . . .'

He thought about that for a while, then he smiled.

'It could be interesting, Mr. Gregory. Yes, very interesting indeed. I may need a little time to consider, and then to put the funds together but, in principle, yes, I should like to begin a negotiation.'

'My lawyer arrives from Sydney tomorrow night. I can put the two of you together and let you work out a deal. You don't need me here for that. I hope to leave on Monday. I have to call into Zurich on the way. Would you like me to visit your granddaughter?'

'It is a kind offer, Mr. Gregory; but in all the circumstances I think it might be better to keep the two families separate. So much water has flowed under the bridges and children love to ferret out mysteries. I'm sure you understand what I mean.'

'Perfectly, General. By the way, will there be an inquiry into the accident?'

'Oh yes, a big one. Our navy is dredging and diving for wreckage. Our aviation experts will be examining every scrap of evidence . . . but it is hard to say what they will conclude. We are not as expert in these things as the Americans or the Europeans. On the other hand, we are not obliged, as they are, to make constant announcements to the press. So, yes an inquiry; but little hope of a conclusive finding. I saw it happen. The aircraft just blew apart in the air.'

'Sabotage?'

'Possibly. We have a small but active cadre of dissidents, mostly of the far Left; but their usual trade is banditry, not sophisticated operations such as this would have had to be. My own view is that the accident was due to some simple but fatal defect or oversight in maintenance. Anyway, it is done. I have been summoned to the conference of the General Staff to discuss new appointments. A way has been opened now for my long-delayed advancement . . . What does the proverb say, Mr. Gregory? "When one man dies, there is always another left smiling" . . . Please call me when your lawyer is free. I look forward to a talk with him.'

When he had gone, I made my way upstairs to check on Laura. She was awake but still drowsy with the sedatives. I sat down on the side of the bed and combed back the hair from her face. She reached out to touch my cheek.

'What am I going to do, Martin?'

'I'm going to suggest you go back to Sydney and pick up your work at the Melmar. It will give you a base and an activity while your father's estate is being sorted out. Arthur Rebus will be here tomorrow. If you like and trust him as I do, I'd recommend you appoint him your attorney of record and let him handle things on your behalf. He's astute and he doesn't frighten easily. My guess is he'll create an enclave of interest that none of your father's associates can invade.'

'I wish you could be with me too.'

'I can't. You know that; but if you want me to act for you in London, or recommend people there, I'll do it gladly.'

'Thank you. Do you love me, Martin?'

'Yes, I do.'

'I love you too. So why didn't it work for us? Why didn't we just toss everything away and run for the hills? We could have, you know.'

'We couldn't. Let's not kid ourselves. There was too much history to cope with.'

She nodded sleepily.

'Too much old-country. Too many old feuds to poison things. I never knew how much hate was in my father until

271

I found out what he had done to you. If you'd killed him in the car, it would have been easy to forgive you.'

This was getting too close to a grimmer truth. I closed her lips with my fingertips and played the old game that I had played with my children: 'I'm pulling the curtains over your eyes.' She asked me what time it was. I told her it was nearly midday. I would come again to see her after lunch.

'Can I sleep in your room tonight? I'm frightened here.'

'Of course you can. We'll dine there. At sleep-time, I'll give you your tablets and tuck you in.'

I waited a few moments longer and then tiptoed out. Miz Burton held me at the door to ask what plans were being made for the staff. I told her she and the masseur could probably leave for home whenever they wished. If they needed funds, I could draw against Melmar's holdings in Chao Phraya. She asked what was happening with Laura. I told her she would probably return to Sydney. Miz Burton looked at me as if I were a weevil in a biscuit. She said, 'I don't understand you, Mr. Gregory. I don't understand you at all. The girl's head over heels in love with you . . . Still, it's none of my business.'

I agreed it wasn't and decided that it was time to take a swim and watch the fillies by the pool. It was a lot less dangerous than falling half way in love or trying to stop a once-good marriage falling apart.

That night was the last time Laura and I slept together. It was a strange loving; quiet, tender, almost passionless, yet deeply comforting to us both. In one of the long, wakeful moments between midnight and dawn, Laura said, 'Martin, I want to give you some advice.'

'About what?'

'When you get home, you must take your wife to the bedroom and tell her, very quietly and very lovingly, that there are no questions, no explanations. Yesterday is dead. There's only today and tomorrow and you want to share them with her. That's all you say. Then you take her in your arms and make love to her in the best way you ever made it together.'

'It sounds great – but what if she doesn't want it like that? What if she says no, she hates me and doesn't want me to touch her ever again?'

'She won't.'

'How can you be so sure?'

'Because I know how I'd feel if I'd jumped over the broomstick with a young lover and then found I'd been set up to alienate my husband and farm him off to another woman. I'd feel shamed and small and dirty like a raga-muffin on a street corner. I'd want to explain, but I couldn't; no words would make any sense. I'd be willing to abase myself before my husband, but that wouldn't help either, because I wouldn't be his mate any more, but a bond-woman working out a debt . . . You have to trust me, Martin. This is love talking . . . And, for God's sake, I'm giving you back to another woman!'

'I do trust you, my love. It's Martin Gregory I can't rely on.'

'Martin Gregory's fine. He just got himself lost for a while chasing after Charlie Cassidy's ghost.'

Once again, my hasty tongue almost betrayed me. I wanted to ask what Cassidy had meant to her and how he had been as lover and whether she had any caring left for him. I wanted to tell her that it was I, the man with clean hands, who had compassed her father's death. I wanted to know whether then she could find it in her heart to forgive me. I didn't ask, thank God. I drew her close and cradled her in the crook of my arm and wondered how I could ever endure to be without her. But, when morning came, she was better. There was colour in her cheeks and a new light in her eyes and she demanded to be taken shopping for silks and rubies and a princess ring and all the shopworn novelties of the curio shops.

After that, she made me buy her lunch on the garden terrace so that we could watch the river traffic while we ate. Then we found a space at the poolside and swam and sunbathed and drank rum punches until the evening wind came searching down the river with a flurry of rain in front of it.

That night she slept alone in the Royal suite. I sat late in the downstairs bar, talked to a pair of business girls from Manhattan who offered to make up a threesome for five hundred *bahts* each. It seemed an expensive piece of nonsense when, two blocks away, there were brothels stacked three floors high with women. So, I sat out in the foyer waiting for Arthur Rebus to arrive.

He was good for us both. His dry, crusty humour made us laugh and cut our giant fears down to human size. Laura liked him. She respected his cool business judgment. She agreed to his suggestion that she resume work and let him act for her with her father's attorneys.

He had good news for me, too: the probate application in Cassidy's Australian estate was proving simpler than he had expected. The files were in order, the schedules accurate, due taxes had been paid. He also managed to teach the General a few lessons in the art of genteel haggling. After only three hours of discussion, a book value on the shares had been settled, a transfer date set, and the General had agreed to a three-year payment period at a handsome rate of interest. Which all went to prove, as Rebus succinctly phrased it: 'The joint stock company was designed by gentlemen to fleece the suckers in all languages, and nobody understands it better than the British or runs it closer to the line than the Australians.'

He told us that the Chinese Government had invited him to Beijing to teach a seminar in British corporate law and he thought he might accept, 'before the Americans get in and plant too many heretical principles'. He thought, too, he might work out a strategy for disposing of the other Cassidy instruments at a handy profit to the trust. By the end of his three-day sojourn he and Laura were warming to each other, while I was beginning to feel a few pangs of jealousy.

When the time came, we rode together to the airport; they to take the Thai flight to Sydney, I to fly Swissair as far as Zurich. Our farewells were strangely anticlimactic.

Arthur Rebus said, 'I'll call you each week to report progress. Think about coming home. There's work to be done there. Good luck on the domestic front and, remember, bite your tongue!'

Laura held me for one last, precious moment and whispered, 'The doors are closed, remember? Lock them and throw away the key.'

Then she kissed me and turned away. Arthur Rebus took her arm and led her off to what was grandiosely called 'The Captain's Lounge'. I had to accost three giggling girls before I discovered that first-class passengers on Swissair took pot luck in the public waiting-room, where the air-conditioning had broken down.

I landed in Zurich at seven o'clock on a morning of driving sleet and slushy pavements. I went straight to the offices of Horstman and Preysing, who turned out to be two youngish gentlemen, very starchy, very correct and singularly unimpressed by the amount of money of which they were custodians.

They received me with impersonal courtesy. They asked to see my passport and my driver's licence. They confirmed that I was indeed their lawful delegate in the Rotdrache trust and that I did indeed have access and operating rights over the trust funds. Then they demonstrated the trust deed and I learned for the first time that the beneficiaries were . . .

'Any institute, society or foundation having as its aim works of charity, social betterment, the redress of injustice or inequity, which, in the opinion of the trustees and/ or their lawful delegate or delegates from time to time appointed, shall merit the support of the trust, save only that if at any time during the life of the trust Martin

Gregory shall divorce his wife Patricia Anne Gregory (née Cassidy) and shall marry, lawfully and according to the canons and rites of the Roman Catholic Church, Laura Lucia Larsen (née Melville or Melitense) the said Martin Gregory and the said Laura Lucia Larsen shall become joint and unconditional beneficiaries, with reversion of benefits to their offspring *per stirpes* . . . Should the trust determine before such marriage takes place, all the assets of the trust shall devolve to the Roman Catholic Archbishop of Sydney, to be used in his absolute discretion for the promotion of the Roman Catholic Faith in the Commonwealth of Australia.'

I folded the deed and handed it back. Mr. Horstman coughed and said, 'It is, of course, an unusual document, not the sort of thing we would recommend for our clients; but Mr. Cassidy was, as you know, an unusual man.' Mr. Preysing added a small rider: 'It is our view that the trust is open to challenge, since it constitutes a direct provocation to disrupt a stable and legal union in which children are involved. So, if you would like us to examine this aspect for you . . .'

'Thank you, no. I don't want Charlie's money; and I'd hate to think I'd deprived him of his passport to heaven. I'll help you to run the damn thing, of course, and we'll see if we can't do some good with the funds.'

'On that point,' Mr. Horstman coughed again, 'we are directed to hand you a personal communication from the late Mr. Cassidy. He wished us to deliver it on the day you assumed your duties as our delegate.'

It was a holograph note in Cassidy's emphatic script. It was dated a month before his final visit to London. It said:

Dear Martin,

See what you missed? Of course, being Martin the Righteous, you'll tell yourself you wouldn't touch dirty money with a forty-foot pole; but you'll happily play Lord Bountiful and dispense it to the poor and needy.

So, I'm giving you fair warning. There are more con-men in the charity business than there are in politics. When you take over, I'll be up there – or down there, depending on which cosmogony you use – enjoying every minute of your discomfiture, as you try to sort out the sheep from the goats.

It's the nearest I can get to a no-win situation for you, sonny boy; because you sure as hell made one for me and I'll never be able to get out of it.

The back of my hand to you!

Cassidy

I tore the note slowly into little pieces. Mr. Preysing handed me the wastepaper bin and a deadpan comment with it.

'We do have a shredder, Mr. Gregory; but sometimes one does need the satisfaction of a really destructive act. Is that not a fact?'

I agreed that it was. The problem was that my act and Cassidy's had been irrevocable and continuous, a plague of malice let loose upon our little worlds, spreading out like windblown spores across the frontiers. It was time – long past time – to call a halt once and for all.

I bade a hasty farewell to Horstman and Preysing, flagged a taxi on the Bahnhofstrasse and made it to the airport just in time to catch the midday flight to London. The moment I cleared immigration and Customs, I was in a flat panic. I dared not go home. Pat wasn't expecting me until the next day. I had forgotten to call from Zurich. The children would not be out of school until next evening. I feared I might lose all control the moment Pat opened the door.

So, I took a taxi into London, intending to go to my office, dump my briefcase, orient myself a little and then head for home. Instead, just as we were coming up to the Natural History Museum, I had a sudden, unexplainable impulse. I told the driver to turn into Exhibition Road, take me round Hyde Park and then to the Jesuit Church at Mount Street.

When we got there, I asked him to wait. When he demurred, I offered him a run back to Richmond and a ten-pound tip on top of his meter fare. A true-blue Cockney, he had his grumble first and then agreed to wait. He did, however, offer me a piece of theological advice: 'You don't have to hang around, you know. If God knows everything, you don't have to give him a big spiel about the price of fish, do you?'

It was still early in the afternoon, but the church was dim and cheerless in the winter light. I knelt in the last pew, where Cassidy and I had sat on the night of his first and last supper in our house, the night he killed himself in my car, the night our marriage began to turn sour.

He had soured a lot of things for me before then. I could not believe that the Church Cassidy belonged to, the one he helped to run, hand-in-glove with the Cardinal, was the one I believed in. I couldn't believe that the wrongs of Ireland were the only wrongs in the world, and that marriage was made in heaven only if you said the right words in the right place in front of the right minister – and you were damned for ever if you got the formula wrong. So I quit; we all quit, because I wouldn't accept that Cassidy and his ilk had somehow pre-empted the Keys of the Kingdom.

But then I remembered the look of him on that last night – the yellow skin, the sunken eyes, the backside too bony to sit on. When I remembered his wry gesture of resignation – 'One of the Almighty's little jokes . . . It's small comfort He's offering' – I was ashamed of my graceless and grudging hospitality, my stubborn insistence on an amends that he was incapable of making. I hoped that his Maker had given him a warmer welcome than I on that bleak winter's night that seemed an age ago and yet was scarcely a month away. Suddenly, my eyes were prickling with unbidden tears – for him, for me, for Pat, for Laura and my children whose faces I had almost forgotten.

There was a light burning over one of the confessional boxes, indicating that a priest was in attendance, offering a shriving to any who needed it. I felt a sudden urge to unburden myself; but I stayed anchored in my place. What words had I left? How could I tell so long and complicated a tale to a stranger? How could I explain the blood on my hands and the scars of old battles on my flesh?

General Rhana had no such problems. He could blow a plane full of people out of the air and then sit down calmly and haggle over a share deal. Marius Melville had none either. He and his kind were coeval with conflict. Murder was as much a tool of their trade as a computer or an accountant's ledger. Cassidy had corrupted a whole series of lives and brought about the death of his own lover. And was Martin Gregory any different? I had become that most magical of men, who could kill with a word, a hint, a wink of an eye. I had proved I could do it – better even than Cassidy. I could do it again and again, without remorse, unless – please God! – someone lifted me out of the frozen wasteland into the sun.

When I climbed back into the cab, the driver gave me an odd look and said, 'You were a long time in there, mate. Are you sure you're all right?'

'I think so. Yes, I think I'm all right.'

'Funny thing, religion. Me, I never had much time for it. My old man had it bad though, real bad. No booze, no cards, no naughty women, no sport on Sundays. Dull old world he made for himself. Often wondered what sort of heaven he expected . . . Where did you say you lived, guv'nor?'

'Richmond.'

'It's a nice place. You're lucky.'

For the first time since Cassidy's death, I began to hope I might be. When Pat opened the front door, my hope looked like an illusion. She was shocked to see me. She burst into a hysterical gabble of apologies and excuses: she

279

wasn't expecting me until tomorrow; the children never came home till Friday; she wasn't wearing make-up; she was trying to clean the stove; there was no food in the house . . .

All the time she was retreating from me into the hallway, her eyes fixed on my face as though it were a Gorgon mask. I kicked the front door shut behind me, then reached out and drew her to me. She didn't resist. She was as passive as a rag doll.

I asked gently, 'Can we go upstairs?'

'Of course.' She reached down to pick up my bag like a servant but I managed to forestall her and she walked slowly up the stairs ahead of me. When we reached the bedroom, she began to babble again.

'Would you like a bath? I'll draw one for you. You must be very tired. Don't bother unpacking. I'll do that. The washing machine was broken but the man came to fix it yesterday . . .'

'Pat, please . . .'

'Please what?'

'Stop talking. Just look at me.'

'I am looking at you, Martin.'

'And listen to me!'

'I am listening.'

'I want to tell you I love you. I know what happened in Klosters. I don't care. A lot has happened to me, too. People are dead because I fought back when our lives were threatened. Everything before today is plague country. I don't want to go back to it. If you still love me, I want us to go forward together.'

My heart sank when she didn't answer me, but sat limply on the edge of the bed, staring down at the floor. Then slowly she raised her head and faced me and I caught a glimpse of the old fiery Cassidy spirit.

'I do love you, Martin. I wish I could say I'm sorry for what happened; but I'm not – not for all of it, anyway. I'm changed. I needed to be changed. You're changed too. I can see it, feel it. We're different people. Better or worse, I don't know, but different – by God, yes! Do you think we can face that?'

'I'm willing to try.'

'So am I . . . Will you tell me about Father?'

'I'd rather not.'

'Why?'

'The books are closed. Just remember that he loved you once.'

'And he never let me love him.'

'You've got to forgive him, my love. Otherwise, you and I will never forgive each other either.'

For the first time, I saw a hint of surrender. Then she reached out to me and said, with an uncertain smile, 'Do you think we could finish this in bed?'

It was a mating different from any other we had known together, a combat of bodies and of will, a rage to possess what had so nearly been taken from us both; and afterwards, no truce, but a surrender that left us both exhausted and triumphant.

We were lying there, in drowsy tranquillity, when we heard the front door open. A few moments later Clare called from the hallway, 'Pat? . . . Farkis is here! Do be a dear. Come down and fix us some martinis.'

To which Pat, pure Cassidy again, yelled back, 'I'm in bed with Martin. Let Farkis fix his own bloody cocktails. He's a big boy now and you're old enough to handle him.'

It had a nice ring of normality about it. It proved I was home again.

MORRIS WEST

THE DEVIL'S ADVOCATE

For Man to be made Saint!

There can be no greater transformation. It is by definition beyond mortal ambition. The process is long, slow and meticulous. All must be examined, nothing may be left hidden from the searching, unblinking eye of the Church.

So it was that Monsignor Blaise Meredith was with due solemnity appointed Devil's Advocate by the Vatican, charged with finding any reason why, in the case of Giacomo Nerone, the process should not be set in train.

Without mercy, without flinching, the truth of a man's whole life was to be uncovered. This was to be the most terrible of examinations.

'Packed with action, character, bitterness and glory'
Daily Express

'Brilliant and deeply disturbing ... a magnificent achievement'

Daily Telegraph

POST A LITTLE HAPPINESS

Post·A·Book

A Royal Mail service in association with the Book Marketing Council & The Booksellers Association.
Post-A-Book is a Post Office trademark

MORRIS WEST

THE BIG STORY

A breathless thriller of vice and viciousness in modern Italy.

Richard Ashley is a journalist whose exposure of graft in Italy's rich and powerful ruling clique will make headlines all over the world.

His big story centres on the corruption of the dangerous Vittorio, Duke of Orgagna. When Ashley falls in love with Orgagna's wife, there's more to the scoop than just newspaper glory. For when the truth appears, it is complicated, passionate and terribly bloodstained. Ashley's big story threatens to be his *only* story . . .

'Mr West lights his work with the sharp hard sunlight of Italy . . . his characterizations are superb'
Los Angeles Times

'A gripping tale . . . a tense climax'
Evening Standard

'Thrilling . . . romance and international intrigue'
New York Telegraph

CORONET BOOKS

MORRIS WEST

THE SHOES OF THE FISHERMAN

The Pope is dead – but the papacy lives on. Already, from all the corners of the globe, grizzled, scarlet-suited cardinals are gathering to elect a successor. Within the hushed confines of the Vatican, the air is alive with intrigue. Then in the midst of the most frenzied canvassing, comes a surprise result. The new Pope, Kiril I, is the youngest cardinal – and a Russian, recently released from seventeen years in the labour camps . . .

'A great writer'

Daily Mirror

'High drama . . . beautifully executed'
The Sunday Times

'Tough, spare, and wholly unsentimental, a brilliant vital, committed novel of our age'

Bookman

CORONET BOOKS

MORE FICTION FROM
HODDER AND STOUGHTON PAPERBACKS

MORRIS WEST

☐	41113 9	The Devil's Advocate	£2.95
☐	40718 2	The Big Story	£1.95
☐	37759 3	The Shoes of the Fisherman	£2.50
☐	27638 X	The Clowns of God	£2.95
☐	37767 4	Daughter of Silence	£1.95
☐	32052 4	The Naked Country	£1.95
☐	26587 6	The Salamander	£2.25
☐	34710 4	The World is Made of Glass	£2.95
☐	37768 2	The Second Victory	£1.95

All these books are available at your local bookshop or newsagent, or can be ordered direct from the publisher. Just tick the titles you want and fill in the form below.

Prices and availability subject to change without notice.

Hodder and Stoughton Paperbacks, P.O. Box 11, Falmouth, Cornwall.

Please send cheque or postal order, and allow the following for postage and packing:

U.K. – 55p for one book, plus 22p for the second book, and 14p for each additional book ordered up to a £1.75 maximum.

B.F.P.O. and EIRE – 55p for the first book, plus 22p for the second book, and 14p per copy for the next 7 books, 8p per book thereafter.

OTHER OVERSEAS CUSTOMERS – £1.00 for the first book, plus 25p per copy for each additional book.

Name ....

Address ....

....